MW00368222

Halos

A Novel

Halos

A Novel

KRISTEN
HEITZMANN

BETHANY HOUSE PUBLISHERS

Minneapolis, Minnesota

CASS DISTRICT LIBRARY
319 MICHIGAN RD 62N
CASSOPOLIS MI 49031

Halos
Copyright © 2004
Kristen Heitzmann

Cover Design by Brand Navigation
Cover photograph by Steve Gardner, PixelWorks Studio
Car provided by Robberson Ford, Bend, Oregon

The Scripture text on the dedication page is taken from the New American Bible with
Revised New Testament and Revised Psalms © 1991, 1986, 1970 Confraternity of Christian
Doctrine, Washington, D.C. All rights reserved. No part of the New American Bible may be
reproduced in any form without permission in writing from the copyright owner.

All other Scripture quotations are from the HOLY BIBLE, NEW INTERNATIONAL
VERSION®. Copyright © 1973, 1978, 1984 by International Bible Society. Used by
permission of Zondervan Publishing House. All rights reserved.

All rights reserved. No part of this publication may be reproduced, stored in a retrieval
system, or transmitted in any form or by any means—electronic, mechanical, photocopying,
recording, or otherwise—without the prior written permission of the publisher. The only
exception is brief quotations in printed reviews.

Published by Bethany House Publishers
11400 Hampshire Avenue South
Bloomington, Minnesota 55438

Bethany House Publishers is a division of
Baker Publishing Group, Grand Rapids, Michigan.

Printed in the United States of America

ISBN-13: 978-0-7642-2826-1
ISBN-10: 0-7642-2826-9

Library of Congress Cataloging-in-Publication Data

Heitzmann, Kristen.
    Halos / by Kristen Heitzmann.
      p. cm.
    ISBN 0-7642-2826-9
    1. Young women—Fiction. 2. Quests (Expeditions)—Fiction. 3. Automobile theft—
Fiction. 4. Victims of crimes—Fiction. I. Title.
    PS3558.E468H35   2004
    813'.54—dc22   2003021868

For Melodie

In thanksgiving for your precious friendship

Put on then, as God's chosen ones, holy and beloved, heartfelt compassion, kindness, humility, gentleness, and patience . . . And over all of these put on love, that is, the bond of perfection.

Colossians 4:12,14

Rocky Mountain Legacy

◆◆◆◆◆◆◆◆◆◆◆◆◆

Honor's Pledge
Honor's Price
Honor's Quest
Honor's Disguise
Honor's Reward

Diamond of the Rockies

◆◆◆◆◆◆◆◆◆◆◆◆◆

The Rose Legacy
Sweet Boundless
The Tender Vine

◆◆◆◆◆◆◆◆◆◆◆◆◆

Twilight
A Rush of Wings
The Still of Night
Halos
Freefall

Secrets
Unforgotten
Echoes

KRISTEN HEITZMANN is the acclaimed author of sixteen novels, including the Christy Award winner *Secrets*. An artist and music minister, Kristen makes her home, with her husband and children, in the foothills of the Colorado Mountains.

One

IT WAS THE HALO THAT CAUGHT her heart between beats and made her breath pause and take notice. The sun in the white sky was a pale face surrounded by a glow, and she let up on the gas and stared one moment before it began to snow. Plump sugarplum fairies, crystalline dancers afloat on the air . . . and she knew, she *knew* it meant something good.

The gravelly shoulder of the highway ground beneath her tires as she pulled over to the side and stopped. She opened the convertible top and, tipping back her head, watched the flakes separate from the gauzy sky like moths from a giant cocoon.

Alessi held her face still to receive the icy kisses on her skin and hair. A car zoomed by, sending the dancers awhirl in a wild tarantella. She traced their motion with a finger in the air, then dropped her hand to her lap and laughed.

What was she doing on the side of the highway with her car filling with snow? She looked again at the sunglow through the thickened clouds. The halo was gone. They never lasted. But their magic did. She felt it now, captured inside her as she activated her roof and pulled back onto the highway.

She'd seen the first halo at seven years old; her father had been gone for three. Mom had shouldered several jobs, and after school Alessi worked with her. They cleaned houses for people with lots of "don't touch" things. Three nights a week they also stocked shelves at a health food market. The other nights they were home, but Mom was often too tired to fuss over dinner.

The night she saw the halo, Alessi had just started to protest Chef Boyardee when her mother reached into a drawer. "Do you know what these are?"

They were the handkerchiefs they'd found at the Salvation Army for three cents each.

Her mother said, "The fine linens of the queen of Sheba."

Mom liked that queen. She always said one day they'd live like the queen of Sheba. But Alessi was tired of canned spaghetti.

Her mother's eyes lit. "They were smuggled out of the country by very smart sparrows who brought them to the fairy queen for her banquet."

Now, that was a queen Alessi couldn't resist. A story about two royal persons meant extra magic. "How did they get here from the fairy queen?"

"A gift, of course," Mom said.

"But we found them at—"

"Because wicked gnomes stole them from the fairy messenger. But their magic drew us to them on the shelf and made us recognize the gift. You will always see the gift if your heart is open to the magic."

Alessi's heart was opened wide as Mom spooned canned spaghetti onto the plate. "And this," she said, "is the fairy ambrosia."

That's when she saw it, her mother's head encircled by light, her golden hair aglow. Alessi's mouth fell open. Mom bent to serve her own portion and the lamp behind spread its light to the room. But Alessi had seen it.

Reveling in the memory, Alessi pressed the accelerator to pass a wooden-sided truck filled with rubber tires. The driver honked and waved as she went by. The Mustang had that effect. It was the nicest thing she had ever been given. That had been a halo day too—her eighteenth birthday.

"A Mustang? For me?" The convertible had sat in the circular drive like a dark candied apple with caramel leather seats.

"Now that you're on your own, you'll need some wheels," her uncle said, *noblesse oblige*. Aunt Carrie flashed her Estée Lauder smile.

"Thank you both so much. Should I . . . maybe I'll just pack up now?" She had entertained thoughts of college, even the possibility Uncle Bob would put her through. But this was reality. "I really don't know how to thank you. For everything. Taking me in and . . ."

"Less . . . you're my sister's only child." Her aunt's eyes moistened on cue.

Uncle Bob nodded. Standing with their two children outside their sunwashed Palm Beach home, they positively glowed. Halos. She had waved good-bye to the Fisher Price family and envisioned their lives sealing up like a knife mark in Jell-O as soon as she was gone.

Now, three and a half years later, her paint still gleamed, the leather was soft as a puppy's underbelly, and two and a half weeks before Christmas, Alessi had reached a place where it snowed. The flakes flew around the Mustang as the sun disappeared in the pasty sky. A halo on the sun, and now the snow. Something good was coming.

The orange gas pump light flashed on the dashboard, and an eighth of a tank would only take her so far. The road ahead was white, with no cars in view, but she knew the tire truck men were somewhere behind, should a true emergency occur. She just needed an exit, the sort with services.

Snow thickening, she decreased her speed. Her needle was close to empty. The wipers *thwack*ed more quickly as she adjusted them. Finally an Exit sign appeared, though the snow obscured the words and almost covered the trusty food and gas symbols. She tapped her fingertips on the steering wheel in time with the turn signal, then eased off the highway, climbing the ramp to the crossroad. Her stomach growled.

She was used to going without, but the snow had conjured images of hot mashed potatoes with melting pats of butter, meat loaf and gravy, and cocoa swirled with whipping cream. Her last great meal had been a Thanksgiving splurge of turkey and dressing at a cafeteria. Her stomach tightened again. She would stop for food this time.

But searching the road ahead, she hoped there really was something out there. The sign at the top of the exit had been equally unreadable except for the bottom stems of several letters and an arrow to the right. Trees thickened; conifers, pines, and a bare deciduous net on both sides. The road began to dip and rise, and ahead she saw a sign, sideways to the wind and at last readable: *Charity, four miles.*

Halo, snow, Charity. How much clearer could it be? Alessi passed into Charity's city limits, noting the first buildings in a daze: a breeder kennel, a hardware store, a mini mart.

There was a small fire station and, next to that, a post office, city hall, and maintenance all in one log building. At the Stop sign were clustered the Hawkeye Gift Gallery, Bennet's Books, and Moll's Café. To her right, Best Beer and Pool, and diagonally, Mr. Gas Garage and Videos. It didn't seem like the setting for a miracle, but what else could be coming with a halo on the sun?

She pulled up to the pumps and got out. The snow fell steadily, with less whimsy than before. She leaned on the car door and looked back the way she'd just come. A few cars were parked along the street, though none putted down the road, and only one man was out in the snow getting a newspaper from the stand outside the mini mart.

It was a scene she'd never experienced: cold, yet warming, each roof and ledge flocked with foam that for a moment reminded her of the ocean. But she was far from the balmy air, the flaming bird of paradise, bougainvillea, and green, waving fronds. And she couldn't help thinking this was what Christmas should look like. No pink flamingos with neck wreaths, lighted palm trees, or Santas in swim trunks.

She shivered. Her cotton top, bought secondhand, was lightweight, and her canvas sneakers were getting wet. She would have to find her jacket in one of the bags in her trunk. But for now, she reveled in the cold. Except for the smell of gasoline, the air was crisp and charged with some energy she'd never felt. Her heart skipped another beat. Almost giddy, she tried to catch a snowflake on her tongue. But they veered away at the last moment, and she gave up, folding her arms across her chest and looking over the last few buildings.

The Charity Community Center, Maple Tree Bakery, and Hair Magic. She could just make out what looked like a church at the end of the block, and on the cross street by the mini mart was Granny's Trunk, clothes and collectibles. It might be fun to rummage through there, but she should stick with what she had in her totes: shorts and tops, another pair of jeans, socks, sandals—and hopefully a jacket, though she couldn't remember what she'd done with the green windbreaker with the broken zipper. She'd been just peevish enough when she packed up this last time to have tossed it. Maybe she'd try Granny's after all.

She wanted to memorize the whole scene, to plant it in her mind. It could be—yes, it could be—her first view of the "place." The thought warmed her, as did the anticipation of a meal at Moll's, and the whole scene, comforting as a children's picture book. She imagined the title: *Charity's Treasure*. She had landed in a fairy tale, and she wished Mom were there to see.

The gas pump clunked. She rehung the nozzle and replaced her gas cap. Looking down Charity's quaint street once more, she tried to absorb the magic, to keep her heart open and recognize the gift. Shivering, she reached past the open car door and took two bills from her purse.

Tucking hand and money beneath her opposite arm, she hurried inside the station. The man behind the counter smiled and stood up from his stool. He was very tall and narrow in the shoulders. "You could have waited in here for the pump."

"I know. But since I've never stood in snow before . . ."

"Never?"

She shook her head. "Nope."

"That's why you were . . ." He lapped with his tongue. "Trying to catch it."

"You saw that?" She laughed.

"I don't suppose there's anyone who hasn't tried it. You have to move slowly so you don't blow them away."

"So that's it."

"It's easier with a really wet snow. The flakes are heavier." He pushed the buttons on the register. "Do you want anything besides the gas?"

She looked around the shelves of oil and automotive parts, racks of snacks and incidentals, to the back wall lined with videos. In the midst of that was a glass case with old photos and movie memorabilia. "What's all that?" She walked back to the case.

"Just a hobby." He joined her there. "That's my favorite." A signed Clark Gable looking debonair as Rhett Butler.

"Do you sell these?"

"Nah. They're keepers." He put his hands into his pockets.

There was Humphrey Bogart and Yvette Mimieux, a Three Stooges Festival poster, a Charlie Chaplin doll, and a playbill featuring the cast of *The Wizard of Oz* with all five signatures, including Toto. But what she really loved was the autographed photo of Rod Taylor sitting in the Time Machine. What a place this Charity was. A lanky grease monkey with a Hollywood collection.

A man came in from one of the side doors, compact and dark with black circles around his nails. He carried the warm oozy smell of grease. "Finished up that V-dub. Running sweet now." He stopped when he saw her. "Oh. Hey. Quite a collection, eh?"

"It's wonderful." She turned back to the first man. "Well, I'm pretty hungry. How's Moll's?"

"It's good if you like real food. If you're one of those Florida gals who only eats sushi . . ."

She smiled. "How did you know I'm a Florida gal?"

"Read your license plate."

"Oh." She followed him back to the counter.

"That and you never seeing snow before." He rang up the sale and gave her seven cents change.

"Not ever?" the short man asked.

"Not actually falling. Well, of course I've seen it in the movies, and you know what? It looked just like this." She looked out the window at the gas pumps growing fuzzy. She blinked. "Did you . . . did someone . . . move my car?"

Her tall attendant leaned to look. "You move her car, Dave?"

Dave paused from wiping his greasy hands on a rag. "What do you mean? I was working on the Bug in the garage."

Alessi pushed through the doors and stood in the lot between the gas pumps and the station. She looked both ways down the street. Everything looked the same, except the snowfall had thickened—and her car was gone.

Two

A CHILL THAT WASN'T CAUSED by the weather found her spine; panic raced through her veins. How could her car be gone? It was all she had, her sum total, including her purse and all her clothes in the trunk. She clasped her arms and laughed. "Is this a joke? Is someone . . .?" Both men looked dumbfounded.

Dave said, "How long was she inside, Ben?"

Ben spread his long arms and shrugged. "Not that long." He searched the ground, but tire tracks circled the pumps both directions, intermingled with footsteps.

Alessi ran to the street and stared both ways. If anything, the cars were fewer and the snow fell more thickly than ever. She rounded the corner and searched the cross street, her lungs squeezing tight little breaths through her throat. No Mustang. She rushed around the back of the building, searched the turnaround at the small house behind it, then the vehicles parked outside the service garage and the other side of the station. No Mustang.

Lungs tighter still, she hurried back to the two men waiting, it seemed, for her direction, their faces as empty as the place she'd left her car. No Mustang there either.

"I'm sure I locked it," she said more to herself than them. But she couldn't actually recall hitting the power lock. She searched her pockets for the keys. Her jeans lay flat to her hips. She must have dropped them in the purse when she grabbed her money. "Keys in the purse, purse in the car. I need to call the police."

"That would be Sheriff Roehr. We can phone from the station." Ben took one more look along the street.

What had she been thinking? Snow. Fairytales. Miracles. She groaned. "This can't be happening. Halos are supposed to be . . . good."

The two men shared a glance. How could they understand? If she tried to explain, their faces would not change, except maybe for the worse. But she knew in her deepest being it was so. Hers was not a charmed life—far from it. But her mother's promise was firmly embedded in her mind. Angels watched over her if she just had eyes to see.

Ben motioned her back inside, went to the phone, and dialed the sheriff.

Alessi chafed her numb fingers. It could be a small-town prank, someone taking a fancy car for a joyride. She could see that. They'd bring it back and she'd be on her way. That halo on the sun must not have meant Charity. Charity was not proving charitable.

Ben said, "Cooper? It's Ben here. A lady's car seems to be gone from the station." He chewed his lip. "No, no sign of it at all."

Alessi waited through the pause, forcing her panic to subside to something closer to concern. Concern was positive, constructive. Panic was helpless.

"Oh, it was here, all right. Couldn't miss it. Shiny red convertible Mustang. GT package."

Alessi reached for the phone. "Excuse me? Do you think you might come now? You see, my purse and everything are in the car."

A heavy sigh came through the receiver. "Well, all right, then."

"Thank you very much." She hung up the phone and looked up at Ben. Standing five-feet-ten herself, there weren't many men who towered over her, but he must be six-six at least.

His face was not unlike Dorothy's faithful scarecrow in the picture at the back, and it pulled now into a sorrowful mien. "I sure am sorry about this."

"Oh . . ." She looked from him to Dave. "I'm sure it'll work out." But her heart jumped around in her chest like a doughball in a blender. "Maybe I should go look around again." *Do something productive.*

Ben said, "Sheriff'll be here shortly."

She looked out. Having checked the immediate area already, and with the snow coming harder than ever, there wasn't much to do but wait. What were the chances she'd chase down her Mustang on foot? If it was a joke, they'd have their spin and bring it back. If it wasn't a joke . . .

A man came in and paid for his gas. "How's it goin', Ben?"

"All right."

All right for Ben. All right for the man heading even now back to his car firmly in place where he'd left it.

Her stomach cinched itself into a knot.

Dave put a hand to her shoulder. "Look, Miss . . . Did you say your name?"

"Alessi. Some people call me Less, like not more." She twisted her hands together. "It's kind of funny, actually. My last name is Moore. Less Moore?"

"Alessi's a real pretty name." Ben motioned her to a high stool beside the counter.

She wanted to run out and search the streets, no matter how futile, but Dave and Ben showed little urgency; concern, but not panic. Exactly what she'd been telling herself to do. She'd take that for what it was worth. The sheriff was on his way. Panic would change nothing. She took the stool. Friends must come and sit there to pass the time with Dave and Ben. She'd pretend she was one of them. "So how long have you had this station, Ben?"

He pursed his lips to the side. "Oh, eight, nine years. Dave and I started working for the original Mr. Gas, James Beale, right out of high school."

"We bought him out nine years ago." Dave brought her a cup of hot chocolate from the machine.

"Thanks." She took the steamy cup and sipped. "Is the sheriff far away?"

"Well, he has a little trouble getting around just now. Had a hip replaced." Ben tore a strip from a roll of paper towels behind the register and handed it to her for the drip on her cup.

"Oh. No wonder he didn't want to get up." She looked out the window.

"He'll be here shortly." Dave offered her a package of peanuts.

She set the cup on the counter and tore the package open. "Just as soon as I get my purse back, I can pay you for these." She popped in a handful and chewed.

"Don't worry. It's on the house." A gap in place of Dave's eyetooth gave him a youthful look, despite his prematurely balding crown.

"That's really nice of you."

She had finished the package of nuts and drained the cup by the time the police car pulled in, sporting a small red light attached to the roof, though it wasn't flashing. The sheriff climbed out stiffly, his white hair catching in the breeze like a wisp of cotton candy. She stood and met him at the door. "I'm so sorry to get you up and out in this cold, especially with your hip."

He looked from her to the men behind her. "It's fine, young lady. You're the one with the missing car?"

She nodded. "Yes, I'm afraid so."

"Ben, you and Dave saw the car?" He pulled a pad from his pocket.

"I was in the garage," Dave said. "Never saw it."

"I watched her put in a full tank," Ben said. "Red Mustang convertible, alloy wheels."

"You left the keys in the ignition?"

"No. I wouldn't do that." Though she could not quite picture dropping them in the purse either. "I took money from my purse and went inside. My purse is in the car and, well, everything I own." She'd been terribly careless. Charity had worked some spell, some . . . hypnotic trance.

"Registration?"

"In my wallet."

"Title?"

"In my car."

He stood eye to eye with her, his cheeks a little jowly, pink from the cold. "I'd say you have a problem, Miss . . ."

"Moore. Alessi Moore."

"No driver's license to prove it."

"No, that would be in my purse. But I think . . . maybe if we started looking soon, we'd find the car."

The sheriff raised his brows. "Hard to say. People passing through . . ."

She looked out into the nearly deserted street. "I haven't seen too much traffic. I think someone in town is pulling a prank or—"

"Don't know much about Charity if you think that, Miss Moore."

She met his blue eyes under shaggy brows. "Maybe not, Sheriff. But someone took my car, and I'd really like it back."

He opened his pad. "License number?"

"It says Less. L-E-S-S. My uncle got me the plates with the car. They called me Less."

"State?"

"Florida."

He nodded. "I didn't figure you for around here."

"No, just passing through." Even though at first glance, she'd thought Charity might be it. The more she'd seen, the more she'd liked—until someone took her car. This could not be the scene of a miracle. She'd taken a wrong turn, a—

"Description?"

"It's a deep metallic red with a tan roof and leather seats. Like Ben said, alloy wheels and fairly new tires." They had cost her, but she kept the car in good condition. Had to.

"You got insurance?"

She licked her lower lip. "Not . . . currently. I had some, but I changed jobs and . . . actually, the store I worked in became a Dippin' Dots and Dogs, so I thought I'd find something else and started driving, and it's been a little while since I worked because I wanted to find a place I could stay and settle in." She swallowed.

The sheriff pursed his lips. "So no insurance."

She shook her head.

"Well." He closed the pad. "I'll see what I can do."

He was not inspiring great confidence. Panic sank fresh claws into her throat. She had thought whatever smart aleck had pulled the prank would have it back by now. Charity didn't seem like the sort of place you had to watch your back. Maybe she'd been lulled by false appearances, but even the sheriff had said no one in Charity would take her car.

Someone had, though.

Sheriff Roehr accepted the cup of coffee Dave brought him. "Where can I find you if I learn anything?"

If?

"You got friends around here?" He tightened the lid over the lip.

She shook her head. "No, I . . ."

"Maybe you ought to call your folks."

"They're dead."

"Your uncle, then, who gave you the car." He squinted one eye and scrutinized her.

She drew herself up, topping him by an inch, though he had her in girth. Alessi thought of her mother dying of cancer and how she hadn't called Uncle Bob and Aunt Carrie. She had accepted their rejection, had not forced herself on people who didn't want her in their lives. It would dishonor her mother's memory to involve them now, if they even would help. Uncle Bob would be furious she'd lost the car. "No, I'm on my own."

"Whereabouts, then?"

She swallowed hard. "Is there a motel?" Could she beg a room until they found her car, at which time she could pay? Provided, of course, they'd left money in her purse—though that possibility seemed slimmer and slimmer the longer the car was gone.

"Closed down two years ago." The sheriff gave her a sour look as though it were her fault for not coming sooner.

"She can stay right here tonight," Ben spoke up. "Steve's gone after more books, so his room's empty."

Alessi looked up at him, seeing *her* scarecrow now. Was there ever a truer face?

The sheriff turned. "That all right with you, Dave?"

"Sure." Dave threaded his fingers together. "We'll hold on to her till you find her car." His gap-toothed smile was quick and sincere. "Call her at the house soon as you have something."

"Miss?"

"If they don't mind having me." Maybe it wasn't the smartest move, but she had known more men like Ben and Dave than the sort who would take advantage of her. Three years of fending for herself had developed instincts for judging character. And what choice did she have? She was getting tossed about like a snowflake on an unexpected wind.

Sheriff Roehr set his cup on the counter and zipped up his coat. "Okay, then. I'll be in touch." He moved slowly for the door. He did *not* inspire great confidence.

Alessi looked from Ben to Dave. Their faces were carefully neutral. Her heart sank. What would she do if her car was gone for good? She'd landed in Oz, with no ruby slippers and no place like home.

Three

ALESSI AWOKE WITH A START. Voices outside her door had broken through the numbed sleep of comfort food from Moll's, courtesy of Ben and Dave. The room was completely dark. It couldn't be morning.

"So you put her in my room?"

She suddenly felt like Goldilocks, but that growl did not sound like Baby Bear.

"We didn't know you'd be back tonight." Ben's voice.

"And where else could she go?" That was Dave.

She climbed out of bed and crept to the door. She pulled down the navy terry-cloth robe that hung there. Ben had offered her a T-shirt and drawstring sweats from the drawer, so adding the robe shouldn't matter. Her height was a definite advantage when wearing men's clothes.

"So where am I supposed to go?"

"You've got the cot over at the store." Ben sounded reasonable, if a little fuzzy with sleep.

"Great. I've been on the road all day, unloaded an entire truck bed myself, and now I get the cot at the store."

Alessi opened the door. The growl belonged to a man who split the difference in height between Ben and Dave. Dark hair in disarray, dark eyes annoyed, and a dark shadow covering his jaw. She pulled his robe closed at her throat. "I'm sorry I took your bed."

He looked down her length, obviously noting the bed wasn't all she had taken.

She said, "I'll just dress and—"

"Forget it." He shoved his hands into his jean pockets. "I'll sleep at the store."

She pushed the door wider. "You shouldn't have to do that. I can—"

"I said, forget it." He hefted his travel bag and cocked an eyebrow. "Everything fit all right?"

She looked down her front, then back at him. "Close enough."

"Good." He almost smiled but caught it in time. He looked at Ben and Dave. "We'll talk in the morning." He turned and walked out.

She had felt safe in his room, sandwiched between Dave's and Ben's. Now she wasn't so sure. He had that unruly, outdoorsy look, but then, she probably looked fairly unruly herself.

"Steve's just tired," Ben said.

"Sorry he woke you." Dave ran a hand over his head.

She was sorry too. All the worry had rushed back in, and she wouldn't sleep again soon.

"Good thing we caught him before he barged in." Ben and Dave shared a glance.

Good thing! Alessi imagined opening her eyes to him in her . . . *his* room. "Is he okay at the store?"

Ben waved a hand. "Sure. He works late sometimes, so he keeps a cot there to crash on."

"What kind of store is it?"

"Books."

She thought back to Sherlock's, where she'd worked in Miami. Those doors were closed up by six every night. "How does that keep him late?"

"Oh, tracking down leads and all." Ben tugged his pajama shirt.

"Leads?"

"Lost books, out of print, rare titles."

"Searching estate collections and such," Dave put in. "That's where he was. Someone whose collection he's been watching died last Tuesday."

Alessi nodded. "Oh. Well . . ."

"You get some sleep now." Dave patted her shoulder.

"You're sure it's okay?"

"Sure," Ben said. "We'll work it all out in the morning."

She nodded. In the morning, her car would be found, maybe even be returned to the gas pumps out front. She'd pay what she owed and head out, through the snow, away from Charity. "Good night." She closed the door behind her and turned on the lamp.

The room was neat, the shelf along one wall holding books, of course. Framed black-and-white photos, mostly landscapes, covered the other walls: cliffs and waterfalls, desert formations, high mountain ridges, icy lakes. The photographer had an eye. Some shots were dramatic, others creative or simply beautiful. She walked from photo to photo, imagining the man she'd just seen behind the camera.

The only pictures of people were an older couple holding hands and a snapshot of a man with gray hair reminiscent of Steve's tousle. Not the type of photography one expected from a young man. But his equipment was in the corner. He must be the cameraman.

Earlier, when Ben had rummaged about for something she could sleep in, she had noticed the clothes in his closet hung perfectly straight. Now she couldn't resist just a little peek. She pulled open the top drawer of his bureau. Socks and boxers. She pushed it shut. What was she doing, snooping through some man's dresser drawers? But the socks were paired and the boxers folded once. Steve was meticulous. Probably disliked surprises, wanted everything in order. Except his hair in that careless state that made him look vulnerable and appealing. Nothing appealing in his scowl, though his angular face had softened by the time he left.

It wasn't personal. He'd been taken advantage of and reacted, probably because he was tired. Understandable. She wouldn't like to find someone in her room and have to sleep somewhere else. He'd handled it generously, all things considered.

She turned off the lamp before she was tempted to snoop further. It was a terrible habit, but you learned so much from people's things and the way they kept them. Maybe cleaning people's houses as a child had fostered the curiosity. In any case, she resisted it now. She took the robe off, laid it across the foot of the bed, then picked it up and hung it back on the door. Lifting the covers, she slipped into his sheets. It hadn't mattered before, when she didn't know whose bed she was taking. It could have been any bed in any motel in any town. Now she had a dark-eyed face to put to it. She sighed.

It was only for the rest of the night. In the morning he'd have his room back, his bed back, his sweats and T-shirt. Closing her eyes, she remembered the feel of those first snowflakes landing on her skin, their swirling dance, the halo on the sun. Halos always meant something good. It might not look like it right now, but it would come. It had to.

Steve let himself into the store, wondering just what had changed his mind: her rumpled blond hair on the shoulders of his robe, the freckles across the bridge of her nose, or the sleepy huskiness of her voice apologizing. He'd looked forward to a good night's sleep in his own bed. He dropped the bag onto the foot of the cot in his store-room, rummaged through, and found his toothbrush.

In the small bathroom he brushed, then scrubbed his face and hands with warm water. No hot shower. Paper towels. He swallowed his annoyance. The guys had meant well, had seen a person with a need and filled it . . . with his room. He turned off the light and went back to the cot. The room was chilly, and he would have liked his robe, but it was in use already.

He took off his sweater and jeans, folded them and put them into the bag, then took out a similar pair of sweats to the ones his guest had chosen and pulled them on. The cot was hard and cold. He considered changing his mind, then settled in and pulled the sheet and blanket up over his shoulder. The things Ben had told him started clicking through his head.

She stops for gas, leaves her keys and purse, gets wrapped up in Ben's collection, and *poof*—her car is gone. Sheriff Roehr was looking into it. Um-hmm. He rolled to his other side. He was not going to get used to this cot. It was his emergency quarters, not for daily use. He never spent more than one night at a time. Never. He rubbed his face and pressed it deeper into the pillow. In the morning they'd settle it, car or no car.

———————

Alessi woke, rumpled and confused, then suddenly too aware that she was sleeping in some man's sweats and T-shirt in a room of the small house behind the garage where her car had disappeared. At the moment, it was hard to conjure hopeful thoughts of finding it waiting at the gas pump or even of the sheriff finding it. The Mustang was registered in the state of Florida. Their records would show it was hers as soon as it was found—unless of course it was stripped of serial numbers or whatever it was car thieves did.

Why hadn't her uncle given her some old jalopy? No one would have stolen it, and at least she'd have transportation out of there. But she'd taken pride in the Mustang. Its beauty alone warmed something inside, and she understood the old Beach Boys song, "I'm in Love With My Car."

She did love it. It was all she had. Many times, when she couldn't pay the rent, she had lived in that car, parked it at nice hotels, away from prying eyes and crowbars. *I'm staying at the Marriott,* she'd tell herself and slip into an obscure slot. Not a room with two queens and a Jacuzzi tub, but a safe place for her and her car. No security guard looked twice at her shiny red car as long as she stayed down low.

Suddenly anger stirred. She tried to resist, but fury boiled up. What right had someone to take her car, even for a prank, even for a joyride? It was hers. So what if she hadn't bought it? She had paid for it in so many ways, holding her tongue against demeaning remarks, trying to make herself as small and unobtrusive as a five-foot-ten teenage girl could, never arguing, never complaining. She deserved that car, even if it was her one-way ticket out of her uncle's home the minute they could justifiably be rid of her.

Alessi sighed. It was her fault. She'd betrayed her car, left it vulnerable. Swept up in hopes for Charity, she'd been thoughtless, uncaring. She pressed her palm to her forehead. What were these depressing thoughts? Of course it would turn out all right. Wasn't this place named Charity, for heaven's sake? Why name a town Charity if it wasn't the most hospitable, caring place on the planet?

She climbed out of bed, took off Steve's clothes, and dressed. She made the bed neatly, folded the sweats and T-shirt, and laid them at the foot. Of course, she had no personal hygiene items—no brush, toothbrush, or cosmetics.

Well, Ben and Dave would have to deal with her *au natural*. She snuck out to the bathroom across the hall. Her cabinet search revealed a bottle of Scope—better than nothing. A comb lay on the counter and she picked it up, scrutinized it, then brought it with difficulty through her shoulder-length curls. Her hair was as fine as Aunt Carrie's but not straight. Most of the time she was glad for that. People paid a lot of money for the kind of attitude that grew naturally on her head. Aunt Carrie added chemical highlights to make her hair glow. Alessi had to depend on the sun.

Judging by the dim gray of the frosted bathroom window, there was little sun today. So who was she trying to impress? She left the bathroom and smelled coffee. Ben was at the circular glass kitchen table, mug between his hands, Bible open to Proverbs. Her scarecrow had a brain.

"Anything in there about lost cars?"

He looked up and smiled. "No. But it says 'A cheerful look brings joy to the heart, and good news gives health to the bones.'"

"Has there been good news?" She clutched the top of the wicker chair.

"Not yet. But I like to start out expecting it."

A man after her own heart.

"You want some coffee?" He made to stand.

"I'll get it." She'd already located the pot. Mugs must be close. The cabinet above. She took down a Garfield cup that said *Got Lasagna?* She filled it with coffee and quipped, "Got milk?"

"Got some half-and-half in the fridge. Dave likes it," Ben said.

So did she, though she usually settled for milk. Her stomach was still content from Moll's meatloaf, so she sat down with her coffee and watched Ben.

He tapped the page with the backs of his fingers. "I read a chapter every day from Proverbs. Some of it's got to stick, don't you think?"

She smiled. "I'm sure."

"It also says 'The fear of the Lord teaches a man wisdom, and humility comes before honor.'"

"Why aren't you married, Ben? I thought all men like you were snatched up."

He actually blushed. "Well, I'm in a situation, see." He closed his Bible and set it aside. "I've been seeing a woman, Mary, for three years. She's got twin girls, Cait and Lyn." He looked down into his coffee. "She had a rough go of it first time around."

Alessi looked into his face and almost saw a halo. It was there, she was sure. Without thinking, she squeezed his hand. "Three years is a long time." She knew. She'd spent her last three doing the best she could with almost nothing to show for it. Actually nothing, now. But she had to stop thinking in terms of that car. It might be gone for good.

"She's got to work out her troubles from that before she can think of remarrying. Her and the girls both."

Alessi nodded. "It can't be easy."

The door opened, and Steve blew in on a cold wind. His hair was worse than the night before, the shadow had become stubble, and his scowl was firmly in place. He looked her over, noting with a quirk of eyebrows her change of clothes. "Good morning."

His civil greeting caught her off guard. "Hi. I left your things on the bed. I'd wash them but . . ." She spread her hands.

"Don't worry about it." He went to the counter and poured coffee into a wide-eyed Tweety Bird mug that read, *I did, I did!* But it was no puddy-tat that gripped him.

"Sleep all right?" Ben asked.

"Sure." Steve sipped his coffee.

Alessi stood, wrapped herself in her arms. "I guess I'll just go see if someone returned my car." She had on the same top she'd worn the day before and felt the chill as she stepped outside. What shirt would she have chosen if she'd known it would become her sole possession? She closed her eyes for half a breath. The ribbon-embroidered cashmere sweater she'd splurged on at the Goodwill. Definitely.

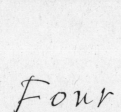

Four

DID I HEAR RIGHT?" Steve turned to Ben.

Ben nodded. "She thinks it might be a prank." He spread his hands. "Maybe it is."

Steve looked at the door she'd exited. What crazy wind had blown that tall, awkward bird into their nest? He went to the closet, pulled on his brown bomber jacket, and went back out. He found her standing at the gas pumps, looking disappointed. Had she actually thought it would be there?

"It's understandable." She looked one way up the street, then the other. "The first time I slid into that leather seat, cranked some tunes, and stepped on the gas, I fell in love."

He'd heard men talk that way. Dave frequently made love to the engines he repaired, even talking to them as he worked.

Her face pinched. "It wouldn't be easy to give it back; I just thought . . ."

He shoved his hands into his pockets. "Do you have a name?"

"Alessi." She still searched the street as though the car might appear at any moment. Then she shivered.

Leaning his head to the side, Steve took off his coat and wrapped it around her shoulders. She turned, startled. Hazel. Her eyes were hazel, a nice blend with her hair. Not too dramatic. He said, "Did you see the movie *Gone in Sixty Seconds*?"

She nodded slowly.

"Then you know the odds."

"But not here." She pulled the coat closed at the neck, just as she had pulled his robe the night before. "Not in a place like Charity."

He scoffed. "What do you know about Charity?"

She dropped her gaze to the snowy ground. He hated to disillusion her, but the sooner she cleared the fluff from her head, the better. He stamped his feet and said, "Can we go back inside?"

"I think I'll just walk around and look. Maybe I'll see it."

He crossed his arms over his quickly chilling chest. "If someone stole your car, they didn't just drive it to Moll's."

"I have to do something." She pulled off the coat and thrust it toward him. Anxiety flashed over her face. Not quite the blind optimist she'd seemed.

He sagged a hip. "At least wear the coat. It's a pretty good fit."

She brought it back to her chest. "Thanks." Then she pulled it on and started off.

He watched her go. Long limbs. His coat was loose in the shoulders and a little bunched at the wrists, but not much. He put a hand through his hair, shivered, and went back inside.

Dave had joined Ben at the table. Steve's coffee was cold. He dumped it in the sink and brewed a fresh pot. As he waited for the carafe to fill, he leaned on the counter. "So what's the plan?"

Ben and Dave looked at him.

Steve spread his hands. "What?"

"We can't just turn her out."

"Meaning . . ." He switched the carafe with his mug, filled it, and switched them back.

Dave said, "She's got no family. Everything she owned was in her car."

"Wait a minute." Steve returned his hips to the counter. "I thought you said she was driving a cherry Mustang."

"It was a cherry all right." Ben nodded. "Red convertible, leather seats. Very sweet."

"Hardly sounds like some indigent waif." He drank the strong brew, which hadn't quite mellowed to a full pot flavor.

Dave said, "She told Cooper her uncle gave her the car."

Steve frowned. "More likely she took it and ran." That explained her strangeness. He'd probably never see his coat again.

Dave scratched his head. "It had her name on the license plate. L–E–S–S. She said they called her Less."

Steve said, "Less, not Alessi. How do you know it wasn't her uncle's name? Lester or Leslie." It was hard to imagine two men more gullible than Dave and Ben. This woman had them totally snowed.

Ben stood up. "That would be one *s*, I think." He carried his mug to the sink. "I'm going to open the station."

Steve turned. "We haven't decided anything."

"Like what?"

Were they intentionally obtuse? "Like where I'm sleeping tonight."

"I guess I'll get after that Toyota." Dave squeezed in and rinsed his mug. "When did Pete want it by?"

Steve spread his hands. "What is this?"

Ben shrugged. "If you want her out, you'll have to tell her so yourself."

"Excuse me, but I'm an equal partner here. I pay you a third of the mortgage, last I looked."

"That's true." Dave nodded. "I guess we could rotate, each of us give up our room for a night until she finds her car."

"She's not going to find her car." Steve slammed his mug, sloshing the coffee over the rim. "And both of you know it."

Dave and Ben exchanged a glance.

Finally he'd gotten through. "How many missing things have been found lately?"

Ben cleared his throat, but Steve didn't give him time to comment. "None. Not one. And I for one am not going to sleep in a cot until Cooper comes up with a good excuse to send Miss Alessi on her way."

"I don't expect you to."

He spun, feeling the chill from her eyes more than the wind from the open door. She took off his coat and held it out. He took it, feeling like a heel. "What I mean is . . ."

"Don't worry about it." She turned to Ben. "I talked to Sheriff Roehr. He's working on it. I was wondering . . . Would you need some help at the station? I asked at Moll's. She was doing a brisk breakfast business, but she didn't need anyone. You don't either. I can tell. Well . . ."

"What about you, Steve?" Dave tapped his elbow. "You could use help at the store while you value and post all that new inventory."

Steve glared. "I'm sure I can break away for the two or three people who might walk in needing books this week."

"It takes you days to catch up when you've done an acquisition."

"That's all right." Alessi pushed her hair back. "Do you think I could take a shower? I might have better luck if I'm not so rumpled."

"Sure. Of course." Dave and Ben all but fell over themselves.

"Thanks."

Steve watched her head to the bathroom, where he had planned to shower. The door closed behind her, and he turned to his companions. "Listen, guys, we need a plan here." He did not like the looks in their eyes. "She's suckered you. She's a . . . sociopath." Anyone who could be that sweet and innocent and cheerful in these circumstances had something going.

Ben shook his head. "I'm going to open the station." He went to the closet, pulled on a coat, and walked out.

Dave pursed his lips. "If I had a cot to sleep on somewhere, I'd sure give her my room."

"Well, why don't you?" Steve wiped the spill from the side of his cup and hand.

"Because I don't have a cot."

"There's a couch." Steve pointed to the navy plaid couch they'd all gone in on last summer.

"I don't think she'd feel comfortable with that. I sleep in my under-wear."

More information than he needed. "Look, it's silly to talk as though she's going to be here any length of time."

Dave swirled the dish soap around the sink, then ran the hot water until it filled with suds.

"I said she won't be here any length of time, right?"

"Where is she supposed to go?" Dave set each cup into the water.

"Dave." Steve drained his mug and brought it to the sink. "I'm not being heartless here. I just think there are better solutions."

Dave swabbed a cup. "Like what?"

"Like the Moto-Lodge."

"In Chambers City?" Dave sounded as though he'd suggested the moon.

"Why not?"

Dave said, "How's she gonna pay? Her purse was in the car."

"How convenient." She had it down to an art.

Dave turned. "Have you talked to her? Spent any time with her? She's real nice, Steve."

"The best cons are." He knew that from experience.

Dave rinsed a mug and set it upside down in the dish drainer. "You should let her work in the store a few days."

"With access to my till? No thanks." Steve jammed his hands into his pockets.

Dave jabbed a soapy finger toward him. "I don't like you calling her a thief. She hasn't asked for anything except just now for a job."

"And a shower." He sounded petty.

Dave shook his head and rinsed the last cup. As the sink water glugged out, he wiped his hands on a towel. With one last accusing look, he grabbed a jacket and headed for the garage.

Steve went to the refrigerator and took out a carton of eggs and a loaf of whole-wheat bread. He dug for a stick of butter. He was not going to lose his appetite over this.

Five

A LESSI STEPPED OUT OF THE SHOWER and toweled off. Sheriff Roehr had been friendlier this morning than the night before. He didn't laugh when she proposed finding a job while she waited for her car to be found. He had tried to convince her to call her uncle, though. Was it pride that kept her from it? No. It was self-preservation, what self they'd left her.

So finding a job was the first order of business. She'd never had a credit card, but all the cash from her bank account had been in her purse; almost a thousand dollars, starting-over money. She'd been especially frugal the last months when Edward Miller hadn't seemed well. His stroke was not a complete surprise.

Poor old Ed. How was he doing? His sons and daughter had swooped in to care for him and found him a decent facility. Alessi had not been needed. She worked the towel over her hair. Nope. Not needed one bit. She did help close down the store, working long hours clearing inventory at bargain prices. It was like selling pieces of Ed.

And the thought of Dippin' Dots and Dogs was just too much. She had left Daytona Beach December 4 and made it all the way to Charity. That, it seemed, was as far as she could go, unless she struck out on foot. Hitching a ride with strangers on the highway was not an option. And living with strangers was?

She clutched the rough towel to her throat and breathed in the soapy-scented steam. It was only the one night, and her instincts had said she could trust Dave and Ben. She believed that still. But she was trouble for Steve. Understandable. She'd invaded his space. Story of her life.

Alessi pulled on her clothes, then searched the cabinet. No hair dryer. But then, neither Ben nor Dave had enough hair to worry about it. Dave's was a black buzzed rim on a bowling ball head, and Ben's was that wispy brown scarecrow hair. If Steve had a blow dryer, he probably kept it under lock and key.

No, that was unfair. She had to see things from his perspective. She worked the comb through her hair again. It would take an hour to air dry. Or freeze into witch hair—maybe she could scare up a job. At least she was clean. She dressed and went out.

The smell of eggs and buttery toast made her stomach clutch up like a fist. She was a morning eater as a rule, though the meal at Moll's had been much more than she usually had in the evening. She'd intended to head right out to continue her job search, but Steve turned from the stove.

"You want some eggs?"

She hesitated.

"Or don't you eat cholesterol?" He looked her over. "Tofu and sprouts more your style?"

"I eat anything." Beggars could not be choosers. And she knew what health food cost from stocking the shelves with her mother.

"Wouldn't know it to look at you."

"Well, I'm from Anorexia Beach. No one eats much when you live in bikinis."

He shot her a glance. "One egg or two?"

"Two. My bikini was in my car."

He almost smiled. "Toast?"

"Just one, thanks. Do you have any juice?"

"In the refrigerator."

She searched the shelves and found a carton of orange.

"Pour me a glass, too, will you?" Steve pointed to the cabinet that held glasses. At least he was no longer growling.

She filled two glasses and set them on the table. He flipped her eggs. Their edges were crispy brown from all the butter in the skillet. A moment later, he slid the eggs and butter over the slice of toast. Her mouth watered. He carried both plates to the table, and she followed.

Laying the paper napkin in her lap, Alessi said, "My mother had this grace she used to say. 'Thank you for this food, O Lord. Make this meal a feast, if only in our minds.'"

Steve scrutinized her. Didn't he believe in grace?

She took up her fork and looked down at her plate. "Of course, this is a feast already."

He said, "Cut the act."

She looked up sharply. "What act?"

He raised his brows. "Your Pollyanna con might fool Ben and Dave, but I see through you."

"Oh." She cut into her meal. Yellow egg yolk oozed over the corner of her toast, and she speared the bite and chewed.

"You have nothing to say to that? No witty comeback, no denial?"

She swallowed and wiped her mouth. "In the three and a half years I've been on my own, I've met two kinds of people. The kind with their minds made up, and the kind who wait and see." She took another bite. It was delicious cooked in excessive butter like that.

"You're not old enough to be on your own three and a half years."

"Twenty-one last June. I was given a car on my eighteenth birthday and invited to hit the road." She took a gulp of juice. It had sat a little long in the carton.

"Why?"

She shrugged. "Guardianship only lasts until then. Aunt Carrie and Uncle Bob had fulfilled their duty."

"So they kicked you out."

A sting touched her heart. "It wasn't like that. I was . . . an embarrassment. My mother eloped with my dad. No one in the family even knew about me until both my parents had died and I had to go somewhere." She pushed damp strands of hair behind her ear. "I was a gawky twelve-year-old. They did the best they could."

He was silent so long she was sure he didn't believe her. He'd already decided she was a liar. So what? People made judgments all the time. That was their problem. They'd judged her mother for choosing her dad. It wasn't her fault he'd drowned five years after they married. So she was a single mother trying to make ends meet. Did that mean she was a loser?

Alessi finished her eggs in silence. "That was good. Thanks." She stood and took her plate to the sink. She dribbled dish soap over the yolky plate and spritzed it with water, then wiped the ragged cloth over it and rinsed. She loved when things came clean. Probably a holdover from all the places she and her mother had janitored. Mom had made it a game: The princess was coming home at last and all the kingdom must sparkle; or the ogre would devour the owner of the dirtiest house; or the prince would marry the damsel who wasn't too spoiled to dirty her hands. Whatever the game, Alessi had worked with a fervor, taking on the devotion or desperation or humility of the theme.

She turned. "Would you like me to wash your plate?"

Though finished, he hadn't risen. He sat watching her, then seemed to realize she'd addressed him. "No. That's all right."

She dried her hands on the towel. "Thanks for letting me use your room last night."

"About that . . ."

"I'll have something else tonight." She wrapped herself in her arms. "Well, bye."

"It's cold out. You should at least take a coat."

She headed for the door. "Cholesterol's a great insulator."

"Alessi, hold it." He went to the closet, took out a thick flannel-lined jean jacket. "This one's short in the sleeves. It'll probably work just right for you."

She took the coat, risking one glance at his face. It was the softest she'd seen it yet. "Thanks. I'll return it when I get my stuff back."

He said nothing. She went out the door, snapping the jacket to her neck. It would have been an awfully cold walk without it, especially with her hair still wet. Snow might be beautiful, but it had its downside. She stuffed her hands into the pockets. Her fingers found something in the right one. She pulled it out. Two ten-dollar bills folded up.

She stopped. Had he planted it there? Her throat tightened painfully. She turned back, knocked on the door. It took a while for him to answer. When he did, he stood in T-shirt and jeans, having removed his sweater, shoes, and socks. He was not ripped in a beachcombing Florida way, but his musculature spoke of healthy exercise and natural strength.

She held out the bills. "I found this in your pocket."

He looked from the money to her. "Keep it. You might need it."

She shook her head. "No thanks."

He pushed her hand back. "Keep it, Alessi. I didn't even know it was in there."

Her ache eased. It was conceivable someone could have money in a pocket and forget. "I'll pay you back when I get my purse."

He nodded. "All right."

She pushed the money back into the pocket and started down the street. She would only use the loan if she had to. But its presence there was a tiny spark of security. She decided to start at the farthest-out point and work her way back to the heart of Charity. The buildings were not tucked up to one another at the fringe. That made for a longer walk than she'd realized driving in.

But she kept her pace brisk, building up some thermal energy inside Steve's jacket. She entered the front of the kennel that smelled of cigarette smoke and tuna. Then slowly she realized it wasn't tuna but dog urine. "Hello?" She waited. Finally a shuffling sound.

A hunchbacked woman made her way to the counter. "Yes?" Her orange hair looked like fake fur, too many chemicals used for too long. A chorus of barks followed her.

"Hi there." Alessi spoke quickly. "My name is Alessi Moore. Could you use help in the kennels, cleaning up or anything?" She'd prepared an oral resume, but . . .

"No. Do my own cleaning. All the dogs are mine."

"That must be very cheerful companionship."

The woman blinked slowly, her neck arched at what had to be an uncomfortable angle to meet Alessi's gaze. The smile she tried to form was a ghastly cross between a grimace and a grin, but her voice sounded sincerely regretful when she added, "I'd help you if I could. I hate to send away a stranger in need."

"That's all right." Alessi wasn't asking for help, just a chance to help herself. "I'm sure I'll find something. Thank you anyway." She went out and the cold snatched her as she moved on to the mini mart. A ponytailed man informed her that he and two others covered all the shifts there.

She crossed over to the hardware store, where a cheerful couple gave her the news that they and their son and their granddaughter ran the store and "thank you very much for asking, dear." He was tall and she was tall, and Alessi guessed the son and even the granddaughter were as well. She'd have fit in nicely there, but they had it covered. "Good luck," Grandma called. "Hope you find something."

Alessi passed a motel that she hadn't noticed on the way in, since it had only two rooms and the sign lay facedown in the tiny front lot. She went into the beer and pool hall. It wasn't open for business yet, but when she tapped the window, the door was opened by a man with blond hair that stood straight out an inch from the sides and top of his head. He had the proverbial broom, his purpose made clear by barrels of salted peanuts in the shell.

Alessi said, "I could sweep that up for you. I'm looking for work."

He looked her down and up. Not unkindly, but with a sort of vague confusion. "And I would do what?" That left her stumped just long enough that he said, "Sorry. Can't help you. Wish I could," and closed the door.

Alessi walked on in the cold. No one needed her, that was plain, but they all sure wished her well. If wishes were fishes, or horses, or fairy wands—or halos? Alessi shivered as her hair glazed. No sense asking at the city hall, with its sign that said call Frank at home with inquiries, so she made her way back to the gas station.

Ben waved her inside and brewed up a hot chocolate. "Any luck?"

She shook her head, the strands faintly clinking. "Not yet. But I've only done half of the town. Once I warm up a little, I'll start on the other." She sipped. "Ben, do you think I could start a tab for a few things like a toothbrush and toothpaste? Just until I get my money back or a paycheck?"

"Get whatever you need, Alessi. We'll just write it down."

She started down the short aisle that held shoelaces, eyeglass repair kits, toothbrushes, and combs. She selected a hairbrush as well as the dental items. Maybe there was somewhere in town with lower prices on those things, but she doubted anyone else would let her wait to pay.

Dave came in rubbing his hands. "Hey there. Is that Steve's coat?"

She nodded. "He's letting me use it."

"So you two made up?"

"No. He thinks I'm a liar. But that reminds me. I can pay for these things." She pulled out the tens. "I thought Steve planted the money in the pocket to see if I'd take it, but he seemed surprised it was there. He said to use it, so . . ."

"You just save that for something else." Ben pushed the bills away and wrote down the items.

She put the money back into her pocket, then rolled the top of the small sack shut and tried to work up the energy to continue her search. "People in Charity must be the nicest people around, but this town seems to be high on help and low on need."

"You ought to talk to Steve at the bookstore." Dave tore open a Danish pastry and took a bite. "He's always over his head when he buys a collection. Spends hours searching out the history and value of each book."

"I think he'd just as soon forget I'm here."

"He's not really like that," Ben said. "It's been a rough year."

Alessi took the stool next to the counter and leaned on her elbow. She might as well thaw out a little.

Ben moved the cardboard display of breath drops. "He was up in Anchorage working as a park ranger, but his dad took a bad turn, and Steve came back to run the store." Ben shook his head. "He wasn't ready to lose him."

Alessi nodded. She could certainly understand that. Her daddy's death had been sudden too. She chewed her lower lip.

"And that's not all." Dave crushed the plastic wrapper and threw it into the trash. "His fiancée came with him, spent one month in Charity, then left him for some other fellow she'd been stringing along. Steve hadn't even known the guy existed."

No wonder he had a poor opinion of women. Some certainly ruined it for the rest of them. "Was she pretty?"

"A knockout." Dave took a minty pick and poked it between his front teeth.

"That figures. Beauty stunts character."

Ben leaned on his elbows. "Well, I hate to tell you this, Alessi, but you're real pretty yourself."

"I'm lanky and freckled. I was taller than everyone in my class until eighth grade."

Dave grinned. "Diana always says she'd kill for five more inches."

"Who's Diana?" She reached over and brushed a Danish crumb from his shirt.

"My girlfriend, sort of."

"How tall is she?"

"Five foot three." He tossed the toothpick into the trash. "Says she'd distribute her pounds better over five more inches."

"That's one good thing about being tall. Plenty of distribution." Alessi scooted off the stool. "Well, I suppose I'll go see who wants me." She tucked the bag inside her coat and went back out. Spoken kindly, the next rejections at the community center and Maple Tree Bakery were as regretful as the rest. Though no one wanted to refuse her, she was learning the downside of a small town. People pretty much ran their own businesses, and business was minimal. There was certainly no tourist traffic, not even much Christmas shopping, though that might be due to the snow falling again. A silent desperation started inside.

Unless Sheriff Roehr came up with her car right away, she needed a job. *"Don't depend on others, Alessi. No matter how bad it gets; God helps those who help themselves."* Mom's way had not worked out well in her illness, but the general philosophy was one to live by.

She crossed the street, but the hair salon wasn't open. It listed hours for Saturday, but Alessi guessed maybe there hadn't been any appointments. Or the person was on vacation. Or any number of scenarios. She couldn't cut hair, but she could learn to polish nails. The fact that no one was there on a Saturday didn't look good, though, not for needing extra help.

Hawkeye Gifts was open, and settled in among the maple syrup displays and handcrafted wooden bowls, trivets, and serving trays were the owner and his cat. He stood up and extended his hand to her. "Doyle Upton." He smiled. "This is Dolly." The fur on the cat's neck and back flattened under his hand, then rose up with static connection as his palm stroked her. "What can I show you? It's all handmade, except for the syrup—that's God-made." He started toward a glass case. "Got some maple fudge the wife stirred up this morning."

Alessi's mouth watered as she accepted the sample he offered. It was good fudge. "Mmm. That is some of the best I've tasted." She thought of the money in her pocket. Did fudge constitute an emergency? The thought sobered her quickly. "Mr. Upton, do you need help here? I'm looking for work."

He looked instantly disappointed she wasn't a customer and shook his head. "As you see, there's not much traffic. Keeping the store moves me out of the wife's way, and the wood gives my hands a thing to do. But no, I'm sorry; I don't need to take someone on."

"Well, thank you anyway. Tell your wife I enjoyed the fudge."

"Oh, I will. Wives like to hear that."

Alessi went outside. Granny's Trunk and Bennet's Books remained. She crossed over to Granny's and inquired of the woman inside, expecting exactly the answer she got. Back outside, she looked across the street to Bennet's. That must be Steve's father's store. As her steps drew her closer, she studied the brick façade and neatly painted window frames adorned with a simple evergreen garland and white lights. She stood there long enough to memorize the window displays, then pushed open the door and went inside.

It didn't smell like Sherlock's, where she'd worked before, with its spanking new paperbacks and a hint of her boss, Ed Miller's, Old Spice. This store smelled of old cloth and leather-bound tomes. Who on earth did he sell to in Charity? She took another step in and caught a whiff of cinnamon and pine from the potpourri bowl in the window. You did not smell cinnamon and pine on the Florida coast, and for a moment she felt completely misplaced.

The front did hold some new hardbacks and also a section of trade paper and mass markets. One woman searched that rack lackadaisically. He had a customer? Doyle Upton would have been courting her eagerly. But Steve was nowhere in sight. Alessi passed into the rows of used books, each section neatly labeled by type, some locked behind glass.

She knew nothing at all about rare books except that it was hard to find one when a customer asked for something out of print. Ed had sometimes done an Internet search, but he hadn't applied himself too diligently and rarely found what they wanted. He sold new quick reads to fast-food readers. Thinking about it now, she would have reversed roles for Ed and Steve. It seemed the old man would have valued the old books, and the young . . . well, she didn't know what Steve valued. He was just running his father's store.

Six

ALESSI STOPPED AT THE BACK CORNER, where Steve worked on his computer. His hair was more disheveled than the night before, and she suspected he did it on purpose. A peppermint aroma came from the lump in his cheek. He looked up, brows raised in that skeptical annoyance reserved for her.

She smiled. "Dave said I should come by and see if you'd changed your mind about needing me."

"You haven't found anything?"

She shook her head. "Most everyone said the same as you. They can handle it themselves."

He took his hands from the keyboard, laid them in his lap. "So?"

She swallowed. "There's a customer up front."

"I know."

"I could see if she needs assistance."

He studied her face as if she'd grown another nose, then looked down. "All right." He turned back to the monitor and replaced his hands on the keys.

She stood rooted. All right—she should help the customer? All right—she had a job? The latter, she decided, and therefore the former as well. She walked to the front. "Hi. Are you finding what you need?"

The woman turned. "I'm . . . Where's Steve?"

"He's working on a new collection."

"And you're . . ."

"Alessi Moore." She held out her hand.

The woman took it stiffly. "You work here?"

"Just started."

The woman looked her over.

Alessi said, "I came in yesterday. I would have left today but someone took my car."

Her brows came together. "You mean your car was stolen? Here?"

"Yes, but Sheriff Roehr's working on it."

The woman's face changed. "Oh." She turned back to the bookshelf. "I'll just browse, if you don't mind."

Alessi wandered back through the store. The only customer in town wanted to browse. Steve was right. He didn't need her. But then another woman came in. Charity must be a readerish place if the bookstore, of all things, was doing the best business. Alessi greeted the new entrant, receiving a nod in return. This woman had an overbite that kept her lips from completely meeting, but her other features were nice: creamy skin and bright green eyes and a smell of almond extract.

The woman joined the first customer. "How are you, Sue?"

"I'd be better if I could decide on something for Noreen. She's always the hardest one on my list."

"Give her a fruitcake."

Sue rolled her eyes. "Who are you shopping for?" Her question sounded innocent until she sent a pointed glance toward the back. "As if I didn't know."

Alessi felt like a snoop. She'd make her offer, then leave them to their schemes. "Can I help you find something?"

They both turned to her. Sue frowned. "Does he have you running interference?"

Alessi stared at her. "If you mean Steve, he's back at his desk."

Sue elbowed her companion. "Go ahead, Deirdre."

Deirdre elbowed back. "Maybe I'll look around a little first."

Alessi left them perusing opposite racks, though it was obvious neither had a serious need for reading material, and returned to the back corner.

Steve glanced up. "Are they still here?"

She nodded.

"Think you can watch the store for a bit?"

"What if they want to buy something?"

"Not likely." But he took the register keys from his wrist. "Here."

"You trust me with your money?"

"I'd rather be robbed than acquired."

She heard movement from the front. He was already heading for the back room with a finger to his lips. This was certainly not what she'd expected. But she took matters in hand and rejoined the women in front. "Does this difficult friend of yours have a sense of humor?" At least she could distract them while he made his escape.

Sue raised her eyes from the back cover she pretended to read. "Not an ounce."

"An inquiring mind?"

"Not unless it's someone else's business."

"Does she cook?" Alessi had noted Martha Stewart's holiday cookbook in the window.

Sue tipped her head. "Yes, she does. . . ."

"What about this?" Alessi scooped the book from the window and displayed it. "Martha Stewart has such good ideas. Except, of course, on investing. But this is all cooking and entertaining."

Deirdre leaned over. "Wouldn't hurt Noreen to realize there's someone better in the kitchen than herself."

She and Sue locked glances. "Not that we all can't grow in humility."

"And discretion."

"And generosity."

Alessi waited while they reminded each other of those valuable virtues. Generosity was her cue. "It's a good deal. Twenty percent off hardbacks until Christmas." Again the sign posted in the window. She was glad she'd stood outside debating whether to go in.

Sue nodded slowly. "Maybe I will." She gave Deirdre a sultry look. "I'll pay for it now. You had your chance." She started toward the back.

Steve was gone, she was sure, but Alessi turned to Deirdre. "Maybe I can help you with something?"

Deirdre was definitely peeved. "Well, maybe a mystery for my father."

Now, that was something Alessi knew. "Rare or new?"

"What? Oh, new, I suppose. Just something in paperback."

Ah. A fast-food reader—at least the buyer was. "Time period?"

"Excuse me." Sue came forward with Martha Stewart plowing the air. "I thought you said Steve was back there."

"Did he step out?" Alessi glanced past her. "Well, I can help you." She took the book and headed for the register on the elbow of Steve's desk. She hoped it was similar to the ones she'd used before. She inserted the key and turned it. Simple enough. She rang up the sale and took Sue's money.

"When is he coming back?" One of Sue's eyebrows had developed a distinct arch.

"I don't know. Sorry."

Sue took her bag and swung away from the counter. She murmured something as she passed Deirdre, still lingering in the front, then went out.

Whew. Alessi went back up. "Okay. A paperback mystery . . . did you tell me what time period?" Ed had specialized in British turn of the century, but he'd carried everything.

"I don't know." Deirdre wrung her hands.

"American, British, or something exotic?"

Deirdre opened her mouth but nothing came out. She shook her head.

"Does he prefer a male author?"

"Why don't . . . you just pick something." The second half of her phrase escaped with a rush of breath.

"Good plan. If he doesn't like it, you can blame it on me." Alessi turned to the mystery shelf. Steve's selection was a fraction of Ed's, but these books weren't his focus. She doubted he had much traffic in his focus, though. She selected the latest P. D. James title and handed it to Deirdre. "How about this one?"

"Well . . . maybe I should think about it and come back later."

"Is your father a serious mystery reader? Does he write down the clues?"

Deirdre's features sharpened. "I have no idea."

"He'll like this one."

"Fine." Deirdre thrust it at her. "Ring it up."

Alessi took Dierdre's payment and bagged the book. "Thanks. Let me know how he likes it." Why did she say that? He wouldn't get it until Christmas, and she'd be long gone by then.

"Do you know . . ." Deirdre gripped the bag. ". . . what Steve's doing for Christmas?"

She didn't know what he was doing at the moment. "No. Sorry."

Deirdre sighed. "I suppose I should have gone right back. But he can be . . . peevish."

Alessi nodded, secretly agreeing. "I'll tell him you were looking for him."

"No . . . well, all right." Deirdre took her bag and left.

Alessi turned off the register and started around the desk, but Steve came toward her from the back room. She glanced quickly toward the front, but Deirdre had already cleared the windows. "That was close. They only just left."

"I know." He held out his hand for the keys.

Alessi handed them over. "Where were you?"

"In the storeroom."

She pictured him huddled among the boxes. "I thought you'd actually gone somewhere."

"Good."

She pushed her hair behind her ear. "I sold the Martha Stewart cookbook. And a paperback mystery."

"I heard." He tipped his head with a speculative expression that seemed to have puzzled him. Was it so unusual to make a sale? Then how did he stay in business?

"While I was in the storeroom I had a thought," he said.

"Shelves and boxes can be stimulating."

He leaned on the desk with the nearest thing to a smile she'd seen yet. "If you need a place to stay tonight, you could use the cot and bathroom back there. It's not the most comfortable, but it's better than nothing."

She drew herself up. "Aren't you afraid I'll run off with one of those seventeen-hundred-dollar books?"

"You won't get far on foot."

"No, I guess not," she said. "If the sheriff hasn't found my car by tonight . . ."

"Alessi." Steve fiddled with his keys. "Cooper Roehr is not going to get your car back."

She folded her arms across her chest. "I think it's here somewhere. There was hardly anyone on the highway; no one got off the exit with me. And someone 'passing through' would have left their car to take mine. No, it has to be here in Charity." She faced him directly. "How hard can it be to search a little place like this?"

"It's not that little. The village maybe, but the township is thirty-six square miles."

"And how many live in those square miles?"

He frowned. "Why don't you call your uncle?"

"I can't. My mother died of cancer before she'd ask them for help."

"But they took you in."

"The social worker guilted them into it."

"But they did it." He closed the keys in his hand.

"That wasn't my fault." Her voice rose in pitch. "I *can't* tell them I lost the car."

He crossed one ankle over the other in a casual pose, then threw out another stinker. "What about grandparents?"

"They refused to attend any family function if I was present."

He whistled. "What did your mother do that was so bad?"

"Fell in love with the pool boy."

He eyed her. "You're either the best liar . . ."

"I know." She raised a hand. "You've made up your mind."

"I thought I had."

She rounded the edge of the desk. "It doesn't matter. The fact is, I can't call my uncle and there's no one else. My best friend had a stroke—"

"More fantastic by the moment. You expect me to believe some girl—"

"He was seventy-four. Owned the mystery bookstore where I worked."

"And that was your best friend."

"Yep. You shouldn't go making assumptions."

He jutted his chin. "I think it was reasonable to assume your best friend was a girl. Not many twenty-one-year-old women call a seventy-four-year-old man their best friend."

"They didn't know Ed." She looked at the floor-to-ceiling case beside the desk. Each book in it had a detailed account typed up beside it. Steve obviously got his meticulous sense of order from his father. The pieces of her story must sound like so much gibberish. She could put it all together for him, but why do that for a man who wouldn't believe her anyway?

A draft raised gooseflesh on her arms. It was the same at the front. The cold that had seemed magical and refreshing in the snow was just chilly inside. She could wear the jacket he'd lent her, but she would look like she was going out the door, and that might give him ideas.

"Could I run over to Granny's Trunk real fast?" She didn't want to tell him his place had the atmosphere of an igloo, but a warmer shirt was required.

"Granny's Trunk?"

She caught her elbows. "Get something to work in tomorrow?"

"I'm not open Sunday." He slipped the keys back onto his wrist, then noticed her shiver. "I guess you'll need something for Monday, though."

"If I don't have my car back. I have plenty of clothes in my car."

He opened his mouth and closed it, then glanced toward the front. "Well, the piranhas have gone for the moment."

Alessi fingered a Venetian-glass paperweight and studied its swirling pattern. "They're worried about you for Christmas."

"They're on the hunt." He was growling again. "The whole pack of them."

"School, you mean."

"What?"

"It's a school of piranhas, not a pack."

He tucked his tongue into his cheek. "School, then. Either way they'll eat the flesh off my bones."

"Why?"

"A bereaved bachelor in Charity is fair game to every divorcée, widow, and single woman within a decade of my age. The holidays just rev them up."

It might have sounded vain, but she'd seen it for herself. "How long do you figure I've got before they circle back?"

Now his mouth did jerk sideways. "Make it quick."

She pulled the two tens from her pocket. "You sure about this?"

"Get going."

Seven

THE COLD OUTSIDE SEEMED LESS SEVERE as she made her way back to Granny's; the string of jingle bells almost cheery. If the woman she'd spoken with earlier was Granny, she held her age well. She'd been polite in her rejection. Definite, but polite. Alessi waved. "I'm back again."

The woman sent her a concerned glance. "I really don't have any positions."

"I'm just going to find a new sweater." Alessi passed the antique glassware, china, and dolls, a trunk of gloves, collars, and scarves, and wove between chairs, lamps, and farm implements. The rack of vintage clothing would be beyond her means, but there was a section marked nearly new and she headed there. "I need something nice and warm to work in."

"You found a job?" She probably didn't mean to sound so incredulous.

"Bennet's Books," Alessi said. "Just temporarily, until they find my car."

The woman didn't ask what she meant. The car didn't seem to be a subject people wanted to discuss. "You're working for Steve?" Granny slipped on a pair of half lenses that added years to her face.

Alessi circled the rack. "At least as long as it takes him to inventory his new stock."

Granny nodded at that. "Yes, I knew he went after an estate collection."

"Well, he got it. Lots of books. They're heaped up in back." She'd caught a glimpse when he made his escape.

The woman must have decided to believe her because she said, "Do you want something seasonal?"

Alessi studied the red-and-green sequined sweater the woman pulled from the rack. "It's really pretty." But considering the limitations of her wardrobe and the few weeks until Christmas, not practical. "I guess not, though." She wished again for the ribboned cashmere. It had been such a find. The thrift stores up the coast were sporadic treasure troves.

"Ah, this one." The woman held out a long winter-white mohair. "This was Amanda Bier's, special order from Saks. I'll swear she only wore it once. She's dreadful in white. But with your height and coloring . . ."

Alessi gathered the sweater into her hands. Soft as the goats it came from. "Do you have a changing room?"

The woman brought her to the back and flipped the light switch on in a tiny booth with a wavy mirror slanting to the left. Alessi closed the door and pulled off her shirt. This pearl-dotted white one rivaled her ribboned favorite. Probably even better quality, certainly less wear. She pulled the mohair over her head and let it fall.

"How's it looking?" Granny asked outside the door.

"It's really nice." Amanda Bier might not look good in white, but she did. She flipped over the tag dangling from the sleeve and sighed.

$39.99. She should have checked before she tried it.

"Let's have a look," Granny said.

Alessi opened the door.

"Oh." The woman clasped her hands. "It's perfect."

"It's really pretty. But I don't have that much money."

"Amanda paid almost two hundred dollars for it new."

Alessi nodded. "I'm sure it's worth your price, but I need something under ten dollars." She'd part with half the windfall from Steve's pocket, but not all. He hadn't even said what he'd pay her for working the store. Maybe he didn't mean to pay her at all—just let her stay there.

Granny tapped her chin with a finger. She looked into Alessi's face, then down at the tag. "Oh, it's a green tag? That's fifty percent off."

Alessi hadn't seen anything about a green-tag sale, but that did make a difference. Unfortunately not enough. She groaned softly. All Steve's money. Her whole windfall.

Granny flicked a fleck of lint from the sleeve. "That's only twenty dollars, a steal for that quality."

It was true, and she'd be tempted under other circumstances. She knew a good thing when she found one. She sighed. "I'd sure like to say yes. But my purse was stolen with my car, and I only have twenty dollars to my name. Do you have anything under ten?" Alessi absently petted the softness of the sleeve.

Granny's features shifted. "All right, you can have it for ten since you're new in town. And Amanda doesn't need the money."

Alessi wrapped herself in her arms. "Wow. That's great. Are you sure?"

The woman adjusted the shoulder. "It's a very nice sweater. But Amanda's things always linger."

Alessi could not imagine why, but she sure was glad.

"I'm Stacie, by the way. Since we're neighbors, by shops at least."

Alessi held out her hand. "Alessi Moore."

"Well, Alessi, you have the long waist to do that sweater justice. Do you want to wear it or sack it?"

Again Alessi petted her arms. "I'll just keep it on." She ducked into the changing room and scooped up her old shirt and Steve's jacket. She paid for the sweater and smiled hugely. "Thank you so much."

"I'll bag that other for you." Stacie tucked Alessi's shirt into a sack. "Tell Steve hello."

Alessi noted the gold-and-diamond band on Stacie's hand. "I'll tell him." She scooted back out to the snow falling in earnest. Stacie certainly had the Christmas spirit, and Alessi found a kindling of her own. She turned her face up, recapturing some of yesterday's wonder, and nearly walked into a heavyset man with a paper bag. "Excuse me. I wasn't watching where I was going."

He said nothing, just scowled as he passed her by. *Scrooge. "Are there no work-houses, no prisons,"* she mouthed after him. Then almost as if he'd heard her, he turned and mumbled, "Pardon me."

She gave him a wave and went back into the bookstore, took off the jacket, and set it behind Steve's desk with the sack. She didn't see him in the store. Was he hiding again? She went through the back doorway and found him taping half a dozen mailing boxes by the door.

She leaned on the steel shelf along the wall. "I thought maybe you were hiding again."

He turned, focused his gaze on her sweater, then raised it to her face. "You got that for twenty bucks?"

"Actually ten, for being new in town and green-tag day."

Steve turned back to the box and stretched the tape over the seam. "Stacie felt sorry for you."

That stung. "Must be the Pity Me sign on my forehead."

He straightened. "More likely she did it to spite Amanda."

"How do you know it was Amanda's?"

He didn't answer, just said, "It looks nice on you."

"Thanks." But she wasn't going to leave it at that. "You must know her."

"Oh yeah." He gripped an armful of books and stood up.

"A piranha?"

"The school marm."

Alessi laughed. "That was good. I wouldn't have guessed you witty."

He stopped and cocked his head. "Just humbug Scrooge?"

"More like Heathcliff. With a gripe against the world."

He studied her a moment. "I presume you mean Bronte's Heathcliff, not the fat ugly cat."

She laughed again. "Yes, I meant Emily's timeless character."

He stacked the boxes and pushed past her toward his desk.

"Are those orders?" She motioned toward the boxes he'd left.

"Yep." He circled around to his computer.

"Rare books?"

"Moderately." He sat.

She looked around for something to do. "Are you getting lots of orders for Christmas?"

"Yes. I still have quite a few to locate and process."

She leaned a hip on his desk. "How do you find them?"

He glanced up. "I have a special database I've built up. Actually, my father started it and joined with people around the world with collections like ours." His attention and his fingers went back to his work.

"Like us, they're constantly on the lookout for estates and collections becoming available. Then we list what we've acquired and, when someone needs a certain tome, we search each other's stock and make a deal."

It touched her that he still included his deceased father in the ownership. "That's a great setup. I wonder what Ed would have thought of it."

"Ed?" He looked up again, his fingers pausing on the keys.

"The man I worked for."

"Your best friend who had a stroke."

Her throat tightened a little at his tone. "Yes. Sometimes people wanted some hard-to-find title, and he'd search the Internet, but he didn't have much luck."

"You have to know where to look."

The little bell jingled on the door and Alessi turned. A very shapely woman entered. Her red cable-knit sweater had what must be a mink collar around her ivory neck and was belted at the waist. Diamonds the size of her earlobes glittered through strands of coifed platinum hair. Her lips matched her sweater, with a glamour dot of gloss centered on her bottom lip, visible to the back of the store. Her eyes were a little narrowly placed, but she extended them a good distance with an artful liner pencil. In Palm Beach she would have been another beautiful face; in Charity she looked gaudy.

Alessi started forward but made it only past the first case from the back. "Hi. May I . . ."

The woman turned and stared. "That's my . . . Where did you get that sweater?"

"You must be Amanda." She said it loudly enough for Steve to make his retreat.

But Amanda was quick. No lingering over racks for her. She swept past on a gale and caught him rising from his chair. "There you are. I heard you were back."

"Just last night."

She stood her red nails on his desk like soldiers at attention. "I will not take no for an answer."

He finished standing and pushed the chair in. "No to what?"

"I insist you have Christmas at my house. No more pining."

Steve clicked his fingers and gave a soft grunt. "Sorry, I've got plans."

"What plans?" She leaned forward. "Ben and Dave will be with Mary and Diana. I asked. That leaves you all alone."

He started around the desk, lifting a book as he went.

"Do *not* tell me you'll be here with these musty old books."

"No." He opened the case and slid his volume between two others that matched, but he was starting to waver.

"What, then?"

"I have a date." Definitely unconvincing.

"With whom?"

A more caustic tone Alessi had never heard, and Steve was crumbling. She stepped into their midst. "With me."

Steve froze midstep, then turned to face Amanda. "With Alessi."

When his hand touched the small of Alessi's back, she managed a smile.

Amanda's eyelids lowered as she inched up to Steve, heat rising from her skin in waves. Alessi imagined touching her with a wet finger to hear the sizzle.

"Fine." Amanda gave her a frosty look and stalked out.

Steve took his hand away. "You didn't have to do that."

"Who were you going to say?"

"I don't know." He studied the bookshelf as though he'd forgotten what he just put there.

"Volume four—between three and five."

He jerked up. "Thank you." He took the next book from the stack, checked the code he'd initialed on the paper he'd slipped inside the cover, and carried it to a shelf midway toward the front. Alessi closed her eyes and drew a slow breath. What on earth had made her step in like that? Her rescue mentality kicked in at the worst times.

Steve came back and glanced her way. "Alessi—"

"I don't know why I said it." She folded her arms. "You just looked panicked."

"I wasn't panicked." He scowled, taking the next two books in the stack. "And now word will spread. Amanda's probably spouting indignation from one end of town to the other."

Great. Now he blamed her. Alessi said, "Well, I'll be gone by Christmas. I might even be gone tomorrow." She picked up a book and read the initials on the paper slip. "You'll have to find another excuse." She started for that book's section, but he caught her arm. She looked into his face, hoping he was not going to scold her further.

"Do you know where to put that?"

She pointed. He let her go, but when she came back, he said, "I was handling it."

"You'd be spending Christmas with Amanda."

"I . . ." He scowled. "Funny how easily that lie sprang to your lips."

She swallowed hard, not even pointing out that it was his lie that started it. And he'd certainly gone right along.

He sighed. "Forget it now. You seem to know what you're doing. Help me shelve these."

They stocked the two piles of books he'd processed so far, then Steve looked at his watch. "It's almost two. Why don't you go get some lunch."

"All right." She put his jacket back on, though the sweater hung down beneath it and looked silly. She didn't care. She walked out, back straight. She had no illusions—Amanda Bier she was not, even in the woman's sweater. And she was certainly not in the school of piranhas. It was a major feat just working with Steve Bennet; any personal involvement would be emotional suicide.

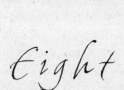

Eight

STEVE WATCHED HER GO. Something in the way she held herself walking out told him he'd managed that badly. Why had she come to his rescue? He looked panicked? Possibly. Like it or not, Amanda was attractive, and he might have found himself in her teeth if Alessi hadn't been there. He'd almost succumbed to her allures the last time, and the only thing that saved him then was contemplating the morning after. And after and after and after.

A constriction not unlike a boa's coils seized his throat. He would never entertain those thoughts again, not with Amanda or anyone else. Spending Christmas alone was just the ticket, though now he was in a different fix. If Alessi left before Christmas, he would not only have no excuse, he'd have a new jilting pumping blood into the water. Amanda would spread word of his involvement with the new girl, and when that girl fled town, it would be just like the last time.

He slammed his fist on the desk. Ego aside, he wanted to walk the streets without compassionate females stalking him. Not that there were so many in Charity, but they came from miles around. There was a solution, and she could hardly refuse since she'd interfered in the first place.

Two and a half weeks wasn't asking much, especially since she'd lost her car and wasn't likely to have it back soon. Of all the things missing lately, Sheriff Roehr had come up with exactly zero. It was something of a mystery, which was hard to accomplish in any small town, much less one with Charity's particular attributes. If there was a culprit in Charity, he or she was closemouthed. Steve shook his head. He had a unique perspective, being of Charity yet estranged, but even he had no quick explanation.

Cooper Roehr would have to make an effort, and maybe he would actually come up with the car. As far as Steve had heard, nothing that large and expensive had turned up missing. In the meantime, Alessi might change her mind about calling her uncle. . . . He'd have to stop pushing that. And she would need certain basics like food, clothing, personal items. . . .

He could offer her paycheck up front, covering the time until Christmas. And he could concede his position in the storeroom. She would be more comfortable in the house with Dave and Ben. Yes, that was the ticket. Keep her safe and comfortable. In fact, she'd be the perfect shield to get him through the holidays with the least interference.

By the time she came back, he was ready. "Alessi, I've been thinking. . . ."

"So have I."

He frowned. If he didn't get it out first, it might not sound right.

She took off the jacket and laid it on his desk. That didn't look good, especially when she reached for the bag that held her other shirt. "I know you meant well giving me this job—"

He held up a hand. "I know what you're going to say, and you're right. The remark about lying was out of line." After all, what did he know about her? Every word of her story might be true, as improbable as it sounded. He stopped that thought before he ended up like Ben and Dave, gulping it whole. "You did what you thought I needed." He stood up and walked around to her. "My personal business is not your concern, and I was wrong to involve you." But her involvement was precisely what he needed.

She pushed her hair back in what he recognized now as a defensive gesture.

"The fact is, I do need your help. This was a huge collection I acquired, and I'll be days researching some of the finds. If you could just stay through Christmas, I won't make you deal with any of the women who come in for anything besides books." He wouldn't need to if Amanda spouted the news as he expected. If any women came in and saw Alessi, it would only enhance the situation in their minds.

Alessi looked at him, hazel eyes penetrating.

"And," he said, "I want you to stay at the house with Ben and Dave. It's more comfortable and safer. I can manage here and go home to eat and shower."

She tipped her head. "You're more full of it than I thought."

"I'm what?" His jaw actually dropped.

"What if I hem and haw?"

He swallowed. She had him. "How about I pay you now for the time until Christmas?"

She laughed. "Holiday overtime?"

"No." He frowned. "I just look like I'm made of money."

She glanced over at the shelf. "Actually, I wondered who on earth you sold this stuff to."

"Not many in Charity." He glanced over his cases. "I get some traffic from neighboring cities, but as I said before, it's an Internet enterprise. People all over the world know what I have."

"Oh." She ran her fingertip over his paperweight.

"I meant that about needing your help, by the way."

She nodded without looking.

"Six dollars an hour plus room and board. I'm open from ten to six every day except Sundays."

"Why not Sundays?" Now she did look, and he guessed there was more in her question than the obvious.

"That was my father's philosophy."

"And yours?"

"Are you asking if I keep the Lord's Day?"

She shrugged. "It's none of my business. You just don't seem . . ."

Now it would come, and he deserved it. But she left it hanging.

"Alessi, I'm sorry. I've been a bear from the start of this."

"Well, I did invade your den," she said.

"Any kind of gentleman would have accepted that gracefully." He didn't want to lay it on too thick, or she'd see through him again. Or maybe he really was sorry he'd been inhospitable. He couldn't quite conjure his previous animosity.

She tucked her hands into her pockets. "I guess if you want my help, I can stay. And I'll accept my pay up front so I can reimburse Ben for my toothbrush and my lunch."

"You had lunch at the gas station?"

"I wasn't sure how long I'd have to stretch that last ten dollars you loaned me. Ben said I could run a tab until I get my purse back." She sighed. "I had almost a thousand dollars in my purse."

He kicked himself for not considering her situation but only said, "That's a lot of traveling cash."

"It was everything I had." Her tone lacked the self-pity he would have expected. Maybe she'd stolen the thousand dollars from her uncle as well.

"What did you eat for lunch? Corn nuts?"

"Cashews."

He snatched his store keys from the desk. "Come on, let's get some real food." He expected a smile or something. Did she realize what a concession he'd just made?

She reached for the jacket and pulled it on. "That should set Amanda on her ear."

"What do you mean?"

"Us having lunch, and it's not even Christmas?" She snapped the top snap and worked down.

He actually hadn't intended the invitation for effect, but it wasn't surprising she'd taken it that way. "If you'd rather not, I understand."

"I'm hungry enough to eat with Hannibal Lecter."

He grimaced. "Thanks."

She followed him to the front, waited while he set his return time on the door sign and then locked the door. He wanted to apologize again but wasn't sure why. None of this was his fault. She'd lost her car, weaseled her way into his store, and pronounced herself his date. He was only going along.

She turned her frank face to him. "You ought to hold my hand. That's a picture that paints a thousand words."

He stopped still, staring at her. He did not want that picture painted inside him. "I ought to?"

"Even if you don't want to."

"What if I want to?" It came out hoarsely.

"Then you're in trouble. After Christmas I'm out of here."

That was just the answer. He took her hand, felt the strength of it, the chill at the tips of her long fingers. How long had it been since he'd cradled a woman's palm against his, carried her along beside him? Alessi was nothing like Barb, her hand larger and firmer than Barb's soft, petite fingers. He had only to turn sideways to catch Alessi's glance, not look down as he had to the heart-shaped face of the woman he'd loved. He kicked himself. What was he doing?

"Where are we going?" Her voice brought him back.

"Moll has killer pot roast."

"Good. You can take the pole out of your back."

Frowning, he let go her hand and slipped his arm around her shoulders. Definitely less disparity in height. It was nice not to have to stoop. She turned, a little surprised.

"Loose enough?" He smiled.

Surprisingly, she smiled back. "I'd almost think you meant it."

"Well, right now I do. I appreciate your help." He steered her into Moll's, raising the eyebrows of the diners inside. Alessi was right. He'd just sent them a Kodak moment. Lonely, jilted Steve Bennet has a new love interest. Oh boy. Lest the drama get out of hand, he let her go and motioned her toward a booth near the back.

She slid into the seat. He liked the way she folded instead of scooching like Barb. But Barb's feet had hardly reached the floor. She loved being tiny, used it to make him feel big and capable and protective. He hadn't realized until it was too late that it was himself he'd needed to protect.

Alessi picked up her menu, then laid it down immediately. "Did you say killer pot roast?"

He slipped his paper napkin to his lap. "I did."

"Then that's what I'll have," she said.

"We'll make it two."

"Just like some old couple." She stashed the menu back behind the condiments.

He cocked his head and eyed her. "I can't imagine you old."

"I probably won't be."

Odd. "What do you mean?"

"My mother died at thirty-two. Breast cancer. It's hereditary." She picked up her fork and balanced it like a tree.

"Hereditary factors, maybe. But that doesn't mean you'll get it. Or that you'll die of it. You said she could have gotten help."

She held the fork upright with one finger across the tines. "I think both parents dying early is a sign, like a warning for me."

"What happened to your dad?"

"Boating accident. The big sailboats that people charter? He took his out one night and never came back."

"You can't call that hereditary."

"No," she said.

"Did they recover the boat?"

She laid the fork back on the napkin. "What was left of it."

Moll came to their table, wiping her wet hands on her apron. "Pot roast for you, Steve?"

"Two." He looked at Alessi. "What do you want to drink?"

"Do you have root beer?"

Moll wrote without answering, then walked away. Steve looked at Alessi sitting across from him, unsure of what to make of her. If she was a con, she stayed more consistent than he would expect. Her car might have been stolen from her in Charity, but as to it being hers in the first place . . . He still suspected she couldn't contact her uncle because she'd taken the car and run. If Cooper ran a check for stolen vehicles, he might just find that red convertible Mustang listed already. What then?

Arrest Alessi? Great. Steve Bennet's new girl in ankle chains. And it would be embarrassing when they could not come up with the car. More likely, Cooper would ask around, search the streets, and conclude it wasn't in Charity. Then what? Would they all pretend Alessi had just arrived with the snow? And would it somehow whisk her away after Christmas?

Moll returned with Alessi's root beer. She brought him a cup of coffee and a creamer.

"Thanks, Moll."

"Pot roast is coming." She tucked a string of red hair into her net.

He said, "It's worth the wait," and received the fake smile, silver tooth and all, that said flattery would get him nowhere. It was almost a game.

Alessi pulled her straw from the wrapper and dunked it into her drink. She glanced at him as she sipped. In some ways she seemed very young, in others older than her years. And this business about dying young . . .

"So what was it your grandparents objected to in your dad?"

"He was the pool boy."

"There had to be more to it than that." Steve peeled the lid from his creamer. He drank his coffee black in the morning but creamed it the rest of the day.

"He was not supposed to entice the daughters of the people he worked for. He could hardly help it, though. He was very good-looking." She rubbed away one of the frosty sections on the glass with her fingertip.

"What's good-looking?"

"In his case? Tall, blond, blue eyes."

"Malibu Ken. I suppose your mom was Barbie." He half believed it, with Alessi herself giving credence to the Barbie-doll shape.

She leaned back against the booth cushion. "My mother was small, flat chested, and curly haired."

"So you got your dad's height and your mom's curls."

She nodded. "What about you?"

"I don't remember my mom."

She frowned. "Why not?"

"She left us before I was three." He sipped his coffee. How had this turned around on him? "So your mom fell in love with Ken and—"

"His name was Brian. He gave her a Bible and said he'd help her read it."

"I bet."

"He told her about Jesus when no one in her family had ever believed. They didn't have to. They had everything they needed."

"He offered her faith in place of the good life." Steve leaned back and folded his hands.

"He offered her truth."

"So she lied to her family and married him." He half taunted, hoping to throw her off her game.

"They eloped, yes. But she tried to reconcile. My grandfather refused to take her phone calls or read her letters. When they came back unopened, she stopped trying."

Steve studied the coffee in his cup. "There's a price for running off."

Alessi studied him a moment too long. He had sounded vindictive.

She said, "Mom was dyslexic. Everyone called her stupid, even my aunt Carrie, who was two years older. People made fun of her. Except my dad. He told her she was exactly what God wanted her to be."

Probably not much discrepancy between her intellect and the pool boy's. Steve caught himself. Why was he automatically disparaging a man he'd never met? Just because he'd won the heart of a woman and lured her away from her family?

"My mom was not stupid. She was brilliant, just not in testable ways."

He nodded, half believing it. Maybe that was the oddness he noticed in Alessi. "How did you manage after your dad died?"

"Mom worked as many jobs as she could find. I worked with her."

"Doing what?"

"Cleaning, mainly. Stocking shelves. Whatever she could do. There was not one day we didn't eat three meals, even if it was from a single can." She dropped her gaze. "I cry when I think of the times I complained." To prove it, her eyes turned glassy.

But he'd seen great acting before. Thankfully, Moll brought their plates before he had to determine if Alessi was for real. The steamy pot roast looked fork tender and smelled rich and peppery, the way he liked it. Gravy smothered the mashed potatoes, carrots, and onions. "Moll . . ."

"I know. You're speechless."

"Again."

She snorted, then left them.

Alessi said, "I guess now I'm invisible." She picked up her fork. "This morning she thought I was contagious."

"Moll's just Moll." Frankly, he found her abrasive personality refreshing after all his plastic, pious neighbors. Courtesy was one thing; Charity was taking its name a bit too seriously these days. Besides, Moll made him look good.

Steve nodded at the bite Alessi had scooped. "Aren't you going to say your mom's grace?"

"I think I'll just be grateful for this food. It doesn't need imagination."

Steve took a bite. It needed nothing but a touch of salt. He reached for the shaker at the same time she did. They both pulled their hands back. He said, "Go ahead."

She sprinkled the salt, then handed it to him. He touched her fingers when he took it. "Are you cold?"

"It's just from the root beer." She touched him with her other hand and it was warm. Too warm. Barb's were perfectly manicured doll's nails. It looked like Alessi bit hers. But maybe that was because her toiletries had been stolen.

"If I give you your pay today, you could go to Wal-Mart and get the things you need." She could also skip town with the money.

"Where's the Wal-Mart? I didn't see one coming in."

"No, it's almost in Chambers City. About thirty miles outside of town."

She scooped potatoes onto her fork. "I'm not sure I'm up for that hike."

He'd forgotten her transportation situation. She'd have a hard time skipping town without a car, unless she'd stashed it somewhere until she had swindled all she could. He said, "I'll drive you."

"You will?" The bite stopped just outside her mouth.

"I'm not always a jerk."

She did a fair job hiding her incredulity. All right, so he hadn't shown his best side. She took the bite and dabbed with her napkin. "This is really good. Moll's a great cook."

"How about you? Do you cook?"

She sipped her root beer. "Well, I flip a mean burger. Fries too. But I haven't had an actual kitchen—"

"No, of course not. You probably lived in your car, this mysterious, disappearing Mustang."

She set down the root beer. "Is there a bathroom?"

He pointed toward the doors next to the counter. She stood up and walked away with the same stiffness he'd seen before. He'd hurt her again. What was it about her that made him strike with both fangs?

Nine

ALESSI CLOSED HERSELF INTO THE STALL. It didn't matter. People judged by what they saw or thought they saw. Steve must have serious abandonment issues if his mother left him before he was three and his fiancée left him for someone else. Of course he wouldn't trust her. She just wished he wouldn't call her a liar every time they talked.

Didn't he see all she wanted was to get her car back and leave? A twinge stung inside. Was that what she wanted? Wasn't she tired of roaming, trying to get by, trying to find someplace she belonged? That was the whole point of this trip, this pilgrimage. To find the place she was meant to be, to know she could stay.

She remembered the first time she'd been asked to leave. She wasn't sure how old she was, but it wasn't long after Daddy's accident. Two men had come to the door and Mom let them in. They sat a long while in the small living room of their apartment; Mom cried. The men had looked very uncomfortable, but when they left, Mom told her they had to find a new home.

It had never been an apartment again. The cost of living was too high on the coast, but Mom was afraid to leave it. Alessi guessed now that she'd been hoping her family would look for her and she didn't want to be far. So it had been motel rooms for them, up along the coast, and nothing like a Marriott.

Years later Alessi had learned that they lost their first place because Daddy had borrowed heavily for the boat and was underinsured. With that debt and no offsetting income from charters, Mom could not make the rent. Any time Alessi needed a doctor or something extra for school or the time someone ran into their car, they'd been set back so far they'd have to change motels. There was always a new adventure to go with it, but Alessi was tired of that life.

Yes, she'd spent some nights in her car. Not by choice, but things didn't always happen the way you wanted. She wasn't complaining, so why should he criticize? She'd had great hopes for Charity, but now she was living with strangers and begging a ride to Wal-Mart. Did he think she liked it that way?

She left the stall and washed her hands, immersing them in the warm water until she found the courage to return to the booth. She looked into the mirror. Mom might not have been Barbie, but she'd had the greatest smile.

Alessi mostly took after her dad, but she had her mom's smile. She practiced until she could make it look real, then straightened. If Mom could smile through it all, she could too. She toweled her hands and went back to the table. Steve's plate was nearly empty; hers was covered with a plastic lid.

He lifted it and set it aside. "I had Moll cover it so it wouldn't get cold."

He must have thought she'd fallen in. "I'll just take it in a box."

"I thought you were hungry enough to eat with Hannibal Lecter."

She had been; he just couldn't tell that he'd eaten her alive. "I've had enough, and you probably need to get back to the store."

He didn't argue, just commandeered a box and waited while she shoveled it in. It would make a great dinner, even cold. She stood. "I'd offer to pay Dutch, but I'd still be using your money."

He smiled. "Some date I'd be."

Date? She was definitely down on her luck.

He took the check and paid at the counter, handing Moll her tip directly. He was generous. Alessi appreciated that, though Moll seemed unimpressed.

Alessi smiled at Moll. "Sure was good."

No answer.

She and Steve walked out together, but he didn't hold her hand. She did not remind him. Two women waited outside the store when they got back, both within a decade of his age. He greeted them by name as he unlocked the door and motioned them in.

"How was your trip, Steve? Find anything wonderful?" The first woman was dark haired and plump with great dimples and very blue eyes.

"Some."

"You'll have to show us." This from her friend, also plump but with the ruddy appearance of energy and spunk.

He flipped the sign around. "I don't have much shelved yet. That's what I'm working on. Alessi can help you find anything you need."

She said, "Hello," and steeled herself as they turned to her, but these two weren't belligerent. If they were dismayed to be pawned off on her they didn't show it.

"You're new here." The first woman's blue eyes were startling against her black lashes.

"I'm just temporary. Until I get my car back."

"Oh, so you're the one whose car was lost." The other woman put a hand to her arm. She was the first one today who hadn't brushed off the mention of her car or changed the subject. Even so, *lost* didn't exactly explain the situation. Alessi knew exactly where she'd left it.

She sighed. "I sure wish Sheriff Roehr would find it." Then she could drive herself to the Wal-Mart. No, she wouldn't need the Wal-Mart; she'd drive right out of town.

"And your purse gone and everything with it?" They were certainly well informed.

"Everything." And she was sure that word meant more to her than to the woman.

"Oh, honey." The ruddy woman pulled out a card. It read Diana Barnes, Cosmetology. "You just take this and if you need anything, give me a call. I'm just down the street at Hair Magic. At least some of the time."

Alessi looked at the card again. "Diana. Are you Dave's Diana?"

She laughed. "If he'd ever get off the stick."

"So that's how you know."

Diana shook her head. "Everybody knows by now."

"I'm Karen." The other woman hugged her. "And what Diana said is true for me too. If there's anything you need, you can find me at the church office."

"The church?"

"Charity Chapel. It's just a block and a half north of here. Can't miss the big cross standing out front."

Alessi slipped the card into her jeans pocket. "Is there anything I can help you with?"

Karen glanced over her shoulder, then whispered, "I just wanted to make sure Steve wasn't spending Christmas alone."

Alessi would not give her the line they'd fed Amanda Bier. "He's dodging invitations."

Karen clicked her tongue, shaking her head. "I know you can't rush grief, and his father was the only family he had after . . ."

"He told me about his mom."

The women shared a stare then turned it on her. "He did? He never talks about it, not even in Bible study when we're all sharing our most painful moments."

Alessi did not picture Steve in Bible study. She'd made the same judgments about him as he had about her. "He only said she left."

Both women's eyes fell. "Walter Bennet was salt of the earth. When she ran off with Randal Potts, he never said a word against her, just took his little boy under his arm and raised him all alone."

Karen lowered her voice. "He didn't contest the divorce papers, but he never signed them either. It passed the date and was a done deal with him never a willing partner."

Diana nodded. "And he had plenty of chances to remarry but never did."

No wonder Steve dreaded the pursuit of all the women in town. He'd already lived through it with his dad. Alessi said, "What Steve wants most right now is to be left alone."

They shook their heads. "That will not happen. A good-looking man like Steve with his own business and a hint of tragedy is just too tempting. I'm surprised Amanda Bier hasn't already snapped him up."

"She tried."

"And?"

Now she had to say it or make Steve a liar. "I'm . . . we're spending Christmas together."

"Well." Diana squeezed her hand. "I am glad. Wait till Dave hears."

Karen seemed a little deflated, but she smiled too. "I'm just glad he won't be locked away somewhere. This will be his first Christmas without Walter, and they were so close."

Alessi remembered the first Christmas at her aunt and uncle's. She had cried inconsolably from sheer loss. They'd finally left her in her room and celebrated without her. It was the best of the Christmases she'd spent there.

"So you don't really need a book?"

They looked at each other and laughed. Karen said, "We've got stacks of things still to read, but if he's feeling assailed . . ." She looked around her.

"Here's a nice one." Alessi pulled a small collection of poems and prayers for the holidays from the shelf. "You could tuck it into a gift basket with a teacup or something."

Karen's dimples deepened. "We are definitely going to get along."

Alessi caught her breath. A rush of warmth filled her as she caught the glow of the window garland behind Karen's head. Karen reached for the book, and the glow was gone, but it had been there. Just like the halo on the sun. Maybe she wasn't in the wrong place at all. Maybe a miracle just took some building up.

She hadn't noticed how dim it had grown outside. The snow now fell like confetti on New Year's Eve. Where would she be New Year's Eve? "I'll just ring you up."

After they left, Steve came out of the storeroom with a full box of books. He slid it to the floor beside his desk and took his chair.

"Karen bought that poems and prayers collection."

"Uh-huh." He took off his screen saver and scrolled down the table that replaced it. "There it is. I knew I had one."

"She thought this Christmas might be hard for you."

"Not if I can fend off the vultures." His fingers clicked on the keys. The piranhas had taken to the air, it seemed. "She meant well."

"She and Diana both, I'm sure. I just don't need their coddling." Nor her platitudes. "Can I shelve some of those?"

He glanced at the box. "Sure. I have some orders here to deal with." He was back to the screen already.

She reached into the box, realizing what he'd said before. His main business was not transacted through the front door. Her little sales might mean nothing at all to him. If he was selling books worth hundreds or even thousands of dollars to buyers all over the world, his whole little store was hardly more than a warehouse.

But she didn't care. It felt good to make a sale, to match a product to a buyer. She had a knack for it. And she had to earn her paycheck somehow, though come to think of it, he had yet to write that check. She shelved all the books in the box, then took the feather duster and went over each row, except inside the locked cases.

The snow came down so hard she guessed they might not see another customer, not even one with hopes for snagging Steve. Whoever had her car better keep the top fastened down tight. And her tires, though new, were not snow tires. Steve came up behind her and took the duster.

Her shoulder bumped into his chest as she turned. "I was just finishing."

"Let's go get your things. The road'll be impassable soon."

She pulled on his jacket and followed him out the back door. His burgundy truck was lathered with snow. He let her into the passenger side, reached over and started the engine, then took the scraper and started on the windows. The snow was light as fluff, and he brushed it away quickly, all those little snowflakes flung from their resting places.

He climbed in and revved the engine, checking his temperature gauge. "We'll have heat in a minute."

"I'm okay."

He half turned. "Do you ever complain?"

"It doesn't do much good."

He reached into his pocket. "Here." He handed her a bundle of bills in a rubber band. "I put it in cash since you don't have a bank account."

That was thoughtful of him to consider. "Thanks." She didn't count the bills. Steve would have figured it exactly, and she didn't want to look too eager, since he already thought she was trying to get something for nothing.

"I didn't bother with FICA or any of that since it's so temporary. You can be responsible for your taxes."

She almost laughed. She'd never paid taxes in her life except the social security the government automatically withdrew. She never made enough to stand up and be counted.

The snow was thick on the road, but his heavy tires plowed through, leaving a double track. It looked as though the snow threw itself at them as they drove, but when she looked to the side, it fell straight. The heat quickly filled the cab.

"Warm?" He reached for the dial.

"Toasty." His truck had a hint of butterscotch from empty wrappers in the console. Other than that, it was as tidy as his room.

The wipers fended off the flakes, but Steve had to strain to see the road. "We should have started out an hour ago."

"If it's too bad, don't push it."

"We'll get through," he said.

Long after all sign of Charity had disappeared behind them, she saw a lone parking lot with its lights each bearing a hazy halo. Had the sun gone down already? The sensors thought so.

Steve pulled into the lot and found a space close to the entrance. Alessi climbed out and shielded her face from the insistent snowflakes.

"Come on, beach girl. Don't just stand there." Steve caught her hand and hurried her inside. The warmth of his grip lingered long after he released it. "I'll be in electronics. You can meet me there when you're done."

She nodded and headed for the health and beauty section. She chose the cheapest blow dryer she could find but got a decent shampoo. She added facial cleanser and moisturizer and lingered over the foundations and eye shadow. An argument of necessity couldn't really be made there. She looked presentable without it, even with every freckle showing.

So she went to women's clothing and searched the clearance rack. She found a pair of extra-long forest green slacks that would look nice with the white mohair sweater. In the dressing room, she realized what she needed most, and she was thankful Steve had not hung around.

She preferred Hanes, so it took her only a few minutes in the lingerie racks to choose what she wanted in underwear, socks, and bra, and to fold them inside the pants. She ought to have something to sleep in, but Steve's T-shirt and sweats had worked so far. She hated to spend the money when she had sleepwear in her car. Maybe he wouldn't mind sharing his a little longer. She found a black cable-knit sweater on clearance for seven dollars, a beige turtleneck for five that would give her some combinations. She added them to her cart and went to find Steve.

He was perusing the CDs. "Get what you need?"

"Well, if you want your jacket back now, I'll have to find something else."

"Keep it. It fits you better than it does me." He picked up a jazz ensemble, glanced at the backside, then returned it to the rack.

"Then I need to ask if I can still use your sweats and T-shirt."

He rested his hands on his hips. "I'll even throw in my robe."

"Wow." She smiled.

He half returned it. "We better hurry before I turn back into the beast." He looked at the things in her cart. Thank goodness she'd hidden the underwear. He said, "Brush, toothbrush?"

"I got them from Ben. Now I can pay him."

"All right, then."

They started for the front. Most of the lanes were empty, and she went right up to the counter. She turned to Steve. "I'll check out by myself."

He stood dumbly, then grasped her point and went to wait by the door. The checker rang up her items, and Alessi paid, then gathered her bag and joined Steve.

"Ready?" He arched his brows with definite amusement.

"Yep."

He pushed open the door and let her through. She was surprised to feel his hand on the small of her back as they made it through the lot to the car. "It might be slick." It was awfully nice to have someone looking out for her, even if he did it under duress. He let her in and again brushed the snow from the windows.

Almost no other cars were on the road. They followed their own half-filled tracks back to town, and Steve turned in at the station and past it to the house behind. "I'll just get some things from my room; then you can make yourself comfortable."

Alessi clutched the bag. "I think I'll stick to your other offer."

"What do you mean?"

"Sleep in the storeroom."

He stopped the truck in front of the house. "Why?"

"I don't want people to get the wrong idea. Diana might not appreciate me sleeping in the room next to Dave, and Ben certainly doesn't need any more complication in his situation. The storeroom's like my own place."

Steve eyed her a long moment, but whatever he was thinking, he kept it to himself. He climbed out and walked around the truck, pulled her door open, and offered her a hand. "Come get what you need, then."

"Just the sweats and T-shirt." She stepped down, her hand in his. He moved aside and closed the door behind her. They plowed through the snow toward the door.

"I've never seen a white Christmas. Do you think it'll stay?"

"If not this batch, then the next." He opened the door. "We usually have snow for Christmas."

She banged her shoes, though the powder stayed around her laces and clung to the tread.

"The carpet's old. Go on in." Again he nudged her with a touch to her back.

She went in, letting the warmth enclose her. She wanted to shake herself, turn around three times, and curl up by a fire. But they had no fire in the small square fireplace. If she ever had a fireplace, she'd use it. And get a dog.

Ten

STEVE TOOK THE T-SHIRT and the sweats from the foot of the bed. It surprised him that Alessi would consider Dave and Ben's situations. Barb would have reveled in the chance to play one man against another, incensing any women involved. Though both men had women they cared about, it was obvious they were also a little smitten with Alessi.

"Here you go." He handed over the clothes and reached for his robe from the back of the door.

"Keep your robe. I'll be fine with this."

"Sure?"

She nodded. "Would it be all right if I still showered here?"

"I doubt anyone will object." He went to the closet, took down a thermal blanket and an extra pillow. "This might help." He knew all too well how chilly that room could get.

She reached for the bedding, but he said, "I've got it." Did she think he was going to send her back to his store alone? He was ready to go, but she looked around his bedroom walls.

"Did you take all these?"

He glanced at the black-and-white photos he'd framed and hung. "Yeah."

"They're great."

"It's a hobby."

She walked to the wall and studied the waterfall he happened to like best. "You could do it for real."

"For real?" He raised his brows.

"Professionally."

He frowned. "So I've been told."

She glanced over her shoulder. "You don't like the idea?"

"I have a business."

She nodded. "But you must like to get outdoors and capture nature on film."

He didn't answer. He loved photography and being outdoors, but he'd resisted Barb's insistence that he start a studio. He knew where that would go. She planned events for a living, and with his photography, they'd be a dynamic duo. Only he couldn't stand her in event mode; she turned into a gushing commandant.

"There aren't many pictures of people."

"What?" he said sharply.

Startled, Alessi turned away from the wall. "You don't take pictures of people?"

His frown deepened. Barb's criticism again. *What is interesting about a hole in a rock? It's people that matter. If you shoot the weddings and parties I plan . . ."* He plowed his fingers through his hair. "I do. Some."

"This old couple is nice." She pointed to the picture on his wall.

"My grandparents. And that one's my dad." The other people pictures had been of Barb, and he'd taken those down and stuffed them in a box somewhere. He set down the bedding, walked to the corner, and took out his Nikon. He adjusted the settings. Then he held it to his eye and framed Alessi, turning it vertically to catch her height.

"What are you doing?"

Did she realize she was naturally photogenic? He snapped, adjusted the focus for a close-up, and snapped again. Her features were arresting, and though he'd initially thought of her as awkward, through the lens she seemed genuine, unaffected. He recalled the poses Barb had assumed to show off her best features, a beauty who knew how to flaunt it.

He lowered the camera. "You're one of the few people I've shot who didn't pose."

Her sober mien surprised him. "I hate being photographed."

"Why? Do you not show up on film?"

"Everything shows up."

He slipped the camera back into its case and set it down. "What 'everything'?"

"My long nose, my freckles, my kinky hair."

Steve laughed. "You're kidding, right?"

She shook her head. "I'm not kidding. I look like a foal still growing into my legs."

He cocked his head. She was genuinely unaware of her attractiveness. It wasn't the kind you'd see in Cover Girl ads, not Barb's sort of beauty. It was an unstudied, unprepared appeal. And he was unprepared for it too. His chest constricted. "Is there anything else you need?"

She shook her head, gathered the clothes tighter in her arms, and walked out.

He scooped up the bedding and followed. Outside his room, his chest eased. He didn't want her evaluating his talent or his choices. It made things seem personal. "We usually keep the kitchen door unlocked. You can come and go that way."

Ben walked in, stamping the snow from his shoes. "Hey there."

"Hey." Alessi's whole face changed. The tightness she'd exhibited throughout the day peeled away. "How did it go?"

"Well, she did say yes to dinner, but she couldn't find a sitter, so we're eating there."

"That's all right."

Steve looked from one to the other. They were certainly candid. After twenty-four hours?

Ben swiped his hair back and nodded. "Yeah. She's a good cook."

"Maybe you should go over early and lend a hand."

"You think?"

Alessi shrugged. "It wouldn't hurt."

She was giving advice?

Ben pulled off his jacket. "What are you going to do?"

"I have dinner at the store. Leftover pot roast."

Ben glanced from her to Steve. "What about later?"

She clutched the clothes to her chest. "I'm sleeping in the store-room."

"Her choice," Steve broke in before Ben gave him the evil eye.

Alessi said, "But if you don't mind, I'd still like to use the bathroom. I'll keep it clean. Oh . . ." She dug into her pocket and brought out the bills. "I can pay you for those things now, and dinner at Moll's last evening. . . ."

"We can settle up at the store." But Ben paused. "Where'd you get all that?"

"I paid her in advance." Steve put a hand to her back and nudged her toward the door. Ben did not need the full explanation of their agreement. He'd done what the guys expected, given her a job and a place to stay. If it happened to benefit him, as well, they didn't have to go into all that.

"You can use the kitchen too," Ben called as Steve got her through the door.

"I will. Thanks!"

Steve closed it behind them. The temperature had dropped dramatically, and the streetlights were globes under siege. He drove her back to the store, even though they could have walked. She gathered up her bag and the things from his room as he walked around to let her out of the car. His foot slipped as he reached the door, and he cautioned her, "It's gotten icy."

She stepped gingerly onto the frozen ground and walked like a new fawn to the door. It was apparent she hadn't seen much weather like this.

He let her in through the back door. "Are you sure you'll be okay here?"

She nodded. "I spent lots of nights in Ed's storeroom with only a sleeping bag."

He frowned. There it was again, her ridiculous story. If she was indigent and helpless, he was Santa Claus. "I'm going to set the alarm when I leave. If you open the door, it'll trigger it."

"Sure hope I don't sleepwalk." She set her things on the floor next to the cot.

"Anything else you need?"

She turned. "I'll be just great. If I can't sleep, I'll read." She picked up the Styrofoam box from Moll's that she had left on the shelf. "I've got dinner and everything."

It was not normal to be so cheerful over so little. Maybe she did mean to rob him blind. But she'd have to break through the alarm to get away. "Okay, then."

"Thanks a lot. I mean . . . for everything."

"It's mutual, remember?" He jerked a quick smile. "You're my excuse."

She nodded. "Good night."

"Here's our phone number if you need anything." He scribbled it on a pad next to the phone at the desk. Then he set the night-lights and the alarm and left her.

Alessi circled the storeroom, then settled on the cot. She opened the box of pot roast and realized she had no fork. Well, she had a sink. She reached in and picked up a bite. Having skipped most of it at lunch, she was hungry, and eating with her fingers didn't change that.

She finished the pot roast and mashed potatoes and carrots, then washed up in the small bathroom. She brushed her teeth and tied her hair back with a string from Steve's pencil cup. She looked into the mirror. Her nose was long, but it fit the rest of her face. If it were short and pert, it would look ridiculous. Her mouth was wide, the smile generous, though she hadn't smiled for the camera. Why did he take her picture? To prove his point? She half wished she had bought the makeup, but in a way that would be worse. It would look like she was trying to be what she wasn't, and she'd given that up years ago.

She wiped a dot of toothpaste from the corner of her lip and studied her freckles. They were the pale sort that spread over the bridge of her nose and across her cheeks, and truthfully, it could be worse. She was too hard on herself, but it came from her years in a high school where looks and connections meant everything. She'd never minded something as inconsequential as freckles until she encountered girls who waxed suicidal over a single blemish. Suddenly her flaws took on monstrous dimensions because she wanted to fit in. And, though she lived with Uncle Bob and Aunt Carrie, everyone knew she wasn't one of them.

That was where she'd first been compared to a horse, where someone said she walked on stilts. She'd grown into her legs since then, but finding a good fit in jeans was always a challenge. Thankfully the rest of her was in proportion, even if it took five feet ten inches to do it. She turned away from the mirror.

Life was too short to worry about looks. It was what she did that mattered. She might not live to a ripe old age, but she'd use every day the best she could. Today had been an interesting one. Not fruitful as far as finding her car, but . . . interesting. She just had to be patient. She might get a call from the state patrol any time now if the thief had taken it on the highway. If the car was in Charity, it might take a while for Sheriff Roehr to question people, but sooner or later it had to turn up. Didn't it?

She could already tell her thoughts would not quiet easily. She went into the store and considered playing solitaire on the computer, but Steve had it all shut down and it was probably password protected, and he wouldn't want her on it anyway. She did turn on the radio, and sultry jazz filled the air. So Steve was a jazz man. Ed had liked big band, but she had introduced him to ska.

She preferred classical and especially the romantics Beethoven, Mendelsohn, and Viotti. So much emotion, so much life. But there was emotion in Steve's jazz too; it just tended to be heavier. Maybe that was why he liked it. She half smiled, then pulled a scowl like Steve's and imitated him nodding to the rhythm, taking the dark tones inside. Suddenly she shook it off and found the classical station and strains of Berlioz. She'd never been to a symphony concert, but she knew the composers from the radio.

Chin high, fingers waving to the notes, she moved between the shelves, thankful there were no motion sensors. At least Steve hadn't

HALOS

mentioned any. She started to search the rare book aisles for a reading selection, then considered the potential buyers who might not want her reading them. She went to the new books and chose Dickens' *Bleak House*. She loved Dickens because he cared about the plight of people. He knew what it was like not to have a home or people who cared, to be trampled and insulted.

She carried the book to the cot and settled in with the single fixture overhead for light. She knew how to read without bending the spine. Ed used to laugh at her peeking between the pages. She wondered how he was doing. Had he learned to speak again? It must be so frustrating to lose your abilities. Maybe it was a good thing not to grow old. She sighed and opened the book.

Chapter 1: In Chancery

London. Michaelmas Term lately over, and the Lord Chancellor sitting in Lincoln's Inn Hall. Implacable November weather. As much mud in the streets as if the waters had but newly retired from the face of the earth, and it would not be wonderful to meet a Megalosaurus, forty feet long or so, waddling like an elephantine lizard up Holborn Hill.

Alessi smiled. There he was painting the ultimate picture of gloom, and into it, *plop,* a humorous image as real as it was fanciful.

Smoke lowering down from chimney-pots, making a soft black drizzle, with flakes of soot in it as big as full-grown snowflakes—gone into mourning, one might imagine, for the death of the sun.

At least the snow in Charity was white. She could hardly imagine black, sooty flakes being anything but bad luck. A flicker of insecurity licked up inside. Her white crystalline dancers had not proved overly helpful either—yet.

Dogs, undistinguishable in mire. Horses, scarcely better; splashed to their very blinkers. . . . Fog everywhere. Fog up the river where it flows among green aits and meadows; fog down the river, where it rolls defiled among the tiers of shipping, and the waterside pollutions of a great (and dirty) city. Fog on the

91

Essex marshes, fog on the Kentish heights. Fog creeping into the cabooses of collier-brigs; fog lying out on the yards, and hovering on the rigging of great ships. . . .

Alessi lost herself in the world of London drizzle, reading until her own eyes grew foggy. Then she turned off the light and pulled the covers tightly under her chin.

Life was a complicated business. Why should she expect it to change now? Time washed over generations of troubled lives, remarkable only in the struggle to keep going on. There were moments of transcendence, but the rest was just hard work. She closed her eyes and dozed on the hard, unfamiliar cot. She couldn't even count the number of strange, hard places she'd slept—most of them preferable to the soft mattress of her Palm Beach bedroom.

Life was an adventure, and this was just one more curve of the yellow brick road. So far Charity had presented no lions and tigers, only bears—one in particular. She could live with that. She drew in the bear's scent, laid down the night before on the cot he'd accepted in her place. It was remarkable, really, how much he'd done for her in just one day. Waves of sleepy gratitude rocked her. She would work hard for him, make it worth it. Even after she got her car back. . . .

Eleven

ALESSI IMAGINED HER MUSTANG sitting out front, draped in fog. No wonder she couldn't see it. But she could hear it, that familiar rev of the engine. Louder now, intentional, telling her it was there, calling her out of sleep. She startled, listening hard. It was still there. She jumped up from the cot, ran through the dimly lit store and looked out the front windows. A car was zooming up and down the street, spinning donuts at the intersection. Under the streetlight, she recognized the red body and tan rag top.

"Hey!" She banged the window. "Hey!" She burst through the door and ran in her socks toward the intersection, waving her arms. "Hey you! Stop!"

But the driver straightened the wheels and took off down the road, spewing snow behind. She tore after him, ran all the way to Ben's gas station, but the taillights were long out of sight. She turned at the gas pumps and ran for the house, banged on the front door before she remembered Steve saying he left the kitchen door open. She ran around and through the door just as he launched himself toward her. In matching shirts and sweats, they grappled, grabbing each other's arms and hollering together.

"My car!"

"The alarm!"

"I saw my car!"

Ben and Dave burst into the kitchen. "What's going on?"

"I saw my car. Someone was spinning donuts in the intersection. It's here! In Charity!"

Dave and Ben stared at her. Steve went to the closet and pulled on his brown bomber jacket.

"Hurry!" Alessi caught his arm. "We have to catch him. And call the sheriff."

Steve scowled. "You already did."

"What do you mean?"

"You set off the alarm. Everyone within six miles is calling him right now." He caught her arm and dragged her with him. Her feet were soaked and her teeth chattering. Steve took off his coat and wrapped it around her shoulders as he tugged her down the street. "Didn't I say not to open the door?"

"What are you talking about? I saw my car!"

"You think you did."

She jolted to a stop and yanked her arm free. "I know I did."

He kept walking.

"You don't believe me? Do you think I'm making it up?"

"I don't know what to think."

After all his kindness, he still doubted her. She pulled off his coat and shoved it at him. "Then I don't need you or anyone else. I'll find my car myself." She stomped up to the store and stormed through the door, her eardrums cringing at the strident tones she hadn't even noticed before. She hoped the alarm woke everyone in town.

She went into the back room, tugged on a pair of dry socks and her sneakers, then threw on the jean jacket and stalked out. Just as Sheriff Roehr pulled up, she pushed past Steve into the frigid night. "The alarm is my fault. I opened the door. And in case you're interested, I saw someone driving my car. But I'm sure that doesn't matter to you or anyone else in Charity!"

She stalked toward the intersection where she'd seen her Mustang spinning under the streetlight. There had to be tracks to prove she was not hallucinating. Sure enough, big circles were churned into the snowy square. If she could match the tread from those, she could follow them out. That was not easily done in the dark with a streetlight on only one corner, but it was the only thing she could think of. While she chased one track after another, the sheriff got out of his car, stiff again and clearly put out.

"Young lady." He joined her in the middle of the street. "I need you to come in now. You're creating a disturbance."

Alessi spread her arms. "*I'm* creating a disturbance? How about the guy in my car? Look at these tracks. What do you think made them, a UFO?"

Sheriff Roehr fixed his hands to his hips. "I don't like your tone. Fact is, no one saw a car but you."

"No one was sleeping in a store but me."

Steve caught up to them and took her by the arm. "Let's go, Alessi."

She shook him loose. "Don't grab me again, or I will not be responsible for what I do." She meant it.

"I'll take that chance." She swung for his jaw, but he gripped her wrist and pulled her close, hissing into her ear, "This is not the way." He held on tight. She meant to fight free and could have, but instead her lower lip shook. Tears filled her eyes.

He walked her past the sheriff, out of the intersection, and back to the store. She went along, angry and confused. Didn't anyone understand? She'd seen her car, and whoever stole it was driving off with it right now.

He brought her back to the storeroom, sat her down on the cot. "Are you all right?"

"No, I'm not all right. I know what I saw, but you don't believe me, and neither does the sheriff or anyone else in this town."

He looked into the shelves. "There are things you don't under-stand."

She felt a chill. "What things?" Had she walked into some crazy scheme? Maybe the whole town stole cars and fenced them.

"You ought to call your uncle and leave Charity."

She bolted to her feet, looking him in the eye. "I am not leaving without my car." Her breath heaved in her chest, but she would not break down and sob. "Why won't you help me?"

"I am."

She shook her head, fists clenched at her sides. He caught her face and held it. His eyes were green, dark forest green with flecks of silver. They closed as he kissed her. Surprise turned to panic, then turned to wonder. He let go suddenly and stalked out without a word.

The door clicked shut behind him. She dropped down on the cot and wrapped herself in her arms. What on earth just happened? Somewhere between falling asleep and this moment, she had left reality and entered *The Twilight Zone.*

Of all the stupid, impetuous, imbecilic things to do. Steve kicked himself all the way home. Ben and Dave were lying in wait.

"Well?" Ben said. "Was it her car?"

"How should I know?"

Dave took his glasses from his T-shirt pocket and put them on. "Did Cooper get a look?"

"No, Cooper did not." Steve flung himself onto the couch. "He almost arrested Alessi for disturbing the peace."

"Disturbing the peace?" Ben sank to the recliner across from him. "What did she do?"

"Pointed out the donut tracks in the intersection and suggested all was not right in Charity."

Dave shook his head. "Something should be done."

Something had, and Steve kicked himself again. What lunatic had taken over his mind?

Ben clasped, then unclasped his hands, then dropped them to his sides. He was the only person in Charity, besides Alessi, who'd seen the car—or admitted it. Steve wished he had more to go on, then wished he'd never gotten involved.

Dave pushed his glasses up the bridge of his nose. He wore them so infrequently he hadn't had them sized right. "This is the first time it's been something big."

Ben's face lengthened. "Stealing is stealing. I just can't believe anyone in Charity . . ."

Steve sank into the couch. How could he so lose control? He wasn't even attracted to her; he refused to be.

Dave leaned forward and rested his forearms on his knees. "Maybe it started as a prank, like Alessi thought, and the person got worried with Cooper called in and all."

Ben shook his head. "That doesn't explain tonight. Who'd rub her nose in it?"

Steve frowned. What on earth had possessed him?

"You okay, Steve?"

He jerked, glared at Ben. "Why wouldn't I be? Just because I'm running the streets in the snow after some lunatic girl you guys let into our lives . . ."

Ben and Dave shared a glance.

"What?" he demanded.

They both looked away.

Steve squeezed his fists. "The question is, what to do now? She thinks the car is here, and she's not leaving without it."

"Why should she leave?" Ben threaded his fingers. "This is as good a place for her as any."

Steve scowled. "Except for the minor matter of her stolen car—and something rotten in Charity."

Dave straightened. "Every place has got problems."

"Yeah." Steve stood up. "But most places admit it." He jammed his hands into his sweats pockets and paced the room.

Ben and Dave stared at him. He'd heard all about the recent dynamics, springing from an incident while he was gone, but it still felt off. Wrong had been done, and Steve was skeptical of the new outlook.

Ben spread his hands. "The pact—"

"Alessi's not part of that." Steve paced back across the room.

"Neither were you," Dave said.

"My father was, and I uphold it for him." He caught his hand in his hair. It wasn't the pact that had him agitated. "I'm going to bed." He did, but it was worse in there.

What had he set in motion? Had he triggered something by pretending with her that afternoon? Holding her hand, holding her. . . . He was a man. Nine years older. That wasn't so much, but she'd looked like she'd never been kissed before.

Impossible. She had the kind of face that needed kissing, demanded it. Not some pouty painted lips like Amanda's . . . or Barb's. Steve had known it would happen when her lip quivered in the street. He'd dragged her along to someplace private, but he'd known what was coming.

She hadn't. She'd been kissed without any warning, any recourse. And just thinking of it made him want to kiss her again. He groaned.

Was it only last night she'd invaded his space? He'd lost his mind. The one good thing was that tomorrow was Sunday. He could hole up at the store, but there was no reason for her to be there. He rolled to his side, forced his eyes to close.

So they'd kissed—in the heat of the moment. Animal instinct. He could taste it still. His hands clenched. If he took those thoughts captive . . . He rolled to his back and stared hard at the dark ceiling.

"The Lord is my shepherd. I shall not want . . . Alessi Moore in my arms right now. I don't even know her. I certainly don't trust her. I don't believe she's as innocent as she looks." Gritting his teeth, he closed his eyes and considered the author of that Psalm and the trouble thoughts of a certain woman had brought him. "I—will—not—go—there." He swallowed, feeling some measure of control return. Temptation and desire were part of his chemistry, but that didn't mean he couldn't govern it.

He shouldn't have taken her picture and given recognition to thoughts of her attractiveness. He shouldn't have given her a job. He should have stuck to his first opinion. His face screwed tight. She was not his problem. He didn't have room for any more problems. Let Charity deal with her.

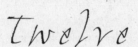

Twelve

ALESSI MADE HER WAY TO CHARITY CHAPEL the next morning. Who did Steve Bennet think he was? She clenched her hands at her sides. Maybe it was adrenaline—some masculine ritual. People lifted cars and all sorts of crazy things on adrenaline. He'd been distracted enough that he left the store in her hands. She could have cleaned him out and walked through the unprotected doors. But had he thought of that? Apparently he had other things on his mind. She hadn't slept much. It had taken hours for her feet to warm and her lips to cool, and she'd had no alarm to wake her once she did sleep.

She reached the chapel and stared at the cross. Karen was right; she

CASS DISTRICT LIBRARY
319 MICHIGAN RD 62N
CASSOPOLIS MI 49031

couldn't miss it. It seemed to be made of some sort of Plexiglas, and it captured the daylight in a way that made it almost glow. It stood a good fifteen feet tall, looking new and untouched by anything as reprehensible as crucifixion. She read the sign for the time of the service, which had naturally started ten minutes before.

She slipped into the back and halfway down the side aisle, where people made room on the edge of a cushioned pew. The church seated over a hundred, and it was packed. Had to be most of Charity's population right there. She recognized a few, including Moll, which sort of surprised her. But a gruff manner did not mean a lack of faith, and the Lord saw the heart.

From her vantage she could see a lot of people with just a little glance sideways. Ben's head was easy to locate, bobbing above the others. He sat singing beside a woman and two little brown-haired girls. It must be Mary. For the life of her, Alessi could not guess why the woman wouldn't snap him up.

The choir finished their hymn, and the pastor rose. People drew a collective breath as he took his place before them. His hair was a deep, rich auburn; two long dimples creased his cheeks, and his nose was straight but humble. Alessi sensed a sincerity that tugged at her insides. She sat straighter as he raised his face and said, "Forgiveness."

The single word marched out alone and stood at attention until all wayward thoughts had been collected. Then the pastor opened the Scriptures and read: "'Peter came to Jesus and asked, "Lord, how many times should I forgive my brother when he sins against me? Up to seven times?" Jesus answered, "I tell you not seven times, but seventy-seven times."'" He let the number rest on their heads like coals, then looked up and added, "Seventy-seven thousand, seventy-seven million, billion, trillion. An infinite number."

He went on to describe the scene. "The Lord was surrounded by crowds, people secure in their righteousness, steeped in the tradition of an eye for an eye, cursing their enemies. Some wore rich robes and rings on their fingers, oil in their hair. Some carried the office of authority. Others were ragged, crippled, leprous. All lived under the oppression of Rome and were waiting for the day their bonds would be broken, the enemy overthrown. They were simmering with righteous anger."

Alessi could picture it: milling crowds in sandals, dust in the air, the smell of animals and sweat, oils and figs. Jesus seated on a rock, speaking simply, yet His words carried to the farthest ear.

"To all of these, Jesus spoke words of revolution: pray for your enemies, do good to those who hurt you. Forgive, forgive, forgive." The pastor looked out at them with his amber-colored eyes. "These blessed words are now for us, the redeemed, set free from evil."

Alessi was caught up in the timbre of his voice, the animation of his eyes, the vitality he exuded—though he stood nearly still. More amazing, though, was the reflection on the faces turned up to him. She'd never seen such rapture.

He spread his hands. "We live together in love and charity. Among us, no offense, small or large, is unforgivable. No offender, weak or strong, is unpardonable. No misunderstanding, no selfish desire nor contrary thought, can keep us from this precious truth: It is sweet forgiveness that frees us to love with the love of Jesus, who even in the throes of death, practiced what He had preached."

Soft sighs of affirmation floated like doves to the rafters and poised there expectantly. Someone coughed, and it felt like a commotion. The pastor sent a compassionate glance toward the offender, then continued. "Consider that when someone has wronged you, it could be in ignorance."

Alessi found the back of Steve's head and sank lower in her seat, memory bringing a flush to her cheeks. Of course it was ignorance. How would he know she'd declared that behavior off-limits? It was probably nothing to him, but he hadn't heard Aunt Carrie in the hall.

"She's just like Shannon, that dewy-eyed slut. She'll throw herself at the first gigolo who bares his torso." Was that why she thought Mom had run away with Brian Moore?

Then Uncle Bob: *"What was I supposed to do, tell the social worker we couldn't afford her?"*

And her aunt's reply: *"Shannon should have drowned her at birth."*

Alessi shuddered. She had spent that night praying for God to let her die. Her mother's consolation through all the horror of cancer was that soon she'd be with Brian. Alessi had wanted nothing more than to join them in heaven.

Instead, she'd made herself invisible, never giving offense or embarrassment, never complaining. As her body changed and matured, she'd banished every thought of love. Not for her sake, but for Mom's. If they were one and the same in Aunt Carrie's mind, then what she did reflected her mother as well. There would not be one smug moment when Aunt Carrie could say "I told you so." Not one.

But now the pastor was saying you couldn't stay mad, that no offense mattered in the face of Christ's message. "Don't assume you know their motivation. They might not even realize they've caused you harm."

That was it. Alessi agreed. Most of the time people went along slashing and bruising with no idea how many they'd laid waste, like the snowflakes last night, crushed under their tires. Even when Aunt Carrie tried to sound kind, there was always the lingering echo. *"Good job, Less." Less than good. If only you'd been drowned at birth.*

But they had taken her in and kept her when they didn't want her. Actions spoke louder than words. That's what she had to remember, and she envisioned the halos again as she'd driven away. Anyone could be a halo person.

The pastor said, "How often we wound without intending to. Yet the balm of forgiveness soothes the ailing heart. You understand and you agree. But there's more." He paused, and not a breath was drawn. "Sometimes people intend to insult, to injure."

Alessi wished people didn't mean to hurt each other, but she knew better. Otherwise, words like *spite* and *malice* would not be necessary.

"So what does the Lord say if someone *means* to hurt us—wants to, sets out to, deliberately intends to wrong us?" The pastor gazed out over them. "He says seventy-seven times."

Alessi swallowed. She really didn't bear a grudge. She wished her aunt and uncle well and was thankful for what they'd done for her. She was even thankful for what she'd learned. Hurt and rejection were teachers if you let them be. And she had. She wasn't stupid—though she'd let people think she was. Aunt Carrie had refused to believe her sister could create an intelligent child, so Alessi had played dumb. And given her current predicament, maybe it hadn't been as much of an act as she thought. But she hadn't walked away bitter, and that was something, considering all the offenses she might have heaped up.

The pastor's eyes searched his flock. "The hardest of all, Jesus knew, was the unrepentant repeat offender."

Alessi jumped as though he'd snatched her thought and shared it with the crowd.

"The one who won't change, who keeps offending, maybe daily, even hourly. That was the justified cry of Peter: when is enough, enough?" The pastor's agonized query drew every face to him. Breathless murmurs. He spoke as though each word meant more than he could express, no matter how he tried. "And Jesus said, never. We never have the luxury of unforgiveness."

Her gaze traveled over the congregation. Heads nodded, others looked down. One young man, about her age or younger, stared at the pastor, and their eyes met with pride and affection. What she wouldn't give to have someone look that way at her. But there she was, coveting a relationship she knew nothing about. She'd had twelve years of her mother's love. That should be enough for anyone.

"We never have the luxury of unforgiveness, because unforgiveness leads to misery, to sin, to death."

Nervous shuffling. The pastor shook his head as though the thought of their suffering caused him pain. Alessi wanted to reassure him that she was responsible for her own shortcomings. Mom had taught her that, without ever once rubbing it in. *"Choices have consequences, sweetie. Don't pick a bouquet of regrets."*

The pastor leaned forward in a professorial manner and went on. "Unforgiveness has many faces: not forgiving others, not forgiving ourselves, not forgiving God."

"Don't blame God, Alessi."

Alessi remembered the sobs that had wracked her chest. *"I hate God, Mom."* Her mother's hand was too weak to stroke her, too feeble even to return her grip. *"Don't hate Him, baby. He's all you have now."* The truest words she'd ever spoken.

Pastor's voice grew solemn. "No matter the look of it, no matter the cause of it, no matter the frequency or the severity of the offense. We who are called by His name, who are set free from the bonds of evil, must allow no fissures in our love, in our charity to one another." He softly pounded one fist into his other palm. "No one can find peace and hold a grudge. Unforgiveness devours joy."

Alessi cringed. Life had enough ups and downs without a joy-devouring element.

Pastor's face darkened as she imagined Moses' might have before he pronounced frogs or locusts on Egypt. "Do you harbor the enemy?" His expression intensified with an almost painful response from the crowd. He looked from individual to individual, gleaning their souls with his glance.

"Harbor the enemy?" A strange phrase for unforgiveness, but it compelled her to search her heart. Whom did she need to forgive? The person who took her car? She could hardly blame him or her when she'd left the temptation right out there, keys and all. She didn't blame anyone, she just wanted it back. Couldn't he see that?

But when his eyes reached her, they clung, and she wondered if the whole message had been for her. Did he know who she was and why she was here? Did he expect her to jump up and confess? Confess what? A lapse in security and a wish for her property back?

But there had been anger and fear . . . and doubt. Did she doubt God . . . and what He had in store? Her throat grew tight and the ragged edges of her nails bit her palms. The pastor released her with a slow blink of his eyes and took his seat. Breath returned to her lungs, and she whispered an apology to Jesus. *I believe. Please forgive my doubt.*

Karen led the choir in "Forgive, O Lord, Our Severing Ways" as a basket was passed, and Alessi was thankful Steve had paid her in advance so she could contribute. She hated to get something for nothing. And she'd gotten more than she expected from a small-town chapel. Why, he could be a televangelist or do crusades. The strains faded and the congregation dispersed, greeting each other as they left. Alessi started to leave but was caught up in the press at the door.

Karen reached her there. "Alessi." She hugged her again. "Thanks for joining us." She sounded so sincere.

"I didn't know what time it started."

"Don't worry about that. I was just tickled to see you come in." Karen pulled her aside to let others out past them. She waved. "Here's Diana."

Diana joined them with Dave in tow. He looked puffy-eyed and yawned when he greeted her. "Sorry." He pumped a fist at his mouth.

"*I'm* sorry," Alessi said. "I shouldn't have woken you last night; I just reacted."

"What's this?" Diana elbowed him.

Alessi saved him the explanation. "I saw my car. Someone in town was driving it last night." It burned her how flagrant it had been, and she realized there might be more resentment in her than she'd thought.

Diana stared at her. "Are you sure it was yours?"

She hadn't gotten close enough to grab it, but . . . "How many red convertible Mustangs do you have in Charity?"

"Well, I don't know. . . ." She looked uncomfortably at Dave. "Do you work on any, Dave?"

He shuffled. "Haven't lately."

Alessi felt a prickle in the back of her neck and turned to find the young man she had noticed before. He wasn't smiling now, just appraising her as he made his way toward the door from the front. Though she thought she had seen a familial relationship, he didn't share the pastor's features or coloring. He was large boned and blond and looked away when she noticed his attention.

Ben joined them with Mary's hand in his. Unlike Diana, whose verve radiated, Mary looked frail in spirit, something in the way her eyes darted about as though anything might happen. Ben said, "Alessi, this is Mary. Mary, Alessi."

Alessi took her hand with a warm smile. "I'm so glad to meet you. I don't know what I'd have done without Ben's help."

Mary smiled up at him, then her eyes darted down again. "This is Cait and Lyn."

"Hi there." Alessi received little more than a glance in response. The girls had too much of their mother's nervousness. They needed Ben as much as Mary did.

Ben didn't look as tired as Dave, but she apologized anyway. "I shouldn't have bothered you about my car. I've caused you enough trouble."

A hand pressed the small of her back, and she knew before he spoke whose it was. Steve leaned into her ear. "We need to talk."

What now? Alessi wished she'd made a quick escape, but Steve's hand was firm. She could barely wave to the others before he propelled her toward the door, where Amanda, resplendent in fox fur, presented an obstacle. Did she wear anything that some creature hadn't lost its life for?

"I understand you had trouble last night." She addressed Steve, though truly, Alessi thought, the trouble had been hers.

"False alarm." Steve tried to keep moving. Did he really think that, or was it only to avoid elaborating for Amanda?

"I'm having a New Year's Eve party. Will you be there?"

"I'll have to get back to you on that." He shot her a smile, then squeezed Alessi past and kept a steady pressure on her back toward the minister and his wife.

The wife caught Alessi's hand between both of hers. "Steve, you haven't introduced your friend." She was petite, dark haired, with skin so gleaming smooth it looked poured on. She had been seated with the blond guy.

Steve said, "Alessi Moore, Madeline Welsh. Pastor Burton Welsh."

She shook the pastor's hand firmly. "You sure do pack a church."

"Not I." He looked up with an expression of true devotion at the gleaming cross. She would have moved on, but he said, "And this is our son, Carl." He motioned toward the blond youth who loomed up from behind her, taller even than he'd seemed earlier.

"How's it going?" he said.

"Well, it'd be better if I got my car back. But at least I know it's here in town. Last night—"

Steve's hand pressed into her spine. "Come on, Alessi."

"Have a great day." Pastor Welsh's smile was dazzling, the sort you'd pay to see on the big screen. Then he was greeting the next person with the same direct attention.

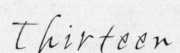

Thirteen

ALESSI SKIPPED A STEP AS STEVE tugged her around the side of the chapel, turned, and pressed her into the wall. "You need to watch what you say."

"What did I say?" And who did he think he was?

He glanced over his shoulder at the people streaming away on foot or bundling into their cars. "Don't talk about last night."

"Why not?" Did he expect her to pretend that nothing happened, that her car was a donation to Charity?

The silver flecks in his eyes gleamed like the ice crystals glittering in the air around them. "Just trust me on this."

"Like you trust me?"

His hands tightened on her waist. "More."

At least he was honest about that. Frustration and confusion draped her. She dropped her head back against the wall. "I thought it would all be different. I thought the halo was a sign from God. It was supposed to mean something good."

"Halo?"

The Lord's reminder of the good, the silver lining, His way of helping her find the magic, the strength to keep on. The proof that angels *were* watching over her. Was it all foolishness? It would sound that way to Steve.

Her throat tightened. "What am I supposed to do? That car is all I have."

He didn't understand. How could he? Six years without love, six years of knowing she was a burden and compensating in every way possible. That car was all she had to show for it. And she was not convinced the Lord was taking it away. It was Steve and the sheriff and Charity and the person who stole it in the first place who wanted her to give it up.

"Come on." Steve took her hand and led her away from the wall, out across the parking lot aswirl with ground blizzards, and back toward his house.

Trust him? It was getting absurd. But his grip was purposeful. They reached the house, and he motioned her inside, saying, "Ben and Dave went out for breakfast. How do waffles sound?"

Waffles sounded fine, but food was not on her mind. "Why shouldn't I talk about my car?"

He went to the kitchen and turned on the coffeepot.

She rested her hands on the counter. "Why does everyone change the subject or act like they don't hear me?"

He pulled a waffle iron from the cabinet and plugged it in.

"Why doesn't anyone believe me?"

Steve looked as though he might answer, then said, "Hand me that red-and-white book."

Alessi reached for the cookbook standing in the corner. "I would have talked to Sheriff Roehr at church, but he wasn't there." Because his sleep had been disturbed? Or he didn't worship God? Maybe she thought he was God, accusing her of disturbing the peace.

Steve said, "I'm sure he's doing what he can."

"He did not even try to follow my Mustang last night." Maybe he already knew where it went. The thought caught her short. Maybe he was in on it, a corrupt sheriff who kept the town in fear. She almost burst out laughing at the thought—old Sheriff Roehr with his replaced hip. So maybe he was just inept.

Steve took out a mixer and bowl.

"You're not going to tell me what's going on, are you?"

He turned from the counter and studied her. "Nothing's going on. There's not some master plot or . . . or . . ."

"Sinister force."

His mouth jerked. "Right. It's just different in Charity."

"Different how?"

He opened the drawer and took out beaters, then inserted them into the mixer. As he flipped the pages of the cookbook, she figured he was not going to answer. But then he said, "Something like this is not supposed to happen."

"Sounds like my line."

He laid the book flat, then turned. "What did you mean by the halo?"

"You won't understand."

"Try me." He combined ingredients while she considered sharing something she knew would make him consider her less reliable than ever.

She drew a breath. "Halos like on angels."

He held up a finger, ran the mixer, then said, "Okay. Go on."

"When I see a halo, I know angels are watching out for me. That something good is going to happen. I just have to watch for it." He could get the laugh over with; then maybe she would get some answers from him.

He didn't laugh. He said, "Maybe you make the good happen because you're expecting it."

She hadn't thought of that. But that would put the magic inside her, and she had no such illusions. Besides, she'd been watching for it when she came to Charity, and if it were up to her, it would have happened already. "No, it's not me."

He took a small bowl and cracked eggs into it, or rather dripped

109

part of the egg in while passing the yolk back and forth between the shell halves.

"Don't you like the yolk?" she asked.

"It calls for whites. You know what happens if any yolk gets in."

"No. What happens?"

He glanced over, expecting what? "They're supposed to beat up stiff."

She nodded. Did he want her to guess?

"You really don't know?"

Now she got it. He was testing her, trying to trip her up. She dropped her gaze. "My waffles come out of a box and cook in the toaster. Sorry to disappoint you."

He had the good grace to look chastened, but she wondered what she was doing there with him anyway. He didn't like her, didn't trust her. Maybe he thought it was his job to prove her a fraud. After beating the egg whites, he said, "Come over here. You can fold these in while I oil the iron."

She joined him in the corner and took the small bowl and spatula. Another trick? How could you fold foam in a bowl?

He opened the iron and brushed it with oil, then noticed her standing there still. "What's the matter?"

"I'm not sure what you want me to do."

He came back and scooped the whites into the batter, working them gently in with the plastic spatula, though they left small, fluffy lumps. He wore an aftershave that made her think of dark, thick woods, moose, and moonlight.

"Do you miss Alaska?"

He shrugged. "Yes and no."

"What do you miss?"

He cocked his head. "Climbing up into air so crisp it catches your lungs by surprise. The rosy glow of sunrise on glacier ice as turquoise as Caribbean seas. The call of moose, lumbering grizzlies, and pine scent so thick it stays in your nostrils forever."

She stared into his face. She'd never been farther north than Vermont, but she felt the scene as though he'd laid it out before her in the kitchen, and it sounded even more wonderful than Charity. "What don't you miss?"

"Barb." He laid the spatula down and handed her the batter bowl from the base of the mixer.

"Your fiancée?"

"My mistake."

No wonder he had so little joy; it was being devoured by unforgiveness. Had he heard the pastor's message?

She saw the light turn red on the machine. "Is the iron hot?"

"Quite." He lifted the lid. "Here. Pour it out from the center or it'll leak down the sides when we close it."

She did as he said, but the batter came unevenly because of the egg whites. One side bubbled out when he shut the lid. Almost immediately the aroma filled her nostrils as the steam heated her face.

He said, "Now we let it toast."

She rinsed her hands in the sink. "How do you know all this?"

He leaned on the counter. "You grow up without a mother, you learn to cook. Dad and I used to have contests, see who could make the meal of the week. Winner got out of dishes."

"You were close to him."

He nodded.

Alessi sighed. "Mom and I were just getting to that stage where we were more friends than mother and daughter." She looked down at her hands in the towel, rubbed slowly. "I wish she'd lived. I miss her so much."

Steve crossed his arms over his chest.

Alessi said, "I'm sorry."

"For what?"

"Your loss is more recent." She hung the towel over the bar.

He frowned. "That doesn't make it worse."

"You haven't had Christmas without him."

"I have every day without him."

She was glad they had the span of the kitchen between them or she would have put out a hand and touched him.

He turned and eyed the steaming waffle iron. "You like them soft or crisp?"

"Either."

He went over and lifted the lid. "Just between, I'd say."

"Okay."

He paused. "How about burnt black?"

She drew her brows together. "Black?"

"Can you form an opinion, voice a preference?"

She swallowed. "I'd rather they weren't black."

He took a plastic spatula and lifted the whole foursome from the iron onto a plate. It was nicely golden, and the warm, grainy aroma wafted through the room. "Perfect. I'm glad you didn't want them burnt."

"Would you have?"

"That's not the point."

"What is the point?"

He poured more batter and closed the lid. "I gave you a choice."

What was he trying to say, that she couldn't make a decision?

"The usual response is one or the other." He broke the foursome into quarters with his hands and put two on another plate.

She said, "I thought you might have a preference."

He shook his head, obviously frustrated. "Take these to the table." He handed her both plates, then followed her with a small jug of pure maple syrup and the butter dish. He went back, poured two mugs of coffee, and joined her at the table. Folding his hands, he said, "Father, bless this food and each of us in need of your grace."

"That's a nice prayer." Alessi pushed back her hair. "I thought at first you were offended by prayer. I guess it was just me."

"I'm not offended by you. I just don't know what to make of you."

Alessi spread soft butter into the squares, then drizzled syrup over. Was she so different, so out of step with the rest of the world? She took a bite of crispy waffle, savoring the sweet, buttery maple. The next bite was as good, and the next. Frozen waffles were no comparison, just as canned spaghetti could never really be fairy ambrosia.

He got up, opened the waffle iron, scooped the next foursome to the plate, then refilled the iron with fresh batter. He brought the steaming waffles to the table, broke them apart with strong yet gentle fingers. She accepted the two he offered. May as well eat up as long as it was free. Again she buttered and drizzled the waffle. The syrup was thinner than the generic brands, and a little tangier, but packed with flavor that filled her tongue with glorious satisfaction. "This syrup is good. I never had the real thing."

"We're in Vermont. Anything else is sacrilegious."

She smiled. "Ben said you were a park ranger."

He chewed his bite, then described some of the territory he had covered, the routine tours that had turned out more adventurous than he'd expected, the scenery he'd discovered.

"That's where you took the pictures in your room?"

"I took them all over." He swigged his coffee.

"If I had a camera, you know what I'd shoot?"

"What?" He cut his fork down through two waffles together.

"Animals. Birds. Dogs especially."

He chewed thoughtfully. "You'd like Alaska. Lots of wildlife."

"Maybe I'll go there." She dragged a bite through the syrup on her plate. "When I leave Charity."

He frowned. "More coffee?" He noted she had not made much headway. "Cream?" He stood and got the cream from the refrigerator.

"Thanks." She creamed her coffee and sipped again. Much better. Her stomach was full, but she lingered over the last of the warm coffee, then wiped her mouth with the napkin. "That was really good."

He reached for both plates and carried them to the sink. She picked up their mugs and the miscellaneous flatware and brought them to him. She liked the way he didn't waste time on small talk. And how honestly he'd answered her questions. They seemed to have skipped a level in communication right from the start.

He made quick work of washing up, then left the dishes to drain and turned. "About last night . . ."

"I'm *going* to find my car." If that disappointed him, she was sorry, but the more she thought about it . . .

"Not that part." He toweled his hands dry.

Her heart rushed. She did not want to discuss the rest. That level of communication was off-limits. "I know you didn't mean it." She turned and reached for the jacket on the back of her chair.

"Alessi . . ."

She pulled the sleeve onto her arm. "Forget it. We were both out of our heads."

"That doesn't excuse my—"

She spun and hurried for the door. "Really. It doesn't matter." She was out the door before he could say another word.

Fourteen

WELL, YOU HANDLED THAT ONE WELL." Steve tossed the dish towel aside. Why had he brought it up, anyway? To clear his conscience? By the way, I only kissed you because . . . because what? He wanted to? No, as she said, they were out of their heads. She was certainly distraught. He'd meant to comfort her. Not that it had. By the way she shot out the door just now, he'd say it had done the opposite.

It was all crazy. She was a stranger, yet he talked to her more openly than he did anyone else. She'd started it, telling him things like her fears of dying young. Maybe knowing she was leaving made her seem safe. She had no designs on him—that was certain. One kiss had proved that. He felt a twinge. He hadn't even really kissed her, not the way he'd wanted to.

Fine. If she wanted the subject closed, it was closed. He put on his coat and went out. He had plenty of work waiting at the store, but he didn't head that way. Instead, he went to the white house at the corner of Hawkeye and Meadow and found Cooper Roehr in his den, a stub of cigar in his teeth.

"How's the hip?"

"Better than the old one." The sheriff motioned him to a chair. "Cigar?"

The air was pungent with cigar, litter box, and body odor. "No thanks. I missed you at church."

"Overslept." Cooper shooed the cat from his lap, and it wended its way to Steve's legs, arching up to rub as it passed. Cooper straightened. "I know why you're here."

Steve took the offered chair, his nostrils adjusting to the onslaught. "What have you learned?"

"Not a whole lot. No one saw anything, except Ben, and the snow was coming pretty hard. I think he watched the gal more than the vehicle."

Probably. But what did that matter? "The car is gone."

"Don't mean it was stolen."

"What, then?"

"She could have been dumped off."

Steve hadn't considered that. Had Alessi been deserted? Maybe the car wasn't even hers. Maybe some boyfriend had ditched her and she was making up the stolen car story. She was stranded, needing help and sympathy. . . . He nodded slowly. "So Ben could have seen the car but not noticed someone else inside." Easy to do if Alessi was standing out in the snow.

He imagined the scene. Then she goes into the store and the jerk takes off. Steve caught himself on that thought. Jerk? The word packed too many assumptions, all in Alessi's favor. Maybe she deserved what happened. Maybe she drove him off—with what? Her niceness? Unless it was all an act. Still, you didn't just leave someone. With nothing.

"What about last night?" Steve scratched the cat's face as it rubbed its gums against his fingers and then leaped into his lap.

Cooper shifted the cigar to the other side of his teeth. "You see anything? Hear anything—before the alarm?"

"I saw the tracks."

Cooper shrugged. "No law against spinning donuts. Don't mean it was her car."

Steve frowned. "She was pretty worked up." So much so, he'd almost believed her.

Cooper drew on the cigar. "She heard a commotion and saw the chance to build up her story some."

Could she be that calculating? He knew firsthand it was possible; Barb had written the script. The cat sensed his irritation and paused its purr, looking up into his face.

Cooper puffed. "Makes more sense than anything else."

Cooper wanted to believe that. Everyone in Charity did.

The cat jumped off Steve's lap and padded under Cooper's chair. Cooper rubbed the feline with one stockinged foot. Had he even asked around, questioned anyone? Whom would Steve suspect? Where would he start? "What if it's true?" He stood up and paced.

Cooper reached to raise the blinds, then settled back heavily into his chair. "Her story's sketchy at best. She could be a runaway."

"She's twenty-one."

"Got proof?"

Steve turned. "She can't prove anything without her purse."

Cooper snorted. "Right."

Hearing his own doubts echoed should have been confirming. But it left him feeling jangled. Steve stopped and looked out the window. "What is she supposed to do?"

"Far as I'm concerned, Miss Moore—if that's her name—should call her uncle, or whoever she's got, and stop casting aspersions on the people of Charity." Cooper stubbed his cigar out. "I know you have feelings for the girl. . . ."

Steve spun. "Feelings for her! I only met her yesterday." Unless he counted the middle of the night before, when he found her in his room.

"Uh-huh."

Obviously word of their "relationship" had reached even Cooper, and it seemed their crazy plan might backfire. "Look, this has nothing to do with me. It's about Charity, about decency and truth. We have to get to the bottom of this."

Cooper shifted in his chair. "I'm not taking the word of a stranger that discredits the character of this town."

"Not the town, Cooper. Someone in it."

"One and the same."

Steve shook his head. What was he arguing for? Cooper's take on it was as rational—or more so—than Alessi's story. And she wasn't his concern anyway. He was trying to make amends for overstepping last night. He'd never behaved like that with someone he didn't even know. Maybe Barb had cracked his restraint, warped his integrity, left him vulnerable to a chemistry with Alessi that he wanted no part of.

Cooper said, "Send her home."

Steve hung his hands at his sides. "She has no home."

Cooper blew through his lips. "My eye. She's all softness and fluff. Probably one of those debbytants out for a fling. She can call her daddy to fetch her, and we'll all be better off."

Maybe. But Steve couldn't see it. Alessi was anything but used to having things her way. She went overboard not to offend, or even let her preference overrule someone else's. Unfortunately, that reflected her version of things more strongly than Cooper's. "Let me know if you learn anything?"

Cooper nodded, and Steve left the sheriff smacking his lips and cutting a new cigar.

———

Alessi figured if she walked the streets she was bound to find her car eventually, and once she knew where it was, the sheriff could not ignore her. As soon as she left the stores of the village behind, she entered a neighborhood. Ben had explained that most of the people in Charity worked in Chambers City, so in spite of the few businesses, there were a sizable number of houses for her to search.

At first they nestled up close to the heart of town, then they grew scattered, tucked back in the trees. She knew they would soon be few and far between. She didn't like the idea of snooping around private property, but what choice did she have? She approached and peeked into the small square windows of a garage door.

"You there. What are you doing?" The man came bustling out of nowhere.

Alessi held her ground. "I'm looking for my car. A red Mustang. Have you seen it?"

The man's face looked like a triple scoop of cherry vanilla, splotchy white and red with cracks and crevices. "Young woman, are you suggesting I stole your car?"

"Someone was driving it last night. I know it's here."

"No one in Charity would take your car." He picked up a snow shovel and dug it into the pile on his driveway.

Alessi had noticed that, while the snow came down fluffy, it packed densely, and after heaving a few shovelfuls, his face was mostly red. She left his driveway and called, "If you see it, would you please call Sheriff Roehr?"

"You have the wrong idea, missy."

Alessi started toward the next house. A large woman was trying to sweep the snow from her porch. Alessi approached. "Need a hand with that?"

Though sweat glazed her forehead, the woman said, "Nope."

"Have you seen a red Mustang? I know it's here in town, and I'd really like it back."

"Haven't seen your car, dear. You're looking in the wrong place." The woman turned her back and swept.

Tucked well back from the street, the next house had only a dirt driveway and no garage. The only car there was a gray Toyota. This whole neighborhood looked too sweet and respectable to be harboring a car thief. But looks could be deceiving. She went to the next house and the next and peered into the garages. No one accosted her, but there was no Mustang either.

A woman at the next house seemed sympathetic as she let her shaggy dog back inside, but she only shook her head. "I'm sure it's not in Charity. No one here would steal."

That was a very broad statement, even for a small community. Maybe they were embarrassed such a thing could happen in their nice town. Steve had said things weren't supposed to be that way in Charity, and that had been her first fatal opinion as well. She had been careless, it was true, and if the car had been taken away down the interstate, she'd blame no one but herself. But it hadn't.

A wave of last night's fury washed over her, and again she recognized her resentment. Someone had intentionally shown her the car. Was it a game like keep away or like a bully holding your hat just out of reach? Well, she had experience with bullies, and she wasn't going to back down. She had spent too many years giving in to do it now. Another streak of anger surprised her. Fine. She'd work on forgiving after she had the car back.

Alessi kept searching. If poor Sheriff Roehr couldn't get around, she'd do his footwork for him. And if people didn't want to talk about it, she'd use her own eyes and ears. She might not have much, and she sure knew how to do without, but as long as there was one option left to her, she'd take it.

She had planned to walk the streets until she spotted her car or it got too dark to look, but as she neared the end of a narrow road, she saw Ben with Mary and Cait and Lyn hauling huge tires—no, inner tubes. Ben caught sight of her and waved. She waved back.

He leaned a moment by Mary's head, then said, "Hey, Alessi. Why don't you come sledding with us?"

Mary gave a shy smile as Alessi approached. The girls' faces looked rosy and eager. People were swooping down a hill to a lumpy field on sleds and inner tubes, arms waving.

Ben's ears were the color of maraschino cherries. "Guess you haven't gone sledding if you never saw snow before."

She shook her head. "It does look like fun, but I'm searching for my car."

Ben's long face sobered. "You won't find it around here."

Alessi squinted up at him. "You know where it is?"

He rubbed his face. "I wish I did."

Alessi sighed. "Someone's got it, Ben. I saw it last night."

"Well, you better leave it to the sheriff."

"That's just it. The sheriff won't do it." Alessi planted her hands on her hips. "I don't know if he's senile or stubborn, but he just doesn't get it."

Mary spoke softly. "Why don't you take a ride." She held out her tube.

"Hey," Ben said. "You both go." He set both tubes down together.

Alessi looked down the hill. It did look like fun. "Well, maybe once. Thanks a lot for asking." She and Mary climbed on and grabbed hands. Ben pushed, and they shot off down the hill, which was steep enough to build plenty of momentum. It was exhilarating. Laughter built up and overflowed as they shot side by side onto the field and twisted to a stop. Alessi leaned back onto the fat, squashy tube and laughed again, the cold seeping into the seat of her pants. "Now I've done everything."

Mary smiled. "Watch out. Here come the girls."

Alessi sat up as Cait and Lyn careened toward them. Lyn spun and bumped backward into her mother's tube. Cait overshot them both and tumbled out headfirst. They all stood up.

"Now what?" Alessi looked up at Ben at the top of the hill.

"Now we walk back up." Mary scooped up her tube.

Alessi lifted hers. The girls' tubes were thinner than the fat ones she and Mary had. They tucked theirs under their arms and hurried up the sidewalk, stumbling and laughing and stomping the snow. Alessi climbed the hill, careful not to get run over or mess up the sledding tracks with footprints. Ben met the little girls halfway down, looped his arms with their tubes, and took their hands.

She smiled. "Ben sure seems fond of your girls."

"He is."

"It's not really my business, but it seems a godly man like that would be just the thing for them. And you." She looked over at Mary, surprised she'd been so frank, hoping she hadn't offended the woman.

Mary looked down at the ground. "I had a godly man before. He pointed out every one of my sins with Scripture to back it."

Alessi watched Ben send the girls back down, this time giving them a spin with the push. "From what I've seen, I'd say Ben's more the find-your-own-splinter-first sort."

Mary stopped walking and looked at her. "Yes, he is. In three years he's never criticized me."

"Then what are you waiting for?"

She shuddered. "If he did . . . I think I'd wither up and die."

Alessi hadn't expected that. "Why?"

Mary clutched her inner tube tight to her chest. "The last one . . . He meted out God's punishment here on earth, so he wouldn't be accountable for my wrongdoing in eternity."

Alessi touched her shoulder. "Love can heal a lot of things."

Mary stared a long moment into her face, then turned and looked at Ben. "I was thinking in church today of how unforgiveness chokes out love and how love casts out fear." She swallowed. "Do you think I have to accept love first, before I can stop being afraid?"

Alessi smiled at Ben's pantomime urging them up the hill. "My mom always said if you have a chance at real love, you ought to take it. It's too rare and precious to miss."

Mary let out a quick breath. "I can't believe you said that. Those were the two words that came to my mind this morning when I looked at Ben in church. Rare and precious."

Alessi felt a tingle up her spine. She hadn't meant to be profound. She'd only spoken from her heart the words Mom had clung to when the loneliness or desperation threatened to overwhelm them. She had refused to regret her choice, even though it had not lasted a lifetime.

Mary clasped her hand. "Thank you."

Alessi smiled. "Sounds like you had it figured out already."

"Race me," Cait said when Alessi reached the top, and then, of course, she had to race Lyn. They spent the next hour sledding down and walking up, Ben taking his turns as well. Sprawled into the tractor-tire tube, he looked as much like a scarecrow as she'd ever seen. And when the girls piled on either side and the three took one tube down, it warmed Alessi's heart. They needed him. She was sure of it.

Tired and hot, in spite of the brisk wind, they trudged to Mary's small house for hot chocolate and sugar cookies. The table was strewn with tubes of frosting and sprinkles. Alessi sat down with the twins while Mary and Ben mixed up the hot chocolate.

Cait slid a cookie her way and said, "Want to frost a bell?"

"Sure." Alessi took the cookie.

"Open this." Lyn handed her a plastic tub that her tiny fingers could not pry open.

Alessi pulled off the lid and saw that it held white frosting. She took the knife that lay beside it and spread the bell-shaped cookie with icing.

"Now use these." Cait pushed over an assortment of decorating tubes.

Alessi made drops and squiggles with the colored gels and smiled at her finished project. She'd made cookies one year at a friend's house. They'd colored their own frosting and decorated with toothpicks, none of these fancy gels in plastic tubes. But the result was the same, a cookie too sweet to eat.

She took the mug of chocolate offered her by Ben. "Thanks." The steam dampened her upper lip as she blew softly, then sipped.

"Can I have the bell?" Cait leaned her elbows into a scattering of red sprinkles.

"No," Lyn said. "That's not fair."

"I'll make you a cookie, Lyn." Alessi handed the bell over to Cait. "What shape do you want?"

Lyn chose a Christmas tree. Alessi spread it with frosting, then sprinkled green sugar all over the top. She dotted it with yellow and red for ornaments, then gave it over to Lyn. "How's that?"

"Pretty."

Mary had hung a miniature candy cane over the lip of the mug, and the peppermint melted into the hot chocolate as Alessi warmed herself with careful sips. The girls slurped loudly on theirs, cooled with milk, and pulled their chocolate-crowned lips away, smacking.

Ben and Mary joined them at the table with a plate of crustless tuna-salad sandwiches cut into triangles. Alessi couldn't be sure, but it seemed some of the frailty she'd noted that morning had gone from Mary. Maybe it was the color whipped into her cheeks, or the way she met and held Alessi's eyes instead of glancing away the minute their gaze met. And she leaned lightly into Ben's arm with her shoulder as they sipped from their mugs and nibbled sandwiches. Alessi felt a glow all through her.

This was better than finding her car. She could look again tomorrow, when she wasn't working for Steve. Maybe on her lunch break. She and the girls decorated cookies until they'd finished the batch. Then she stood and looked out the window. "Look at that!" It had started snowing great lumpy flakes. "I'd better go back now."

"Do you want Ben to drive you?" Mary cleared the sandwich plate to the counter.

"No thanks. It's not far."

"You sure?"

Ben had Lyn on one knee. She was trying to feed him a star with enough yellow sprinkles to choke a horse.

Alessi smiled. "I'm sure. Thanks for the sledding and all."

Mary walked her to the door. "I'm glad you joined us."

"Me too." Alessi touched her arm briefly, then let herself out into the cold.

She figured it couldn't be more than a mile or so back to Steve's store, and she would keep her eyes peeled for her car along the way. There was still plenty of daylight, even with the snow coming down. But it was hard to walk with the flakes in her face, and she began to consider the snow enough of a good thing.

As she walked she felt a sudden chill in the back of her neck and spun. Nothing but snow. Shaking her head, she went on, passing a few people heading home with sleds and children in tow, but as she left the neighborhood behind and reached the shops, there was no one but herself out on the street. Of course, the stores were closed on Sunday, even Moll's. The Best Bakery and Espresso had been open after church but was closed as she approached it now.

Again Alessi had the sensation she was being watched. She resisted turning and acting like a paranoid fool. But as she started past the Laundromat, the creeping sensation up her spine grew, and when she heard a sound, she shot a glance over her shoulder. She thought she saw something move into the shadows between the Hawkeye Gift Gallery and the Bennet's Books front awning.

She walked faster toward the Mr. Gas station and pulled Steve's jacket close around her neck. She was probably catching a chill, and that accounted for the quivering in her spine. She focused on the station. She'd have to go past it to the house to see if Steve was there with the key to the store. Just as she reached the gas pumps, a snowball whizzed by her head and smacked the pump with a hard crack.

She spun, but there was no one in sight. She stared down the empty street, then looked at the ground where the snowball had burst apart to show the rock. She crouched down and felt the sharp edges of the projectile. If that had hit her head . . . She jerked herself up and hurried around the side of the station toward the house, heart racing. A mean joke? The bad feeling in her spine made her run. She reached the kitchen door and went inside, fighting tears. Why would someone target her? What had she ever done to this town?

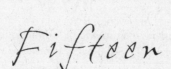

Fifteen

STEVE HAD GONE FROM HOME TO HOME as people in Charity frequently did Sunday afternoons. His intent had been less social connection than trying to get a pulse on the situation. Some people, like Stacie, were more sympathetic to Alessi than Cooper Roehr had been, but no one believed, or could admit, her car had been stolen from Ben's station—except Ben and Dave. And even they doubted the car was in Charity or had been taken by someone from Charity. They would believe it had been lifted by aliens before they would doubt their neighbors or call Alessi a liar.

Ben did admit there'd been other strange goings-on lately. He had lost some videos from the station, and Dave was replacing tools he was sure he never misplaced. They were all little things, and no one talked about it much, but auto theft was not little. Steve wished he had asked Cooper whether he'd checked with the Chambers City police, but he guessed he had. Even if he didn't believe her, Cooper would want an answer to the missing car. Probably hoped it would show up somewhere with someone else inside.

Steve stopped now at Pastor Welsh's house, and Burton welcomed him with his perpetual warmth and concern. "How are you, Steve? Holiday getting you down?"

"No," Steve said. "I'm concerned about Alessi."

"The young woman with you this morning?"

Steve nodded, then said, "Not *with* me."

Madeline joined them. "Come in, Steve. Your young lady seems quite nice."

"She's—"

"Very attentive, I noticed."

Burton brightened. "Was she? I hope she took the message to heart." He motioned Steve to a chair. The stereo played, *"Good Christian men rejo-i-ce, with heart and hand and vo-i-ce."* A trio of red candles scented the air with something fruity.

Steve sat down. "It was an appropriate message if her car's been stolen."

Burton's countenance dimmed. "I don't doubt she's had trouble. Cooper believes she was deserted."

Steve jerked his mouth. "He also thinks her a princess out for a fling."

The pastor threaded his fingers around one knee. "Either way, there have to be hurts to make her behave like this. She deserves our compassion and assistance." His voice grew rich. "We know the life-changing power of kindness."

Madeline handed Steve a mug of spiced cider. "It was good of you to give her a job and a place to stay."

Steve was hardly surprised by their knowledge. Even more than small-town dynamics were involved in ministry connections. Burton Welsh and his wife were told everything. "Well, I did have extra work with the new estate collection I acquired. And there's no lodging in Charity."

Burton said, "I suppose she could be taken to Chambers City."

"She thinks her car is here. She saw it last night."

"She's obviously mistaken." If you could visualize blind faith, the pastor wore it now. Burton Welsh did not want to hear that anything was awry in his little kingdom. Nor, it seemed, did he leave any opening for doubt among his flock. Steve drank the cider without arguing.

"How is business? A new collection, you say?"

Steve nodded. "It's one my father watched for several years. The owner named him in the will as having first rights to buy. That included me as his successor." Steve's throat tightened up. Why did it still hurt?

"This is a hard time for you. Where are you having Christmas dinner?"

Steve smiled. "Believe me, I'm not out in the cold."

Burton returned his smile. "Good, good. Well, that's what we're about in Charity. If we can't help each other, what else is there?"

"And now you've reached out to Miss Moore." Madeline gave him a knowing smile.

"Well—"

The door opened and Carl came in, chapped from the cold. He came to stand beside Madeline, whispering, "What's for dinner?"

She laughed and squeezed his arm. "We have a guest, Carl."

"Hi." Carl smiled with a little too much polish for a seventeen-year-old, but Steve guessed that came with the territory, at least the new territory. Carl had grown quickly and matured early. Steve guessed him thirty pounds his better, though he had yet to fill out his substantial bone structure.

Carl said, "I've been meaning to go in and see what you have."

Steve raised his brows. "At the store?"

Carl nodded. "I'm getting into literature."

Steve stood up. "Well, I mostly carry rare editions, but if you had particular titles you wanted, I could look them up for you."

Carl said, "Maybe I'll come in sometime."

"Sure." Steve made his good-byes and left. That was probably the first time he'd spoken with Carl since he returned from Alaska. Not once had Carl come into the store, but then, old books didn't do much for most of Charity's youth. Steve had loved them because Dad loved them. But Carl? With his start? Maybe the pastor was working even more of a miracle than it already seemed.

Steve shook his head and walked to the truck. Maybe he was the only one out of step with it all. Even his father had signed on. *"Yes, I signed, son. They are my neighbors and friends, people among whom I've lived every day, people who supported us in the loss of your mother."* Loss—not desertion, not betrayal. Even on his deathbed, Dad had not maligned her. And all he would say regarding the pact was, *"We all acted in anger. Therefore we share the responsibility. More than that, we have a chance to make a difference, to save a life . . . in place of the one that was lost."*

Dad had given his word with the others and to the others. Steve recalled all the lessons on honesty, integrity, decency. *"Your word is your bond, son. Give it with pride, and never take it back."* Dad had lived by that, in the pact and before.

His dad had been eighteen years older than his mother. She had drifted into Charity, and into Walter Bennet's heart, like a spring breeze, and had blown out the same way. Yet he'd never said a disparaging word about her or the man she'd run off with. He'd gone to the grave with his wedding band on.

Steve frowned. What did that have to do with anything? His purpose today was to learn what he could about Alessi's situation and hopefully settle his own mind on the matter. There was one person in town who usually had a broader view of things. That would be his last stop.

Steve parked the truck in the broad tree-lined drive. He climbed the impressive stairs and rang the bell. The door opened to cleavage and pearls. "Hello, Amanda. Is your father home?"

Amanda led him into the spacious entry of their three-story house looking every inch the actualization trainer she was. "May I take your coat?" She had already slipped her hands into the shoulders of his jacket. "Though I do love a man in leather." Having annihilated every inhibition she may have had, she amused herself by provoking his.

He suffered the removal of his coat, but she didn't leave it there. She slid her hand over his sweater. "More?" Her mouth turned tease, just as it had from fifth grade on, after she realized the power she had over the boys.

"No thanks." He wished like crazy he hadn't led her on the last time they were alone together. They had no more than kissed in his truck in her driveway, but it had been a stupid move nonetheless, a knee-jerk result of his breakup with Barb and Amanda's failed marriage to a corporate team builder.

"Are you sure it's Daddy you wanted?" She pressed in close, smelling of musk and skin and forbidden fruit.

He forced his eyes to stay on her face. "Yes, your father."

"You used to be more fun." She pouted, an exotic bird preening on a temporary perch.

He had no idea what she saw in him except maybe a challenge, the ultimate aphrodisiac for a chronic dominator. He said, "I need to see Ernest."

She pushed away, looking bored. "He's in the gym."

Steve headed past the atrium and pool to the well-equipped home gym. An Amoco wildcatter and petroleum engineer, Ernest had retired early with seemingly no diminishment of income. People laughingly spoke of illicit connections to OPEC or, on the flip side, secret involvement with the CIA or the FBI. Ernest Bier neither denied nor confirmed anything.

He jogged now on the treadmill, looking ten years under his age. Amanda got her looks from her dad, though her mother was no slouch.

Ernest said, "Take off your sweater and try the bike."

Would everyone in this house invite him to take his clothes off? "I wanted to talk to you about the stolen car."

"What stolen car?"

Steve gripped the treadmill handrail. "The red Mustang taken from Ben's station two days ago." As though Ernest didn't know all about it.

"Amanda ask you to dinner?" he puffed. "Marlo's got Cornish hens roasting."

Steve's stomach growled in response. He'd spent hours trying to figure things out. But he shook his head. "I thought you might know something."

Ernest swiped his forehead with his arm. "Me? I've got nothing to do with it."

"We've all got something to do with it. Isn't that what the pact means? Keeping evil away? Looking out for each other."

"Each other, yes."

Meaning Alessi was not included. Steve frowned. "We can't just pretend she's not here, that nothing happened."

Ernest hit the Cancel button on the treadmill. "The pact doesn't include an outsider's car, or an outsider for that matter. It's Charity's business."

"But if someone in Charity took the car . . ."

Ernest reached for a towel and swabbed the back of his neck. "Steve, I like you. I wish you and Amanda would get something going. But you're on the wrong track with this."

"I just thought—"

"I don't have any inside information or any reason to doubt the people of this town and the good work of the pact."

Steve wasn't sure what he'd expected from Ernest, but not the same pabulum regurgitated by the rest.

Ernest stepped down from the treadmill and pulled off his shirt. "I'll need to shower before dinner. Shall I have Marlo set an extra place?"

Steve shook his head. "No thanks, I have to get back." He retrieved his coat from among Amanda's furs and left. What had he achieved? Nothing that would bring a solution to the situation. Either Alessi was a fraud, preying on the town's sympathies, or she'd been put in a desperate situation and was lying her way out of it. Or she was telling a truth no one in Charity would admit.

———

The house was empty. Alessi turned on lights in the kitchen and den, certain the men wouldn't mind if she stayed there until she could get into the store. She closed the front curtains and turned on the outside lights as the daylight continued to diminish. She had just heated a mug of water in the microwave for tea when she heard shuffling at the front door.

She froze, staring as the knob turned. The door swung open and, puffing, Dave tugged on a cut tree. Relieved, she hurried over and held the door open for him. "That's a nice one, Dave."

"Yeah." Dave jerked it through the door, almost toppling backward.

Alessi lifted the tip end and helped him get it to the corner and into the stand he already had positioned. The tree was a few inches shorter than she but nicely shaped. "I didn't expect three bachelors to have a Christmas tree."

"If it weren't for me, we wouldn't." He crawled under the tree and started tightening screws.

Alessi held the trunk in place, with her arm engulfed in prickly needles. "It smells nice." She breathed the pungent pine aroma and thought of Steve's description of Alaska—*"Pine scent so thick it stayed in your nostrils forever."*

"Is it straight?" He tugged it slightly toward the wall.

"Let me see." She backed away and eyed it from three sides. "Looks good."

He crawled out. "There. Now Diana can't complain."

Alessi stroked the pliant needles of one branch between her fingers. "Why would she complain?"

"She says men have no sense of ceremony and that if women weren't in charge there'd be nothing festive in the world."

Alessi could picture Diana saying that. "Do you have lights?"

"Out in my trunk. Just bought 'em." He took his keys and a moment later came in with a Wal-Mart bag bulging.

"That's a lot of lights."

"It's the whole ball of wax. Lights, ornaments, tinsel." He set the bag before the tree.

She peeked inside. "Didn't you have anything from last year?"

"Didn't have a tree last year."

"So without Diana, there'd be nothing festive?" She elbowed him.

He ducked his head to the side. "Don't you start too."

She laughed. "I was so tired from sledding and walking back, I didn't think I could do anything more. But just looking at this stuff . . . Can I help you?"

"Help me! You can do it."

"What fun would that be?" She pulled out a box of lights. "I think these should go on first."

He took the multicolored strand from the box and plugged it into a wall outlet. The string burst into a brilliant array of ruby, amethyst, topaz, sapphire, and emerald—luminous jewels to bedeck the tapered tips of the valiant fir.

Alessi was enchanted by the colorful glow. "White lights are nice, but these are more fun."

"Watch this." He flipped a switch and the string began to dance, the lights blinking individually. "And this." He switched it again and they ran in a line. "It's got speeds too." They ran faster.

"Makes me dizzy, Dave."

"Yeah." He flicked it again and they grew still. "I should have just spent four dollars on the plain ones."

"Well, Diana might like variety. Here you are." She handed him the end.

Starting at the bottom, he wrapped the tree, and Alessi prepared the next string. "Looks like it plugs right into the last one." He was ready, so she connected them, and again her palms glowed green and gold and red, warmed by each tiny bulb.

"Why don't we get a Christmas tree, Mom?"

"Because the trees are so sad to be cut."

Then, of course, Mom told Hans Christian Andersen's story of *The Little Fir Tree*. Alessi had tried to be sad for the trees, but she wanted one so much. This tree looked anything but sad as Dave wove back and around with the lights. There had been, of course, the extravagantly beautiful trees Aunt Carrie decorated with glass ornaments from Tiffany's, 24-carat gold poinsettias, and billows of ribbon.

But those weren't hers. This tree wasn't, either, but she could pretend. She dug into the bag and pulled out a deluxe set of fishing lures. "What's this for?"

"I figured after I took them off the tree, I could fish with 'em. Get double use for the money."

Alessi looked at the beaded and feathered lures. "That's great, Dave."

"You think?" As he poked his head between the branches, the lights framed it in a flamboyant halo no one could miss.

Grinning, Alessi held up a lure by the barbed hook, watched it turn, then hung it upside down on the end of a branch. "You know what I love most about Christmas? The anticipation. Joy and peace and hope renewed." And she would not let today's scare change that. So someone had played a joke on her. Maybe the same someone who had her car. Christmas was coming. That baby in the manger awaited a place in her heart, and she'd prepare it.

"Uh-know-whu-yu-min." Dave had the end of the string between his teeth, circling the top with the last of the lights.

She translated his agreement, then hung a second lure on a branch. "I once heard a pastor say the event happened two thousand years ago and the only reason we celebrate is to remember the price the Savior paid for being born." She dangled another lure. "But I think Jesus came as much to live for us as to die for us. If His whole purpose was to die, then Herod could have accomplished that with his soldiers long before Pilate with the cross." She hung the lure beneath a tiny green glow.

Dave tucked the plug end down the back of the tree. "You've got a point there."

"It's His *life* I think about at Christmas." She handed Dave a lure. "Jesus died young, but think of how much living He did first!" She glanced up. "Did that sound irreverent?"

"Not at all." He reached for another lure.

"Part of the reason I can understand His sacrifice is because Mom sacrificed every day for me. Like the times she made dinner when she was too tired to stand, just like Jesus. After tramping around all day, healing and preaching, He still managed to whip up loaves and fishes for five thousand."

Dave grinned. "Never heard it told quite that way."

"And when He finally did get to sleep, His friends woke Him up because they were scared."

Dave chuckled. "Where'd you learn your stories?"

"My mom." She hooked a blue beaded lure. "Oh, I heard them in sermons and Sunday school, too, but when Mom told them, they came alive." She sighed. If she could do as well before her time was up, she'd be grateful. "I think joy really is reborn at Christmas, even though it's hard to find when you're alone or you miss someone you love."

She handed him the last lure and watched him tuck it under a red light, then reached into the bag and took out packages of plastic bobbers, the red and white halves seasonally appropriate. "I'm surprised more people haven't thought of these." They filled the branches with bobbers. Mom would have liked this tree, even if it was cut. How she would have laughed at the bobbers.

Last of all they added silver tinsel, hanging the strands straight at first, then tossing. She caught Dave's arm, laughing as the last strands left her fingers. "I can't thank you enough. That's the first tree I ever decorated." She leaned over and kissed his cheek.

A sudden draft from behind them caused them both to turn around as Steve came in and took in the scene. His scowl drained her joy. She let go of Dave's arm.

"What do you think?" Dave waved toward the tree.

Steve eyed it. "Going fishing?" He went into his room and closed the door.

Dave stood silent.

She said, "The first holidays are hardest. You remember everything you did together."

Dave frowned. "Maybe I shouldn't have gotten it."

Alessi shook her head. "No, you should." She pushed her hair back. "May I take a shower?"

"Sure, go ahead. It's my night to cook. I'll have something ready when you're done."

She had meant to shower and go straight to her room at the store. But dinner would be good. She'd eaten only two of the tuna triangles and one frosted sugar cookie for lunch. She stood in the shower, lathered and rinsed, then toweled dry and dressed.

It took a while to blow her hair, and she hummed "O Christmas Tree" and thought of the lures and bobbers. Dave might have meant it practically, but to her it was magical, something she'd always remember. The whole exercise had rejuvenated her, made her forget her troubles and remember what really mattered.

Steve's door was open when she stepped out, and she glanced into his room.

"Come in." He turned from the dresser.

She didn't want to, but his tone was commanding.

"Here's a key to the back door of the store. You can let yourself in and out."

She took the key. "What about the alarm?"

"I won't arm it while you're there."

"Is that safe?" She tucked the key into the pocket of her pants.

"Nothing's safe with you around."

His words stung. *Is nothing safe with you around? Look at this. I paid ninety dollars for this tablecloth.*" Aunt Carrie had been livid, but Alessi never breathed that it was Brittany who'd cut the linen in a snit. No one would have believed her, just as anything she said to Steve would be pointless. She turned before the tears betrayed her, straightened her back, and walked out.

Dave was cooking something that smelled like chili, but she walked out the front door and didn't look back. She let herself into the store and locked the door behind her. She set the key on the edge of the shelf in the storeroom, then sank to the cot and curled up.

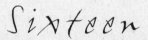

Sixteen

OUTSIDE HIS ROOM, STEVE DID a quick search to make sure she had left. He went to the refrigerator, poured a glass of milk, and drained it.

"This is about done." Dave put the lid back onto the pot. "Is Alessi out yet?"

"She's gone."

Dave turned. "Gone?"

Steve refilled the glass and set it on the table. "Where's Ben?"

"With Mary." Dave spooned two bowls of chili and brought them to the table. He laid out a package of crackers. It would not make meal of the week, but it was hot and Steve was hungry. He'd forgone

Cornish hens and hurried back to the cozy little scene he'd walked in on.

Dave took his seat. "Wonder why Alessi left like that. I told her I'd have it ready soon."

"Three's a crowd." Steve picked up his spoon without uttering a blessing.

"I made plenty."

He blew the steam, then chewed sullenly and swallowed. "Sorry I broke in on you."

Dave looked up. "What are you talking about?"

"You, arm in arm with Alessi. Her little peck on the cheek." He had her pegged now. Same ilk as Barb. Never mind that Dave cared for Diana. She'd wheedle in with her innocent eyes and add Dave to her string. She already had Ben, though Mary needed him badly. Steve frowned. She'd almost suckered him, too, with those doe eyes when he'd kissed her.

Dave buried his spoon in his chili. "She'd never decorated a tree before. It got her excited, that's all."

"Sure."

"Well, you didn't see how big her eyes got when I brought in that bag of lights and trinkets."

Steve wiped his mouth. "I'm sure she played it just right."

Dave shook his head. "I don't get you. Last night you're fighting *for* her, now you're against."

"Not just last night. I spent the whole day trying to find answers. What a waste." He jammed his spoon in and gulped the bite. He should have gone to the store and worked on inventory. Instead he had tried to verify her story, to whip up support and action on her behalf, to convince himself and everyone else she was telling the truth.

Dave tossed his napkin. "You can't stand to see her happy, can you? You had to walk in and spoil it. That's why she left, isn't it? Now she's going hungry because you got a grudge that won't let go."

"I have no grudge against her."

"No, just every woman who breathes."

Steve shoved his bowl away. "That's not true."

Dave stood and cleared their bowls. Obviously he'd lost his appetite as well. "You can clean up." He walked down the hall to his room and shut the door.

Steve scraped and washed the dishes mechanically, trying not to think of Alessi at the store. Had she eaten lunch? Was she going hungry because he'd insulted her? What was it to him if she hung on Dave's arm?

Or had he misread it? Had it been as Dave said, excitement and happiness? He felt like a fool, a jealous ridiculous kid. If Alessi was a fraud he wanted her unmasked, but Dave's description of what led to the scene was a little too real. Steve grabbed his coat and went out. The streetlights revealed spheres of swirling snow. They might have half a foot by morning, maybe more. Somewhere a dog barked. Steve's breath showed white.

He tromped through the clotted snow to the back door of the store and unlocked it with his main key, then pushed it open to find her standing with a document mailer like a baseball bat. "What are you doing?"

She lowered it with a sigh. "I sure didn't think it was you." She stood the mailer against the wall.

He eyed her. "Why not?"

She walked away. "I figured you'd drawn enough blood for one night."

Touché. He expelled a slow breath and stepped inside.

She turned. "I know this is your storeroom, but I'd appreciate some privacy while I'm in it."

He stopped. "I'm sorry. I'm sorry I said what I did, and I think you should come back and eat." He closed the door behind him.

"No thanks." She sat down on the cot.

It *was* his storeroom, but he felt an invisible barrier keeping him next to the door. It was probably just as well, because he wanted to yank her up and repeat last night's folly. "I thought you were playing Dave. It reminded me of . . . someone."

She shook her head with a roll of her eyes.

"I shouldn't have jumped to conclusions."

"Why not?" She looked at him. "You've made up your mind from the start."

"Alessi . . ."

"Look, I'll have to work with you tomorrow, and I need to build up my resistance."

"Ouch." He'd never had anyone put it so brutally, though plenty had probably thought it.

She drew her knees up.

"I admit I was a jerk. But can't you come back to the house and have some food?"

She dropped her face into her hands, and he sank lower in the mire. He didn't want to believe she was as innocent as she made out, but his intuition kept buying in. "I promise not to draw blood. I won't even show my fangs."

She glanced up over her fingertips. "I shouldn't have said that."

"No, you were right. I had no business coming off that way."

She wrapped her knees in her arms. "Anyway, I'm not hungry. I'm not just saying that either."

"You don't want to spend the whole evening in the storeroom." He leaned on the door.

She shrugged. "I don't mind."

"We're watching *It's a Wonderful Life*. Starts in twenty minutes."

She looked up. "You and Dave and Ben are watching *It's a Wonderful Life*?"

"Ben's still at Mary's. I doubt Dave'll come out of his room unless I bring you back."

"Is that why you came? For Dave?"

It had sounded that way, but it wasn't. "I came because I was wrong. Now, the sermon today suggests you should forgive me. Even a repeat offender."

She formed a halfhearted smile—it was small but there nonetheless. "All right."

His chest eased as he stepped closer and held out his hand, doubtful he would have responded as well with the positions reversed. But she took it, and he made a quick exit with her in tow. He would be civil and kind for the time remaining until Christmas. Friendly. He could manage that.

They got back to the house, and he nodded his head toward the back hall. "Tell Dave you're back. He'll join us." Steve hoped so, at least. An evening alone with her, watching a heartwarming tale he and his father had loved, would not be wise. He heard her tap on Dave's door, and Dave's response. Yes, it was eager and glad, but nothing more. It was his mind that had made the leap to something improper, not Dave's or Alessi's actions.

Maybe Dave was right. Maybe he did have a grudge—or a definite bias. Barb had set him up. And his mother before her. His dad hadn't allowed bitterness in, but Steve seemed to have. Maybe because his father was gone. He sighed, relieved when Alessi returned with Dave.

Dave padded forward. "You want some chili? I can heat it up."

"No thanks." Alessi smiled for real at him. "I'm not hungry."

Steve let Dave have the couch with Alessi. He took the chair across from them and stole glances throughout the movie. A few of them she met, but mostly her attention stayed glued to Jimmy Stewart and his plight.

"He doesn't see how much the little things matter." She wove her long fingers around one knee, a pose completely suited to her shape.

Steve fixed his attention on the screen. "People usually don't."

"Unless it's all little things."

He didn't ask what she meant. He guessed. Once life was reduced to the most basic elements, as hers was currently, everything mattered. Maybe that's why his remarks hurt her. She didn't have much to fall back on. He felt bad again. He hadn't been so convicted in a long time. First the day's sermon, then Dave's grudge comment, then Alessi's: *"I need to build up my resistance."* It was definitely time to look inside and clean house.

His father used to remind him to "dust the cobwebs off his conscience." A serious pang seized Steve's chest. Christmas without his father was too hard. If Alessi hadn't come and thrown everything off kilter, he'd be depressed.

"Zuzu's petals! Zuzu's petals!" Jimmy Stewart ran to his home and found his family and his neighbors and all the people whose lives he'd touched.

Steve wanted his life to matter. Closed up with his father's books, he'd done the least interacting he could get away with. Unlike his dad, who always had a kind word, a helpful hand for his neighbors—even the women who stalked him with casseroles. He watched Jimmy Stewart take his little girl into his arms and felt the sting of tears. Dad had always teared up at the end of that movie. Because Jimmy was reunited with his wife? Or just because goodness prevailed?

"*Atta boy, Clarence.*"

Steve swallowed the tears back with a vengeance. Alone with his dad it hadn't mattered. But across from Dave and Alessi it sure did. He risked a glance. Alessi's eyes were more than moist.

She sighed. "I love that story."

She would, with her penchant for halos and angels watching over.

Dave rose and shut off the TV. "Well, I'm turning in." He yawned hugely.

Alessi stood and stretched. "Guess I'll go back now."

"I'll walk you." Steve stood up.

She didn't argue. Jimmy's wonderful life had mellowed her. They walked together across the street and down to the store, stopping outside the back door.

He leaned on one arm against the wall. "Will you be all right?"

She nodded. "I'll be fine."

He bent and kissed her cheek. "Good night."

She stood there speechless as he turned back toward the house. He'd done it again. But this time he didn't kick himself.

Seventeen

THE NEXT DAY ALESSI WENT OUT EARLY to cover more neighborhood blocks before starting work at the store. She shuffled through four inches of fresh snow, going the other direction this time, searching houses set farther apart. How did one hide an automobile? It had to be somewhere close enough for the person to play in the street outside Steve's store, though last night had been quiet; no Mustang sighting, no disturbing of the peace.

And peace was what she found in the streets as she walked. All of Charity seemed at peace—no gang symbols marking territories, no profane graffiti, no questionable goods and services being peddled on corners. It seemed Charity was everything she'd expected, except that the choice to leave had been taken away. She could be at peace with that if the Mustang didn't mean so much to her. It was more than a car; it represented her triumph.

Could God want her to give it up? Had she made it an idol? Could the one thing of value a person possessed be a stumbling block? It didn't seem right. Some people had so much. Giving her the Mustang had not fazed her uncle. It showed his friends and neighbors his generosity and attention to duty, but it was no hardship. He could afford the purchase. She could not afford the loss. Didn't God see the difference?

She sighed and walked back toward town. It was time to go to work, and that prospect was daunting enough. She'd ponder the state of her soul when she didn't have to guard her psyche. It was not easy to guess what to expect from Steve. He obviously doubted her, yet he trusted her with a key to his store. He suspected her motives but gave her a job, groused at her, insulted her, then kissed her. The man was clearly confused.

She would only think one day through, then face the next when it came. She was not giving up that Mustang until God left her no choice. In the meantime, it seemed she was stuck in Charity. And looking around her, that was not such a bad thing. Maybe she was following the halo after all.

Steve was focused at his computer when she entered. His face, caught in the bluish glow of the monitor, looked stark, though his hair was in some semblance of order. By the aroma, it must be a red cinnamon disk bulging his cheek, and a slow sucking was his only motion besides the clicking of his fingers on the keys. She didn't bother him, just took off her jacket and arranged the display of holiday books that had been messily perused.

Then she busied herself studying the titles on the rare-book shelves. After a while, the first male customer she'd seen rushed in. He had the look of a pigeon: round bulging eyes, a tiny beak of a nose, and a declining chin; his head bobbed forward in little jerks as he walked. He said, "I need a book for my wife's stocking. If she doesn't find one in there Christmas morning she'll never forgive me."

Alessi smiled. "Pastor Welsh said seventy-seven times, and I'll bet you're not even a repeat offender."

He laughed. "She would definitely have an opinion on that."

Alessi helped him choose a humorous holiday romance from the paperbacks, then asked what he liked to read. Taken aback, he said, "I haven't thought about it."

"If your wife's a reader, she'd probably love a cozy companion on winter evenings. With snow like this and two good books . . ."

He glanced around the store. "I really haven't read since high school."

But she could see his interest was piqued. "Steve has some great classics. When people like a book for a long, long time there's usually a reason." She pulled a hardback off the shelf. "Take this one by Cervantes. Who hasn't heard of Don Quixote? And can't you just see the knight with woeful countenance?"

He looked uncertain. "I guess so."

She took another from the foreign author section. "Or *Les Misérables*. That one makes you cry and cry. Well, it might not make you, but it did me."

He laughed. "I guess I'm just not much of a reader."

"Have you tried the American classics? Maybe you're more of a Hemingway guy—*A Farewell to Arms* or *The Sun Also Rises*—or Steinbeck's *The Grapes of Wrath*. That one got a Pulitzer and they made a movie out of it."

"I'll try that last one. I've heard of it, anyway."

She showed him several copies from the used-classics shelf. "This one's in good condition."

He took the book and studied the cover, then nodded.

As she completed the sale at the register beside Steve, he stayed focused with his usual brusque, preoccupied manner. Not at all the mellow companion who had brushed his lips on her cheek last night. Maybe he was bewitched, only showing his true self in magic moments that she must watch for to set him free. She was just the sort of hapless heroine the fairy tales called for, and he'd already admitted himself the beast. Or was it Dr. Jekyll and Mr. Hyde?

"You know your literature." He spoke without looking away from his screen.

She half turned. "I've read a lot."

"Not everyone reads classics."

She slid her fingers over his smooth glass paperweight. "Mom and

I spent a lot of time in the library. We started with fairy tales, stories she hadn't been able to read as a child. She had made up her own versions from the parts other kids talked about, but she loved hearing the real stories. When I'd read most of those, she got a list from the librarian, and we moved on to literature."

Steve turned from the screen. "You read Hemingway at eight and Steinbeck by nine and a half?" Not quite sarcastic but clearly skeptical.

"Ten or eleven. We started with *Johnny Tremain, The Secret Garden, Jane Eyre,* and *Wuthering Heights*. We read at least something by most of the names people recognize. When Mom got sick, she wanted more hopeful themes. So we read *The Pilgrim's Progress* and *Hinds' Feet on High Places*."

"And *Les Misérables*?"

Sadness slid over her like a tight-fitting sheath. "I read *Les Misérables* by myself."

He eyed her a moment, then said, "Can you package the orders I've started in the back room?"

"Sure." She guessed he didn't want to hear about her loss or think of his own. She could understand that. It had taken a long time for her to talk about her mom. Of course, that was partly due to living with Aunt Carrie. Alessi had guarded her mom's memory like a holy secret.

She boxed the orders and turned them over to the UPS driver who came to pick up. The store was surprisingly busy with people ostensibly coming for gifts, but by the overheard comments, curiosity about Steve's Christmas date was much more of a draw than his books. Alessi wished she'd never started that business. But she had, and now it was like the make-believe scenarios she and Mom had devised to get through less-than-delightful duties. They'd been masters of imagination, and she was glad she'd honed the skill. It took some stellar acting.

She lifted the stack of books Steve had processed, and as she shelved them, she wondered what made them important. Was it age or scarcity? The words on the pages or the date of publication? The author or the message or the story? And who was out there looking for this book or that? She imagined someone learning the very copy in her hands was found and available, maybe a title the person had despaired of finding. Maybe one with a deep and personal meaning, memories of someone special or a time looked back on fondly.

"Why, yes, we have that book. I know right where it is." Her placing the tome in his hands would be as momentous as dipping the cup into the pool that would heal the ailing mother or the mute child or the dying father. Dropping to her knee and parting with the most precious—

Steve touched her elbow. "Let's get some lunch."

She jumped, then clutched the book to her chest, reality flooding in. "I was going to search for my car over lunch."

He slid the book out of her hands and set it on the small end cap. "You do have to eat."

She had skipped breakfast to search earlier. "I'll just grab something while I look."

"A good hot meal will hold you better. My treat."

He had provided most of the meals she'd had lately, and she guessed another free meal was worth the time she'd lose in searching. He motioned her toward the door and set his return time on the sign. It didn't seem to occur to him that if they went separately he could keep the shop open, but that would mean leaving her alone with access to the register—a little different than having everything shut down and locked up when she slept there at night. He led her down the sidewalk toward Moll's.

It was the first time she'd seen Charity in the sunshine. Every snow-covered surface was dazzling bright, more so than noontime glare on the beach. It made her think of the light in C. S. Lewis's *Voyage of the Dawn Treader* as the adventurers drew nearer and nearer Aslan's country. Mom had loved that story best, and Alessi imagined her now, seeing everything with perfect, brilliant clarity. Her own eyes, however, squinted nearly shut until they stepped into the relief of Moll's dim interior.

Alessi ordered through Steve—who had direct communication with Moll—a meal she'd never eaten before: chicken fried steak. It was sinfully good. She'd have had enough comfort food by the time she left Charity to last her a lifetime. Steve laughed when she told him that, then grew pensive and dropped his gaze.

"Although, there is something to be said for avocado and sprouts, hummus and tofu," she added.

He winced. "You're speaking a foreign language."

"You don't get fat on that food." She dug into the crispy edge of her steak.

"You'll be back to your bikini in no time."

She shook her head. "I'm not going back to the coast."

"Been there, done that?"

"Bought the T-shirt." She laughed. "Or rather I sold it—about a hundred times." She dipped a wad of mashed potatoes in the creamy pepper-flecked gravy. "There's too much else to see."

"In what direction?"

"I think I'll head for Alaska. You made it sound stupendous."

He sipped his coffee. "You know your way around?"

She shrugged. "Have any maps or travel books?"

"Only a few hundred." He wiped a drip of coffee from his chin.

She smiled. "I'd love to find that waterfall on your wall."

He didn't reply. Maybe the place had painful memories. Maybe he thought Alaska was another place she didn't belong. But she was getting pretty good at drifting. People around them sent curious glances but didn't come forward and congregate as they did at some of the tables. Alessi guessed Steve might normally be something of a loner, and people seemed to accept that, especially since they'd warned the ladies off with their supposed holiday liaison.

Alessi liked people. Except for the years with Uncle Bob and Aunt Carrie, she had never been without friends. None of them knew her real living conditions because, if she wanted to bring a playmate home, Mom always suggested a park or a beach instead and adjusted her work schedule to take them. The hard part was that she never kept her friends for long because they'd have to move. There'd be days with no school while they looked for a different place to live, and then she'd have to start all over in a new school.

She learned to make friends quickly—until she'd been rendered uncertain she deserved friends, and then her grief had closed her up in a way that warded people off. But after leaving Uncle Bob's utopia, she had chosen a broad spectrum of companions. It seemed people her age were either college bound or self-destructive. Being neither, she got along better with people like Ed. Here in Charity, she had already connected with Ben and Dave and even Diana and Karen. And, though

based on their early interaction she would not have named Steve, there
he was.

If she got her car back and headed for Alaska, his life would go
back to normal. But could she actually tour the wilderness and not
wonder about Steve any more than she'd not think of Ben and Dave
every time she pulled into a filling station? So many lives had touched
hers and melted away, walk-ons in her memory. But these people were
sinking in.

Moll brought a box for the rest of her lunch as soon as she noticed
Steve was done. Alessi thanked her even though she would have liked
to finish it there. "It was delicious."

No answer. Alessi hardly cared. Whatever the woman's issues, she
sure could cook. They walked out and Steve hooked an arm over her
shoulders, obviously convinced their charade was working. She had to
remind herself it wasn't real. What he did in public was no more than
hanging garlic around his neck.

Eighteen

STEVE RESTED HIS ARM ON THE SHOULDERS just inches lower than his. His stride matched Alessi's. He smiled at the neighbors they passed: Benjamin Stone, an elder in the church, Judy Soren and her three toddlers. His stomach was full, his gait easy, and his mind . . . Well, he wasn't trying to think too hard.

Working with Alessi was making the assimilation of the new estate easier than any he had done before. He no longer considered the job a favor he'd done her. Besides the obvious interference factor with the women of Charity, she did have the training to handle the store and help with his orders and inventory during the only busy time of the year. It probably was true that she had worked in a bookstore, and maybe even the part about the old guy she called her best friend. She was certainly strange enough to be best friends with a seventy-year-old man.

He hated to admit he found her strangeness refreshing. Even things like reading Steinbeck with her mother—before the age of twelve. He'd have liked to be a fly on the wall for that one. Pretty heavy-duty language and subject matter for a little girl, but then, he couldn't picture Alessi as a young child any more than he could imagine her old. She seemed sort of ageless. And that was very strange, since she was twenty-one and he was almost a decade older.

He took his arm off her shoulders. She was a young woman, stranded, maybe deserted, maybe in trouble, maybe trouble itself. He knew nothing about her. As Cooper said, they had no proof of even her name. Yet he kept acting in ways he couldn't fathom, playing a role he had rejected completely. His arm had gone around her with no effort from his mind. As their fingers brushed now, he thought of clasping her hand in his, then realized he already had.

Thank God they had reached the store. He unlocked it, then stood, half blocking her entrance until she looked up. Her hazel eyes were laced with green, the lashes a light brown only slightly darker than the freckles across her nose. Her brows were peaked and tapered and rose now with consternation. She thought he was going to kiss her.

And he was, but she slipped inside and held the door for him. He needed a book on parapsychology, unexplained mental phenomena. She was a mind snatcher. Yet it went deeper than that. He slid her jacket from her shoulders and carried it to the desk. The sooner he got back to work the better. But he couldn't concentrate. Something was not copacetic. He sensed it, even if he couldn't put it to words.

Yesterday he had visited people he'd known most of his life—and felt a disconnect. Now he spent an hour with someone he'd met only days ago and experienced a bond of supernatural intensity. He was way off course. He forced his mind to tackle the facts.

She had drifted into town with enough sun streaks in her hair to make Florida a possibility. Ben had seen the car; the car had disappeared—until the other night. Did he believe her? Say he did. What then? A missing car was not a lost wrench. It was criminal. So what again?

Charity had developed a mindset that didn't allow for this scenario. The pact had created expectations, and no one wanted to admit there was trouble. It all came back to the premise: If evil no longer existed in Charity, then a crime could not have happened.

But if it did . . .

Steve shook his head. He wasn't sure if people truly believed the pact on a spiritual level or if the idea was simply enough to determine behavior. Was there a difference? Ben and Dave had reached out to Alessi, had given her assistance. He provided employment and shelter. If Cooper—

The front door opened and Carl came in, his eyes scanning the dim room like a waking owl. Steve had suspected he was only talking about an interest in literature to make an impression, but there he was. Steve started to go forward, then realized Alessi would handle it just fine. He glanced around the back shelves but didn't see her.

Carl, however, seemed to. At least something had attracted his gaze, and Steve doubted very much it was a book title that drew that particular expression. He frowned. Carl was what, seventeen? Perhaps Steve was making more of it than there was, but the kid ducked behind the front shelf as Alessi rounded the corner into the aisle. She looked forward, expecting a customer no doubt, and started that way.

"Alessi." Steve stood up as she turned. He thought fast. "Can you get something for me?"

She came, and he felt an inordinate relief. Ridiculous.

"I need a ream of paper. For the printer." He handed her the truck keys. "Remember the way to Wal-Mart?" He had lost his mind.

Her brow puckered. "I don't have my license."

He frowned. "If Cooper stops you, remind him he's supposed to be finding it."

She chewed her lower lip. "He'll think I stole your truck."

"Just go. He's home napping with his cat." He nudged her toward the doorway to the storeroom. "The truck's out back."

"One ream of paper?"

"Get another bag of these." He held up the bowl of hard candies.

As soon as she was out the door, he started for the front. He was making a total fool of himself. The kid only wanted a book to read. Maybe he was shy; maybe he was . . . gone. Steve scanned the front.

He circled the racks, the tall shelves, all the way to the back. He rushed through the storeroom and pushed open the back door. The tiny lot was empty; Alessi had taken the truck.

He scanned the area, then walked around to the front, looking both ways along the street. What on earth was he thinking? He had provided her with new transportation. She could take his truck and head for Alaska. He had panicked because the pastor's son looked funny at her.

Steve rubbed his face and wondered once again if something had taken over his brain. He went into the store and paused where Carl had stood with that strange expression. There was a direct line of sight to where Alessi had been working. Steve narrowed his eyes, counting off the seconds Carl had stood there watching and then ducked aside.

Steve cocked his jaw and considered the situation. Why would Carl come in, then leave like that? Maybe he forgot something. But why would he hide from Alessi? Steve paced the aisle. Twenty-nine miles there and back, time to look for the two things he'd requested and maybe browse a little herself . . . It could take two hours.

He set the time on his door sign, then locked up and walked to the station. Ben was talking with Matt Smith. Steve went through and looked into the garage. Dave had a Buick in the bay and was up to his elbows in grease. Steve circled the video wall until Matt left.

Ben joined him. "What's wrong?"

Steve turned. He'd probably telegraphed his foolishness to everyone. "Tell me about Carl, Ben."

Ben looked at him with the slow, measuring gaze that questioned his sense, then said simply, "What about him?"

"Does he have a girlfriend? Is he dating?"

Ben slid his hands into his jeans pockets, obviously unsure how to answer. "Well, I . . ."

Steve spread his hands. "He was looking strangely at Alessi, then he hid behind a shelf when she started toward him." Steve knew how it sounded. "It's nothing personal, Ben. I'm just curious."

Ben swallowed. "Pastor recommends courting, and only after eighteen. If Carl's got a girlfriend, I sure don't know it. He's . . . really come along."

Yesterday Steve had noticed the kid's polite behavior, his almost slick demeanor. He hadn't looked that way today. There'd been something feral in his look. "It was pretty strange."

Ben scanned the store, then returned his gaze. "I thought your Christmas date was just to ward off the gals."

He had expected Ben would take it that way. "This isn't about me, or our date, or anything like that. I'm just not sure . . ."

Ben looked as though he didn't really want to know.

"I'm not sure all is right in paradise."

"Alessi's fine. She's got good sense, even if she did lose her car."

Steve closed his eyes and expelled his breath. "Listen to you, Ben. You won't even consider the subject. Something's wrong here."

"Carl's had it pretty bad. I'd hate for people to start pointing fingers."

"Yeah. Maybe Dave pinched the Mustang. You know how he is with cars."

Ben frowned. "We don't know anything for sure."

"I thought we did. I thought we believed Alessi's story."

"Well, I do." Ben ran a hand over his strands of hair.

"Then someone took it, Ben."

Ben dangled his arms. "You think it's Carl?"

He hadn't. He'd only wondered why Carl had acted so strangely. "I don't know. I didn't see it in their driveway."

Ben smiled. "No, I don't suppose so. Pastor wouldn't feel right in a sporty little number like that."

Steve returned the smile. "Wonder how Alessi likes my truck." At Ben's raised eyebrows, he explained her mission. "Think I'll ever see it again?"

"Yes, I do." Staunch and steadfast.

Steve's concern eased. "I just wish we could figure it out."

"There's an explanation, I'm sure. Maybe Cooper—"

"If you say that one more time, I'm taking you down." Steve glared. "You know I can."

"You think you can."

Actually, wrestling Ben was like tackling an octopus. "Cooper is not the answer. He's an old man with a bad hip and less inclination than a sloth."

"Then you figure it out," Ben said. "But watch that you don't jump to conclusions."

Steve pictured Carl's face again when he hadn't known anyone was watching. Maybe it was the wrong conclusion, but he had to start somewhere. He went back to the store, unlocked a case that held valuable inventory and one thing that wasn't for sale. He took out his father's scrapbook.

The pain was too sharp to start it at the beginning. But he opened to a place nearer to the end, then turned pages looking for anything to do with the pact. A newspaper clipping caught his eye, and a chill washed over him. *Beth Hansen Missing.*

Steve stared at the picture and understanding flooded his mind. No wonder Carl had looked at Alessi that way.

———

Alessi pulled the truck up to the back of the bookstore and parked. She had not been arrested or questioned or even looked at twice. Steve had forgotten to give her money for the purchase, but she'd had the wad of bills in her pocket since she was not about to leave it behind. She considered circling to the front but tried rapping on the back door first. Steve ought to hear it from his desk.

The door opened a moment later. She handed him the paper with the package of candy on top. He took it with a strange look on his face. What now? He motioned her in and closed the door behind them. When they reached the desk, he said, "What was your mother's name?"

"Shannon."

"Your aunt?"

"Carrie."

"Any other sisters?"

What on earth? Alessi frowned. "No, why?"

He shook his head and set the things on the desk. "I forgot to give you money."

She pulled out her bills. "I had it."

"That's yours. Got the receipt?"

She took that out and handed it over. He stooped to open the small safe under the desk, took out a cash box, and gave her the amount on the receipt.

"It sure was different driving that big truck."

He glanced up. "Does that mean you backed into something?"

"You're a very suspicious sort."

"Well?"

She opened the package of candies and refilled the bowl. "No, I didn't back it into anything."

"Good." He lifted a large album and locked it into a glass case.

She patted the candies into an even mound. "Did you do much business?"

"Not much."

"That's good."

He turned from the case. "Why?"

She held up the register key dangling from her wrist. "You'd have had a hard time ringing up the sales."

He looked from the key to her face. "I stepped out for a while."

So that explained it. "Didn't want me here, robbing you blind?"

"What?"

"I wondered why you sent me out when there's most of a ream there under the printer and no one eating the candy but you." Why did it hurt every time she saw what someone thought of her? She should be used to it. Especially from him.

He balked. "No, I . . . If I thought you'd steal something I would hardly have handed over my truck."

She swallowed. That was a good point. But he'd definitely made up some silly excuse to get rid of her. A thought dropped like a coin in a slot machine. "Do you know something? Did they find my car?"

Steve shook his head. "No." He jammed his hands into the pockets of his jeans. No car, but there was something he wasn't telling.

Frustration crawled her throat. "What's going on?"

He glared. "I was worried."

She stared into his face. "About me?"

"Yes. Sort of."

She scanned the store, confused.

"It doesn't matter; I figured it out." He circled the desk and sat down.

Figured what out? She stood her fingers on the desk. "You know something."

"No, I don't. I was on the wrong track." He looked up. "I read it wrong and reacted."

Her fingers softened. He'd been afraid for her. He had protected her. Never mind that he'd been mistaken. Warmth poured over her like molasses. "Well . . . thanks."

He bushed his hair up like a shaggy hedgehog and started typing.

———

With Alessi busy at the front of the store, Steve accessed the library files of the *Chambers City Chronicle* dating over five years ago. There was the article his father had clipped noting the disappearance of one of Charity's citizens. Beth Hansen was reported missing by her husband, Duke. A search had been organized but proved unsuccessful.

Steve studied the enlarged photograph on his screen. The similarity was less in features than in type: blond curling hair, thin neck, and something vulnerable in the expression. It had been a lot of years since he'd seen Beth in person, and he hadn't paid much attention since she'd been older and married. He hardly remembered her, but what he recalled was the sense of someone waiting for calamity.

A subsequent article was only a couple of paragraphs. They had found a letter stating Beth's decision to leave Charity and her husband, Duke. The search had been discontinued.

Steve leaned back in the chair, his chest constricting, though not by memories anymore. He couldn't access the loss he'd felt when his mother left. It was more the lingering questions, the anger, the sense that he was in some way deficient. No wonder Carl had stared at Alessi with a look of hunger and disdain. He'd been seeing his mother's face.

It must have been a jolt. Steve rubbed his hand over his eyes. How many times had he imagined his own mother's return? He'd looked for her in every new face, wondering. Carl had eleven years of recognition to draw on. He could not have missed the likeness between Alessi and his mother. Even the obvious age difference might not have registered, since Carl's memories would be years old. No surprise that he'd frozen and hid. Steve wished he could have talked to him, but what would he have said?

He got up and watched Alessi working on a shelf he rarely bothered with. The books there were in poor condition, not worth much.

But she was taking each one, wiping it clean of dust and cobwebs, and carefully replacing it as though they were all priceless. He supposed she couldn't tell the difference.

She took one out and started to wipe it, then paused, running her finger over something on the cover. Curious, he approached her. The book was *Religious Art of the Renaissance,* the cover Filippo Lippi's *Adoration.* Alessi was tracing the halo around the Madonna's head.

Steve leaned over her. "Is that what you see?"

She shook her head, glancing up. "No. I just see light."

He nodded. "Those are symbolic. A halo motif."

"Oh." She opened the book and paged slowly through the fragile leaves. The binding was all but shot, though the pages were in fair condition. She turned to *The Madonna of the Rocks* by da Vinci and paused.

Steve waited curiously to see if she would pick up on the accepted halo elements in the work, the diffused light around the Madonna's head, her cupped hand suspended over the infant Jesus.

She studied it a long time, then turned the page.

He said, "I guess you're not alone in your angel sightings."

She balanced the barely hinged book across her knees. "I don't see angels—just halos and the good that comes after."

Steve rolled her words over in his mind. Definitely not the language of a T-shirt mongering beach babe, yet there was a lack of sophistication, almost ignorance, in spite of her knowledge of stories. Maybe gaps in her education, like migrant workers' kids. She was a study in contradictions—either the most real person he'd met or the con of all cons.

As it was, the last few days had been interesting to say the least. Certainly distracting and not unenjoyable, which was saying a lot since the grief of Dad's passing pressed in. It was also the first Christmas without Barb, but he didn't miss her. He did, in dark moments, hope she was shivering in some shack, but he doubted it. The poor sod she chose had probably taken her out of Alaska to the big city, where he carried her design books and took pictures of her events.

More power to you. My blessing on you both. And my deepest thanks for returning my sanity. He squatted next to Alessi and flicked the book's flimsy spine. "I ought to have that bound. Dad used to do the repairs himself, but I never learned how."

"Things get lost between generations."

He looked into her face. "What did you lose?"

"Family."

Nineteen

ALESSI APPROACHED BEN AT THE COUNTER as he closed out the register for the day. He looked up. "Hey, Alessi."

"Hi, Ben." The picture of Clark Gable as Rhett Butler lay on tissue at the counter. "What's this for?"

"Mary's Christmas present. She won't say it, but I know she likes that piece of my collection best." He formed a wry smile. "Most gals would, I guess."

"That's really nice."

"She's got one of those Barbie dolls dressed up as Scarlet. So I think she could hang this near the doll."

Alessi nodded. "That'd be great. Sort of like he's the big dream in her mind." She had loved *Gone With the Wind*. Scarlett's "Tomorrow is another day" had resonated somewhere deep inside her. No matter the obstacle, the setback, she could dig down and face another day. That was when she learned to stand up straight and stop hunching her shoulders.

"Ben, I was hoping you could do me a favor."

"Sure."

She laughed. "You haven't heard it yet."

He gathered the picture with the tissue and tucked it all under the counter. "What is it?"

"Would you drive me around to find my car? I've gone about as far as I can on foot."

"You want to look in the dark?" He glanced out the station windows.

"Steve doesn't close until after the sun's down, but I have been searching in the morning before he opens."

Ben frowned. "By yourself?"

She sighed. "I hope I'm not the only one looking, but I'm not too confident Sheriff Roehr is putting out his best effort."

Ben took his keys and headed her toward the door. "I'll drive you around some."

The gasoline-scented air bit when they stepped out, and Alessi pulled her collar close. After Ben locked the station, she climbed into his Jeep Cherokee. She might not be able to see much in the dark, but she'd at least get a feel for the area and where she could look in the daylight. Then again, she might actually see the Mustang. You never knew if you didn't try.

Ben's radio played "Sultans of Swing," then Roy Orbison's "Crying," followed by the Beach Boys and Kansas, as he drove slowly around the outlying areas. She breathed the lingering aroma of coffee and French fries. Ben's car wasn't too tidy. But she noticed a kid's-meal box and guessed part of the clutter was Cait's and Lyn's. Ben's stomach growled.

She turned from the window. "You're hungry."

He tipped his chin. "I can't say no when my stomach just said yes."

"Let's go back. I'll look again tomorrow."

Ben brought the car around and drove them to the house. "Sure am sorry about your car."

"I know. But I'll find it." It was getting harder to sound confident. But tomorrow *was* another day.

———————

Steve drew the fry basket out and tipped the crisp, battered fish and chips onto the paper towels. He glanced up when Ben and Alessi walked in together. She had slipped out from the store without his noticing, and it irked him now to see her with Ben. He ought to be glad she hadn't gone off alone in the dark as he'd thought. But she had snuck out without a word. Weren't women supposed to be the great communicators?

Alessi went into the bathroom, and Steve accosted Ben. "Where were you?" He had checked the station and found it locked up.

Ben whispered, "She wanted to look for her car. I drove her around."

Steve frowned. "Where?"

"South side mainly."

She could have asked him. Maybe it was just that he was occupied. Or she didn't trust him to help. "Did you see anything?"

Ben shook his head. "It was pretty dark. And I doubt it's here."

Steve rumpled his hair. Alessi hadn't chased it in the street lately. Maybe she had been mistaken the other night. Maybe the car was miles away. He almost hoped so.

Alessi came into the kitchen. "Sure smells good."

Was there any food she didn't like? "It's not bikini food. Except the salad." He pointed to the chopped tomato and cucumber in vinaigrette.

Dave came in and washed up at the sink with his green bar of Lava soap. "Smells like fish."

Steve had to admit this meal would be with them for a while, but sometimes on a cold night there was nothing like the crisp, greasy taste of battered cod and fries. And on his night it was his choice. Alessi pitched in by setting the table, and he carried the platter of fried food. They gathered and Ben said a blessing. Alessi murmured a caveat to help her find her car. Maybe that was the answer: God.

Dave might not appreciate the smell, but he dug into the meal.

Steve watched Alessi as they ate. She seemed subdued, probably from her fruitless search. He had a sudden urge to drive her around himself. Not with any expectation of finding it, but just to show he was willing to try. Why had she gone to Ben instead?

Dave wiped his mouth. "Diana's coming over to play dictionary."

Steve shared a glance with Ben. Not exactly his plan for the evening, though he wasn't sure what he'd do instead. Probably go back to the store and work. Except that was Alessi's space after hours. She'd probably play the game, though.

"Karen's coming, too, Steve."

He jerked up his head. "What's that supposed to mean?"

"We'll be outnumbered if you run off."

He frowned. "You won't beat them anyway."

"We might."

Alessi laid down her fork. "What's dictionary?"

Dave pushed his plate aside. "We make two teams, guys and gals. One team chooses a word from the dictionary and writes out its definition. Then they make up three more. The other team has to guess the right one."

She nodded. "Sounds like fun. Why don't you like it, Steve?"

"No one said I didn't." He looked at the guys. "I just have work to do."

Ben sighed. "You're worse than Dave on an engine. At least he knows when to quit."

Steve dragged his last bite of fish through the malt vinegar on his plate. It hadn't always been this way. He had never been one to sit around, nor was he plagued with tunnel vision. Only since Dad's death and Barb's desertion had he learned to hibernate.

Okay, maybe he wasn't the most gregarious man by nature. Barb had driven him crazy with her constant social needs. Companionship was fine, but did everything have to be a party? He met Alessi's gaze. "I'll play." She might guess him incapable of fun, but he was good with words and conniving. Nowhere near Karen's proficiency, but no matter.

He had barely finished cleaning up the kitchen when the women arrived, Karen bearing her two-volume Webster's tome. That was another inequity. She probably studied the thing at night like a Bible, so she'd know where to look for the most insidious words. They clustered in their teams, and he noted again how Alessi had connected with the two women. No doubt all of Charity would have embraced her— if it weren't for the car.

In his visits he'd sensed almost a resentment of Alessi for accusing Charity of something impossible. Or at the least for bringing temptation in the form of her shiny red car. He wished she'd never lost it. Did he wish she'd never come?

"You haven't written yours, Steve," Dave hissed in his ear. "Are you drawing a blank?"

Steve shook his head. "Just let me see the word again."

They played until ten o'clock, when Diana yawned and said, "I have an eight-o'clock perm. Gents, this is your last chance."

Several times they had drawn their score close to the women's. But they were still trailing.

"Find a good word," Karen's eyes gleamed, "and we'll give you double points."

"We could tie it with that," Ben said.

Steve took the dictionary, holding Karen's eyes. "You're sealing your fate."

Karen folded her hands. "We'll take that chance." She glanced at Alessi. "With our new secret weapon."

Alessi's definitions had been easy to discard, but she had an uncanny knack for ferreting out the right one of theirs. Steve could swear she didn't know the words, practically didn't listen to the definitions. She just watched whichever of them was reading.

Steve scanned the pages and came to *xenogenesis*—the production of offspring entirely unlike their parents. He showed it to the guys and got their nods. He said the word aloud to the women, and none of them knew it. So he quickly jotted the real definition and one of his own as the other two made up their versions. He took the papers and mixed them solemnly while Diana giggled.

"You'd make a great undertaker with that face, Steve."

He flicked a glance to Alessi, who was studying him closely. Undertaker face or not, he was giving nothing away this time. He pulled the first paper and read it, careful to do nothing with the inflection that would indicate its veracity. He slid the slip to the bottom and read the next with equal aplomb.

His false one was next and he stumbled a little but got it out, then read the last. They got no points if all the women guessed the right one, double points for whichever decoys any of them fell for. Diana had to guess first this time. She chose Dave's, as she had with regularity throughout the evening. Either their minds worked alike or she felt sorry for him.

Steve noted her vote and went to Alessi. She stared into his face and said, "I'd like to hear them again."

He frowned. This time he would only look at the papers, no glancing up at all. He read through the choices in the same order, and he didn't stumble on any of them. But when he met Alessi's eyes, he sensed her confidence. She chose the right one and Karen parroted her answer, leaving the guys four points short of the tie.

"Well, of course you two got it." Steve handed the dictionary to Karen. "Next time we're blindfolding Alessi." He had no idea what she'd seen, but she was some kind of clairvoyant if she'd read anything from his expression that last time.

"The Lord loveth a cheerful loser, Steve." Karen took the books with a laugh.

"Find that chapter and verse."

She laughed harder. "It's implied."

"Your interpretation." Let her laugh. He didn't care about losing; it was Alessi's uncanny ability to read him he didn't like.

Diana stood and stretched, and Alessi unfolded beside her. She'd have a dark walk back to the store. He stood reluctantly. "I'll walk you back."

"Oh, we'll give her a ride." Diana took her arm. "Good night, Dave." She smooched his head. "Nice tree, by the way." She and Karen giggled, and Dave reddened.

A twinge of disappointment stung Steve as the girls walked out the door. Had he wanted to say good night to Alessi outside the store? He frowned, watching Dave wipe lipstick from his crown.

"I wish she wouldn't do that," he mumbled. But the goofy grin said otherwise.

Just another example of female brainwashing. And after Alessi's demonstration tonight, he intended to keep his brain to himself.

Twenty

STEVE WAS BACK TO GROWLING, Alessi noted the next day. After grousing at her all morning, he responded to her current question with a sarcastic, "Can't you read my mind?"

He was either a sore loser or had something on his mind she didn't want to read. "If you ever looked away from your monitor I might."

He turned and glared. Definitely moody today. "What was your question?"

She repeated it.

He took the three books she held, checked the codes, and expelled his breath. He took out the slips and threw them away, then penciled the correct codes and held the books out. "Thank you for catching that."

"You're welcome." She turned.

"How did you do it last night?"

"Do what?"

"Know the right answers."

She clutched the books to her chest. "Lucky guessing."

"Hah."

There he was, calling her a liar again. She started toward the correct shelf for the recoded books, but he caught her arm.

"Look at me."

What on earth?

"Guess what I'm thinking."

"I can't." She pulled her arm free. "But I could sure say how you're feeling."

"How?"

"Angry. Resentful."

He looked away. "That's only what you see."

"I'm not psychic, just observant. You're not comfortable with untruth."

"As you are?" He scissored her spirit.

For a while there she had thought he might believe her. Now she realized she had only wished it.

He dropped his hands to his lap. "I don't like someone thinking she knows what's in my head."

"Then you shouldn't play guessing games."

He scowled. "It was about words, definitions. You're the one who took it further."

So he was a bad loser. "Sorry."

"I'm not looking for an apology. I just want to know my mind's safe from you."

And they were back to that. She set down the books, took the register keys from her wrist, and laid them on his desk. "There. You're safe from me." She started for the door. She could use the day to find her car, and by nightfall . . .

"Alessi." He caught her arm. "I'm sorry."

She closed her eyes. *Seventy-seven times*. But this wasn't about forgiveness. It was about self-preservation. She had promised herself never again to stay where she wasn't wanted.

"It's not my best day." He admitted this last under his breath, which made it somehow more believable.

"We all have bad days."

"Do we? Have you ever had a bad day?"

Her throat tightened. That recitation would take way too long. "The one when my car was taken didn't exactly shine."

"And did you snap and growl at everyone?"

She shook her head. "I think I was too stunned."

"You're too nice. That's the thing. No one believes it."

"Guess I'll work on my act." She tugged her elbow out of his grip and tried again for the door. There were only so many times she could—

"Wait. I don't mean that. You are nice."

"I'm not fishing for compliments." She reached the door.

He blocked it. "We had a deal."

She dug into her pocket and pulled out the money. She had earned part of it, but she didn't want his money.

Someone tried to come in, but Steve barked, "I'm closed," and pressed the door shut again.

She thrust the money toward him. "I don't want the job."

"You're not a quitter."

She crossed her arms. "And how would you know that? Maybe I'm . . ." She swallowed hard against the tears.

"Look, I didn't mean to upset you. I want you to stay."

She closed her eyes. If he'd said anything else she could have walked out. But she wasn't a quitter, and he'd just removed her excuse. If he wanted her to stay, she could not justify ditching. She raised her chin and opened her eyes. "What do you need me to do?" Maybe it was stupid, but she had taken the job and accepted his money. If she couldn't handle a little rudeness, she hadn't learned anything.

"You can unpack some boxes and look for a couple things that got separated."

"Okay."

He showed her what he needed and even gave her an explanation of what he and the others in the network did. It was almost like Go Fish. A complete three-volume set was worth more than the individual books alone, so if he had two and someone else had one, he could buy it or trade for it. *I'll give you my Wordsworth for your Shakespeare.*

She found the books he wanted, boxed up his express packages, and turned him down when he suggested lunch.

"What?"

"I said, no thanks." *No need to stare with that non-comprehending expression.*

"I know you haven't eaten."

"I'm going to look for my car." In the daylight, she might just see that red, shiny convertible with *LESS* on the license plates.

"If you're tired of Moll's, we could do something else."

She tugged on her jacket. "If I don't find my car, no one's going to." And sitting across a booth from Steve again was not her idea of fun.

"You won't get far on foot."

"You'd be surprised. These shanks can cover some ground."

He expelled a slow breath. "We can grab sandwiches from Moll's and take the truck."

She stared at him. "You'll drive me to look for my car?"

"You asked Ben."

"Ben believes me."

He frowned. "We'll see more in the daylight."

So he couldn't say he believed her, but if they found the car, he'd know she wasn't making it up. And she would get farther driving than on foot. "All right."

Steve's truck died in front of Moll's. Alessi sighed. "So much for that idea."

"No fear. It does this sometimes." He stepped out and opened the hood, then turned back. "Here." He pulled some bills from his pocket. "Get us lunch while I fix it."

Since his head was deep under the hood, she guessed she'd choose the fare. She went inside with the money and stopped at the counter. Moll scooped a burger onto its golden toasted bun, did a single pirouette to the counter, and set it before the man in overalls. She ran her gaze over Alessi during the motion but didn't acknowledge her. Catching up the spatula, she scraped thin brown curls from the grill.

"Excuse me." Alessi folded her hands on the counter.

Moll turned, spatula ready.

"Could we get a couple sandwiches, please?"

Moll put her wrists to her hips, eyebrows raised.

"Oh. Um. Roast beef?"

Moll slid the spatula into the slot beside the grill and took down two plates.

"Oh. Could we have them to go?"

Moll stared at the plates, her tongue making a lump inside her lower lip. Then she whisked them back to the stack and replaced them with Styrofoam boxes. There were several kinds of bread, but she grabbed white and smeared it with mayonnaise, layered lettuce leaves, mounds of roast beef, still pink, and salt and pepper. She clapped the lids on, stuck in the pickle spears, and shut the boxes.

Alessi gave her the money at the register. "Those looked really good."

Chin down, Moll raised her eyes through her ample eyebrows and silently counted the change.

"Could we get some napkins?"

Moll snatched a couple and laid them atop the boxes she handed over.

"Thanks so much."

Moll's tongue found the corner of her mouth as she turned back to the grill.

The entire process without speaking to her once. That had to be an art. Alessi called, "Bye," at the door, just for the ornery pleasure of having the last word. Again.

Steve had the truck running by the time Alessi came out. She got in and handed him his box. "Hope you like roast beef."

"Nothing Moll serves I don't like."

"She sure seasons it with love."

"At least she can cook." He hadn't meant it as a commentary on Alessi's lack, but she obviously took it that way. She stared out the window, eating in silence. Her body language was all "back off." And he deserved it. He had hurt her again.

What—Mr. Wonderful? If he did inflict himself on one of the piranhas, she'd have indigestion for life. He rubbed his left eye and drove the long stretch of road between houses within the township. Charity was rural outside the village, and mostly woods. Even if her car were out there, they could easily miss it. He chomped his sandwich and slapped his chin with a slice of beef. *Elegant, Steve.*

Alessi handed him a napkin.

He gave his chin a swipe. "Thanks."

"Thank you."

He glanced at her. "For what?"

"Driving." She went back to staring out the window.

Her expectancy filled the cab like fog, until he drew it in with every breath, hoping fiercely to see her car. But it didn't happen. The thief might be bold enough to tease her with it in the dark, but he wasn't so stupid he'd leave it out in plain sight. Had she thought he would? Steve scanned the next property they approached. Phyllis Bartle lived there with her Down's syndrome daughter and three dogs. She would not have the Mustang stashed away, but he drove up to the house so Alessi could ask if she'd seen it.

He waited in the truck as Phyllis shook her head, holding two of the dogs by the collar and one between her ankles. Her daughter, Debbie, rounded the corner in mittens and a knit cap, barrel-shaped in her parka. She went straight for Alessi, patting her with the mittens, then pulling one off to feel her hair.

Alessi didn't pull back. She smiled while Debbie patted her arms again and then closed her in a hug. Debbie was affectionate, but he'd never witnessed that demonstration, not at first sight. Even Phyllis seemed surprised, but the twenty-five-year-old child hugged Alessi as though she'd known her forever. Something in that stood the hairs up on his neck. He'd always believed in the intuition of simpler people. But what did it mean now?

At last Debbie released her. Alessi waved, then climbed back into the truck. "They haven't seen my car."

That was it? No comment on being pawed and squeezed by a total stranger? He put the truck in reverse.

She sighed. "I guess we have to go back. We've used up the lunch break."

Steve sent her a sideways glance, reluctant to return to the store. It was easier to be civil in the truck, and it had raised his spirits to help her. "We can look a little longer if you want."

"You only put an hour on the sign."

Contradiction again, showing diligence and dedication to the job she almost walked out on just hours ago. He was still surprised she'd stayed, but then, he had an unfair advantage. She had nowhere to go.

He pulled around and stopped. "Alessi, I'm sorry for what I said before. The mind reading and all."

She didn't answer.

He had definitely punctured her spirit. "I don't open up easily. Barb called it the 'Secret Steve'—all the stuff inside me I wouldn't share."

Alessi actually turned, no longer giving him the back of her shoulder.

What was he doing telling her this? "It scared me to think you could see inside." Way too open.

Her face softened. "All I saw was your discomfort when you read the wrong answers."

He nodded, his chest tightening. "Honesty was a big deal in my house." He ran his hand over the curve of the wheel. If Barb had told him up front about the guy, if his mother had not sneaked away . . . Dave was right. He did expect the worst from women. He'd thought Alessi had some trick he couldn't withstand. But all she saw was his own need for truth.

"I've been a jerk."

She smiled. "I've seen worse."

He tucked his chin. "You make excuses for everyone."

She braced herself as though what came next might be hazardous. Some accusation of too-niceness.

He caught her eyes with his. "You need to know some people are exactly what they seem." He reached over and squeezed her hand. "Please don't assume the best of people who don't deserve it."

She held his gaze, but for the life of him he could not see that she understood. Maybe she had a dose of her mom's disability. Maybe Debbie had sensed it too. He put the truck in gear and headed for the store, confident now that he could once again treat her right. But the reality was she only seemed too nice juxtaposed with his meanness. And if someone had taunted her with her car, that person was meaner still.

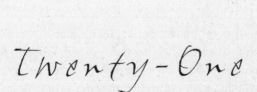

Twenty-One

THE FRIDAY EVENING SERVICE WAS MORE PACKED than Sunday's had been. Pastor Welsh had a loyal following. Ben had told her the village population was only eighty-seven, with the other eighty on the Charity population sign accounted for in the thirty-six square miles of the township. The count hadn't been updated since the last census, so a few births and deaths might have changed the figures some.

Although she'd been born in Miami and spent the first years of life there, she and Mom had wandered among the small beach towns after Dad's death. But they were hardly more than tourist stops and didn't feel the same as Charity. It was easier where everyone was a stranger passing through. Charity had a unity and singleness of purpose she hadn't seen anywhere else.

She leaned over to Diana, who had invited her to sit with her. "I wouldn't have guessed all these people went to the same church."

Diana whispered, "They've got the denominations in Chambers City. Some go there on Sundays. But most everyone comes to hear Pastor Welsh on Friday night."

And he was in prime form, standing before his flock, looking sublime in a camel-hair jacket that set off his auburn hair and amber eyes. His looks alone would bring them in, but it was his voice you remembered. His wife looked like one of those shiny Lladró statues, and Alessi wondered how it would be for her to hear "Pass the salt" in Burton Welsh's Mosaic tones.

What kept a minister with his skills in a little place like Charity? She could see him in some big cathedral, stretching his hands out to the masses with television cameras moving in for the close-ups, catching the fire in his eyes, the dimples in his cheeks, his voice carried out over the radios and TVs of thousands, maybe millions of people. He must be the most humble, obedient man to stay in such a little place and affect so few. But she had to admit, he sure did affect the ones he had.

His son, Carl, sat on the platform with him. Again she noticed he took his looks from neither his dad nor his mother. Maybe they'd adopted him. They didn't have other kids, as far as she could tell, and they actually didn't look old enough to have a son that age.

The music tonight was contemporary, no hymns, contrasting with Sunday's more sedate tone. Tonight's service had more the feel of a revival, only not the old tent style where they dunked you in the river. This was more youthful, and she realized that many of the seats were filled with teens and young adults.

Actually, the seats weren't filled, because the worshipers were on their feet for the first twenty minutes. Karen was at the piano, but there was also someone on electric guitar and a drummer. People were clapping and dancing in their places. Alessi couldn't help but smile. They seemed to have a real joy in the singing, but she guessed it was also the thrill of being part of such a believing group.

The pastor said, "Carl," and his son took the podium. A hush fell over the crowd, though it had a different feel than the hush Burton Welsh inspired. This one seemed cautious and tense, like a parent at a child's musical recital. Would he play it well, as he did at home, or make a mistake with so many faces watching?

Carl opened his Bible and read, "'Blessed are the poor in spirit, for theirs is the kingdom of heaven. Blessed are those who mourn, for they will be comforted. Blessed are the meek, for they will inherit the earth.'"

His voice was nothing like the pastor's as he read on, but his mannerisms and delivery were similar enough that she wondered if he might be their biological son after all.

"'Blessed are the merciful, for they will be shown mercy. Blessed are the pure in heart, for they will see God.'"

Some girls in the front row whispered something and covered their giggles with their hands, but their eyes never left him. Alessi wondered if they thought they were seeing God. Carl did have strong Nordic good looks. Not the magnetic attraction of the pastor but a strapping farm-boy build and carriage. His large hands and broad shoulders looked anything but meek, and he wasn't through growing yet.

"'Blessed are the peacemakers, for they will be called sons of God.'" He looked up and startled Alessi with a direct glance. His blue eyes were cold, though his face warmed. "'Blessed are they who are persecuted because of righteousness.'"

She felt something sink inside and squeeze. How could Jesus' own words be haunting? She was in a predicament but hardly persecuted. Not like people losing their lives and loved ones.

"'For theirs is the kingdom of heaven.'" Not even the attached promise chased away the chill that crawled up her spine. But it passed as Pastor Welsh thanked Carl and took his place front and center. Carl sent a sideways smile to the front-row girls and sat down with his mother.

"Whom does the Lord bless?" Pastor's voice carried powerfully after Carl's adolescent pitch. "The rich and powerful? The proud? Those who live the 'good life'?" He looked over their faces. "Whom does the Lord bless?"

He raised a finger and pointed to them individually, then collectively. "You—the poor in spirit, the meek, who hunger for righteousness. You merciful, you clean of heart. You—the children of God. Ours is the kingdom of heaven, for we have closed the gates of hell, locked them fast, and thrown away the key."

His glance brushed her but didn't stay. "We, the redeemed, are the living embodiment of these beatitudes. Who is proud among us, let him confess it now. Who mourns without comfort? Hungers and thirsts and is not satisfied? Who has not seen the mercy of our God? Call out if you are peacemakers!"

The assembly roared.

Certainly a different treatment than she'd heard before. Instead of a call to holiness, it seemed a confirmation of a given state. She looked at Steve, sitting with Stacie and a small walnut-skinned man who must be her husband. Sheriff Roehr was next to them and looked away from her glance. He resettled in his seat as though his hip pained him, but she guessed it was probably her.

"We who mourned have been comforted." The pastor walked a few steps to the side and said, "We who were persecuted for the sake of righteousness have inherited the kingdom."

There it was again, those words taking extra meaning. It was almost as though he referred to something specific, but whatever it was, she didn't know. Maybe the things Steve alluded to that she didn't understand. She wasn't part of Charity, only marooned there. She sighed. Being with Ben and Dave and even Steve had given her some sense of belonging. But the whole of Charity at once . . . Her throat tightened. It was worse than the cliques at Palm Beach Gardens High School.

"We were shown mercy and are now the merciful. Praise God!" The roaring echo filled the rafters. "Praise God!" he hollered again and again as they echoed louder and stronger. The body around her gained energy, but Alessi felt leached by the time the pastor stopped speaking and the music began again. While it continued, people went forward for prayer, and Pastor Welsh sure did groan in his spirit over some of them. No question how deeply he cared. She felt emptier still.

Once the final song ended, she made her way to Sheriff Roehr. He did not look happy to see her. And she was sorry to spoil his evening, but something had to be done. "It's been a week now, and I wondered if we should get help from someone to find my car. Does Chambers City have a police department?"

"They do, and I've consulted them. They haven't seen your car, and it's not their jurisdiction."

Steve came up beside her. "Do you have anything at all?"

The sheriff scowled. "Well, it wasn't listed stolen before I did it myself."

Alessi pulled herself up. "Why would it be?"

He cocked his head and the tuft of hair lifted and dropped. "You've provided no form of I.D. and no registration. I don't know you from Adam, except for some obvious differences. It was just as likely you'd taken the car as anyone else."

She could not believe he had thought she stole the Mustang. No wonder he wasn't trying too hard. "Now that you know I didn't steal my own car, what are you going to do?"

He took a cigar from his pocket, then seemed to realize he was still in church and replaced it. "It might be your car, but that doesn't mean you're telling the whole story. I think you should come clean with the rest of it."

"What rest?" She fought a rising indignation.

"Maybe you were with someone. Maybe that someone went off and left you."

Was that the story going around? That she'd been ditched? She swallowed hard and gained her composure. "There was no one with me, and I've never found a place so ready to condemn the innocent and excuse the guilty. If Charity is God's kingdom on earth, it's got some flaws, in my opinion."

Steve pressed his hand to her lower back, and in a minute he'd suggest she shut up and leave. So she stalked up to the platform while people were still milling around, laughing and visiting, the younger ones making eyes at each other in clusters. She stepped behind the podium and cleared her throat.

Several people turned her way, and she said, "Excuse me. You may not all know me yet. I'm Alessi Moore and I came to Charity a week ago. I know it's hard to believe, but somehow in this fine place my car was stolen. So far nothing much has been done about it. I'd like to ask you all to look for a red convertible Mustang and give Sheriff Roehr any help you can. And just in case you're the one who has it, I'd sure appreciate it back." She started to step down, then added, "Actually, the sooner I get it back, the sooner I'll be out of here. I guess that'll be better all around."

All the faces stared at her, but Carl's had a look of pure spite. Okay, so she'd ruined his daddy's show. She got down and walked for the door as fast as she could go. No one moved to stop her.

The night was cold and clear, and her breath made a cloud as she stalked out. But she was glad no one offered a ride. It was only a few blocks back to the store, and not long enough to dispel the furious tension that reached the farthest points of her chilled fingers and toes. But better she stomp it out alone than inflict it on anyone else.

It was one thing to know she didn't belong, another altogether to have people thinking that someone would have been so sick of her that . . . She clenched her hands and strode fiercely. It didn't matter what they thought. She just wanted to get her car and leave. God's halo must have meant somewhere down the road. The good was out there; she just couldn't get to it. Frustration threatened to strangle her. Wasn't she doing her part?

Or maybe . . .

She stopped and clasped her hands at her chin. Maybe it was a test. A trial. She breathed tightly, suddenly pensive and expectant. Maybe a miracle took more than just seeing. If keeping her heart open helped her see the magic, maybe something this big called for more. But what?

Steve looked from Cooper, whose face had gone crimson, to Carl, standing like a wax figure. Was it shock? Confusion? Or malice in his face? Alessi's likeness to his mother must churn inside, and at the moment Carl looked more like Duke than ever. He had a personal stake in the pact that no one else could match and had, by far, the most to lose if people started doubting. Surely he would want the car found and Alessi out of there.

Burton Welsh stood to the side, staring at the doors she had disappeared through. He had said she deserved compassion and assistance, and Steve saw that in his expression, but there was also a calculating tension that made Steve glad he hadn't heard her opinion of Charity's kingdom of heaven.

Voices broke into a buzz, and he could guess the comments. She had made her point in spite of his urging caution, and Cooper wasn't the only one on the hot seat now. The pastor's face came alive and his voice, though not his words, carried through the room as he did damage control for the fledglings of feeble wing. But Steve couldn't help wondering, if the pact crumbled and the premise proved false, what was left but guilt? And what strides would people take to avoid it?

He caught Ben's eye and shared a shrug, then turned to Cooper, who was searching for something meaningful to say. Steve saved him the trouble. "It would be a good thing to find her car."

"You think I'm not trying?"

"I don't know, Coop. But I have a bad feeling."

Cooper Roehr took out his cigar and stuffed it unlit between his teeth. "I've had a bad feeling ever since she got here."

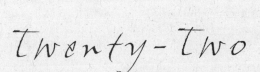

Twenty-Two

THE NEXT MORNING, STEVE PULLED into the parking space behind the store, pensive and tense from a night of subconscious activity not conducive to rest. Alessi hadn't come to the house for breakfast. If she was out somewhere, fine—but he hoped she wasn't stirring the pot she'd set to boiling last night—if she was sleeping, he could be quiet. He climbed out of the truck and stopped. The item hanging from the back doorknob did not belong there.

He glanced both ways—the alley was empty. The others usually moseyed into their businesses around ten, and it was only half past eight. He'd expected to slip in and work without notice, but he did not know what to make of this particular surprise.

He took it from the knob and unlocked the door. Alessi was neither gone nor asleep but up and dressed and brushing her teeth. She froze. "Where did. . . ?" She turned and spit, swiped her mouth with the back of her hand, and said, "Where did you get that?"

He held it up. "Is it yours?"

She snatched it out of his hand and put it behind her back. "I asked first."

"Hanging on the door."

Her gaze jerked to the back door, and she stalked over and pulled it open.

Curiosity and amusement warred inside as he tried very hard not to imagine the article in use. "There's no one out there."

She spun, brandishing her toothbrush but still concealing the other item. "It was in my car."

He sobered. "Are you sure?"

Glaring, she stuffed the mint green bra into her waistband and thrust past him to wash out her toothbrush at the sink. "Sheriff Roehr can't ignore this."

Steve winced. "He won't be up yet."

"Well, he deserves a wake-up in more ways than one."

When had she gotten so feisty? "Alessi, you're not really going to go dangle that under his nose."

She flushed. "Well, it wouldn't be my first choice, but it's tangible proof—"

"It's a bra."

Her flush deepened.

"Even if it had your name all over it, you can't prove it was in your car. Cooper won't take your word for it."

"Then you tell him. You found it."

Steve considered that. "But I don't know how it got there."

"How do you think?" She paced across the room. "He put it there."

"Or you did."

She spun. "What?"

He shrugged. "I'm pointing out the possibilities."

"You think I hung my . . ."

The way she was guarding it from sight, he couldn't say he did.

"No, but Cooper might. He'll think you're beefing up your story."

Her jaw dropped. "What does it take around here to get proven innocent?"

Steve sighed. "He doesn't have much to go on, Alessi. You're the only one who's seen the car since it disappeared, and it's just your word that bra is even yours."

She stood speechless, then rendered him the same with, "What do I have to do, try it on?"

He shot his gaze to the ceiling and did violence to his thoughts. "I'm not telling you what to do. I'm just suggesting you save yourself the embarrassment."

She flounced down on the cot. "No one wants to believe me." She spread her hands. "I don't understand it."

And he couldn't enlighten her. He held his fist to his mouth, then said, "The good thing is you have something back."

She pulled the silky bra from her waistband and tucked it under the pillow.

He rested his hands on his hips. "I guess I'll go to work. Were you heading for the house?"

"I'm not hungry." She stood up and put on the jacket he'd lent her.

"Where are you going?"

"To find my car."

He knew better than to argue. He dug his keys from his pocket and held them out.

She looked from them to his face, then took the keys. "Thank you." She stopped at the door. "I'll be back by opening."

He nodded. "Be careful."

With the computer booting up, Steve stared at the screen and wondered. Was it just a joke? Someone milking a prank with little fear of consequence? Hanging her bra out there smacked of locker-room humor. Maybe they'd have their fun and then give it all back. He jolted. He was sounding like Alessi.

———

In Steve's truck, she did cover ground. The hilly forest around the village spread out in places, and several homes dotted those acres. She stopped at each one. Many people weren't home, but the ones she talked to were almost hostile.

"You've got the wrong idea, young woman."

"Don't project your problems on us."

"You've got a lot of nerve walking up to my door to accuse me of stealing."

Alessi blew on her cold fingers. "I'm not accusing anyone. Just trying to find my car."

But the door slammed in her face anyway. She had put them out of joint with her speech last night. She did not have Pastor Welsh's way with words. But then, he told them what they wanted to hear. They were special, they were good, God's redeemed. She must seem like the devil tempting Jesus in the desert, trying to shake him from what he believed.

Mom had told that story so well. *"There He is, so hungry the lizards are looking like steak dinner, and up comes the devil in a chef's hat, one rock in each hand, and says, 'What'll it be? Hot crusty rolls or cinnamon raisin bread?'"*

Alessi smiled. She'd always thought at that moment she would have crumbled. *Make sure it's buttered.* But Jesus stood firm. He told that devil where to go, as these folks were telling her now. She could see why they'd be upset. She didn't like to be accused or even doubted. They'd feel the same way. It was understandable.

Though she did see one vehicle covered in a tarp, the shape of it could not be her little Mustang. Steve's truck roared back to life, and she drove through woods as dense as hopefuls in a ticket line. There were some tracks through it, but she didn't want to risk Steve's truck leaving the road. Not until she'd exhausted her other possibilities.

She had hoped that making her announcement might scare the culprit into returning her car. Instead, he'd hung her bra on the door. Then it hit her. He'd been right outside the place she slept. And she hadn't heard a thing. She sighed. What more could she do?

As she pondered that thought, it came to her that maybe searching for the car should not be her primary focus. Maybe there was another task, something hidden, like in the story *Niccola's Grapes*. His kindness to the old woman had cost the family what money they would have earned for their grapes, but the old woman was really a fairy. He hadn't known there was magic ahead, but he had seen someone in need and shown kindness.

Maybe someone in Charity needed kindness. Maybe she had to look for that instead. It sure hadn't helped to stomp her foot and demand her car back. Alessi brought the truck around and headed for the store. She wasn't sure how to accomplish her quest, but things mostly happened when a person wasn't looking. If she simply did her job, her part in the miracle might become clear.

A deep peace settled inside. She'd been selfish to focus so completely on her car. If God wanted to hide it for a while, He could do it right under her nose, and no amount of browbeating her neighbors would make it appear. She'd just forget it. A pang squeezed her stomach. Okay, so she couldn't actually forget, but she wouldn't focus on finding it.

She pulled the truck into the lot. Steve had the door open by the time she reached it. He'd been right there packing boxes. She wouldn't think rare books were in such demand, but it was right before Christmas.

"Any luck?"

She smiled. "Well, I didn't find my car, but I guess that's all right."

"It is?"

She shrugged. "I must not be supposed to have it right now."

He stared at her. "Right. Well, I have three more cratefuls to process, and you can clean the books up and shelve them."

Alessi pulled off her jacket. Wouldn't it be funny if Steve was the good fairy? She almost giggled at the thought. That would be one great disguise.

She worked with him well into the morning, feeling a fresh anticipation after her morning's revelation. She shouldn't have doubted just because things looked grim. That was how magic was. You couldn't expect it—only be ready when it happened.

Alessi's cheerfulness flummoxed him. She had gone out the door embarrassed and frustrated, determined to find her car, then come back resigned. More than resigned; serene. What could possibly have wrought the change? Or was it just the way her mind worked?

Maybe she couldn't hold on to anything that troubled her. It could be some defense mechanism, or true delusion. Maybe she wouldn't look at things she didn't want to see. She glossed it with a platitude and went about as though everything had just come right.

But while she was out finding sunshine, he'd grown concerned. Yes, it had seemed funny, finding her bra on the door. And her reactions had amused him as well. But the more he thought about the situation, the less he liked it. It was one more indication that someone in Charity had her car.

The bra had felt like a prank, but it was also a message. In spite of her speech, this person would not be intimidated. Instead, he would humiliate her. He was in control. He'd said in essence, "I have it, and I'll do what I like with it, and no one in Charity will believe you no matter how many speeches you make."

What was he thinking? His scenario assumed the person who took the car was at the church to hear her. He couldn't believe that. It was like imagining Dave or Ben had taken it. He'd grown up with these people. He knew them. Or did he?

Hadn't he told Alessi what a poor judge of character he was? He wouldn't have believed Barb could treat him as she had. He really knew nothing at all about people, what they were capable of. That's why he steered clear of any relationship deeper than the friendships he knew and trusted.

Mary came in with Lyn and Cait, and Alessi greeted them at the door and brought the girls over to his candy bowl. He watched with his peripheral vision as Cait took butterscotch and Lyn went back and forth between cinnamon or blue mint, then settled on butterscotch like her sister.

Mary said, "Hi, Steve."

He said, "How are you, Mary?" without stopping his fingers on the keys.

"Just fine." She turned to Alessi. "Could you help me choose something here for Ben?" She glanced over her shoulder as though he might find her out. "I want to get him something meaningful."

Alessi smiled. "I'm sure we can find him something."

Mary took Cait and Lyn by the hands. "Here I work at Wal-Mart with tons and tons of stuff, but Ben just isn't that sort of guy."

Alessi nodded. "Not the kind to give a set of screwdrivers to."

Steve wondered what she based that on. She'd only known Ben a week.

"I want something special," Mary said. "I've been saving."

He couldn't help turning to see what Alessi would recommend as they made their way forward from his desk.

She said, "Steve has some nice books that aren't too steep. Just don't look in the glass cases." But then she paused. "Except there is one. . . ." She went to a case he did not keep locked but that did protect some valuable books and took one out. "This is a pictorial history of Hollywood with some great old photos."

He could hardly have chosen better, and he'd known Ben all his life. But the book, with its dustcover in perfect condition, was over a hundred dollars. Mary could not afford it.

She took the book and turned the leaves with reverence. "Wouldn't he just love it?"

He would. Ben hardly ever came into the store, but if he'd seen that book, he'd want it.

"What were you looking to spend?" Alessi asked.

Steve got up from his desk. "You can have it for thirty dollars."

Alessi turned to him, eyes shining. She knew what was penciled inside the cover.

Mary smiled, then dropped her eyes. "Thirty's about what I hoped to spend."

She had Cait and Lyn to make a special Christmas for. Ben would hate for her to take away from that on his account. "Ring it up, Alessi."

She did, then tucked another butterscotch in each girl's hand. They smiled and waved as Mary took them out.

Alessi turned. "That was nice."

"Mmm." He sat back at the computer. "Do you know every book I have?"

She laughed. "Hardly."

He didn't believe her for a minute.

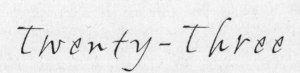

Twenty-Three

THE THOUGHTS WERE GETTING HARD TO CONTROL. He hadn't started with a plan, had just seen his chance and done it. More of a risk than he'd ever taken. But he wanted it. Want worked in him like a parasite, growing and filling and sapping until it controlled.

He hadn't even realized it was hers. He didn't care whose it was. And it had been so easy. She was stupid. That thought felt good. Stupid and helpless and trapped. She couldn't leave, because he had her car. He had it, and he'd keep it. But that wasn't enough. Not since he'd seen her.

His throat ached, and the pain of it made him angry. It was the

KRISTEN HEITZMANN

angry thoughts he wasn't sure he could control. They worked their way down his arms to his hands, made them tight and hard. And strong. She might be tall for a girl, but she was still nothing.

———————

Alessi wore Amanda's sweater to church on Sunday. She thought maybe they wouldn't let her in, but Steve met her at the door and invited her to sit with him. By the disappointed looks in many of the female faces they passed, she guessed his plan was twofold: keep her under control and use her as a shield.

He stood beside her and held the book for the opening hymn. He sang it nicely too. His singing voice was a lot better than his growl, though lately he'd seemed more confused than grumpy.

Pastor Welsh looked a little tense as he took his place before them, his stance just a touch defensive, as though he'd fend off usurpers to his podium if he had to. But she had no intention of disrupting things again. She was hoping for direction and maybe even confirmation of her new perspective.

"Our text today is Paul's letter to the Philippians, chapter two. 'If you have any encouragement from being united with Christ, if any comfort from his love, if any fellowship with the Spirit, if any tenderness and compassion, then make my joy complete by being likeminded, having the same love, being one in spirit and purpose.'"

His voice gained strength as he read. "'Do nothing out of selfish ambition or vain conceit, but in humility consider others better than yourselves. Each of you should look not only to your own interests but also to the interests of others.'"

Steve had demonstrated that with Mary yesterday, discounting the book so she could give it to Ben.

"'Your attitude should be the same as that of Christ Jesus: who, being in very nature God, did not consider equality with God something to be grasped, but made himself nothing, taking the very nature of a servant, being made in human likeness.'"

Beautiful words, and so appropriate with Christmas on the way. The thought of God becoming a tiny baby, as helpless in every way as any other, made her heart swell with gratitude. He knew what it was like to have nothing.

"'And being found in appearance as a man, he humbled himself and became obedient to death—even death on a cross.'"

She hated to think what He suffered. What her sins and all the world's had brought upon Him. The hairs on her neck rose, and she turned to find Carl glaring. Good grief, was he still fuming? Steve caught the look, as well, and nudged her with his knee. She saw the warning in his expression. He didn't want her to make trouble. Well, she wasn't planning on it.

"'Therefore God exalted him to the highest place and gave him the name that is above every name, that at the name of Jesus every knee should bow, in heaven and on earth and under the earth, and every tongue confess that Jesus Christ is Lord, to the glory of God the Father.'"

She hadn't even thought about the pastor or his voice, those words were so compelling. But he stepped out now and said, "Do nothing out of selfish ambition or vain conceit." His hands opened. "Our attitude should be the same as that of Jesus Christ. That of a servant, humble and thinking more highly of others than ourselves. Not finding fault and accusation." He looked at her directly. "Not demanding what is ours, but surrendering all to the glory of God the Father."

Alessi caught her breath. It was confirmation all right, but it didn't bring the peace she'd hoped for. Could she surrender the Mustang forever? How could that glorify God? But she had no doubt that was exactly what Burton Welsh wanted. Why else look at her with that fire in his eye? Anticipating God's miracle had given her hope, but there was no promise in the pastor's face now, only a fierce expectation.

She ducked her chin and tried to feel humble. Jesus had better material to work with. He didn't battle selfish ambition or vain conceit. Was it selfish to want what was hers? Vain to hope for a positive resolution . . . a miracle? Did God want her to give up her hope for a miracle?

An awful squeezing made her stomach ache. Give up on the halo?

"If we are God's people, this is our model, being like-minded, having the same love, being one in spirit and purpose. And not allowing anything to come between us, but standing firm on what we know. We have the victory."

The congregation stirred.

"We have the victory." This last was spoken with brash assurance.

Steve held the book for the next hymn, but she couldn't sing it. She might have the final victory, but right now the strongest thing she felt was loss.

———————

Diana had invited her to dinner Monday night, and when Dave dropped her off, Karen was there as well. Alessi hugged them both. After the growing hostility from most of the town, their acceptance was extra sweet.

"Come in, come in." Diana waved her through the door. "We're having hors d'oeuvres."

Diana must do well with her cosmetology. Her house was larger than Mary's or the men's. And there was no lack of festivity. Everywhere Alessi looked there were bows and poinsettias, snowmen, Santas, reindeer, a crèche in two rooms. One tree was done in blue and gold with clear glass ornaments, and the other was entirely penguins. Personally, Alessi preferred Dave's fishing lures, but she didn't say that, just, "I guess Dave's is a theme tree too."

Karen and Diana both laughed. "Quite a piece of work. Here." Diana handed her a small plate with four different hors d'oeuvres.

It was just the light supper she needed after all the rich, heavy meals she'd had lately, especially the lunches at Moll's with Steve. He seemed to think the midday meal was part of the deal. He did eat slower now that he'd realized they'd be cleared out the minute he finished and that usually meant there was still food on her plate. But that left more time for questions and scrutiny.

Even at the best of times, eating with him was nothing like the peaceful times with Ed. They had shared their sack lunches nearly every day. She remembered him peeling his boiled egg, one small fleck at a time, then salting it and slicing it bite by bite with his pocketknife. She missed him.

Swallowing the ache, she picked up the strange airy cracker with a pair of tiny pink shrimp settled atop a blob of something creamy. She bit in. "Mmm."

"Those are sesame rice crackers."

The texture was like a Styrofoam egg carton, but they were packed with flavor. Alessi tried the jumbo stuffed olive next. "How do you come up with these ideas?"

"Oh, I love to experiment."

Karen nodded hugely. "And it's not always successful. Remember the tongue soufflé?"

"We don't need to go into that." Diana waved her off, caught Alessi's arm, and tucked her onto a low-backed stool at the counter. A floral spray ran along the center of the counter, complete with glass balls and shiny plastic beads. Even the microwave door had a red velvet bow and plastic mistletoe. "Now, I will admit the soup might be a little unusual."

"Soup?" Alessi looked at Karen as Diana walked to the refrigerator. "The soup's in the refrigerator?"

"It's a chilled sour cream beet soup." Diana took out the tray holding three small bowls.

At least she knew enough to serve slim portions of her experiments. "Does Dave like interesting meals?" She thought of his chili, about as basic as you could get, but which had reheated nicely for breakfast the next morning.

The women shared a look.

"He'll learn." Karen slid one bowl to Alessi and took up her spoon. "Let's bless this course." She uttered a short pleasant prayer of thanks.

Bending her head over the swirled purple in her bowl, Alessi silently added, *Please don't let me hurt Diana's feelings.* But the soup was delicious. More like pudding, in her opinion, but if Diana called it soup, who was she to argue? Her experience was the generic form of Campbell's. "You have a real talent for food."

Diana beamed. "So does Karen. That's why we look this way." Diana patted her hips.

Though plump, both women were attractive, more so than Amanda Bier, in Alessi's opinion. Their figures fit them as she supposed her own did. She'd had a year or two where she wished she were petite, then gave that up and accepted her height. And Karen had lovely eyes. Steve should take notice of that. It was obvious that they knew each other well. And Karen had just the sort of heart to handle Steve.

Diana gathered the bowls. "Now the salad."

Alessi closed her eyes. And here she'd thought the hors d'oeuvres were supper. Again the salad was a miniature portion. A few crisp, scraggly leaves with two sections of grapefruit, a single slice of avocado, and a spray of tiny mushrooms that looked like white balloons on strings. She lifted her fork in anticipation, but before she took a bite, Diana drizzled it all with Russian dressing.

"Now try it."

They ate the course with murmurs of appreciation. It was fun and crazy to eat such elegant servings at the countertop, but Diana's table held a vast miniature snow village, complete with tiny streetlamps that really lit. Next came rolled salmon filets stuffed with lobster and dill Havarti and, beside it, three red potatoes the size of shooter marbles sliced and fanned and drizzled with butter and fresh snipped parsley. Alessi had never tasted anything so good. But she couldn't help wondering how Dave would like it.

Lastly, Diana served a praline mousse parfait; fluffy clouds of chocolate mousse layered with pecan caramel filling. Karen lifted a spoonful. "This is the real reason we're shaped this way." Her blue eyes danced as she took the first bite. "Two hundred sit-ups tomorrow."

"Three miles." Diana indulged herself in a dainty bite.

Alessi tried hers and sighed. At last she'd found it. Fairy ambrosia. *Oh, Mom. No disrespect, but my imagination never got this good*. The mousse blanketed her tongue, awakening every taste bud. She closed her eyes and saw the fairy court, her mother presiding. Tears sprang up and trickled out the corners of her eyes. She opened them, embarrassed.

Karen and Diana were staring at her. "My praline mousse has never made someone cry before."

Karen touched her arm. "What is it, honey?"

Alessi tried to smile. "My mother and I played a game, that whatever we were eating was ambrosia from the fairy queen. If she'd ever tasted this"—Alessi dipped another spoonful—"she'd never have to imagine again. But maybe in heaven she tastes it every day."

Diana's eyes teared up. "No one's ever paid me such a compliment."

"Now look what you've done." Karen dabbed her own eyes.

They laughed. Alessi caught both their hands. "Thank you for having me."

After singing carols at the piano, Karen drove Alessi back to the store. "You'd be welcome to stay with me if I weren't leaving town tomorrow. I'd even let you stay without me, but I've got someone house-sitting already. For the dog."

"I'm fine here." Alessi looked at the storefront, elegant and festive. Steve had done that without feminine prodding, though probably following his father's tradition. She smiled. "Diana offered too. But it's only for a couple of weeks."

"Then what?"

She shrugged. "I don't know."

"You could stay."

Not if someone had taken her car, pitted her in some way against the town, or at least the sheriff. He'd been markedly cold since she'd asked people to help him do his job. She opened the car door and found the store key in her pocket. "Thanks for the ride."

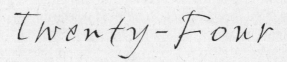

Twenty-Four

ALESSI LET HERSELF INTO THE FRONT DOOR and locked it behind her. It was strange to live in a bookstore, but at least she was earning that space. She didn't freeload easily, and with Diana's extended family coming in tomorrow, it would be too reminiscent of the six years with Aunt Carrie, everyone belonging but her.

She took off Steve's jacket and headed for the back. Diana's meal had left her satisfied but not stuffed, in spite of all the courses. She hung the jacket on the nail inside the storeroom and settled onto the cot with Dickens. She opened to her place mark and jumped at a car horn out front. Had Karen forgotten something?

The night-lights made traversing the store easy, but they cast eerie shadows between the shelves. She hurried forward to the window and stopped short as her Mustang swung onto the sidewalk and jerked to a stop. The top was down, and she stared at the driver.

In the half light his head seemed misshapen and enormous. She screamed when he turned, then realized it was a mask, a horrible rubber mask with one side of the face peeled away to reveal gore and bare eyeball; the other half leered. She staggered backward into the rack of paperback mysteries.

The driver raised a black-gloved hand and pointed at her, then put the car into reverse and pulled off the sidewalk. She stood unmoving until her heart stopped thumping her ribs like a rabbit in a cage. She would not chase after him, not give him the satisfaction of her desperation. He was sick.

She stalked to the desk, found the phone number, and dialed. Someone had to be home. It rang twice, then, "Hello?"

"Ben?"

"Is that you, Alessi?"

She pressed the phone to her ear. "Ben, I—"

Then Steve came on. "What's wrong?"

Her voice shook; tears had sprung to her eyes. What was she supposed to say? "He's out there again. In my car."

Steve was quiet a long time. If he asked whether she was sure, she'd hang up, but he didn't. Instead he said, "Don't go out. I'll be right over."

"You don't have to come. I just thought someone else ought to know." Though what possible good would it do? She drew a jagged breath.

"I'll be there in a minute. Don't bean me with a mailer." He hung up.

She felt like a fool, but she was shaking and the tears came harder. Good. Get them out before Steve got there. She searched his desk for a tissue box, found none, and went to the bathroom for toilet paper. Pressed against the bathroom wall, she cried, then blew her nose and assessed the damage. She splashed her face with cold water, then papered it dry.

She jumped, then realized she'd heard Steve's key in the lock. She drew herself up tall and met him at the door. He stared into her face, reached for her shoulders, and pulled her to his chest.

Steve sensed her fear. Anger he would understand, fury of the sort she'd shown the other night. But fear? "Tell me what happened."

She sniffed and drew away. "Karen drove me back from Diana's dinner. I'd just come back here to read when I heard the car horn. I thought it was Karen, but it wasn't. He pulled the Mustang up to the window."

"The store window?" He would check the sidewalk to be sure.

She shuddered. "He had a horrible mask on."

Steve seethed. "He thinks it's a prank. Did he see you?"

She nodded. "He pointed at me and then pulled off the sidewalk. I heard him spinning out in the intersection."

At least she hadn't chased him again. But there was no doubt he knew whose car it was and where to find her. The bra incident no longer seemed a joke at all.

She gripped herself in her arms. "He was gruesome, all mangled and gory."

"He's trying to scare you."

"He's doing it." Her throat worked. "Just like the snowball."

"Snowball?"

"Someone followed me home from Mary's a while back. I sensed it, but he stayed out of sight. Just before I reached your house, a snowball flew past my head. It had a rock in it."

"Why didn't you tell me?"

She shrugged. "I forgot about it in the fun of decorating Dave's tree."

His mind went back to that day when he'd put in a stellar performance of jealous accusation. But the situation was escalating if she was being followed on foot and frightened through the window. She had stirred up the kind of trouble he'd feared.

He cupped her shoulder. "Come back to the house."

She shook her head.

"Why not?"

"Then he wins." Her face was frank and determined.

Steve released a slow breath. "Look, Alessi . . ."

"Who is it, Steve?"

He glanced away. "I don't know."

"But you can guess."

He had leapt to one wild conclusion recently, even acted on it and made a fool of himself to Ben. "My last guess was wrong. My perceptions are not very accurate."

She looked into his face, her eyes absorbing him in a dangerous way. "You should trust yourself."

He half smiled. "I just don't want you to think I'm holding back. If I knew, I'd tell you."

Her throat worked, and for a moment he thought she might cry, but she said, "Would you? Because I don't get the feeling that anyone really wants to know what happened. Everyone's sorry, but . . ."

"No one wants to think badly of his neighbor."

She shook her head. "It's more than that. I feel it in the way people look at me—or don't. They wish I wasn't here."

Steve couldn't meet her gaze. He could probably count on one hand the people who weren't wishing her gone. And that didn't include the one who was playing cruel games. She shouldn't stay alone, but she was obviously determined. "If you need anything, hear anything, call me."

She swallowed but didn't answer.

"You don't believe I'll help?"

She dropped her gaze.

"Alessi, I'm trying to. There's—"

"I know. Things I don't understand."

How could she? She was not part of Charity, not one of them, not bound by the pact or delivered from evil. All the frustration of his efforts to reach people flooded back to him. He'd tried, but they were of one mind. Nothing bad could happen when you'd slain the devil and cast him back to hell. No one washed in blood would violate the new covenant.

In renaming the town Charity, they'd made their mission clear: Love, faith, and righteousness. Charity could not produce a thief. But after tonight, Steve wondered if theft was the worst they had to fear. Taking something in secret was not the same as terrorizing. And if the culprit knew they'd all turn a blind eye, how far would he go?

Steve frowned. It struck him that Alessi was the perfect target. No family. Drifting. Something had certainly happened. Her fear was tangible. She'd been targeted, but by whom? Steve wanted to take her with him by force if necessary. Adrenaline surged. "Alessi . . ."

She closed herself in her arms. "I'll be fine."

Maybe that really was all she had, the determination to stand her ground. He admired her resolve. In fact, he admired *her*. These last ten days she'd done her best in the situation, with precious little to go on.

And he could be way off base with his concerns for her safety. Besides, it wasn't his decision. He hardly even knew her. He sighed. "Okay. Good night." He locked the door and stood outside a long minute before getting into his truck. He'd talk to Cooper in the morning. Like it or not, Cooper was the one with legal authority. He should at least know about this incident.

He looked at the store through his rearview mirror as he pulled out of the small back parking lot. Shadows around the Dumpster could hide a man, or that alley between the stores. . . . He'd drive himself crazy. He had to let it go. She wanted to stay there. He pulled around and parked a short distance from the front of the store. He didn't want her to see him checking, but he had to know. There on the sidewalk were tire tracks right in front of the window. She was telling the truth. He straightened. The relief of believing her was countered by a renewed concern. Someone had been out there, and whoever it was didn't seem to understand the pact.

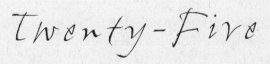

Twenty-Five

STEVE WENT TO SEE COOPER AND TOLD HIM about both the bra on the door and the tire tracks at the window. "Don't tell me she's making it up, Coop. I felt her trembling."

Cooper scratched the cat under its chin and didn't ask how he'd felt it. He chewed the stump of his cigar. "What if I believed it? What then?" The cat made a rolling motion under his hand and flopped onto its side in Cooper's lap. An open can of cat food added ocean whitefish to the scents of Cooper's office. "I can't question people as though there's a guilty party. Not with the pact."

"But there is a guilty party."

Cooper let the cat down. "Bring it to the pastor. If he says we're wrong . . ." He spread his hands. "That opens a whole new can."

"You're sworn to uphold the law."

"There are some laws higher than others. I filed a report. I've looked for a lost car. Anything more goes against the pact."

Steve expelled a slow breath. He understood Cooper's position. It had been easier when he didn't believe Alessi either. His reasons had been different from the rest of Charity's but were just as valid: an innate distrust. After seeing the tracks last night, he couldn't find the skepticism that had sustained his distance, and it was beginning to feel personal.

He went again to Pastor Welsh's house, but he was out on calls. Pretty early for that, but Madeline sent him sweetly on his way. And it was time for more coffee. He headed back to the house. Maybe Ben had some ideas. But Alessi was there when he went in, and they could hardly discuss the pact in front of her.

They had Dave's Bisquick pancakes, but she didn't eat much. She didn't look as though she'd slept well either. At least it wasn't his fault this time. He'd handled last night with the utmost integrity, only later wishing he'd kissed her teary face. Definitely better than the other time he'd gone to the rescue.

As soon as she went in to shower, Steve faced Ben. "What happens if someone proves the pact false?"

Ben frowned. "It's not about proof. It's belief."

Steve tried again. "What if it's wrong?"

Ben glanced at Dave, who worked on his fourth pancake. "If it's wrong, we're in a world of trouble."

"Not everyone. Every single person cannot be responsible, no matter what the pact says."

Dave swiped his mouth with a napkin. "Pastor says, 'Inasmuch as we wished it in our hearts, and stoked it with our lips, we share the blame for the actions taken.'"

Steve rubbed his face, then eyed them both. "Okay. Say everyone's guilty. Why not just accept that and forget the rest?"

"It's the rest that matters." Ben's face pulled down long. "It's the good that came of it. A whole lot of good, Steve. People like they never were before."

"One in particular," Dave added. "And that's nothing short of miraculous."

Steve pushed his plate away. "You mean Carl."

They nodded.

He pictured the young man as he'd been in the pastor's study. "Well, he's improved for sure."

"Delivered," Dave said.

Steve couldn't argue, since he hadn't been around for most of the transformation. Duke's son had been a terror, and now it seemed he walked toward sainthood like his "father," Burton Welsh. But he'd seen some expressions on Carl's face that made him wonder. And Alessi had told him to trust himself. "What if he's faking it?"

Ben tossed his head to the side. "There you go, Steve, thinking the worst of people. That boy's had a lot to deal with. His mom running off and leaving him to—"

"Did she?" He surprised himself with that one.

"Did she what?" Dave said.

"Run off."

The two men shared a look, then turned to him with pure exasperation. Ben said, "What are you saying?"

"She disappeared. And there was some letter, but . . ."

Dave clanked his mug against his plate. "They verified her handwriting."

It hit Steve low. Had he somehow wished that Beth had not willingly deserted Carl to the likes of Duke, saving only herself from abuse? Old feelings churned. At least he'd been left to a wonderful father when his mother decided she didn't care. Who was he to doubt the good that had come to Carl?

"Someone was out there last night with Alessi's car. Someone who enjoys tormenting her."

Memories arose in all their minds as they shared looks all around. Maybe they'd slain the devil, but his works were not forgotten.

Alessi sensed Steve's concern as they walked to the store under cloudy skies that held a smell she guessed might be snow. "Is it going to storm?" Two steps. "Steve?"

"Yeah?" He jolted.

"Are you okay?"

"I should be asking you that." Definite strain in his tone. She appreciated his concern, but it made her uneasy. It wasn't his problem.

"Well, there are a few things I'd change, but I don't guess there's anyone in history who hasn't felt that way."

He stared at her. "That's it?"

Uh-oh. She'd set him off again. What did he want from her anyway?

"What things, Alessi? Tell me what you'd change."

If she said he already knew, he'd bite her head off. She looked straight ahead toward the place her Mustang had jumped the curb. "Well, I'd have my car back, for one. And a place of my own and people who wanted me around." She couldn't help the sinking stone in her stomach.

He frowned. "And how much of that is your fault?" His tone was clipped.

If they were laying blame, she'd have to look no farther than herself. "All of it, I guess."

"You're serious, aren't you."

She swallowed. "No one forced me to leave a perfectly good opportunity at Dippin' Dots and Dogs. I've made all the choices that put me here."

"So you chose to lose your car." He hedgehogged his hair again.

She shrugged. "I guess whoever took it chose that too."

"And last night?" He was practically barking. "You chose to be scared silly?"

Why was he making this an issue? The reminder of that dreadful, helpless feeling was not pleasant. "I'm not responsible for other people's choices. But I got myself in this position. It's no one else's fault." Mom had never made apologies for her choice. *"I knew what I wanted and what God wanted for me. I left and never looked back. One choice leads to another, and regret is worthless."*

Steve reached the door and jammed in the key. "So if you found your car, you'd just say 'thank you very much' and be on your way?"

She swallowed the tightness in her throat. "That's about it."

"No charges, no recriminations." He pushed the door open.

What good would pressing charges do in a place where she was guilty for just living? "Maybe he'd be more inclined to bring it back then." She stepped past him into the store.

"Bring it back?" He turned her toward the window where her car had been, with that horrible face in it. The hands clasping her shoulders from behind were tight and definite. "Do you even remember last night? Or am I the only one?"

Her lungs tightened on her breath. "I remember."

"It just doesn't matter?"

She closed herself in her arms. What good would it do to dwell on it? "It matters."

He turned her. "Last night you wanted to know who it was. Now you say it's all your fault anyway. You get behind a podium and demand action, then say you're not supposed to have it right now. You can't have it both ways. Either you want your car or you don't."

She looked into his face, pain crawling into her throat. "I want it." She squeezed her arms, wanting it so much, just because it was hers. No, it was *her*; something more than anyone expected, something lovely and worthwhile, fun and jazzy and strong. She had never driven it with the reckless detachment this thief had shown. She'd babied and lavished it with meticulous care. Yes, she wanted it. How could Steve think otherwise?

There was some disconnect. There had to be. Steve stared at her, trying to grasp her conflicting moods. She had stalked out the other day, insistent on finding the Mustang—he'd even lent her his truck— and had come back peacefully claiming she wasn't supposed to have it. Now it seemed as though the scare last night that had set her shaking was no longer registering in her gray matter. It had to be a disability, though not one he could easily put a name to.

Maybe there was some disorder that made a person take the blame for anything that happened. He caught that thought and pondered it. Not so far from Charity's own position, as Dave and Ben had expressed. Maybe he was the only one who put blame on others outside himself. Was he out of step?

Was it his fault his mother walked out? Must be. He'd been there. It happened. Was it his fault Barb left? More of a chance on that one.

He hadn't always given his best. But this idea that everything was of your own choosing. . . .

He expelled a slow breath. "For what it's worth, I informed Cooper about last night . . . and the other thing too."

She flushed. "Oh." She dropped her hands to her sides. "Did it make any difference?"

"Probably not."

She smiled. "At least you're honest."

He softened his hands on her shoulders. "So you trust me?"

"I don't have any reason not to. Unlike some people around here, I start out thinking the best."

And it must take something astronomical to shake her from that resolve. "While I'm grateful for that on my account, I think you need to consider that someone out there is not behaving well."

She sighed. "I know."

He let go of her. "Be careful."

She nodded, but once again it was as though his words bounced off her. He was not at all sure she did know.

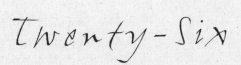

Twenty-Six

STEVE'S CHRISTMAS SHOPPING LIST WAS as basic as it could get. Some little gadget for Dave, a hat or socks for Ben, chocolates for Karen and Mary and Diana, and dolls for the little girls. He'd also give Stacie and the other shopkeepers a scented candle or decoration of some sort for being his neighbors. That was it. No extravaganza, no shipping dozens of packages, no stuffing things under a tree.

He paused. Should he get something for Alessi? She had been helpful. And it would be glaring to leave her out. But what would he get? He was notoriously bad at choosing. Barb had returned most of his gifts for something she actually liked.

He frowned. He could just do chocolates as for the other women. But that didn't seem right somehow. Alessi's comment about Ben stuck in his mind. If she was the kind who matched a person to a gift, a generic box of chocolates might not seem special. Not that it had to be special. He pulled that thought out by the root.

Nothing extravagant, certainly. A book? Too easy. And then it came to him. While Alessi watched *The Bishop's Wife* with Dave and Ben and their respective lady friends, he drove once again to Phyllis Bartle's house.

Debbie met him at the door with a smile, but no hugs or patting followed.

"Hi, Debbie. Is your mom home?"

"Sure." She scooped up the pug and started down the hall. The other two dogs, a shepherd mix and a tawny mutt, bounded over and sniffed him. By their breath, he guessed they'd just eaten something he'd rather not know about.

Phyllis was in her sewing room, machine whirring and piles of fabric cut in small squares all around her, like the peasant daughter in Rumpelstiltskin trying to spin gold from heaps of straw. She looked up. "Steve, I don't have that gal's car."

He smiled. "I didn't think so."

"What brings you back, then?"

"Angels." He looked at the shelves around the walls, stuffed with cloth angels in myriad colors. Some wore little country dresses; some were lace and ribbons. Some had tiny wigs, others yarn hair, and a few were topped with something that looked like dried grass. "I'd like to buy one for Alessi for Christmas."

Phyllis stopped the machine. "Take your pick. I'm making a delivery tomorrow and those shelves will be bare."

She sold very well out of a gift shop in Chambers City, and he was glad he'd caught her before she took this batch out there. But looking at the dozens and dozens of angels on the shelves, he froze. How did he know what Alessi would prefer? Phyllis started the machine again, unconcerned by his inertia.

Debbie set down the pug and walked over to the shelf beside the window. She took down an angel in stiff white fabric with thin lacy wings. Her hair was shiny strands of curling golden thread and her face had sweet, painted features. Debbie handed it to him, and he touched the halo made of twisted gold wire.

"She's my favorite," Debbie told him. "Give her to Alessi."

Steve cradled the angel in his palms. Yes, it was a good choice. And he had no doubt Debbie knew who it was meant for. He smiled. "Thank you."

"Eighteen dollars," Debbie said.

More than he'd intended to spend, but Phyllis and Debbie lived on the proceeds from their angels. He took out a twenty. "You keep the change for helping me choose."

Debbie smiled broadly. "Thanks." She folded the angel in tissue, then put it in a paper bag. Steve left there, certain he had exactly the angel that was meant for Alessi.

———————

Steve was still out when *The Bishop's Wife* ended, but Alessi had her key, so she headed for the store. If the moon was there, it was muffled in thick wooly clouds and gave sulky light at best. Good thing she knew the way.

The warmth and joy of the old movie stayed with her. She imagined the ice rink with strings of white bulbs and the angel Dudley making everyone a great figure skater. She laughed at how easily they believed it was their ability. If you didn't recognize the magic, you could get conceited. Like the princess who refused to marry the frog in *East of the Sun, West of the Moon*. She sure paid for that mistake.

She crossed the intersection where the streetlight showed the heavy sky with no stars breaking through, passed Hawkeye Gifts, then turned into the narrow alley to go in through the back of Bennet's. The tiny lot was dark and silent, her steps in the snow the only sound. Not even the cloud blanket took the edge from the cold. It would probably snow soon. And like anything else that came too regularly, it was losing its magic.

She had the key ready when she reached the door. She inserted it. A sound like wind, and she was struck and engulfed by cold; shocking, stunning, soaking cold. Gasping for breath, she looked up through dripping hair. A blazing light glared, sending needles to her brain.

She raised an arm to fend it off, seeing nothing but orange spots behind her eyelids. She jerked the door open and flung herself inside, slamming it and panting and shaking so hard she thought her teeth would come loose from their sockets. Her spine stiffened and trembled at once, causing spasms to connecting tissue.

She pulled Steve's jacket off, and her wet hair slapped her neck. She stripped the black cable-knit sweater and groped for the blanket on the cot. Her hands were palsied and stiff, and pain shot up her arms. If she ever wanted to know how a coach felt after victory, she knew it now. Only it had been so cold to start with, the icy bath was nothing short of cruel, and she had no victory to soften the blow.

She didn't have to wonder who did it. The person who had hung her bra was on the roof. He'd waited there for her with his ice-water tub, waited for her to stop beneath him, unsuspecting. He knew the shock would paralyze her. And the light. It was calculated cruelty beyond a rocky snowball.

Alessi grabbed a wad of paper towels and mopped her hair as she headed for the telephone. The skinny directory lay beside it, and she flipped through for the sheriff's number. He would never get there before the person escaped the roof and fled into the night, but he could see her soaked things and . . .

Steve's words came back to her. *"You're the only one who's seen it. It's your word alone."* And his telling the sheriff about the other times hadn't mattered. Cooper Roehr would think she'd soaked herself, set it up to beef her story. No witness. And she'd be dragging him out of bed and creating a disturbance. She hung up the phone and drew the blanket tighter around her. Dragging back to the cot, she stripped her wet jeans and created uncontrollable kinetic energy inside her own skin.

Ben and Dave were taking Mary and Diana home. And what would be the good of troubling them anyway? Whoever did this was gone. They might find his marks in the snow, where he huddled on the roof and even how he got up and down. But there'd been the tire circles, too, and that hadn't mattered.

She pulled on Steve's sweats and the dry T-shirt, then squeezed out the wet clothes over the sink. She wasn't injured. It could have been worse. And from now on she'd use the front entrance. There might not be anyone around, but the light from the intersection gave some illumination at least. And maybe she wouldn't stay out past dark or go to the house at all after work.

She frowned. It wasn't right. She should have the freedom to come and go like anyone else. Her shivering increased, and suddenly the word *persecuted* seemed appropriate after all. But why? What.had she done but follow her hope?

Steve went into the house and found the television off and the room empty. He had tucked the little package inside his coat just in case, but no one was home. Or the guys had gone to bed. But as he stood there he heard a car outside. He went to the front door and held it for Ben.

The sky had lowered with clouds, heavy with snow. All day they had fattened, but no snow had fallen. It would be a good one when it came. "Got Mary home?"

Ben nodded.

"Did you or Dave run Alessi back?"

Ben pulled off his jacket. "She went herself, as soon as the movie ended. Dave was getting cozy with Diana, and . . ." He shrugged and reached for a hanger.

Alessi had felt extraneous. Nothing like a fifth on a double date. He shouldn't have left. Not that it would have been a triple, but it might not have felt as awkward for her. "She walked to the store?"

Ben nodded. "It's not far."

It wasn't. But Steve was not easy about it. He went to the phone and dialed the store. After two rings Alessi picked up. Her greeting sounded shaky.

"It's Steve, Alessi. I wanted to make sure you made it in all right."

There was a sound that might have been chattering teeth. "Yes. I did."

"Everything all right?"

She sighed. "Yes."

Okay, so his perceptions were poor, but he could swear things were not okay. He waited for something to come into his head. Communication had never been his strong suit. "Are you sure?" The pause was long enough for him to wonder if he'd insulted her. Then she started to cry.

He hung up and took his keys from his pocket. Something had told him to call; something had made him doubt. He didn't usually trust his intuition, but in Alessi's case, he seemed to hit it pretty close. The cold struck him as he got back to the truck, then drove to the store and parked. A wind had come up and bit the back of his neck.

He reached the door and smacked into it with an elbow and forehead as his feet went out from under him. The whole stoop was ice, wet glare ice and what looked like cubes, the sort you bought in a bag. He gripped the knob and pulled himself up.

"Alessi, it's me," he said before opening the door.

She was huddled in a blanket, her hair wet and lips a lavender gray. Tears beaded her lashes like dew, but she wasn't sobbing. She said, "He was on the roof with a bucket."

More than a bucket by the spread of ice outside. "You saw him?"

She shook her head. "I looked up, but he had a light. Really, really bright."

Steve crouched down and took her hands between his. They were ice-cold and shaking. He chafed them gently. "You're freezing."

"I'm getting warmer."

"You should come back to the house."

"No."

So that was still a stubborn point. She did not want to be scared off. But this was more than scaring. He'd started with a snowball, teased her with the bra, and scared her with the mask two nights ago. You could call those pranks, but this had progressed past taunting. "It's gotten physical. I'm not sure you're safe."

"I have a right to be here." Her face pinched with pain and indignation. "It might be nothing more than my own little corner and my own little chair, but can't I ever have my own place, somewhere I belong?"

"Yes." Steve cupped her hands and blew on them. "But I want you safe." More than she wanted what mattered to her? She had admitted wanting her car back; now she wanted a place to belong. But what if both those things made her a target?

She sniffed. "Could you set the alarm?"

He looked at the door and sighed. "I guess I could." Why this person had targeted Alessi, he didn't know. Maybe for no reason except that she was new. And alone. "But I wish you'd come back with me."

"I'm sure he's long gone. He probably expected me to call the sheriff."

"Did you?"

She shook her head. "I'm not stupid."

He set her hands into her lap but kept them covered with his. "Could it be someone you know? Someone who followed you with a grudge?"

"The one who ditched me?"

"That's not what I meant."

She slipped a hand free and pulled the blanket closed around her neck. "If anyone took the trouble to follow me here, that'd be the most attention I've had in years."

Steve sat back on his heels. "But is there anyone at all?"

Alessi shook her head. "I've had friends most of my life. The only people who hated me were kids in high school, and they're all off at their private colleges making something of their lives." She didn't say it bitterly, just another case of the way it was. "It's no one I know."

He'd have to take her word for that. She didn't seem to be shivering as badly now, and he would set the alarm. Whoever had soaked her had probably run off and wouldn't mess with her again that night. And in spite of the fact that she had little more than two outfits and some personal hygiene items, she seemed to consider his storeroom home. "You sure you'll be okay here?"

"I'd be naïve to say yes, but I swing a mean mailer." She almost smiled.

He had to admire her spunk. And that spunk was one of the things that made him look to her lips with anticipation. He'd better get moving. "I'll set the alarm."

That might be the most he could do in reality, but all night he dreamed of keeping her warm.

Twenty-Seven

ALESSI WOKE UP SHIVERING from what patchy sleep she'd managed. The dream images were all too fresh; that monsterish head leering at her through the window, the glass shattering as the car burst through on an icy wave that engulfed and stole her breath. She shivered again. Didn't Steve heat the store? She blew out her breath in a cloud.

Something was wrong. It had not been this cold the other nights. Even the extra blanket was little help. She climbed off the cot, tugging the blanket with her, and shuffled out into the store. Pale daylight spilled in through windows etched with fronds and swirls of ice. Enchanted, Alessi went to the front and studied the designs, such intricate, lacy crystals turning plain glass into magical mirrors. Beautiful!

She could not attribute it to Jack Frost. He always seemed menacing in pictures and poems. This was too beautiful, too wondrous. Angel breath. Angels had breathed on her windows last night; angels watching over, guarding her.

Outside, the wind coughed gusts of snow from roof and street, tossed it against the glass, and she realized the sound had played a part in her dreams, howling and moaning. She pulled the blanket tighter to her throat, but she'd been safe and guarded. *"Sleep my child and peace attend thee, all through the night. Guardian angels God will send thee, all through the night."*

She hadn't thought of her mother's favorite lullaby in a while, but it came to her so clearly now she could almost hear Mom's voice. The ceramic tiles chilled her feet, and she went back to the storeroom and flicked the light switch. Nothing. The power must be out. No wonder it was so cold.

She dropped the blanket and dressed, shaking with chill. The black sweater was crisp and cold where she'd hung it, but the beige turtleneck and white mohair would be warm, and she put on the dark green pants and two pairs of socks. Her teeth chattered as she brushed them and washed her face. She used the last of the paper towels.

Was it too early to head over to the house? The wall clock had stopped near three. If it was too early, she could sneak through the kitchen door without waking anyone. Steve's jacket was damp and frigid but would have to do against the wind. She should have bought gloves at Wal-Mart. She blew on her fingers, then zipped the coat and spun at the sound behind her.

Her heart thumped, but it was only Steve coming through the door. She smiled to cover the panic she was sure he hadn't missed. "Hi."

"Good morning." His breath pooled in the air.

"Is it as early as it looks?"

"Seven-thirty."

Later than she thought. She was glad she'd dressed and washed up. "You must be freezing."

She shivered on cue. "I used the last of the paper towels. Do you have another roll?"

"Forget the paper towels." He jerked his chin toward the back door. "Let's get out of here." He opened the door to a gusting cloud of ice crystals, then closed it again. "It's nasty out. Here." He pulled the scarf from his neck and wrapped it around her face.

"Thanks."

"Ready?" His eyes crinkled slightly at the corners, as though it were an adventure. Maybe the weather reminded him of Alaska.

Mush, Alessi, mush. "I'm ready."

He opened the door again, ducking his head. "Get in the truck. It's running."

With the damp jacket in the wind, she didn't argue. She ran for the truck and climbed into the cab that was as toasty as a mouse nest in a furnace room. She shook off the cold and basked.

He climbed in behind the wheel and shut the door. "Whew!"

She blew on her fingers. "Is the house warm?"

"Power's out all over Charity. Wind probably took something down." He put the truck in gear. "But Ben's got a kerosene heater."

"Can't we light a fire? In your fireplace?"

He pursed his lips. "I guess we could. Hadn't thought of it."

"Don't you use your fireplace?"

He pulled out of the back lot. "We haven't."

Alessi dropped her hands to her lap. "I do not understand men."

He grinned. "I had a wood-burning stove in Anchorage."

"Well, that's something."

"I know how to light a boy-scout pyramid." He pulled out onto the street.

She laughed. "Do you have any wood?"

"No. But Ben has those prefab logs at the station."

The gusting snow was blinding. She could see nothing through the windshield. He stopped until it passed, then pulled forward slowly. This snow was not magical. There was a threatening element that chilled her in spite of the cab's warmth. "Do you think it'll keep falling?"

"It's not snowing much. Just blowing what got dumped last night."

"Could've fooled me."

"The snow expert." He caught her knee in his palm, then let go.

Alessi stared at the place as though she'd find a handprint. Every time he'd grabbed her elbow or squeezed her hand it was as though his touch sank inside her. It was strange and scary. People had come and gone in her life like characters in a book. She never shut them out, but she knew not to get attached. Now it seemed Steve left his mark with every brush of his fingers.

He stopped outside the station. "Stay here where it's warm."

"Then here." She took the scarf from her neck and wrapped it around his, tucking it into the front of his leather bomber.

"Thanks." He climbed out and hurried for the station. He unlocked the door and went inside, then made several trips to the truck bed, arms filled with packaged logs. He staggered against the blasts of wind, until he finally got back in with her. "Think that'll do? It's all Ben had in stock."

She laughed. "I think it'll be plenty."

He looked at her a long minute before putting the truck in gear and backing away from the station. He pulled around to the house and parked. "Go ahead in. I'll get the wood."

"I can help." The wind caught her breath away with icy malice as she jumped down. It was like a giant frozen respirator blasting in and sucking out. But she hurried around to the bed and loaded up with paper-wrapped logs.

Steve grabbed up half again as many, and they ran for the door. He grappled with the knob, then it was opened from inside.

Dave pulled it wide. "Hey." He took the logs from her.

Ben stood in the kitchen looking sleepy. "Those from the station?"

"Just cleared your inventory." Steve went back out for the rest.

"This your idea, Alessi?" Dave said.

She nodded. "I cannot believe you don't use your fireplace."

"Got the kerosene heater." He thumbed toward the heater smelling up the den.

"Mind if we turn it off?"

He shrugged. "Whatever you want." He put down her load of logs by the fireplace and ambled over to shut off the heater. "Just hope there's no nests or anything in the chimney."

"If there's a nest, the birds are long gone."

"Pretty good fire hazard, though." Dave eyed the opening as though doom awaited.

"Just light the fire, Dave," Ben called from the kitchen. "I'll get our

Coleman stuff from the closet and make some coffee."

Alessi clasped herself in her arms. She was thankful to finally be out of the cold. The wind howled in gusts that shook the windows, and she could not imagine angel breath in that. Vicious wolves huffing and puffing and hoping to devour the three little pigs and Goldilocks, but no gentle angel breath.

Steve came in twice with armloads of logs and stacked them along the brick hearth to the side of the fireplace. He pulled open the screened doors and placed a log on the pristine grate. "Anyone have matches?" He looked around the room.

"I'll fetch 'em," Ben called from the hall, then appeared with a box of waterproof matches from their camping kit.

In seconds Steve had flames licking around the log. He sang, "Oh, the weather outside is frightful. . . ." He was certainly in a fine mood today. Or the fire had bewitched him.

Dave glanced at his heater ruefully. "Hope the heat doesn't all go up the chimney."

Alessi clutched her hands together at her throat, saying nothing, just drinking in the scent and warmth emanating from the neglected orifice. Ben came in with a metal stand that fit over the log and a blue speckled coffeepot, the old-fashioned kind with a percolating insert. *Little House on the Prairie.*

Looking around the room at her three friends taking to the idea of a fire in their own fireplace, she bit her lower lip. If the power stayed out for days she wouldn't mind, she was so warm inside. Last night had been horrible, but it was Christmas Eve, she was with friends, and the magic of the Savior's birth would soon be upon them. Anything could happen. Anything at all.

Steve backed out of Ben's way, stopped beside her, and brought his arm around her shoulders. He hadn't touched her before with Ben and Dave around. They didn't need the charade. "Do we have a skillet, Ben?"

Still in his crouch, Ben glanced over his shoulder. He took in their linked position but only said, "Yeah. I'll grab it in a minute."

Steve turned his head. "Eggs in butter, Alessi?"

Her mouth watered. "Twist my arm."

Instead he cupped the back of her neck and turned her. "Come on. You can help make them." He directed her to the kitchen with his hand. It might have been obnoxious, but his touch was warm and gentle.

She restrained her heart and made it behave. She could have frozen last night, but the Lord's angels had kept her warm, wrapping the store with their wings, breathing onto the glass. The alarm had been worthless, yet no harm had come through the doors, even though dreams of evil had tormented her. There was no evil now.

Steve took out a carton of eggs and a tub of cottage cheese. He pulled a bunch of green onions from the vegetable drawer and closed the door. "Get a bowl from that cabinet next to the sink."

She did as he said and set a medium-sized bowl on the counter.

He opened the carton. "Know how to crack an egg?"

She nodded.

"Do nine of them."

They worked together, whisking the eggs with cottage cheese, snipping green onions, seasoning with salt and pepper and a dash of Tabasco. Then Steve brought the mixture to the skillet heating on the fire and dropped a chunk of butter into the pan. When the butter sizzled and bubbled, he poured the eggs into the middle of it. Ben filled mugs of coffee while Steve stirred the eggs. Dave gathered plates and flatware and set them on the hearth, and Alessi felt superfluous.

In moments Steve had filled their plates, and they gathered near the fireplace as Ben offered a blessing. Alessi sat cross-legged with her plate in her lap and took her first bite. Fairy ambrosia . . . again. The scent of woodsmoke aided the scene in her mind, but this time it was Steve presiding, regal and strong, like one of Tolkien's elves.

She played the scene out in her mind as they ate in companionable silence. Woodland creatures played flutes and danced, and Steve ordered nectar passed in carved wooden goblets. Then he stood and came to her. . . .

Throat tightening, she sipped her coffee. Those imaginations were dangerous. Steve brought his plate to the sink, breaking the scene. No elf lord, just a man who made great eggs.

She joined him with her own dishes. "Let me wash. I haven't done anything."

"I wouldn't say that."

"I mean anything to help."

"So do I." He started the water in the sink, felt it with his hand. "We'll need to heat it on the fire."

The fire she'd thought of. "Isn't it useful?"

He smiled, shut off the water, and trapped her in the corner of the counter. "Useful, warm, lovely . . ." His eyes trailed her face. "And it smells a whole lot better than kerosene."

Ben circled them to set his dishes by the sink, but Steve didn't move. Alessi glanced past his shoulder and caught Ben's smile.

He shuffled. "I'll be heading to Mary's now, make sure she and the girls are all right."

Steve said, "Okay." But still he didn't move.

Dave pressed in past Ben and put his mug and plate on the counter. "Diana's got her family coming. She'll be in a panic with no power. Guess I'll see what I can do over there."

Steve didn't even answer, just kept looking at her. Ben and Dave bundled up and went out. Alessi heard the door close behind them, but the loudest thing was her heart pumping in her ears. The energy between Steve's chest and her own could supply Charity for days. He didn't move even after the others were gone, just kept looking at her with his enigmatic eyes.

She drew a shallow breath. "What are you doing?"

"Trying to make sense of you." An almost pained look came into his face.

She wasn't hurt this time. There was need in him. He was facing hurt he'd stuffed inside too long. She knew how that felt.

He cupped her face. "Tell me you're real."

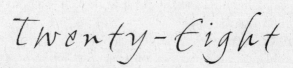

Twenty-Eight

THOUGH SHE DIDN'T ANSWER, HE FELT her pulse under his fingers. She was flesh and blood, but there was something unworldly about her. She made him see things, think things, know things he hadn't before. She awakened his soul, and he hadn't known it was sleeping. She convicted and entranced. Last night had left him aching to know her.

He leaned in and kissed her mouth, wanting but restraining. He didn't want to scare her, and again he sensed her innocence. Her hands were between them, flat to his chest, not fending him off, but protective, careful. He kissed her again, deeper. What was he doing? He didn't know and didn't care.

Her eyes had closed, and he tasted her lips, feeling a need he'd denounced after Barb deserted him. He could not be in love. It wasn't possible after only two weeks. And he'd sworn off it anyway. What, then? It was not the animal attraction he had for Amanda. He did want to hold Alessi, touch her. But . . . it was her he craved.

He closed her into his arms and kissed her neck. She sucked a sharp breath, but he didn't stop. He didn't want to. He found her mouth and claimed it harder than before. He wanted to kiss her until neither one of them could breathe. He loved her. No. But he did. What he'd felt for Amanda was carnal; what he'd felt for Barb, a wish for something more.

This was real. He clutched her between the shoulders and let his mouth show what he couldn't say as well. He wanted every day with her. She changed people . . . if they were willing to change. Stacie had practically given her that soft sweater he hugged now, and Stacie never discounted. Ben said Mary was a new woman after sledding with Alessi, and those timid little girls had taken to her like a sister. Debbie had seen it; so had Ben and Dave.

He kissed the space between her eyebrows, clutching that wild, wonderful hair, then looked into her face. Not terrified exactly, but close. He forced himself to back off. "Treacherous ogre?"

She shook her head and her throat worked. "I just don't do that."

His heart rushed. "Ever?"

"Well, I hadn't."

That thought almost set him off again. She was so pure, so . . . "I find that very hard to believe."

She looked away.

He'd hurt her. "What did I say?"

"Nothing."

He caught her shoulders. "What did I say, Alessi?"

"Aunt Carrie called my mother a slut. She said I was the same."

He was suddenly keenly aware of her youth. He was less experienced than he might have been at his age, because his nature was to find the one woman he could love, not play the field, not play around. His father had taught him how critical that choice was, and he didn't want to blow it. But he felt miles ahead of Alessi right now.

"You proved her wrong." There wasn't a vampish cell in her body.

"And I didn't mean I thought you were experienced. I just can't believe others haven't felt what I feel." What was he doing?

"What you feel?" She looked more insecure than ever.

"I don't explain it well."

"It's probably grief. Your first Christmas without your dad or your lover."

"She wasn't my lover." Her assumption was understandable after his behavior moments ago. "Our engagement was commitment enough for Barb, but I needed the covenant first." He cringed inside. Alessi didn't need to read his mind; he just blurted everything out. "Guess who proved right on that one?"

Alessi's eyes held him bound. He was under control now but surprisingly not chagrined that he'd kissed her. Whatever was going on was beyond him. He wouldn't fight it. He ran a hand through his hair. "We should heat some dishwater."

She nodded, relaxing at last, unaware that at any moment he might give in and kiss her again. Her height was a wonderful fit with his, her skin soft yet not overly moisturized. Barb's had been almost spongy. He emptied the coffeepot and filled it with clean water, then set it over the fire and tucked a fresh log underneath.

The house was still cold, but in front of the fire it was hot. That could account for the heat inside him, but he knew better. Alessi wandered over from the kitchen. She stopped at the tree and fingered one of Dave's fishing flies. Steve left the water to heat and went into his room. He snatched his camera and went back.

She didn't see him at first, and he snapped one shot of her looking up into the branches, toying with the feathers of a blue fly. It wouldn't show blue because it was black-and-white film in the camera. She turned. "Don't start that again."

But he snapped off three more shots in succession. Let her complain. He wanted to see if she came out on film. If she were some phantom or angel, he'd prove it in black-and-white.

She jammed her fingers into her hair. "I really don't like it."

He snapped.

She put her hands to her hips. Great angles on her elbows. Her arms were almost as long as his. He snapped again. She put her hands over her face and he even snapped that.

She took them away. "Let me take you." She reached for the camera.

He lowered it, trying to remember if Barb had ever asked to take his picture. They'd asked people to take them together, but she'd loved her end better, posing and preening for the lens. He handed Alessi the camera. "Here's the focus. Touch here to snap the picture."

She held it up to her eye. "Go over by the fire."

He walked over and crouched, tested the side of the waterpot while he was there. Hardly warm. He heard the shutter click and turned. She snapped another. He smiled, and she took that too. He stood. "Come here." He sat her on the hearth by the fire, took the camera and set its timer. He left the camera on the table and sat beside her on the hearth, encircling her in his arm. "Now who's the one with the pole in the back?"

She turned to him and the camera clicked the picture.

He looked into her face—hazel eyes, long freckled nose, broad generous lips. "Can I kiss you?"

"You did."

"May I?"

Her heart hammered. "I'm not sure."

He pressed his palm to her cheek. "Still think I'm the big jerk?"

She shook her head.

"Heathcliff?"

She shook it again.

"Do you play chess?"

Her eyebrows raised.

"Chess. King, queen, bishops, knights."

"No."

"Want to learn?" He removed his hand.

"Well, I . . ."

He stood up and took the chessboard and pieces from the shelf beside the fireplace. "If I win—I claim a kiss. You win—you name the penalty."

"I think you'll have an advantage."

He sat down on the rug in front of the fire and laid out the board. "But you can name any prize you like. I've already told you mine."

She sank to the rug across from him, watching as he set up the pieces.

"Now, this is the king. He's the most important. But this is the queen. She's the most powerful." He showed her each piece and described how they moved. By the few questions she asked he guessed her a fair strategist. Of course, chess was a game it took years to master.

She put her hands on her hips when he mated her king in only five moves. "You didn't tell me everything."

"You think I cheated?"

"How can you get my king already?" She frowned at the board.

"He's boxed in. The only move he has is into check again."

She stared hard as though that would change things. "But I've hardly moved anything."

Steve spread his hands. "Sounds like sour grapes to me. But in the spirit of Christmas, I'll give you another chance."

"What's the catch?" She looked into his face.

"No catch. Same terms." He smiled. He really was enjoying this.

As an answer she reset her pieces. He did the same. This time, it took eleven moves to put her king into check and thirteen for mate. She cocked her head at the board. "Best of five."

He pulled a sideways smile. "Okay." Barb had sniffed at his attempts to teach her the game. She thought chess was for old men and geeks. Was there anything they'd agreed on? There must have been some basis for their relationship. "Would you like to go first again?"

"No. You go first."

He moved a pawn. She moved a pawn. He moved a knight; she moved a knight. Instead of following a strategy, he simply moved pieces, amused when she did the same. Once, he opened up his queen dangerously, but she didn't see it, and when she copied him, he swooped in and took her queen instead.

"Oh! That was so mean!"

He laughed. "Sorry."

"I know all about that sort of sorry." She spoke without taking her eyes from the board. With her bishop she captured his knight. "Not a fair exchange, but I'll settle for it."

He positioned his queen. "Check."

With her eyes, she followed the threat to her king, moved him to the side.

"You should castle him." He pointed to her rook.

She looked up. "Maybe I should, but I didn't."

"You can take it back."

She shook her head. "I'll beat you fairly."

"You won't beat me at all."

She tucked her knees to the side under her. "I'm doing better every time."

"But this is your last chance."

"Only if you win." The freckles across her nose gave her a sassy look.

Sighing, he positioned his knight. "Check."

She scowled at the knight. "He's no gentleman at all."

"He's following his queen's orders."

She moved her king one square forward.

He positioned a pawn. "Checkmate."

With her mouth forming a determined line, she made an even row of pawns, reset her back row and looked up. "Best of seven."

"I'd only have to win one more."

She folded her hands on her knee. "I have it figured out now."

"Do you?" The thought intrigued him. "Double or nothing."

She tipped her head confidently. "I better start thinking of what I want."

His mouth twitched. "Pride goes before a fall. Or do you mean to keep increasing ratios until you win?"

"Best of seven, double or nothing." She moved her center pawn two squares forward.

Out of curiosity he let her control the match, playing defensively without pursuing the kill. A few times he did take a piece, when he had to, and once when she was too satisfied with herself. She scowled. "You did that on purpose."

"That's the point of the game."

She pushed back her hair. "You're toying with me."

He crossed his legs and rested his forearms. "Why would you think that?"

"It's obvious. You've had no sneak attacks, no attacks at all, actually."

He reached over and placed a fresh log into the fire. "I think it's your move."

"You won't admit it?" She moved her bishop to the edge, pinned her fingertip to his head, and scoured the board around him, then lifted her finger.

He studied the board. "You have my king in check."

She furrowed her brow. "How?"

"Your bishop."

"Ha." She clasped her hands. "Check."

He castled his king and winked at her. She swooped in with her bishop and took his rook, as he'd known she would. He answered by capturing her bishop with his knight.

She frowned. "Now you've taken them both."

He spread his hands. "Your turn."

She brought her queen into position. "Check."

"Are you sure you want to do that?"

Again her brow furrowed. "I've done it now. Why shouldn't I have?"

He captured her queen with a pawn.

"But they go forward."

"They move forward, capture diagonally." He glanced up. "We can reset that if you didn't remember."

She huffed. "I should have."

Steve cradled the queen in his palm. "Put her back?"

She looked like a child desiring a treat but said, "No. I've lost her."

"If you get a pawn all the way across, you can have her back."

She looked up. "You didn't tell me that."

He shrugged. "I didn't want to overwhelm you with too much information at once."

"So you have been holding back."

"If it had mattered, I would have told you before."

She leaned back and rested on her palms, another great picture pose. "Why didn't it matter?"

"Because the matches were over before it became an issue." He framed her in his mind. She was no great beauty, but there was something irresistibly photogenic about her.

"I might have done things differently." Her hair dropped off her shoulder with a soft springy bounce.

He wanted to clutch it in his hand. "All right, then we'll wipe the slate clean. Whoever wins this match takes it all." And he would make those kisses count.

She returned her attention to the chessboard. She was competitive, no doubt about that. It surprised him in a way. She was so non-confrontational in her other interaction. Had she trained herself to back off because of her circumstances?

He waited for her to move. With neither bishop and no queen, her options were limited. She moved a pawn forward, and his mouth quirked. So her peons were on a mission. He positioned his knight. She moved the pawn again. He moved his knight. Once more the pawn advanced.

He put his knight where he wanted it. "Check."

She looked startled. She'd been so focused on getting her pawn across she'd forgotten her king. "Should I castle him?"

"You can't. He'd be in check by my rook."

She moved the king one square to the side.

He brought his bishop into place. "Check again."

She looked at her pawn, waiting to become a queen, then frowned at her king's plight. She moved him one square forward. Steve moved his other knight. He was down one bishop, a rook, and several pawns. But it didn't matter.

With her king safe for the moment, she nudged her pawn another square forward. Steve brought his queen across. "Check. Mate."

She crossed her arms, glaring at the little pawn as though he were personally to blame.

He smiled. "That's why I said it wouldn't matter."

She picked up three pieces and laid them in the box. "What else didn't you tell me?"

He scooped a handful of pieces and laid them into the slots above hers. "There are many strategies I couldn't go into right off the bat. But I gave you all the basic information."

She laid the rest of her pieces into the box. He closed it, took it with the board, and replaced it all on the shelf.

She stood up. "Well, you won."

"I have to say you learned quickly."

"Not quickly enough." She shoved her hair back. "So claim your prize."

He wanted to but shook his head. "Not just yet."

"Why not?"

He shrugged. "Taking it now would be too mercenary." He'd wait for a spontaneous moment, such as they'd shared in the kitchen. Maybe then she wouldn't resist. No, she didn't resist, it was just . . .

He took her hand and led her to the front window. The snow blew in blasts, no cozy snowfall that. Rather a brutal cold that would spoil services and celebrations if it kept up until tomorrow with no power. Charity had spent days with no power at times, though not over Christmas that he could recall.

And then he realized the next day was Christmas. He had flippantly claimed to be spending it with her to get rid of Amanda. Alessi's suggestion, but now he wanted it to be real. Should he ask her? Or just make it happen? And after Christmas. . . ? He glanced over. What was she thinking as she looked out into the blowing snow?

"Alessi . . . I know our agreement went through Christmas—the employment, that is."

"And protection."

He raised his eyebrows.

"From piranhas."

"That too." It seemed ridiculous now, with the sort of protection she needed. They had started out pretending, but having all those hours together had formed a real bond. He'd spent time with others and had not lost his head. But Alessi was like no one else.

He rested his hand on the small of her back. "What if you don't get your car back by Christmas?"

She stared out the window. "I don't know."

"Would you stay?"

She moistened her lips. "I don't know."

"Why would you have to go?"

She pressed her fingers to the glass, melting small circles in the frost. "I need to find where I belong."

He took her fingers from the glass, felt the chill of their tips. They belonged in his. The thought triggered his desire to keep her close, to know all there was to know about her. "It could be Charity."

She shook her head. "Not without my car."

"It's just a car."

She looked up at him. "Then why won't the sheriff get it back?"

"Because he can't."

She turned away, walked back to the fire. He stayed at the window. What if he told her? It was breaking the pact to do so. And it was questionable whether she'd understand even then. It was, as Ben said, a matter of believing. He looked through a white blast to Ben's Jeep pulling into the circular driveway. A moment later Ben emerged and unloaded Mary and the girls. Steve looked behind him toward Alessi at the fire. Too late to kiss her now.

Twenty-Nine

ALESSI STARTLED WHEN THE DOOR BURST OPEN and Cait and Lyn blew in on a blast of white. Steve tugged them out of the way so Ben and Mary could follow, then closed the door behind them. Her heart swelled at the sight of those chapped faces and Mary looking like a little match girl herself.

Ben came in, stomping and huffing. "Their house is too cold. No fireplace." He closed the storm out. "I hope we're not . . ."

"We were playing chess." Steve turned. "You girls like to play games?"

Neither one answered. Steve had a knack for striking people speechless. Alessi motioned them over to the fireplace, where they stood shivering, their little faces pink and their bangs clotted with snow. Alessi stooped to tug off mittens and hats, then laid the girls' things on the hearth to dry. "You want something hot to drink?"

Steam puffed from the pot Steve had filled but never used. Dishes could wait. With the potholder Ben had left on the hearth, she lifted the pot out and carried it to the kitchen.

Mary went with her and set a large paper sack on the counter. They whipped up cups of hot chocolate for the girls, then Mary took a tin from the sack. "Would you like to try this chai tea? It's instant but tasty."

"Sure." Alessi glanced at Ben and Steve speaking low together by the front window. "Would you guys like something hot?"

"You all go ahead," Ben said. "I'll brew up some more coffee later."

Cait crept into the kitchen and whispered to her mother, "I'm hungry."

"I know. It's lunchtime." Mary took a loaf of Wonder Bread and a package of wafer beef from the sack.

Just the sort of lunch Alessi had lived on most of her life. For a moment Mary's face was replaced by her mother's. Such loss and longing as she hadn't felt for a while seized her. She closed her eyes. When she opened them again, Mary was spreading the bread with Miracle Whip and both Cait and Lyn hovered at her sides, sipping their mugs.

Alessi pulled herself together. "Can I help?"

"You can peel the cheese." Mary handed her the package of Kraft singles.

Alessi pulled the plastic off each slice and laid the cheese on the bread. Then Mary added a few slices of wafer beef and the top bread. She handed them over to the girls. Mom had always cut them diagonally into four triangles. Alessi had nibbled the soft inner corner first and worked her way to the crust.

She put two of the sandwiches on plates and carried them to Ben and Steve. Ben said, "Thanks, Alessi." Steve just looked into her face with something like disappointment and anticipation at once. She doubted it was the sandwich he anticipated.

His asking about Christmas and what happened next had changed the mood, made her realize she was still drifting with nowhere to belong. Maybe she never would. It was as pointless as trying to cross the board with a pawn. Or maybe she was the pawn, trying to be a queen while everyone who mattered was being taken off the board.

She turned away and caught Ben's glance, watching her curiously. He murmured something to Steve after she passed, but Steve's answer was too low to hear. Cait had eaten into her sandwich until it framed her chin like a beard. Lyn ate all the crust off and was now biting toward the center. Alessi joined Mary in the kitchen and received her own sandwich. She took a knife from the drawer and cut it into quarters, then slowly, deliberately, she nibbled the innermost corner.

Mary touched her hand. "I want you to know something."

Alessi laid down her sandwich. "What is it?"

"I told Ben yes." Mary's cheeks flushed and red ran down her neck, but it was not an awkward or embarrassed flush.

Alessi stared at her, seeing now that it was peace she'd noticed, peace and joy as deep as any Christmas promise. "When did he ask you?"

"A year and a half ago."

"He's just waited for an answer?"

Mary nodded, then turned and scooped the chai powder into their mugs.

Alessi's heart soared as she tucked the end of another triangle into her mouth and poured hot water into the mugs. Gentle, patient Ben and fragile Mary. She refilled the pot and put it back over the fire. Mary carried their mugs in, and they sat down on the couch.

The tea tasted spicy and mellow at once, a wonderful blend. Alessi murmured, "Did you set a date?"

"Not yet."

"Do the girls know?" She watched them sip their cocoa on the hearth and finish the ends of their sandwiches.

"No. I just told Ben last night."

Looking across at him still by the window, Alessi's spirit danced. How glad he must have been to hear the answer he had hoped for, that he'd waited so long for. "I'm glad, Mary."

Mary stared at her steaming mug. "After you and I talked the other day, the fear seemed to lose its hold."

"Ben will be wonderful for you."

Mary nodded, still staring into her mug. "I already knew that. It's whether I could be any good. . . ."

"Forget those lies. Ben's not like that."

"But they stick, you know."

She did know. Every one of the things Aunt Carrie had said were lodged somewhere inside her. Some had been carelessly dropped and sunken innocuously inside. Others had been driven directly through her heart. Alessi fought to ignore them, refused even one gaining entrance into her mind now. That was done. She would not spend what years were left to her being poisoned by them.

The fire crackled and popped as she ate the next quarter of her sandwich and watched the twins play with the Beanie Babies that had made the trip in their pockets. "I wonder how Diana's going to manage with all her family coming for a big gourmet meal."

Mary blew on the surface of her tea. "Dave'll rig up something. I wouldn't be surprised if he's got a generator running all her lights and appliances."

"Could he do that?"

"Sure. He's a mechanical whiz."

Alessi looked out at the swirling wind. "Where would he get one today?"

Mary sipped. "From the garage. He has everything you'd ever need in there."

Lyn jumped up. "Can we play in Ben's room?"

"No." Mary shook her head. "It'll be cold."

Cait landed a soft unicorn on Mary's knee. "We want to play under the covers with our Beanies."

Lyn leaned into her mother's lap. "Please."

"I'm sure Ben doesn't want you in his bed."

"It's all right with me." Ben turned from the window where he still stood with Steve. What were they discussing? "If it's too cold, come out."

Alessi looked at the men in sober-faced discussion, yet Ben had heard as soon as there was need. He was so right for Mary, for her little girls. A painful, ignored longing twisted inside her.

"Mommy, why don't they want us?"

"Who, honey?"

"*Our family.*"

"*Because they don't know what they're missing, sweetie.*"

And Steve had kindled feelings and thoughts that only made the longing worse. She finished her tea in silence, closing her eyes and letting the fire's warmth lull her. She stirred when the cup was removed from her hands but didn't open her eyes. She'd slept so poorly the last few nights. It was catching up to her. . . . She drifted again and imagined Steve's arms around her.

"*I'm sure Steve doesn't want you in his bed.*"

"*It's all right with me.*" *He turned and one side of his face peeled down, exposing an eyeball and gore. She screamed and struggled, but he wouldn't let her go.* "*I won a kiss.*" *Backing away, she saw the hurt in his one good eye, smelled the unforgiveness rotting his flesh. She struggled to escape, but a hand gripped her shoulder and she clawed at it.*

"Alessi."

Her eyes flew open to Steve's face, whole and unmarred, but she shook with the residue of fear as she drew woodsmoke into her nostrils. It was worse than a dream; almost a premonition. It left a dread that didn't fade with waking.

"Are you all right?"

There were voices and shuffling in the hall, but only Steve was in the den with her. "I must have fallen asleep."

"You've napped four hours."

Alessi bunched her hair with one hand. "Four hours?" The light had changed, shadows grown.

"Slept all through dominoes and charades. I'm sure you needed to." He cocked his head. "Though it wasn't all that peaceful from the sound of it."

She rubbed her face. "I had a dream."

"Bad?"

She nodded.

"You want to talk about it?" He stretched his arm behind her shoulders.

Would he take his kiss? The dream images returned with a vengeance. "No."

"Might help."

She shook her head. That would definitely not help. Not with Steve's being the face in her dream, and her dream so close and real. Sudden dread coursed her veins. Could it be a warning? Steve couldn't be . . .

Her thoughts flew. She hadn't looked at anyone and thought: Is it him? Is it her? Why would she think it now? And about Steve! But he'd been so angry to find her there in the first place. And the night of the donuts? He had pulled her out of the street, stopped her searching. Add to that the almost predatory kiss.

Alessi trembled. The mask? He would have had only minutes to get in to the phone, but Ben had answered first. Had there been time? She couldn't think clearly. He had gone out before she was doused with ice water and had shown up shortly after. To view her misery?

She must be losing her mind. The stress of it all was catching up with her. But he had discouraged her at every step from talking about things and going to the sheriff with more. He knew her comings and goings better than anyone. But why? He had no reason to hate her. Unless it was some way to strike back at Barb or his mother? She'd seen his unforgiveness. Was it neurosis? She started to shake. He'd asked her again and again to trust him. Part of the thrill?

She shot a glance to the window. It was growing dim outside. She must have slept as long as he said. He brushed the hair back behind her shoulder. She shuddered.

He turned her to face him. "What's the matter?"

"I dreamed you . . . your face was like the mask." She searched his eyes as she said it, searched for any sign, any . . .

He took her hand and brushed it over his cheek. "It's just the way it should be."

Was she crazy to even think it? Steve had helped her more than anyone. Yet . . .

Cait peeked around the corner and crept over, Lyn on her heels. "Are you awake?"

Steve eased back.

Alessi nodded. "I'm awake."

"Look what I made." She pulled from her pocket a candy cane turned into a reindeer with pipe-cleaner antlers and a tiny pompon nose.

"I made one too." Lyn pulled hers out, though the nose was gone.

"Your Rudolf's nose fell off." Cait pointed.

Lyn frowned, digging around in her pocket. "Here it is. Ben!" She took off down the hall. "I need more glue."

"Let me see that." Steve reached for Cait's candy cane reindeer. "Do you know the song?"

Cait nodded.

"Let's hear it."

Cait shrank inside herself.

She's afraid of him. The thought was clear and obvious. She had obeyed in surrendering her reindeer, but she couldn't sing, not in a million years. Alessi said, "I'll sing with you, Cait, but I'm not sure I know it all." She began, "Rudolf the . . ."

Softly, almost in a whisper, Cait joined in. Lyn came back around the corner, watching and listening while she held the newly glued nose in place. Steve added his voice.

Alessi glanced at him when Lyn joined the singing. The girls must know him a little if he'd been back most of a year and Ben had dated Mary all that time. Maybe they hadn't spent much time together. Had Steve's grief made him gruff and scary—or was he truly scary?

Lyn crept closer, her voice stronger than Cait's.

"Then one foggy Christmas Eve . . ." Steve held out his hand and Lyn stepped into it, snuggling up against his knee. "Santa came to say . . ."

He stopped singing and both girls continued, "Rudolf with your nose so bright, won't you guide my sleigh tonight." Their voices were precious.

Alessi stopped and listened as they finished together with a gleeful "His-to-ry."

Lyn climbed into Steve's lap, holding her reindeer sideways to keep the nose from sliding off. Steve's hand supported her waist. How could she even be thinking such horrible things? It hurt to doubt him. Her heart quavered, and she looked away. Steve and the twins sang "Jingle Bells," ha-ha-ha-ing, but she stared into the fire, trying to catch hold of Christmas hope and peace. And trust. The trust he kept asking for.

She was always an uneasy napper and usually woke discombobulated. But this was worse. This was as though a heavy pall had been cast over her. He had toyed with her in chess, leading her to a point of confidence, then revealing something she didn't know. It had seemed playful, but could it have been something else? Something sinister, when it had felt so . . . affectionate? A hollow opened inside.

Ben and Mary came back, arms laden with sleeping bags, blankets, and pillows. Ben said, "We'll just set you all up near the fire. You'll be warm enough there."

"Can we make our beds now?" Cait tugged his sleeve.

"Not yet. You might get walked on."

The small room was nearing capacity. Alessi felt stifled.

"And we need to get through to make your dinner," Ben said.

"What are we having?" Lyn looked into his face.

"Let's see . . . worm stew, crispy crawlies, and—"

"Eww!" Both voices squealed.

Alessi's heart squeezed. What a great family they would be. Gloom such as she rarely experienced gripped her. She had to go. Any minute she'd be in tears, and she could not bear Steve's comfort. She had felt too much in his embrace, and now her doubts were eating her up. The smell of the fire was suddenly thick in her nose, and she wanted air.

She had to be crazy to think there was something wrong with Steve. She was the one out of sync. The Christmas tree, scenting the room with subtle pine and hung with fishing flies, the singing voices of children— once again she was the one looking in with longing. Like Dickens's Ebe-nezer outside his nephew's party. She grasped at past memories of her mother, of other Christmases, of games and imaginations, but they only made her want to cry.

Ben said, "I've got some canned stew or spaghetti we could heat up without too much fuss."

Alessi's chest quivered. She had to go. If Ben opened one can she would fall apart. What was happening? She slipped out of Steve's arm and went to the window. The wind had died down while she slept, only occasional gusts tossing the snow now. The sky was clearing, too, though it was still cloudy near the setting sun.

She thought of the sun's halo that had brought her there. Where was its promise? Angels could not guard her heart. They might keep her safe from harm, but they could not shield her from her own hurt. She had to do that. And she couldn't do it with all the crazy thoughts spinning in her head.

She went to the closet and took out Steve's jean jacket. While every-one argued over what to heat for dinner, she slipped out the front door.

thirty

STEVE WATCHED HER WALK OUT. Story of his life. She had seemed all right earlier, then she'd fallen asleep and woken miserable. A bad dream. And he'd been in it. Maybe the threat of another kiss was just too much. He should not have leveraged it, made it seem rapacious. He'd been playing, but she obviously hadn't taken it that way.

He'd driven her out of the warm house into the cold. Maybe she just needed some space. Then he shook himself. She shouldn't be out there alone. He wouldn't expect anyone to bother her today, but he hadn't anticipated any of the other times.

Was someone out there watching her, stalking her? She'd been followed home from Mary's. Steve eased Lyn off his lap and stood up. Ben was insisting worm stew built strong bones. The girls were not buying it.

Steve put on his leather coat and went out. The air, between gusts, was not too cold, and the wind had definitely lost its punch. He searched around until he saw Alessi standing near the gas pumps in front of Ben's station. Had she thought her car would be back? She lowered her head and started toward the store.

He'd give her room, just keep an eye out. He reached the pumps. If she turned around she'd see him, but she kept her gaze forward and walked on. She stopped outside his store and looked into the window a long time. It could not be the display that had her entranced; must be something in her own mind. Probably wondering why she ever walked through the door and put herself at his mercy. It had been one hurt after another ever since.

He waited. Would she be upset he'd followed her? He just didn't want her frightened or hurt. He wanted to guard her. Why? And from whom?

She started down the side between the stores, and he tensed. It appeared no one was out except them, but he couldn't be sure. He hurried across the street and past the gift store. Her shriek shot fire through his veins, and he ran.

Alessi dropped the sleeve of the sweater, the ribboned cashmere she'd wished to have back. But it wasn't the sweater that had wrenched the scream from her. She pressed her hands to her face, shuddering. That poor animal.

Why—who?

She sensed, as much as heard, someone lunging at her. Adrenaline spiking, she spun, fists ready, but he caught her arms. *Steve! Fight— run—cry.*

"What's the matter?"

Shaking, she pointed to the snow-blown bundle on the stoop outside the door. "That's my sweater."

"From your car?" He looked down and kicked the bundle open. The skull was fresh enough to have flesh and fur still clinging. The arms of the sweater had been tied around it, and when she'd stooped to pick it up . . . Why would someone do something so horrible?

Steve caught her shoulders. "You're staying at the house. I'm not taking no for an answer."

He tugged, but she stood rooted. Fear worse than ice water chilled her spine. Was it a dog? She tried to shake away the horror, but it clung. Cruelty she could not grasp.

"Come on, Alessi." He tugged her arm.

She didn't move. Who could do that? Rivers of ice water wouldn't hurt as bad. Steve tugged again. If someone would hurt a creature just to terrify her . . .

Steve made her look at him. "Alessi, come with me now."

She swallowed. "I need my things."

"Okay." He took the key from her hand and let her into the building, but he didn't follow immediately. The Dumpster lid clanged outside.

Steve came in as she took down the stiff frozen things she'd hung last night and folded them. He grabbed her toothbrush, hairbrush, and dryer and put them into a packing box. Then he folded the blankets from the cot and laid the pillow atop. "What else?"

"Nothing." She clutched her clothes to her chest. What else did he think she had?

"Come on."

Her teeth were chattering when they returned to the house, but she hardly felt the cold. She stopped at the door. "Was it a dog?"

"I don't know."

She couldn't believe he could hurt something. But she couldn't believe it of anyone, so what did she know?

Ben had carols playing and the tree was lit. The power must have come on between their leaving the store and getting home. Mary gathered up her girls, and it all seemed as cheerful and warm as when she'd left.

"Sure you won't stay for worm stew?" Ben helped Mary on with her coat.

"I have things to do still." She gave him a meaningful look. "And the girls have to hang their stockings for Santa." Mary gave her a little wave, and Alessi raised her fingers automatically.

Steve added the things she held to his box and set them on the table. It would take a while for the house to heat up again, but near the fire it was baking. He seated her on the couch and crouched before her, chafing her hands. "Can I get you something?"

She shook her head, unable to stop her imagination. "It was a little dog." She sank back, stunned afresh.

"Don't think about it."

But the animal was dead, and whoever did it must not care at all.

Steve didn't like her fixation. It was almost hypnotic, the grip this incident had taken on her mind. None of the insults and attacks on herself seemed to have hit her as hard as seeing that skull. He had to admit it was grisly. Who in Charity would do such an ugly thing? Maybe everyone else had it right; it couldn't be someone he knew.

Alessi groaned. "Why are people so cruel?"

Another thing he couldn't answer. "I don't know. I wish you hadn't seen that."

Grisly as it was, it seemed to have had a much more troubling effect on her than it would on someone else. He sensed an overwhelming innocence, as though evil astonished her every time she encountered it. Even his unkind words had caught her off guard, and she wasn't protected for the next time. The ugliness in the world left no mark on her, nothing she could use to understand the next encounter. What had she said? She needed to build up her resistance? How would she? How did she keep darkness from tainting her?

The CD soloist sang, *"O holy night, the stars are brightly shining."* The fire crackled and its scent filled the room. Steve wanted to hold her, but if he did he'd never let go. He turned and stared into the flames, willing the urge to pass. They sat for long slow minutes.

Ben came in and closed the door. Seeing them, his face sobered. "What's the matter?"

Steve squeezed her knee and stood up.

Ben sat down beside her. "What's the matter, Alessi?"

The door opened, and Dave came in, stomping the snow from his shoes and puffing. "Boy, did I get—" He took in their expressions and stopped. "What's wrong?"

Well, good, they'd only have to go through it once. Steve said, "Someone wrapped a skull in one of her sweaters."

"My best one." Her hands squeezed white.

It wasn't the sweater that was stunning her, but somehow the scum had added insult to injury by choosing that particular sweater.

Dave pulled off his coat and hung it. "What sorta skull?"

Steve frowned. "Probably a dog."

"That's just mean." Dave went over and flanked her other side.

Alessi pressed her hands to her face. "I wish he hadn't hurt that poor dog."

Steve paced. "He could have found the skull. Maybe a fox or raccoon. Roadkill." He'd rather believe that than the alternative. If someone could kill an animal . . .

Ben looked at Steve. "Should we call Cooper?"

Steve shook his head. "I've tried that. He's not willing to break the pact."

Ben frowned. "Let's not—"

Alessi looked up, grabbing him with her gaze. "Pact?"

Steve searched her face. Why had someone targeted her? Did evil sense her innocence? Or was she just in the wrong place at the wrong time? Her car, her misfortune.

Ben and Dave squirmed, but she needed to understand why nothing was being done to help her. "Six years ago, something happened here in Charity—before it was called Charity."

Ben said, "Steve, I—"

Steve glared him down. No one else would tell her. They'd given their words. He had come into it after the fact and only partly bought in. "There was a guy, Duke Hansen. I know we say there's good and bad in everyone, but if Duke had good, we never saw it." He looked from Dave to Ben, confirming it. Neither one could say otherwise. "Duke beat his wife and son, and anyone who tried to interfere would have trouble—pets killed, fires, brake lines cut." He motioned to Dave. "You can vouch for that."

Dave nodded. "I replaced them."

Steve shook his head. "He was sneaky and clever. People felt helpless. It was a cancer, but they couldn't treat it without risking themselves and their loved ones."

Ben spread his hands. "Pastor Welsh tried to talk to him; the next day his wife's car ran off an embankment. His first wife."

Steve watched Alessi grasp the point. He might have shielded her from that, but maybe it was important she know the gravity of the situation. "Duke wasn't the kind of bully who ran if someone stood up to him. He got even. Decisively."

Alessi's eyes were fixed on him. Her shaking had stopped, but her stillness was almost worse.

He wasn't really the best person to tell it. He hadn't been there. But he doubted the others would break the pact. They had sworn not to tell. Steve drew a breath as he got near the bad part. "One day Duke's wife disappeared. There was a search, but all they found was a letter saying she was leaving." He looked at Dave, suddenly doubtful again. Beth hadn't seemed the type to desert her boy. But what was the type? He swallowed.

He had to be careful now. The less detail she had, the better. "Duke barged in on the church picnic and went berserk. Started smashing people's cars and anyone who got in the way. I guess it was just more than people could stand. They took him down, and when it was over, he was dead."

Alessi raised her fingers, then dropped them. No other motion or sound.

Dave cleared his throat. "We were shocked and panicked. But Pastor Welsh said we'd slain the devil and were delivered from evil." He looked at Alessi as though he could make her see. "We renamed the town Charity and made a pact to live in victory, everyone throwing in together, sharing the guilt and the freedom. Making God's kingdom on earth."

There was more to it than that, but Steve was reluctant to tell about Carl, and he knew the others wouldn't.

Ben said, "It's been real good."

She collapsed a little at that. "Until I came."

Steve said, "It's not your fault."

She straightened. "That's why no one believes me? Because the whole town wants to believe no one in Charity would do something wrong?"

"Because if Charity didn't cast out the devil . . . they had killed a man." An evil man, a purely wicked man. Maybe he was the devil, and that was enough to excuse it. But they hadn't left it there. The heart of the pact was to redeem his spawn.

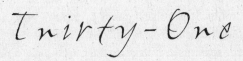

Thirty-One

ALESSI FELT HERSELF SINKING, collapsing inside. Had she ever felt so empty? Her presence in Charity had awakened the devil himself. Ben's words showed that much. *"It's been real good."* Until she drove in, they had lived something beautiful, the warmth and comfort she'd sensed when she stopped and took her first look. The magic she'd recognized in the quaint snow-covered scene. The peace as she walked the streets, even after her car was taken.

She had criticized what she didn't understand, and all the time it was her own fault. Charity. Halos. Magic. It was silly superstition. Something tore open inside, some veil that had protected her, kept her from losing hope, from seeing things the way they were. She saw now.

She had brought evil back to Charity.

Despair caught her throat like a wolf. No matter who the culprit was, she had brought out the worst in him. Steve, or someone else. She stood up. "I'm tired." It was early, but even her bones were tired. She'd slept four hours that afternoon, but it might have been days ago.

Steve said, "We'll figure it out in the morning." He got her things from the table and walked her to his room. She didn't argue.

"With the furnace on, it should be warm soon."

She nodded, but that didn't matter.

"Are you okay?"

Another nod. She closed the door and sat on the bed, feeling ripped like a piece of tissue with ragged edges. All the hurts she'd held inside stabbed her one by one. The people she'd lost, the ones she had hoped might love her, those she'd considered friends but had to leave behind. Even Ben and Dave . . . and Steve.

He had not been part of the pact. Six years ago he'd been in Alaska. So he wasn't there when they became the redeemed. She shook her head. Her suspicions no longer mattered. If she had brought out the evil in someone, it would end when she left.

The night dragged on and the house grew silent, except for Dave's snores. She had to be certain Steve was asleep, though she suspected sleep might be as elusive for him as for her. The weariness inside her did not lead to rest. It was like a cloud over drought-scorched land that dropped nothing but dust.

She waited, soaking in hurt after hurt, no longer fending them off, no longer able to. When she sensed enough time had passed, she put the black sweater on over her other. She folded Steve's jean jacket on the bed with his sweats and T-shirt and left most of the cash, keeping only enough to start somewhere else. If she wasn't keeping her word to stay through Christmas, she wouldn't keep the money either.

She cracked open the door and listened. All was still except the strangely tuneful snores from Dave's room. She crept out to the main room. The smell of the fire lingered even though the ashes held no glow. Steve's breath was soft and even. She slowly turned the front door lock, glancing over her shoulder, then opened it and went out.

Steve heard the click and raised his head, trying to place the sound.

He pushed the blanket back and sat up. All was still, except for Dave's snoring like a squashed harmonica. He searched the darkness, listening again for anything out of order. His mind was over-amped. He lay back down. What was he going to do?

He had told Alessi they'd figure it out in the morning, but how? He shouldn't make promises he couldn't keep. He just wanted a solution so badly. If he could make it right, get her car back or at least learn what happened to it, maybe she would stay.

Was that what it came down to? What he wanted with her? Were his motives that selfish? He could not get out of his mind how it felt to hold her. His kisses might have scared her, but they should have scared him worse. Only they hadn't. Kissing her had been the most right thing he'd known. And if his feelings for her were driving him now, maybe it wasn't wrong at all.

Explaining the pact had made him wonder all over again. Who had the most to lose? Carl. Who'd acted strangely—Carl. Maybe Alessi's likeness to his mother was not a discounting factor but a mitigating one. He wished he knew more about that incident. If Carl harbored rage and feelings of betrayal . . .

Steve knew well enough how destructive those emotions could be. Dad had worked him through so much. Carl was eleven when she disappeared and his father was killed. Pastor Welsh had taken him in, and all those under the pact were committed to his welfare. Redeeming Carl had become their hope. A life saved, for the one that was lost.

Now Steve wondered. Should he speak to Burton Welsh? Tell him his concerns? Could the man look at it impartially—or would he reject the scenario that could mean the crumbling of all he'd built?

————

Alessi trudged along the route they had traveled to Wal-Mart. At least the wind had almost stopped and there was a moon to light her way. A tear slid down her cheek, and she wiped it away with her shoulder. With her gone, Charity could go back to how it was. The one who took her car would not be found out, and no one would have to face the truth of it.

No doubt what had happened had been horrible. She understood the pastor's position. His own wife had been killed. Maybe there'd been no way to prove it, but he must have known who was to blame. He might have seen what followed as just retribution. Who could blame him?

And then he'd made it right for Charity. Bound them together in spirit and purpose—until she'd come and ruined it all.

Who'd have thought her little car could cause so much trouble? If she had known it would come to this, she'd have begged a ride to Chambers City and started from scratch. She wouldn't have come to know the people of Charity: Karen and Diana, so warm and fun loving. Mary and her little girls, finding happiness at last with Ben. Dave always pulling something from the shelf for her to eat or filling a cup with chocolate.

And Steve—that hurt too much for words. Maybe the dream was just a dream. She put too much stock in signs and wonders. If the halo wasn't real, why would the dream be? She could ignore it and imagine . . . No, she couldn't. She'd lost the capacity.

She pressed her eyes shut against fresh tears, too many years' worth. She felt ancient. Her fingers ached from cold, her heart from loneliness and rejection. She'd been walking at least an hour. If she sat down in the trees on the side of the road would she freeze to death, simply fall asleep and drift away?

Would that be taking her life? Or letting God have it? But she kept on, step after step, until she heard a car. Steve? She looked quickly for a place to hide, then told herself no. She kept walking.

The engine revved, and she spun at the familiar tone. Her Mustang zoomed up alongside and skidded to a stop. The driver pushed the button to lower the passenger-side window. It was dim inside, but she made out . . . the pastor's son? Her stomach clutched. No mask, no ice water or rotted skull, but dread filled her. It wasn't Steve. He had only helped. But she'd left him sleeping.

Carl leaned. "Want a ride?" In her own car?

"No thanks." She started walking, stepping into the snow alongside the road. *It does not matter. Let it go.*

"Arf, arf, arf."

Horror shot through her as the image of the poor dog's skull imprinted. She trembled. Would he run her over? But he gassed the car and zoomed past. She stared until the lights were out of sight around a bend. He was ahead of her now.

She stopped walking. What should she do? She knew who it was now. She could give the sheriff a name. And get her car back? She looked back toward Charity. She must be more than two miles out, long past shouting distance.

———————

Steve tossed. Sleep was better than brooding, but it wouldn't return. He sat up, tossed off the blankets, and stood. He looked around the room, then walked down the hall. Dave's snores proved at least one of them had accessed his REM sleep. He hoped Alessi had too. He would just peek, make sure she was fine. If she couldn't sleep, they'd talk, try to find a solution. He knocked softly, then turned the knob to Alessi's door.

The room was dark, and he opened the door farther. He couldn't see her in the bed. It seemed too square and flat. He stepped in, crept closer. He reached. The bed was empty.

He searched the room in the dark, then flicked on the light. She wasn't there. Only folded clothes and cash lying on the bed. *No!* He rushed out of the room, fumbled for his shoes. How long since he'd heard something? An hour? More? She had run out, left on foot rather than . . .

He banged Dave's and Ben's doors. "Get up, guys! She's gone."

"Gone?" Ben threw his covers off while Dave stumbled into the hall.

"Gone where?"

Steve grabbed his coat and keys. "I'll check the store." He could only hope as he ran for his truck. Maybe she'd gone there, just needing to be alone or . . . sleep on the cot instead of his more comfortable bed. Then why leave the money? Still, he checked there first. But the storeroom was empty, as he'd known it would be.

He swung back by the house for the guys. "She can't have gone far."

"But which way?" Dave rubbed his head.

"I don't know." Steve swallowed. "Dave, take your truck and check the highway. She might try to hitch a ride."

"In the middle of Christmas Eve night?" But Dave headed for the garage.

Steve climbed back into the truck. "Let's go, Ben." He grabbed the gearshift and headed toward Chambers City. "Look for footprints." He doubted anyone else had tramped off through the drifts formed earlier by the wind. Would she take cover if she heard him? She obviously didn't trust him to help. The thought sobered him.

Why should she? He'd repeatedly stabbed her underbelly. After his behavior today she'd need an antidote. He hadn't intended to scare her off, but that's exactly what he'd done. He sure did have a way with women. He smacked his steering wheel. Ben glanced up but said nothing.

Alessi walked doggedly back toward Charity, though fear crawled up her spine. Too soon she heard the sound she had dreaded and turned into the glare of headlights. He gunned the engine. She stiffened, ready to dive. Just before she lunged, he slammed the breaks and cranked the wheel, spinning right beside her and jerking to a stop. Snow flew into her face.

He leaned toward the open window again. "Get in. I'll take you for a spin."

She backed away. "Leave me alone. You have the car."

He jerked it into park. She started running before his door was open but heard him coming behind. Her legs were long, and fear compelled her. But she could hear his breath puffing as he closed the gap. He was big.

Lord, help me! It struck her that she didn't want to die, not like this, like the dog whose skull had made her think crazy things. He grabbed her, crashing to the ground on top of her. Her face dug into the snow, filling her mouth and nose. She sputtered and spit, writhing under his weight. He bent her arm and wrenched it back.

She tried to throw him off, but he increased the pressure and the pain. It would break! She stopped fighting. "What do you want? Leave me alone."

"Oh no." He stroked the snow from her cheek, slowly pulling her arm tighter, bringing pain she couldn't hide. "You're the one who does that."

Does what? What was he saying? "Please."

"I saw your letter."

"What letter?"

He jerked her arm and a searing pain filled her shoulder. "You should have stayed dead." With his other hand he ground her face into the snow.

She couldn't breathe. Her lungs burned and screamed for air. She thrashed, but he pressed his knee into her spine and jerked her head back by her hair.

She gasped a breath before he smashed it down again, laughing. "Let me hear you beg. Arf, arf. Don't chop my head off."

Oh, God!

He jerked her up and rolled her over, cramming his knee into her belly. Again she couldn't breathe, though her airways were freed.

"Let me hear it. Arf, arf."

She gasped, grabbing at his leg, then aimed a swing at his crotch.

He dodged and caught both arms, pressing them down into the snow. "For that, it'll be slow." He ground his knee harder, jammed it into her solar plexus.

Her diaphragm froze. Her head grew thick. Mom and Dad in heaven. She'd have a place there. But he lifted his knee, and her breath returned with a sucking groan.

He laughed. "Now you know what it was like. To be left with him." Her chest heaved with panicked breaths. She wanted to cry out, but no words would come. She heard a car, something louder, bigger than her Mustang. He heard it, too, and with a look of pure evil closed his hands around her throat. She arched and thrashed, but his knee pressed in with all his weight and kept her pinned. Her senses paled. Why were her hands twitching?

Steve caught the red Mustang in his headlights and it all became clear. The car was real; Alessi was real. He'd believed, but not viscerally, as he did now. Something moved, a dark form on the side of the road.

It separated, and part rose up into a man running. The other part didn't move.

Steve jammed on the brakes, shoved the gearshift into neutral and set the brake, then lurched out as Carl ran for the Mustang. Every killer instinct said chase him down, but he ran instead to Alessi on the side of the road. She lay like a discarded mannequin, and he dropped down beside her. "Alessi."

She wasn't breathing. *No!* He grabbed her up into his arms and shook her. "Alessi!"

"I don't think I will grow old. I think both parents dying early is a sign, like a warning for me." He clutched her tight as the awful ache grew inside.

———

The light was more beautiful than any she'd ever seen, aglow with colors she couldn't name, yet at the same time whiter than white. A longing so deep, a surety of love unsurpassed drew her forward, up and away from the fragile shell that had held her. She no longer needed it. She was lighter than air, swifter than wind. And love encompassed her, touching the places she'd been pierced with light like fire that sealed them shut and made them whole.

Nothing mattered anymore, nothing hurt. She soared, she flew, carried on balmy air, yet she didn't need lungs to draw it in. The horror of not breathing left her. It was all right now. Nothing marred the perfect peace surrounding her. No sorrow, no fear. Yet she was alone. She searched the light, but though it seemed a tangible presence, it was at the same time empty of form. She was alone.

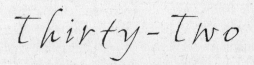

Thirty-Two

"LET HER GO!" BEN WRENCHED HER from his arms and pressed her to the ground, shoving Steve out of the way. He watched, desperation mounting as Ben pressed his mouth to hers. Didn't he realize it was too late? They were too late. Ben puffed and pressed as the moments passed. Was her windpipe crushed? Was there internal injury?

Tears burned Steve's cheeks, and he wanted to punch Ben and scream "Leave her alone!"

A faint sucking wheeze. Air passing through her throat? Steve pressed in as Ben raised his face from hers. More wheezing. Not normal breath. But she was alive. Steve caught up her limp body. He chafed her face. "Alessi."

No response. Her skin was freezing, but she didn't shiver.

"Get her in the truck," Ben said. "I'll drive."

Steve grabbed her up into his arms and carried her to the truck, terror making him strong. Ben opened the door, and Steve slid into the seat with her still limp in his arms. She might be breathing, but it was not right. Ben ran around to his side and jammed the truck into gear.

"Chambers City," Steve rasped, though why he was giving directions was beyond him. Ben was the one thinking clearly. Steve had given up the moment he saw her lying there. The Chambers City hospital was small but the best they had. And there was at least one doctor he trusted. The woman who had seen his father through his last days. Was he bringing Alessi there to die? *Lord, no.* He clutched her tighter as Ben drove. *Hang on, Alessi. Hang on.*

Ben pulled up to the emergency entrance, left the truck running, and burst inside. Moments later the staff rushed out with him, and Steve surrendered her. They laid Alessi on a gurney and rolled her into the hospital, though she still showed no response. Steve stayed beside her as an IV was inserted, and he considered it God's hand when Dr. Liz Deklin came in.

He clenched his hands and blurted, "She was attacked and strangled. She's breathing, but it's not right."

The nurse handed over the chart with Alessi's vitals. Dr. Deklin ordered a respirator. Steve paced. A respirator was not good news, but in Alessi's condition . . . He glanced at Ben, thanking God one of them thought positively. Where he had assumed the worst, Ben had taken action. Steve kicked himself. He was the ranger; he had the training. But when it came right down to it, he'd collapsed.

"Steve." Dr. Deklin laid a hand on his arm. "Go out to the waiting room."

"Is she going to be all right?"

"I need to assess her condition." She pushed him out of the cubicle after Ben. They found their way to the waiting area. A vanilla-scented candle muted the antiseptic smell of hospital and fear.

Steve ran a hand through his hair. "Ben, I—"

"Good thing you woke up when you did."

Steve stared at him. Sure, he'd played a part, getting them out to search. But Ben had saved her life. "You got her breathing. I thought she was gone."

Ben nodded. "I thought so too."

But he'd acted anyway. Steve pressed a hand to his eyes and rubbed his face. "You kept your head."

"I'm not as close to it."

What did that mean? But he knew. He wasn't hiding anything from Ben. If he loved her, why wasn't he the one to give her breath? He'd assumed she would be taken away. He always assumed the worst. What reason did he have not to?

Ben said, "I'm gonna call Dave. He'll be wondering."

Steve tried to focus on his words. Dave. Was he still driving the highway looking for her? Or had he gone back to the house? It didn't matter. Steve paced the small room, waiting. What could take so long? Dr. Deklin was treating Alessi's injuries. He had to be patient.

Ben spoke into the phone on the corner table. "Dave? Alessi's been hurt. We're at the Chambers City Hospital."

A pause, then, "She's hurt real bad."

Steve snatched the phone. "Call Cooper and tell him . . . it's Carl." Steve hung up, shaking. He had guessed Carl and had been too weak to act on it, too insecure to believe his own intuition.

"Don't go there, Steve. No one expected this."

Steve shook him off. "Why not?"

Ben tucked his chin. "We're just ordinary folks."

That didn't excuse it. He should have known. Somehow. He went to the machine and got a cup of coffee.

Two bitter cups later, the doctor came out. Her face was grim. He did not want to see her face so grim. Her hair was soft gray curls around a square jaw, and her indistinct blue-green eyes were carefully guarded.

"Well?" Steve said.

"If there was something surgically or even neurologically that could be done, we would airlift her to a bigger hospital."

He nodded. They could take Alessi anywhere as long as they helped her. Then he realized she had said if. Cold dread crept through his limbs.

"I'm sorry. She was too long without oxygen."

He was suddenly airless himself. Dave rushed in as the doctor continued to speak.

"There is very little brain activity, only the most basic functions. We intubated her before we knew the full extent of the injury, or I might not have."

Steve stared into her face. "Is she going to make it?"

She laid a hand on his arm. She had to have something more useful to tell him. "We've made her as comfortable as we can."

She'd spoken those very words about his dad when there was nothing more they could do. But Dad had been seventy-three with hypertension and a weak heart, not a young woman with her whole life ahead. Not Alessi, who hadn't even seen it coming, who had no resistance to cruelty. Not the madcap, crazy-haired girl who wanted to see his waterfall.

Dave looked from him to Ben, not comprehending the awful news he'd walked in on.

Steve squeezed his empty cup. "So what do we do?" The doctor must have some plan, some go-ahead formula.

Dr. Deklin studied him. "It may require a decision, but I doubt it."

Decision? What decision?

"I think she will drift away."

That penetrated. He'd imagined her drifting away ever since she came. But not like this. Forever but not . . . from life. He swallowed the pain in his throat. It didn't matter that Ben had made her breathe. She would still drift away.

Dr. Deklin had a hint of medicinal halitosis, a scent he associated with his father's death and which he supposed would now be part of his memories of Alessi. "You can see her in a few minutes." She squeezed his arm and included the others in her glance. "I've alerted the police. They'll want a statement."

And he would give it, the pact be damned.

After the doctor left, Dave cleared his throat. "What happened?"

Steve's voice had rusted. "She left." That was the crux of it. She had walked out.

Dave shook his head. "Why would she leave?"

And then the searing started. There was a reason, always a reason. He just couldn't ever find it. Why did his mother leave? The strain of a two-year-old? Regrets about marrying a man twice her age? Poison coursed, then passed. Had she been broken herself? Confused, insecure, unstable? He would never know. Might never know Barb's reason either.

She had said she felt stifled in the backward town. Hated the way people looked at her. He'd been so focused on keeping his word to his father, grieving the few moments they'd shared before his death. Maybe she left because he pulled away.

Ben said, "We can go in now."

They went into the ICU cubicle where Alessi lay with a machine breathing for her and wires attached to her head. Steve clenched his hand, wanting to smash something.

Dave looked at her and swallowed. "What happened to her?"

All he could think to say was evil. But while that was true, it told Dave nothing. "Carl strangled her. He had her Mustang."

"Carl Welsh?"

"Or Hansen." Steve glanced up. "Duke's son."

Waves of agony crashed upon him as he thought of Alessi's terror. Ben sank into the metal chair as though the reality was only now hitting him as well.

Steve's throat worked against the lump. He dropped to the rolling stool beside the bed and reached through the rail to her hand. Too long without oxygen. If they'd gotten there sooner, just minutes sooner . . .

Her hand was cool but not as icy as it had been. He held her wrist and found a pulse. Her heart pumped; circulation warmed her. He could believe strength returned. What did the doctors know? But the electrodes on her skull told the story. Her brain was dying. Her wonderful, fanciful mind.

Tears came, and he didn't stop them. *Lord God.* Is this what Charity's pact would cost them? A life for a life? Carl Hansen had seen his father fall, watched Charity's citizens bludgeon him to death. Whether he loved or hated his father mattered little. He was already twisted inside. He must have been.

And the rest of them? They'd become righteous, gnawing the pact like a holy bone until a stranger's misfortune became her death. He dropped his head and stroked Alessi's fingers, which had placed the pieces on his chessboard, moving her pawn forward in a dogged but futile attempt to reach the end. In the same way she had pushed forward, trying to find her car, the one thing she had in the world, and no one had seen the move coming where Carl took the queen. Steve rubbed his face and sniffed.

Ben spoke softly. "The police are here."

Steve and Ben told what they'd seen, whom they'd seen. It would be a blow to Burton and Madeline and all the others who believed. But making the statement felt good. He wanted them to suffer. And then he didn't.

The police left, and Steve wondered who had jurisdiction, control of dark empty roads at night. He pictured Alessi crumpled on the snowy ground and waves of fury smothered him. He shook.

Dave had pulled an extra chair in from the empty cubicle next to theirs. "I just don't know why she'd go." He glanced at Steve as though Steve had chased her off again. Maybe he had.

Ben said, "She was probably scared. We shouldn't have told her about the pact."

Dave shifted in his seat. "We should have gone to Cooper."

"I did," Steve snapped. "The old fool wouldn't listen."

Dave shook his head. "She would have been safe with us."

They stopped talking. What else was there to say? They could beat themselves up and try to figure out Alessi's motives forever. It wouldn't change anything. They sat as the night passed and dawn must be breaking outside on a grim Christmas morning. Alessi had promised to stay through Christmas. Steve clung to her fingers and whispered, "We had a deal."

The others stirred and shared a glance. The dawn should have been a beacon of hope and promise. A fresh start. Instead . . . Steve lowered his head and continued his vigil.

Some time later, Ben crossed over to him and squeezed his shoulder. "We ought to go to the church."

Dave nodded. "Get everyone to pray."

Steve scowled. Hadn't they heard the doctor? There was nothing to be done. Her brain was dying, dead except for the most basic functions. Prayer did not bring people back from the dead.

"It's Christmas. Everyone'll be there." Dave looked like he might find a miracle in his stocking. As though the pact were still real. And they had power and victory.

Steve wanted to knock their skulls together. "So go."

Again Ben's hand on his shoulder. "Come with us, Steve."

"I'm not leaving her." All that was left was for him to be there.

Then Dave cleared his throat. "She doesn't know we're here."

Steve shot a glance and saw the tears in Dave's eyes. They were hurting too. Did they really think there was something they could do? Maybe they needed to believe that. Maybe he needed it too. He rubbed a hand over his face. "All right."

Ben drove them to the church in the truck. He had kept the keys, and Steve didn't argue. Already people were gathering for the Christmas service. Had Burton been informed? Steve looked at the pastor's house tucked back behind the church. Other lives were shattering today.

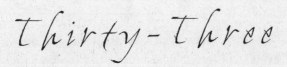

Thirty-Three

CARL DROVE THE MUSTANG INTO THE CAVE, a dugout, really, that they had timbered inside. But it felt like a cave. And from the outside, when he'd pushed the timbers across the bottom and released the boughs of the overhanging fir, it looked like little more than a depression. He'd brushed out the snow where he left the road, and no one came this way without a reason. It was cursed ground.

He pressed the emergency brake and sat there, shaking so hard it took him three tries to get the keys out of the ignition. He hadn't intended to be seen, not by anyone but her. Steve and Ben were not supposed to be there. *Stupid. Stupid.* He made a fist and punched his face. Blood spurted from his nose. Pain cleared his head. He gulped air and looked at the blood dripping into his lap.

He climbed out of the car. The first-aid kit was easily accessible. He could find it in the dark. And it wasn't just Band-Aids. It held tourniquets and needles and high-potency antibiotics and even anti-venoms. He fumbled as he tore a piece of bandage and held it to his swelling nose. How would he explain that? But then . . . there'd be no explaining now.

He had to just hide, lay low until they stopped looking for him. He could do it too. He had everything he needed. And he knew how to survive.

Nose throbbing but no longer gushing, he went to the front. No moonlight penetrated. He reached for the propane lantern and carried it past the Mustang, feeling only lightly as he went. He knew his way.

Confidence built as he lit the lantern. He needed a plan. The light illuminated the space, much larger than a person would guess from the opening. And it was stocked. Oh boy, was it stocked. Duke's paranoia had started it. When the government tried to take away his freedom, he'd be ready. And Carl had added things himself, taken them just as he'd taken the car. So easy.

He'd be okay. Yes, he would. He'd be okay.

The chapel was festive with Christmas finery. The decorated trees seemed overbright and gaudy, bows and garlands superfluous and insultingly joyous. Nearly every seat was filled, people who had snubbed or ignored Alessi. Steve could not judge them. No one had done more to break her spirit, to drive her out, than he.

Karen was at the piano, her eyes red puffballs, but she didn't play any of the carols she must have planned for the gathering. She played nothing at all as the people looked around and began to whisper. Pastor Welsh was not on the podium. It was Christmas morning. Where was their pastor?

They depended on him, thrived on his message, opened their throats and were fed. Now his podium stood empty and the piano was silent. What was wrong? What had happened? Panic rose in the room like flames licking at the rafters, building and spreading from one heart to another. This wasn't what they'd anticipated when they dressed this morning in their reds and greens and glittering gold.

Steve sat silently, dreading each minute that passed. He should have stayed at the hospital. These people were sheep. What could they do? What could any of them do? Karen looked his way with flooded eyes, but no one else seemed to know. They shifted in their seats and looked at their neighbors.

Then Ben stood up. He made his slow way to the front and didn't stop even then. He climbed the platform stairs and stood behind the podium. Murmurs of shock and anticipation. Steve studied his face, long and serious, yet . . . compassionate too. Ben was doing better with this than he. But, as he'd said, he was not as close to it.

He cared about Alessi, had right from the start. But he hadn't fallen in love with the angel who tumbled into their midst. What would Ben say? Would he just blurt it out?

Ben dropped his head in silence, then looked up and said, "Two thousand years ago a stranger came to Israel."

He was going to preach? Give a sermon while Alessi lay dying? Steve felt betrayed. He couldn't look at Ben, who seemed more concerned with ceremony than a dying woman.

"Came with nothing to recommend him, and every door was closed except a hillside stable. Though the heavens opened in song and even the night sky proclaimed his birth, only a handful of outcast shepherds paid attention. The innkeepers were too busy, the Pharisees too important, the scribes too learned. They had no interest in an inconvenient stranger."

Steve wanted to shout, "That was two thousand years ago! What about now?"

Ben said, "A little more than two weeks ago a stranger came to Charity, came with little to recommend her, and what little she had was taken away."

Steve's throat went dry.

Ben looked directly at him. "Some of us did a little. But mostly we ignored the stranger in our midst, hoping her trouble would not become ours. We wore our freedom like a badge, like membership in the Charity Club, only we'd forgotten the meaning of the word."

Steve could hardly believe it was Ben up there speaking so truly, so eloquently.

Ben looked over the people. "'I was a stranger and you did not invite me in.'" He bent his head. "Father, forgive us for not recognizing you."

Moments stretched in silence. Steve felt each beat of his heart. Did Alessi's still beat? He ought to be there beside her.

Ben looked up. "Last night Alessi Moore was viciously attacked."

Gasps filled the chapel. Heads turned and people whispered frantic questions.

Ben hadn't given any details, hadn't even named Carl. Maybe that was better. Keep the focus on Alessi and nothing else.

Ben said, "It doesn't look good. In fact, it's medically hopeless."

Now there was silence as those words sank in. Steve felt them take hold and drag him down somewhere cold.

"But we are not people without hope." Ben's voice rang out.

False hope. Maybe her body systems would drag on awhile. What life was that? Would they pray to prolong it? Yet his throat tightened at the thought of letting her go. Just a little longer, then he could let her go. Or could he?

Ben said, "We have a God who surpasses hope, and so we turn to Him, the One who cares for even a sparrow who has lost her way."

Not a sparrow, a dove. Pure and innocent and unsuspecting. A sacrifice. Steve's throat tightened so hard it almost closed up.

Ben said, "Some of us got to know her, and it might help us pray if we shared our stories."

Stories? Where was he taking this?

But Mary was right there with him. She stood up from a seat near the front. "Alessi changed my life. She gave me courage to love again, made me see the good and put the bad behind me. She said love was a rare and precious thing. She was right." Tears streamed down her cheeks.

Dave stood up. "Alessi had a way of making things matter. Stuff you wouldn't think was special mattered a lot to her, and then it sort of mattered a lot to you too. She helped me decorate our tree; first time she'd ever had one. I think her face lit up better than the lights." He cleared his throat. "And she said Christmas was not about Jesus' dying for us so much as His living for us. How He blessed people while He lived. I can't tell it like she did." He cleared his throat again, tried to say more, then sat back down.

Karen said, "Alessi Moore was the sort of person you felt like you'd known forever. There wasn't anything false or fake about her. She was real." She dabbed her eyes and leaned against the piano.

Steve's chest constricted. *"Your Pollyanna con might fool Ben and Dave, but I see through you."* How blind he'd been.

And it just went on. People who'd only moments with her, sharing their comments, their impressions.

"I went in to buy a book, and she spent all kinds of time making sure I found what I really wanted." Dierdre Gaines sniffed. "I wasn't even friendly."

Sue Jolsten added, "She helped me at the store too. Looked right into my eyes when she talked, and explained why I ought to choose one thing over another. As though it mattered to her what I walked out with."

Moll stood up, clutching herself.

Moll?

"She always said my food was good. Even when I wouldn't talk to her." She sat down, stone-faced and probably a little stunned.

He was stunned too. He wanted to shout for them all to stop it, just stop it.

Diana said, "Alessi called my praline parfaits fairy ambrosia. And she said it with tears in her eyes." Diana sobbed. "I've never known anyone like her."

Debbie said, "She was my friend."

And those few words were the most devasting of all.

Down, down he sank. The service had become a wake. Of them all, he could say the most. He'd spent the time with her, knew her story, the things she'd told him. All she'd wanted was a place to belong, to be loved and trusted. He'd been the one to kiss her. His throat squeezed, remembering Ben's mouth puffing air into her lifeless lungs, an action that a machine now repeated. Too late. It was all too late.

Ben folded his hands on the podium. "Alessi Moore came to Charity for a purpose. Nothing happens by chance, nothing in this life. We can ignore her appearance and pretend it never happened. People have ignored Jesus born in that stable." He pointed to the plaster nativity beneath the cluster of Christmas trees. "But in the Lord's own words, 'Whatever you did for one of the least of these brothers of mine, you did for me.'" He looked around the room.

"I don't know how we can make it right, except by taking to our knees right now and begging God's mercy."

Steve stared at him. Mercy, yes. Mercy to end her suffering. Yet selfishly he wanted more. Just through Christmas. If he could just look at her, hold her hand . . .

"Mercy for Alessi Moore, and mercy for ourselves because . . ." Ben let the word hang. "One way or another, our lives have changed." He meant the pact was over.

Steve didn't care about any of that. He had to get out, had to get back. But Ben had his keys. He got up anyway and made it to the back door. He knew from personal experience that prayer didn't change things. He had prayed for his mother to come back, prayed that Barb wouldn't leave. He had prayed for Dad to recover. Maybe prayer helped in unseen ways, gave strength or comforted, but it didn't change what would happen anyway.

It was like children throwing themselves against a bulldozer. Prayer gave the dozer rubber bumpers to limit their injury, but it never changed direction, never halted course, just kept pressing through their lives. He staggered, and Amanda was at his side.

"Steve, are you all right? I am so terribly sorry." Her sincerity caught him unawares. She walked outside with him. "Is there anything I can do?"

He looked back at the church, guessing she wasn't inclined to bend a knee in her white wool pants. But maybe she was the answer to his prayer. "Will you drive me back to the hospital?"

"Of course." She slipped her arm through his and guided him to her Lexus. As they climbed in she asked, "Do you want to stop for flowers?"

He turned and stared at her. Alessi wouldn't know one way or another. She would neither see nor smell them ever again. He said, "Yes. Thanks."

She started the engine. "Oh, nothing will be open. It's Christmas."

"That's all right."

"Wait. I have something. We'll swing by my place." She drove smoothly to her home, left him staring out the window, and went inside. She returned with a winter bouquet of evergreens, red roses, and white poinsettias, accented with gold and purple berries. So beautiful—Alessi would have loved it.

"Thank you." He breathed its rose and juniper scent as she drove once again.

She pulled up to the entrance that was nearest the ICU and put the car in park. "Do you want me to come in?"

He shook his head, then leaned over and kissed her cheek. "Thanks, Amanda." He carried the bouquet inside. He should have offered to pay her for it. She probably had it for a table piece. But he headed to Alessi's room and carried the flowers to a shelf that didn't seem to be needed for anything at the moment.

It was a large, expensive bouquet that spread out at either side. He imagined Alessi's expression if she could see it, the one she had worn for Dave's Christmas tree, before he crushed her spirits. "Hey, Alessi. Brought you some flowers." He sat down beside her. "I bet you can smell them from here." He swallowed. "To be honest, they were Amanda's."

He took her long fingers in his. "Hope you don't mind. No place was open to buy some. Oh. Merry Christmas." Why was he babbling? Even unconscious she drew him out. He stared down at her as she lay still, the respirator bulging her lips out as it noisily put her lungs through the motions.

Steve tightened his clasp. "I was just at the church. You should have heard the nice things people said about you." No one had said them to her face. Well, maybe Karen and Diana and Ben and Dave. Maybe Mary and the girls. They'd done well by her. "You've given Charity back its heart." And annihilated his.

How could he go back to the store and not have her working on the shelves? How could he enter the storeroom and not see her sitting there, elbows to her knees, telling him off as he deserved. That was where he first kissed her.

Pain squeezed his vocal cords. How must it have felt to have Carl's hands crushing hers? "I'm just sorry I . . ." He was going to say he was sorry he hadn't stopped it from happening, but there were so many things he regretted, he didn't know where to start.

He stroked her hand as tears fell. "We get in these tunnels, and it doesn't seem there's any other way to go but one." He sniffed. "Mine's dark and long, and I don't think I can come out of it alone." Then he felt like a scumbag complaining to her. He thought his tunnel was bad?

He shook with the tears. "I'm sure you want to go." He brought her hand to his lips. "But I can't say good-bye yet. So I'm holding you to our bargain. We'll spend Christmas together, like we said."

He hadn't planned the date. What would they have done? Gone into Chambers City for dinner? Or cooked it at the house and played chess. He might have let her win. But she'd have noticed. He smiled, but it brought fresh tears.

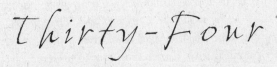

Thirty-Four

BURTON WELSH HAD FELT THIS WAY one other time in his life—when they told him Sarah was gone. Impotence as all encompassing as death filled his mouth with questions, yet he couldn't utter one. He'd been in prayer when the police came, polishing his triumphant Christmas message, when they asked if Carl was home.

Carl? Of course he was home. But the bed was empty and the racing bike gone. Where had he gone, what mischief committed? But the police had sat him down with Madeline and explained, and every sense of victory had crumbled to dust. He looked at his wife now and murmured, "Did you know?"

She dropped her gaze to her hands.

"Madeline, tell me."

"I didn't know. But . . ." Her eyes held agony, and he knew it was for him. "I suspected some things."

"What things?"

"Sneaking out. Stealing things."

Stealing things. Like cars? A pain throbbed in his temple. Had he ever suspected? At the start he'd been vigilant, firm, ever present. Until Carl made his commitment to Christ and Burton dared to believe. In his audacity he believed he had worked a miracle. "Did you see him?"

She shook her head. "I didn't want to . . . doubt."

Pain and guilt. How many others had he called to blindness? A pharisaical pact of righteousness in the face of truth. He had condoned murder. Not wanting good people to suffer, and knowing that, though he struck no blow, in his heart he cried for blood more loudly than the rest, he had condoned what should have been confessed.

The man responsible for Sarah's death had lain in his own blood, bludgeoned by the crowd, and with his own vengeance slaked, he had proclaimed it an act of God. Then in a tremendous act of love, he had taken the man's son as his own. He called the people to share in the redemptive work of saving Carl from Duke's curse.

Eleven years of abuse would not go away easily, but he would be a father to the boy; he would be Christ to him. They would all be Christ to him. And for the life they had taken they would present Carl, pure and unblemished. Burton dropped his face to his hands. Madeline cried softly.

"Do you know where he is?" His voice was a ghost, no longer vital.

She shook her head and sniffed. "How far could he go?"

"He has the car." Had it all along, while they pretended no one among them could have taken it.

A well of despair opened up. He had told Alessi Moore to relinquish it, to stop accusing and accept that the Lord giveth and the Lord taketh away. And now he thought of her, lying near death in the Chambers City hospital. Another sacrifice to his pride. *Lord God*. He was empty of words, empty of promise.

Jesus. Oh, Jesus. He had betrayed his Lord and betrayed his flock. He had raised the scepter and ruled God's kingdom on earth. Where else would he find such devotion, where such hunger for his words, such commitment to his charge? He could redeem them, shepherd them into the kingdom, and present them blameless.

Burton groaned. Six years he had justified the blood lust and preached freedom and redemption. What had Carl heard? That God condoned murder, considered it triumph? That Duke's life had been righteously trampled out like grapes of wrath before the Lord? How deeply he had failed. When Alessi died, he would carry her murder on his own heart.

Madeline came and knelt at his side. She didn't say he couldn't have known or that he'd done the best he could. She said, "I love you."

Ben and Dave came back. The service must have ended. Steve was glad he hadn't stayed. He swiped at his eyes. "Look, guys. You both have people to be with. Go spend Christmas with your loved ones." No one knew how many special times they would have.

Ben shuffled. "We don't want you alone here."

"I'm not." He looked into Alessi's expressionless face. She had agreed to Christmas together. He'd hold her to it.

Ben and Dave shared a look. Steve guessed what they were thinking. *The poor sucker. He thinks she cares. He thinks she knows he exists.*

Dave rubbed his shiny head. "Diana said she'd come by later with some food."

Steve nodded. Food was irrelevant. But he remembered Diana sharing Alessi's comment. Fairy ambrosia. Alessi was a girl who appreciated her food. Barb had picked and commented on every calorie. Being short, it probably did matter more. But there were times he'd wished she would just enjoy the meal he was forking out for.

Alessi had savored every bite as though she'd never tasted something so good. She was grateful. Actually, she'd made gratitude an art.

"I'd pay Dutch, but I'd still be using your money." Barb had never considered paying. Not that he meant for her to—it was just that she took everything as her due. Alessi didn't seem to think she had anything coming her way. And it surprised her when it did.

Ben said, "Steve, are you okay?"

"Yeah. Go take care of Mary." Life was too fragile to miss a day.

"Those little girls need their presents."

Ben smiled. "I got a hat and beard. I'm gonna ho-ho in with the whole bagful."

Steve nodded. "That's good." He hoped Ben could pull it off in spite of it all. Ben loved the girls enough to do it.

Dave touched his shoulder. "We'll check back in a while."

Steve nodded again. He wished he knew what the lines and numbers on the monitors meant. Alessi's hand was still warm, her face completely still. No fluttering in her eyelids, no quiver of the brow. Her hair was a rippled mass on the pillow. Blond from her dad, curls from her mom. His dark, unruly hair was from his mom. He hadn't told her that. There were so many things he hadn't told her. Two and a half weeks was not long enough to cover much personal history, although he knew so much of hers. He could fix that now.

"I don't really remember my mother. Dad kept some pictures around so I'd know what she looked like. Maybe so I'd recognize her if she came back. I think he believed she might someday. Maybe he just wanted her to."

Steve looked around the cubicle. They seemed to be leaving Alessi pretty much alone, probably since it was nothing more than a death-watch. "Dad told me some things, like how they met. He saw her chasing her hat, some big floppy thing, down the windy street. And it was as though Mary Poppins had flown into town." He sang, " 'When Mary takes your hand, you feel so grand, your heart starts beatin' like a big brass band.' "

As his had done when he held Alessi's. As he held it now, knowing she didn't care one way or the other. "He told me the good things and kept the rest to himself. I guess he was like you that way. Focused on the positive." He stroked her arm. "There must have been bad times too. Clues and indications that all was not well."

There had been plenty with Barb and him. He was just so wrapped up in her packaging he didn't want to see it. "Barb was no Mary Poppins." His heart had beaten for all the wrong reasons. It was probably good God hadn't answered that prayer.

He frowned. Maybe in some way he couldn't see, there was good in all of it, his mom leaving, his dad dying. Maybe things that felt like catastrophe were blessing somehow. He looked into Alessi's face. Then there were the things that were just plain wrong. *God, what are you thinking? How can you destroy something so beautiful?* But God hadn't destroyed her. Carl had. Evil had. They all had in one way or another.

His tears came again. *I'd pray, Alessi, if I knew how.* What would he ask? For her to live? To lie there day after day as her muscles atrophied? He swallowed. Christ had cured the paralytic, the blind, the lame. Steve shook his head. Nothing in his experience told him that still happened. Brains did not regenerate.

"She went too long without oxygen." Was Carl sitting in a cell thinking about what he'd done? Steve doubted he had the capacity for remorse. Was he scared? Had they even apprehended him? Steve pressed his hands to his face.

If only Alessi hadn't come to Charity. How would things be then? But you never could see the rest of the picture, couldn't know how a decision you made today would change tomorrow. They were flying blind, all sparrows who'd lost their way. But if God truly cared, why did He let them get so messed up?

One decision could change your life forever. Or end it. Alessi had walked out. He told her he would help, but she ran out on him. She ran out into the cold, the danger. Was he such a daunting alternative? He pressed his hands to his face. Was there some Leave Me sign he wore?

Okay, so he hadn't been approachable. And maybe he didn't really let people in. Barb had complained about the Secret Steve, the man behind the mask. Maybe she was right. Maybe he did hold back. At first it made him intriguing. Women wanted to unlock him. But once they found he was a lock they couldn't crack, they took it personally. Then he was the bad guy, uncaring, untrusting, insensitive.

Fine, he was all those things. Alessi should never have expected more. And she wouldn't have, if he hadn't led her to. What woman had he ever kissed after only two days' introduction? And yesterday? He gripped the metal rail. "You found the key, Alessi. You stole it and broke in. I didn't ask you to come, didn't want you at the store. I never made you wear my clothes and sort my books."

He stared into her unresponsive face. "You should have seen what everyone else saw, not imagined some real person, some . . . pool boy giving you truth." He swallowed.

"Steve?" Karen came in quietly. "I brought you lunch." She held out a box she had no doubt prepared herself. "Oh, what pretty flowers."

"They're Amanda's."

Karen broke into a smile. "Alessi would appreciate that."

He didn't know which way she meant that and didn't care. As she pressed the box into his hands, he growled, "Thanks." *Now go away.*

"I can sit with her while you eat."

He couldn't sit and eat at the same time? "Karen, I'm not really hungry."

"I know. But you won't do her any favors getting weak."

"Do her any favors?" He pushed away from the bedside and rotated the stool. "What exactly do you think I can do for her?" He swallowed the sarcastic examples that wanted to follow. Take her dancing, hiking, exploring?

Karen touched his shoulder. "With Charity Chapel praying for a miracle, one never knows."

"Yes, Karen, one does. Have you ever seen a miracle?"

She tipped her head. "Christy Gaines needed surgery for that twisted intestine. Pastor prayed, and the intestine untwisted all by itself."

He scowled. "And that's a miracle? It's a fluke of physiology." He looked back at Alessi. Was she listening? No. Her brain no longer received signals. She was dead in every way except a beating heart and a machine that made her breathe.

"God can do anything."

"He can, but He doesn't." Steve looked for a place to stash the box.

"I'm not leaving until you eat something."

Who did she think she was, his mother? No, his mother didn't care if he ate. She ran off with her own meal ticket. God didn't stop her. But it didn't matter because Dad was there. People helped people. And sometimes they couldn't.

He opened the box. A fresh roasted turkey sandwich, well peppered, with crisp lettuce and mayonnaise, some pink, frothy salad with fruit in it, and a wedge of homemade pecan pie. She meant well, and she was a good friend. He'd known her from birth. He took a bite of the sandwich. "Okay, I'm eating."

Karen had insinuated she'd leave, but she sat down in the metal chair with a cushioned seat. It couldn't be much more comfortable than his stool, so she might not stay long. "How's she doing?"

He scanned the pulsing, processing machines, the tubes and wires, and Alessi. "I haven't noticed any change." His throat constricted.

"Prayer is a mighty tool."

He didn't answer. Maybe her prayers would help in some unfathomed way. He munched another bite of sandwich. Let her see his obedience and go away. Fresh tears threatened, and no one was going to see that. He ate in silence. A nurse came and recorded something from the monitors, then left. He glanced at Karen and guessed from her expression she was praying for him.

He rubbed a hand over his face. "You don't have to stay."

"Have you asked God to heal her?"

He shook his head. What would be, would be.

"Some things are bigger than us."

And all the more futile. He spooned a glob of pink stuff. It was tastier than it looked, but he only wanted it over with. Once he'd emptied the box she would have no reason to hover. He did not class Karen with the piranhas, but given the chance, she'd just love to take care of him. He couldn't even think about that.

He worked his way into the pie. "This is good, Karen. Thank you."

"Diana's bringing dinner."

He didn't want dinner. But stopping the flow of the meal brigade was as futile as asking for miracles. His lower back ached. He stood up and threw the box away. "You can report to the troops now. Meal launched on target."

Standing, she reached into her monstrous shoulder bag and brought out her Bible. "I didn't know if you had yours with you. . . ."

He shook his head wearily.

"You don't have to study or search. But it might help to just read."

Once again there was no point arguing.

Her gaze melted over him like warm butter. "Is there anything else I can do for you?"

"Nope."

She squeezed his hand. "Don't lose hope."

How could you lose something you didn't have? When Ben had forced his breath into Alessi's lungs he had hoped with everything in him. For what? The chance to watch her slip away, lose the minimal function that remained? He nodded, doubting he'd fool her for long.

Thirty-Five

STEVE SAT DOWN AGAIN WHEN KAREN left and took Alessi's hand. "They're at it now. Operation fortification. It must feed a woman's soul to fill a man's belly. How else to explain the automatic meal mode?" He stroked her fingers. "Tragedy triggers *kitchen* in the female mind." He recalled the laughs he and Dad had over some of the offerings.

"*Oh, this one's serious, son. She's included the recipe.*"

"*That's good,*" he'd said around a bite. "*Then we can make it without her.*"

Steve smirked. They had become excellent cooks in spite of the never-ending flow of good intentions. He could have taught Alessi more than flipping burgers. He closed his eyes until the wave of pain passed.

The meals had continued nonetheless. Not every night. Sometimes no more than once a week, but never ceasing, year after year. And those were the days before Charity took its new name.

With his stomach full, he grew drowsy. He'd been awake most of the night one way or another. He pressed Alessi's hand. "Mind if I rest a little?" Dropping his chin onto their entwined fingers, he propped himself on his elbows and closed his eyes. She might feel him there if she didn't hear him talking. It was all useless, but he didn't want her to be alone.

Waves of exhaustion rolled over him, but he kept jerking back at the thought of her "drifting away" while he slept. Finally not even that could stop the weariness.

He woke to Diana's hand on his shoulder. Dave was with her, holding an insulated case that appeared to contain a banquet.

Dave grinned. "Diana brought you Christmas dinner."

Steve rubbed his face and caught a moist spot at the corner of his mouth. He hoped he hadn't drooled on Alessi's hand, but he guessed she wouldn't mind, even if she knew it. Diana moved Amanda's flowers to the top of the console that held the monitors and used the shelf, which Steve now realized was on wheels, to make him a table.

It would raise up to fit over the bed for Alessi, but he didn't suppose people in intensive care ate much. Must serve multiple functions.

"How's she doin'?" Dave kept his voice low, as though he might disturb her.

"The same." Although as he looked at her now, it seemed her eyes were more sunken, her face less expressive, as though her essence was leaking out.

"Come and eat, Steve." Diana nudged his arm.

He took the metal chair over which she had angled the shelf. Steam rose from a slab of prime rib, whipped potatoes, and creamed spinach. Some sort of nutty green salad was in a separate Tupperware, as was a jewel-red dessert with meringue peaks. He could not begin to eat it all, but argument, he knew, would prove fruitless.

"It's real good." Dave stood near the stool Steve had vacated.

Steve had a sudden urge to push him out and say, "That's my place."

But that was ridiculous. Dave had as much right beside Alessi as anyone. He and Ben had been her first and best friends in Charity. If not for them, he would not have found her in his bed and had the opportunity to demonstrate his magnanimity.

He looked down at the food. *"My mother had this grace she used to say. 'Thank you for this food, O Lord. Make this meal a feast, if only in our minds.'"* This meal was a feast, yet now he prayed for the strength to get it down. He murmured, "Amen," and took a bite of beef. Dave would be well fed if he took stock of his possibilities.

Steve almost choked when he tried to swallow, then forced the bite down and ordered it to stay. No way would he manage all of it. Dave and Diana spoke in low voices over Alessi, and he realized they were praying. He should leave the room so his lack of faith didn't poison their hope. Hadn't Jesus barred all the naysayers and brought in only His most trusted friends when He raised the little girl?

But those were the miracle days when God did that sort of thing. Steve took a bite of potato and noticed the crisp, buttery roll. He managed a bite of that as well. The potatoes went down easily, as did the spinach. Hardly more effort than shoving a bite and swallowing. Then Dr. Deklin came in, and he pushed the shelf away, relieved.

She studied the group a moment, then said, "Has anyone notified Ms. Moore's family?"

They shared a glance around. Steve said, "She has an aunt and uncle, but I don't know who or where."

Dave pursed his lips. "I think she mentioned Palm Beach. We could look up all the Moores."

Steve shook his head. "It's her mother's sister. She won't be named Moore."

Diana looked up. "Maybe Cooper got something when he ran her through the system. Her parents or—"

"Her parents are dead." *"I think my parents dying young is a sign."*

Dr. Deklin scrutinized them. "There's no one at all?"

Steve frowned. "There's us."

She gave him a soft smile. "I know. But I need someone who can make legal decisions in this case."

Steve looked from her to Dave. Dave cleared his throat. "What decisions?"

"Her condition is deteriorating."

So he hadn't imagined a decline. It was real.

"I think it's time to remove the IV and the resp—"

"No." Steve's tone left no room for argument. Christmas was not over. Alessi was staying through Christmas.

"Steve, I know this has been a hard year for you."

"It's not about me." But it was. He could hardly pretend Alessi needed this time. "I think we should wait until Ben's here." Ben should be part of any decision, especially one that would tick away the moments Alessi had left. Especially after he'd been the one to bring her back from the brink. He swallowed hard. "We can talk about it in the morning." She had only agreed through Christmas. *After Christmas I'm out of here.*

He rubbed the back of his neck, determined to stand his ground.

Dr. Deklin nodded. "All right. We'll talk in the morning."

By then there might be no decision to make. Steve stood, silently aching.

Dave broke the silence. "You want to go home, Steve? Get some sleep?"

Steve pulled a wry smile. "I've slept."

Diana shook her head. "All hunched over there on the stool? It's a miracle your neck's not out of whack."

His neck was sore. But he'd have plenty of time to work that out. "Let Ben know he needs to be here in the morning."

Dave nodded grimly. Maybe the fact that God was not answering their prayer was finally setting in. Dave teared up again, and Diana wrapped his waist in her arm. He forced the words, "See you in the morning." They had never held so much meaning.

Diana said, "I'll leave the dinner things. . . ."

"Take it." Steve sat back down on the stool, and for once Diana didn't argue. She packaged up the food and prepared to go back to her extended family.

Except for the bruising on her neck and arms, and probably places he didn't see, Alessi looked like the woman who had stepped into the hall in his robe. She did, and yet she didn't. Something essential was slipping away. Thought? Or spirit.

"God . . ." He gripped Alessi's hand. "You don't make it easy."

Dad's faith had never wavered, at least not that Steve could recall. He had taken the lot dealt him and faced it with dignity. To have his young wife run out on him and her own child must have been a crushing blow. But he had attended church every week and thanked God for his blessings.

Steve did not feel thankful. Resentful, yes. Furious. Devastated. But not thankful. That was Alessi's forte. He looked at her lying there. What good could she possibly find in this? He shook his head.

"I won't let her go. You'll have to take her." Not that it had ever stopped God before.

This crazy girl had come into his life when he hadn't been looking for her, but she would leave like all the rest. And though she hadn't chosen to die, she had walked out the door. Why was he clinging to her like the two-year-old child still crying for his mother? Why not let Dr. Deklin put a stop to the effort? A few hours, more or less—could they really matter?

He picked up the Bible Karen used to teach her studies. She knew her stuff. But she had told him he didn't have to study or search. She knew he had no heart or energy for that. But read? He turned to the Gospels and picked out the miracles. Sometimes there was mud and spit, sometimes just a word. But it was the word of God in the person of Jesus. He didn't have quite the access that centurion had.

Of course, there was the book of Acts. The great men, Peter and Paul, doing the same things Christ did. But they'd been there, directly commissioned. As all believers were commissioned? Didn't the Gospel of John say anyone who had faith in Jesus would do what He did and even greater things than that? Somewhere down the line things had fizzled. It just didn't work that way anymore. He set the Bible down and returned his focus to Alessi.

The clock ticked away the time. Machines kept her body going. He had to work to find her pulse. He pressed her hand to his cheek. What was she to him anyway? Hardly more than a stranger. Why prolong the inevitable? If she were a stray dog, hit by a car, he would have her put down. Was he less merciful to a woman?

He pressed her fingertips to his lips. "What do you want, Alessi?" But she couldn't want anything. Her mind was no more than animal function. He pressed his eyes shut. How could he even think like that? This was Alessi.

Only it wasn't. The part that made her special was destroyed. Yet, looking at her there, he could almost pretend she slept. If he called her name, she would open her eyes and tell him the bad dream she'd had. *"It was only a dream, Alessi. I won't let anything happen to you."*

He sniffed the tears he hadn't noticed. He hadn't even cried like this when Dad died. But then he had Barb there. No man would cry in front of his fiancée. Or maybe he'd blocked the emotion, just as he'd blocked the hurt of her leaving. Why couldn't he block it now?

That key Alessi had turned. She had unlocked his heart and hidden the key in her own. When hers stopped, he'd be laid open. He swallowed the pain filling his throat. *Lord, why?* But that wasn't the question, he knew. Why was for people who didn't believe God knew best. That's what Dad always said. *"Not why, son, just what do I do now?"*

"Okay, God," he whispered. "What do I do now?"

Nothing miraculous. No hand writing on the wall. No burning bush. But he did sense that things would play out as they had to, and somehow he would go on. Two weeks with Alessi had broken his angry shell. Maybe he would form it again after she left him for good. Part of him hoped not. He'd rather be like Dad.

"I'm glad you came, Alessi." And he was, even with all the pain he felt now and the worse pain ahead.

He turned at the motion behind him. Burton Welsh. What was he doing here? Unbearable sadness washed in like a wave. It wasn't the pastor's fault, but Steve wanted so much to blame him, to blame someone.

Burton said, "How is she?"

"Dying." What good were platitudes?

The pastor's hue was already gray. He didn't pale or slump. Just took the chair across from Steve's and studied her still face. After a while his eyes closed, but his lips didn't move, and whether he prayed or just sat there Steve couldn't tell. They kept silent vigil until nine, then Burton stood up.

Steve had to ask. "Where's Carl?"

Burton's face creased with grief. "I don't know. I wish I did."

Thirty-Six

THE ARMY SUPPLY COT WAS SUFFICIENT. What he couldn't stand were the nightmares. They hadn't gone away. He had tried to end them, but they had come back worse than ever. His mother crying, pleading. "Please, Duke. Please." And blood. Carl tasted it still.

"You got a thing for the preacher?" Duke's face like a boiled ham.

"No. It's not like that."

"I saw you." Blows and more blood, and Carl shrinking into the wall. He'd been angry too. How could she leave him with the monster? She must hate him. And so he dug into his own hate. Bottomless wells of it.

His mother gasping, "Pastor only wanted to help."

But help was not something they were allowed. Carl watched the evil take over Duke's face. His knee in her belly. "For that, it'll be slow."

Mind numbing, Carl watched until it ended. Then Duke grunted. "Open the hatch."

Carl had held it open as his mother was tumbled under the floor. Then Duke shoveled in the lime and said, "We won't be coming here for a while." And when he saw tears on Carl's face he punched him.

Carl shivered. The sleeping bag was good to twenty below, but the cold he felt was internal. He lay unmoving, wondering what condition the body was in. And if she'd come out once, what would stop her from coming back again?

———

The morning light had never been so unwelcome. Steve was almost angry when Ben walked in with Dave, as though his presence somehow caused the climax it now facilitated. He had told Dr. Deklin they would decide when all three were present, but now that it came to it, he could not say yes.

Ben spoke low. "How're you doin'?"

Steve didn't answer. What difference did it make? What he felt or thought was irrelevant. He clenched his hands.

Dave handed him a cup of coffee. "Heard about Carl?"

Steve's jaw tightened. What did he care about Carl? "Do they have him?"

Dave shook his head. "It's like he just disappeared."

Steve narrowed his eyes. "Are they looking for the car?"

"Yeah. But they've been looking for two and a half weeks already."

Not very hard. Not hard enough. Not enough to stop . . . Steve ran a hand over his face. "He must have it hidden. And it can't be far if he could get at it."

Ben shrugged. "Where's he gonna go? He's just a kid."

Just a kid? A murderous, malicious, twisted kid.

Dave said, "I'm sure they have an APB on him."

Why were they talking about Carl?

Ben shook his head. "I sure wish none of this happened."

Understatement of the year. Steve sipped the hot coffee, willing the caffeine into his bloodstream. Though he wished he could remain fuzzy and disconnected, he owed Alessi better than that.

Ben stared down into her face. "When I first saw her out there at the pumps, trying to catch the snowflakes on her tongue, I thought, that one's special."

Steve's throat tightened. Had Carl seen it too? Was that why he singled her out, chose to destroy her?

Dave ran a hand over his forehead. "The church is praying. I don't remember the last time there was a vigil sign-up."

"What?" Steve glanced at him.

"That's right. We started a sign-up sheet for people to choose a time to pray so there wouldn't be any hour she isn't covered."

Steve stared into his cup. "What are they praying?"

"God's will."

Steve took a swallow. "God's will happens regardless of prayer."

Dave shook his head. "Not always. Sometimes evil gets in the way."

Ben said, "Like in Daniel, when God answered the prayer but the angel couldn't get through for twenty-one days."

Steve shot his breath through his teeth. "You think He's sending an angel?" They sounded like Alessi with her halos. And where had the angel been when she needed protection?

Dave said, "The point is we can't lose hope."

Lose hope? Steve took Alessi's hand. What exactly did the guys think they were gathered there for?

Dr. Deklin came in. "Good morning."

Steve didn't look her way. He didn't want to see the grim compassion she would show for the decision they must make. He kept his gaze on Alessi, her face angelic as she lay there. Halos meant something good would happen? She looked anything but hopeful, and yet . . .

"I appreciate you all being here. I know this is difficult. But I need to tell you things have changed since we spoke last."

Steve turned in surprise. Was she going to say Alessi had improved, that somehow a continuance of care might help?

"We traced her uncle through the license plate records."

So the uncle was real, another true part in Alessi's story. Now the family would get involved. At least there would be time for them to come and see for themselves what her condition warranted.

Dr. Deklin's aqua eyes softened momentarily. "The decision to terminate heroic measures has been made."

"What?" Steve gripped the bar beside the bed.

"I spoke with the family this morning, and they gave permission to remove the respirator."

"Of course they would." He hadn't meant to raise his voice. "They don't care about her. They haven't even seen her."

Dave and Ben looked apologetic, but Steve was not about to let it go. "They're not really family, not the way it's supposed to be. They took her in, but—"

"They assured me her grandparents would be in agreement. Steve . . ." Dr. Deklin took a step toward him. "There is nothing to be gained by prolonging extraordinary measures."

"You don't know that."

"My years in medicine indicate it."

His argument was pointless, he knew.

"I'm very sorry, Steve. But the decision has been made." As she spoke, a nurse and a technician joined them. Steve had to step aside to let the young man through, but the nurse went to the other side of the bed, disconnected the IV, hooked the tubes over the swing arm, and rolled the unit out of the cubicle. Alessi never stirred.

Dr. Deklin said, "After the respirator is discontinued, she may stop breathing at once or she may continue on her own. I don't think she will have the strength to go on for long, but sometimes we're surprised." She looked at Steve with that last comment.

He stared her down. Did she think he didn't understand reality? Maybe he'd sounded that way. He just felt someone had to stand up for Alessi, no matter how futile. At the doctor's nod, the chunky technician turned off the machine and removed the tube.

Suddenly the light took form. A being more wonderful than she could imagine in any of her woodland scenes reached out to her. Alessi wanted to step forward but could not find a foot to move or a hand to reach. She tried to explain but had no mouth. She was no longer alone, but she had no way of connecting to the being before her. Longing seized her. *Don't leave me.* Not even her thoughts could reach him, yet he seemed to know her need.

He moved toward her without walking. In his hand he held a fiery stone, like a coal from the heart of a volcano. As he drew near, the heat from the stone reached her, yet she didn't recoil. Still closer he came, until the stone burned, and she seemed to burst aflame.

She gasped in wonder. . . .

Steve closed his eyes as the monitors toned. *Lord . . .* Dave and Ben were silent, but he sensed their distress. None of them had wanted this; no one could have foreseen it. Alessi had come in with the snow like a puff of magic. Now she would be gone, crushed like a snowflake underfoot. And Christmas was over.

But she breathed. With a quick sucking sound, she breathed. Steve opened his eyes and stared. Her face had not changed; she didn't move, except for the tiny rise and fall of her chest. He wanted to cheer. *Go, Alessi! You show them.* Her uncle, her grandparents, Dr. Deklin and her years of medicine. *Breathe, Alessi, breathe.* Ben hadn't put his breath in her for nothing. Steve looked at his friend. Was he remembering?

Yes, the doctor had said she might breathe on her own, and he knew it didn't change anything. It almost made it worse, but he didn't feel that way. He exulted. Swallowing back the tears, he looked at Dave, read in his face the same hopeful anticipation. It was stupid. It defied everything he knew by experience, but hope bloomed inside him.

Lord, let her live. It was cruel, unconscionable to want her to linger as she was. But she breathed. A rush identical to the one he'd experienced on the side of the road when Ben made her breathe lifted and carried him. He'd be dashed, he knew. But right now he rode the wave.

Silently the technician wheeled the respirator out. Dr. Deklin waited a short while, then told them she would check back. Steve knew she was doing her best, and it must be bad knowing her training and skill could not change things. But he hadn't expected Alessi to breathe, and she did, better and stronger than the first time. The tube must have opened the airway.

Steve took his seat again beside the bed. "You guys don't need to stay."

Ben shook his head. "We'll sit awhile."

Steve looked from one to the other. "Guess she's made of tougher stuff than they thought."

"Yeah." Dave pulled a chair in as he had the first time they sat there together. "Or maybe God's not finished with her."

Steve's heart pumped faster. *That's right, Lord. You're not done yet, not by a long shot.* The hurt would be far more devastating if he allowed himself to expect anything but the worst. Was he willing to open to that pain? He'd been so well insulated by the time Barb left him that it hardly did more than confirm his morose condition. But every breath Alessi took seemed a bellows to his soul. Could he pray for a miracle? It was safer not to ask, but . . .

A single flicker under her eyelids stopped his breath. "Did you see that?"

Ben leaned close. "See what?"

"Her eyelids moved." Steve stared, but Alessi might have been a wax statue in a museum, she lay so still. He remembered touring one with his dad. *"They look so real,"* he'd said, even glancing over his shoulder to see if they moved once he passed by. This time he was sure he'd seen it, but there was nothing more.

She had been comatose now for thirty-one hours. One flicker of an eyelid changed nothing. Her brain scan would still show minimal function. He knew the reality. But Jesus raised Lazarus.

Steve clasped his hands together. *Lord, you can do this.* Everything inside him knew it wouldn't happen. It would be as Dr. Deklin said; she would breathe for a while, then slowly slip away. *You can, Lord.* Just as it might have been different with his mom leaving, his dad dying, Barb breaking their engagement. His hope sagged.

Ben shifted. "We could pray."

Steve glanced sidelong. They had attended the same church since they were small but had never prayed aloud together, the three of them.

Ben glanced at Dave. "The Word says where two or more gather . . ."

Steve took Alessi's hand. "Go ahead, Ben."

Dave reached out and took Ben's hand, then reached for Steve's. "Sort of solidarity like."

Steve took his hand. The other two closed their eyes, but he kept his on Alessi.

"Oh, Lord," Ben said, "we don't know what you intend to do with all this. But we sure care about Alessi, and we're asking for a miracle."

There it was, what he'd been afraid to voice even in his thoughts. Doubt gripped Steve's heart. It wouldn't happen, didn't happen. It never happened. He watched Alessi for any sign, but there was not even the flicker of an eyelid.

Dave cleared his throat. "I believe in miracles. I believe in you, Jesus."

Steve's grip tightened on Alessi's hand. Could he say the same? It wouldn't be true, so he gave it his best shot. "Please, Lord."

Ben said, "Amen," and they all dropped hands.

Not the most eloquent prayer of all time, but Steve was glad they'd done it. "People are really praying on a schedule?"

Dave nodded. "Around the clock. Even through the night."

Steve smiled. What would Alessi think of that? And then it hit him again that she couldn't think. He kept drifting into the hope zone and imagining the impossible. That was Alessi, not him. *"Maybe I'll just go see if someone returned my car."* He could still see her standing at the pumps as though she really thought it might have been there. And of course it wasn't.

He cradled her hand with his palm. It was crazy. But maybe some of her had rubbed off, because he kept looking for signs of revival. Ben had made her breathe, then the machine, and now she kept breathing. What was to say she couldn't recover? What did science know; or medicine? What did anyone know for sure? He was back in the hope zone, and this time he'd try to stay there.

Ben stood up. "You want to go home and clean up?"

Steve shook his head. "I'll stay here."

Dave said, "It wouldn't hurt to give us a turn."

Steve looked up. He had been territorial. On second thought a shower and breakfast might be nice. Unless she . . . Fear gripped him. Couldn't he resist it a minute or two? His trust was pathetic. Maybe it was time to develop it. "Okay." He stood up. "Call me if there's any change."

If she stopped breathing they would not resuscitate. He would not be there to give her breath as Ben had.

Dave said, "Go."

He nodded. By the time he reached the truck, he wanted to run back in. He forced his key into the lock and turned it in the ignition.

He left the lot and drove home, went inside, and called the hospital.

"She's still breathing, Steve." The ICU nurse had called Dave to the phone and his tone was impatient. "Have faith." Easy for Dave to say. His life may not have been spectacular, but he'd certainly had fewer challenges.

"I'm getting in the shower now. Let it ring if you call."

"All right." Dave hung up.

Steve knew how he sounded. At any other time they would tease him mercilessly. But as the water washed the fatigue from his back, he realized grimly there was nothing funny about falling in love with a dying woman. There was something diabolically macabre in that unless . . . unless it was all he could do for her.

The water ran over his face, and he held his breath. Everything said she was dying, and yet his newfound hope did not relinquish its hold. *Live, Alessi.* He scrubbed his hands over his face. *Lord, let her live.*

It was easier now to ask the impossible. If she died, it would not be because he hadn't asked. The phone rang and he dropped the soap. It hit his small toe and sent a pain up his foot, but he hardly noticed as he scrambled out, grabbing a towel and running for the kitchen wall.

He grabbed the phone and pressed it to his ear. "What happened?"

"Steve?" It sounded like Karen's voice.

His heart was wedged in his larynx, and for a moment he couldn't speak. "Yeah."

"I'm in the driveway with a casserole, but I saw your truck and thought I'd let you know I was coming in."

He gripped the towel to his chest. "Unless you want to see me in the buff, you'd better let me get back in the shower."

"By all means, get." She laughed heartily.

Very funny. Everyone's a comedian, as Dad used to say. Steve slipped on the wet, soapy linoleum, picked up the bar of soap, and climbed back into the water he'd left running. He stayed in long enough for Karen to drop her casserole and leave. But when he got out, toweled dry, and dressed, she was waiting still.

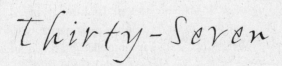

Thirty-Seven

"DO YOU HAVE A MINUTE?" KAREN SAID.

Steve finger-forked his hair and said, "What's the casserole?"

"Sausage and egg."

"Perfect. Grab a plate." He dished two servings and set them on the table as he had with Alessi the few wonderful times they'd breakfasted together. He murmured a blessing, raised his fork, and took a bite. "Thanks. You saved me making something." The sausage was savory and the eggs fluffy with a browned cheesy crust. He washed the swallow down with the juice Karen had set beside his plate.

"Steve, my heart's troubled."

"You should try mine." He couldn't believe he'd said that, given her a peek inside him. Alessi rubbing off again.

"I'm terribly concerned for Alessi. Breaks my heart to see her like that. But the burden that's been laid on me is . . . Carl."

Steve stopped eating.

"I know it's a horrible hateful thing he's done. But with everyone else in vigil for Alessi, the Lord's charged my heart with Carl."

He could not believe she was telling him this. The casserole turned in his stomach and left his mouth sour. She caught him with her eyes, and while he didn't look away, he could not find words to respond.

Finally he ground out, "Why are you telling me?"

"Because I'm hitting a wall."

Steve got up and walked to the end of the kitchen, rubbing his forehead with his fingertips. "You can't expect me to help." He met her careworn eyes. "Carl can go to hell for all I care." His own vitriol surprised him.

Karen stared, no doubt uncertain she'd heard him right. But he meant it. "Steve, I . . ."

"Don't lecture me, Karen. I know it's wrong. But so help me, I mean it. I even want it."

"Well, that explains the wall." She took a bite and chewed slowly. She was going to sit at his table and ask him not to block her prayers for Carl? Was that how it worked? One person's hatred blocking the flow of grace? Weight like a lead apron pulled on his shoulders. Could someone stop the prayers for Alessi? Or did God just make a judgment call over conflicting requests?

"You should finish your breakfast."

Steve looked at his plate and sat down obediently. But he could not take the food in.

She forked up the last bite of hers. "Unforgiveness devours joy. Gives the devil a foothold."

He wasn't the one declaring there was no devil in Charity. "I can't help it."

Karen dabbed her mouth with the napkin. "You don't have to feel like forgiving, Steve. It's a choice."

Now she sounded like Alessi. *I made all the choices that put me here.*

It's no one's fault but mine." She couldn't possibly still think that. She couldn't think anything.

Karen didn't prod. But he sensed Alessi, forgiving him for all the hurtful things he'd said and done.

Karen spoke softly. "She wouldn't want you bound up."

A second lead apron almost staggered him. Would Alessi forgive Carl? She wasn't able to. She couldn't want one way or the other. Could he do it for her? "They've removed the life support." His voice broke.

Karen leaned forward and took his hand. "You love her, don't you?"

He swallowed the pain. "Yes."

Karen sighed. "We're praying hard. Storming the gates."

His eyes teared, but he didn't bother to block them. "I wish I could believe it would make a difference. I keep trying to hope. . . ."

"You don't have to hope. You love." She squeezed his hands. "Faith, hope, and love. And the greatest of these is love."

A tear broke free and sallied down his cheek. Was it true? Could he simply love her and not keep fighting to find a faith deep enough or hope strong enough? If he let himself love her until she died, it would hurt more than anything he'd known. *The greatest of these is love.*

Who else in Charity would give her that? Who else could? Her own family had said pull the plug without even seeing her. He closed his eyes and fresh tears pressed through. Karen got up and hugged his shoulders. It was such a motherly thing to do, it cut him close.

He dropped his chin. "I'm not proficient in the love department."

Karen laughed softly. "You just need the right inspiration."

He swiped the tears from his face and sniffed. "I have to get back."

She patted his shoulder. "You tell Ben and Dave this casserole's here."

He nodded, then hugged her. "Thank you."

She smiled. "You go pour it on, Steve. Then see what God can do."

He wiped his face on his sleeve, grabbed his jacket, and went out to the truck. As Karen went to her own car, he backed out and headed for the hospital. Every moment hung swollen and suspended. The longing for Alessi's face filled his stomach more completely than the eggs and sausage. Ben and Dave had had their turn.

He parked and jogged in, took the elevator to ICU, and strode to her cubicle. The men were talking softly to each other, and Ben sat on the stool. Steve tapped his shoulder. "This is my dance."

Ben looked up, then stood, comprehension dawning. Let them see it; he didn't care.

"Karen has a casserole at the house."

They shared a look. Ben simply said, "Okay." And they shuffled out.

Then Steve had her to himself. He sat down on the stool and took her hand, brought it to his lips with a groan. "I love you, Alessi."

No response, of course.

"Your crazy hair, your long limbs, the way you look in my clothes. Your innocence, your expectation, your wonder and your dreams. I love the way you look in my camera lens and the way you talk and the way you want to see things. I love your faithfulness and your friendship."

He kissed each finger one by one. "I love that you love Moll's pot roast and you got a discount out of Stacie. I love how you see what others ignore." He kissed her palm and pressed it to his cheek. "I love you."

He leaned over and kissed her lips. He was no Prince Charming. Her eyes didn't flutter open and look into his. The pain of his situation rushed in, and he sank back with a shudder in his chest. Could he do it? Could he love her until she drew her final breath? Could he give her what she'd lacked when it mattered? He stood up and paced.

Why was he even thinking that way? What difference did it make to her? Karen had some romantic idea of how the world worked. How God worked. But that wasn't the point. There must be a reason he loved her, because it sure didn't make sense in any normal scheme of things.

He stood over Alessi and took her hand again. "I want to show you all the things you haven't seen. I want to smell the pines with you and hear the bugling elk. I want to sleep under the stars with wolves howling at the moon. I want you to see my waterfall." He kissed her knuckles.

"I know you've only known me a short time, and for most of it I was a jerk. And I guess you know I didn't make a very good fiancé the first time. I probably won't be the greatest husband. But I want to marry you, Alessi." He could not believe he was proposing to her like this, but what difference did it make?

If he never got an answer, it wasn't for not asking. He'd done his part; now it was up to her. Hardly fair, but what else was new? He never pretended to be a great catch. Alessi knew exactly what he was. She'd seen inside him from the start.

He got up and walked, went to the machine for coffee, where Moll surprised him with a boxed lunch. "How's she doing?"

He could have said no different, but "Hanging in there" came out instead.

"She's undaunted, that's for sure." Moll's cheeks reddened. "She sure gave me what for."

"Alessi told you off?" He couldn't begin to imagine it, though he'd been chastised himself. Just not in the normal sense.

"More like killing me softly with her love."

The lump filled his throat as he nodded silently. "Yeah. She could do that."

Ever since Moll's daughter was killed on the highway, hitting a deer in her VW bug, she'd been gruff and bitter. Now it looked like years had left her face. "I've been praying. First time in years."

Steve smiled bleakly. "Thanks." He accepted the box lunch from Moll and returned to the cubicle. He paced and he sat, and Alessi never moved. Her breaths came quietly, but they came. Her heart beat weakly, but it beat. Dr. Deklin checked in and went out again.

Steve stopped beside the bed. "Lots of people are praying for you." And one at least was praying for Carl. He didn't want to be a wall, an impediment to God's grace. He could not feel compassion for him, not with Alessi on the brink. But could he choose? Could he forgive for Alessi's sake and his own?

She should be the one. She would do it better. Alessi knew how to dig deep and find compassion and understanding. She'd done it with him. He looked down at her. "If you can hear me wherever you are, would you come back now?" Oh, that was loving. That was the old Steve. No, that was the real Steve. He forked his fingers into his hair.

"Look, I know I said a lot of things, and you might not want any part of them. So if you're scared to come back 'cause I'm here, don't worry about it. You can say no." He hung his head. Right. Just speak up, Alessi.

He sat down and slumped against the bedrail. He had hardly touched Moll's lunch. It wasn't food he wanted. It was some sign, any sign from Alessi. He pressed his hands to his face.

Dr. Deklin came in and informed him the hospital was writing off her bill.

"What about her uncle?"

"He assured us he was not financially responsible for her in any way."

Steve shook his head. But he had the right to end her life?

"Steve, you'll have to decide on funeral arrangements." She spoke gently as always. "You won't have any assistance from the family."

Funeral arrangements. Was that the best he'd do for her? "What would you do if no one was here?"

"Humane cremation."

He ground the butt of his hands into his eyes. "I'll handle it."

He brought Alessi's palm to his cheek and closed his eyes. He was tired, but he'd heard that most people died at night. If he slept with her hand on his face, would he feel her leave? *Lord, let me say good-bye. If that's the best you can do, at least let me say good-bye.* He gave in to the weariness of grief and dreamed of waking up to find his mother gone. He jolted awake in the dark, but Alessi still breathed.

He whispered, "I love you," and went back to sleep.

Pastor Welsh opened the door, surprised to see Nita Miravella. His day had been one weary procession of people needing his direction when he had no direction to give. Nita was a Friday night participant, a front-row girl, who experienced the Spirit in an enthusiastic way. Whatever she needed from him, she probably had in greater degree herself.

"It's late for you to be out, Nita." He had been up himself because sleep was an elusive foe, encumbered with dreams. But Madeline had succumbed hours ago, perhaps bouyed by the cluster of faithful women who upheld her now in spite of everything.

"I had to talk to you."

The clock ticked loudly in the hall. "Do your parents know where you are?"

She shook her head, and color drained from her cheeks. "I need it to be like confession."

He was not a priest. "I have no vows that contain that."

"But can't we just do it that way? I think I know where Carl is."

The jolt almost staggered him. He took a shaky step backward to admit her. All day detectives had come by to see if they had seen or heard anything from Carl. Charity had been searched and patrolled, highways monitored, even the FBI alerted in case the boy crossed state lines.

But no one had seen anything of him. Now Nita thought she knew. He took her into his study. "Let me get Madeline."

"No!"

"Nita, it's not proper to be alone with you."

"I don't care. I can't tell anyone but you, and you can't tell anyone I told you."

He swallowed. Her distress was real.

She tensed. "I'll leave."

The threat was needless. He had to hear her out if there was even the smallest chance. "Tell me what you know."

"Promise first."

"Yes, Nita, I promise. No one will know you told me." He was too weary to fight.

She swallowed, clasping her hands under her chin. "Carl has a secret place. It's where he hid the car."

Burton tipped his head. Was this a game? She might burst out laughing any moment with all the youth watching outside his window. Was she mocking him? "You'll have to tell me how you know."

Her face pinched. "I don't want to say."

He spread his hands. "Then I can't . . ."

She gulped. "Okay, okay. But you can't tell anyone."

"I've given you my word."

"We snuck out." She couldn't meet his eyes. "He would tap my window, and I'd meet him somewhere. I know you didn't want us dating."

That was by far the least of his concerns.

"But it wasn't just me. Like, all the girls went when he tapped."

Burton's heart sank. "All the girls?"

"You know, the Friday night crowd."

Carl had been enticing his youth? The ones he held in his heart as on fire for Jesus? How blind he had been. "So you snuck out." He had to hear it, no matter where it led. Carl wasn't the first P.K. to trade on his position. He would have been hard to resist.

"One time he took me to this place. He was all mysterious, said he'd have to kill me if I told." Her eyes shot up. "I thought he was joking. Like, he laughed when he said it."

"Why did he take you there?"

She burned scarlet.

"You don't have to answer." Burton walked to the window. "Can you show me where it is?"

"I'll tell you." She wrung her hands under her chin. "But you have to promise, 'cause now I know . . . he meant it."

Burton's breath seized. He hadn't considered that the girls might have been in danger themselves. He'd been so proud of Carl, so convinced . . .

"Nita, I promise." Whatever she'd done with his . . . son, she was still his spiritual responsibility. And his civic responsibility was to find Carl by any means. "Tell me where."

"Just past the turnoff to the old Hansen place, there's a trail through the woods. You turn off there and just kind of go where it takes you. You'll get to this big tree—"

"The whole area is forest."

"But this is a totally big old tree, like, a giant one." She drew a quick breath. "It's under there."

"Under?"

She nodded sharply. "It's a cave they built."

"They?"

"Carl and Duke."

Burton cringed at Duke's name. "Carl told you that?" He and Carl had decided early on that Duke was behind them. They never brought him up unless Carl's nightmares forced a discussion. And then it was only to confirm that the Lord had dealt with the man and Carl had nothing more to fear. He never asked about his mother.

Nita squeezed her hands together. "He said Duke thought the government might come after him or something, and he could, like, live there for years."

So Carl had made it his hiding place. His legacy from Duke? Burton said, "Thank you for telling me, Nita. You should go home now."

"You won't tell, right?"

"I won't tell." Burton closed the door behind her. Should he wake Madeline? He coveted her prayers. Her love sustained him as he stumbled through this valley. He went upstairs and touched her shoulder, knowing it would end her night's sleep. She startled awake and he told her. She cried, but she would pray while he did what he had to. He stood up like an old man.

Next he woke Cooper Roehr, and together they drove out toward the old Hansen place. It wasn't a direction people took by choice; the Hansens had lived deep in the woods and far from their neighbors. Probably why Duke got away with so much. The sheriff's car took the track better than Burton's sedan would have, but even so it was slow going.

"Big tree, huh?" Cooper chewed his cigar. "She say which side?"

Burton hadn't named names, but he had to give Cooper the gist to get him out of bed. Now Cooper drove the trail like a hound, obviously wanting to be the one to bring Carl in. At least he'd agreed to let Burton talk to him first. If he could convince Carl to give himself up, it would be better all around. Maybe there were indications the boy was not in his right mind. Certainly, he'd been haunted. Burton could attest to that.

And when it came out how he'd seen his father killed and the town had called it justified . . . that had to mean something to a judge. Burton ducked his chin. He wasn't making excuses. He was horrified by Carl's attack on Alessi. He was simply trying to make sense of it.

Ahead there stood a monstrous fir with branches that draped like fabric. It had to be the one. Cooper came to a stop. "Don't want to get closer and scare him off. This cave got back doors?"

"I don't know." Burton stared at the tree. It was dark, but even in the daylight he doubted you could tell there was anything in that rise.

He closed his eyes. *Father* . . . Words had not come for two days now, but there was a groaning in his spirit. He had taken the son of his enemy to raise as his own. He had tried to bring light to the darkness of Carl's mind. If there was any grace in that, any consolation . . .

"Let's go." Cooper eased out of the car and settled his hip.

Burton climbed out. "Let me go in alone, Cooper."

Cooper unsnapped the gun in its holster and nodded.

The moonlight barely illuminated the ground through the trees. Carl had been afraid of the dark, at least those first years. He'd been afraid of a hand on the shoulder, a step behind him, a harsh word. He responded with anger, tried to hurt something or someone.

When Burton married Madeline, he warned her not to be alone with the boy when he was in a dark mood. To walk out of the house if necessary. But her gentle presence had seemed to help. It was her devotion that melted his heart and prepared it for his Savior.

Burton faltered and rubbed a hand over his face. *Father* . . . He reached the base of the tree and stopped. "Carl, can you hear me?"

The silence took on a tensile strain.

"I want to talk to you."

There was no response for so long he wondered if he was simply talking to a tree. Then slowly the lowest branches rose up. He saw an opening and went toward it. If Carl meant to kill him, so be it.

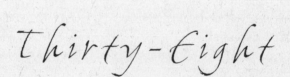

Thirty-Eight

CARL COULD HAVE GONE DOWN THE HATCH and crawled out through the sewer. That had always been the escape plan, and Duke had laid cement pipes big enough to fit through. It came out near the creek under another old tree. But hearing his father's voice—Burton's voice . . .

He pulled on the rope, half expecting the blaze of police lights, the clicking of rifles. But there was only Burton Welsh standing in the dark without even a flashlight. Had God brought him there?

Carl clicked the igniter on the propane lantern. The air pipes going up through the forest floor kept it from asphyxiating him when he had the opening closed. Now he held it for his father to climb over the lower barrier. Bringing the pastor into Duke's place seemed wrong. Carl started to shake.

The hand that gripped his shoulder poured strength into his soul. But he had lost all that, and he started to cry. His father pulled him close and held him as though he weren't the monster he'd become.

They stood that way a long time, then Carl said, "She wouldn't stay dead."

Burton pulled back and looked at him, confused, and sickened, it seemed. "Who?"

"Mom. Beth. She's under there." He waved his hand toward the hatch. "But she keeps coming out to blame me."

"Beth?" Burton staggered. "Your mother?"

Carl sat down on the cot. "She was leaving me to the monster."

Burton sat down beside him. "Carl, your mother was not leaving you." The pastor's arm came around his shoulders. "I advised her to go directly to a shelter. But she wouldn't leave without you."

The shaking intensified. "He showed me her letter." Duke had waved it in his face, holding her by the hair. *"Look what she says! She can't live with us no more."* He hadn't read all the words but he could tell by his mother's face that she'd written the letter, that she was leaving.

Burton held him. "She was leaving Duke. Finding a place of safety. I told her we'd get you somehow, but she said Duke would kill you before he'd let you go."

Carl crumpled. "No." It came out of him like a groan. He couldn't be the reason, the cause . . .

"It's true. She went back for you the day she disappeared."

Carl gripped his head, filled with images of blood. Fear in his nostrils, in his groin. The sound of blows, and cries, then only the thud of flesh. His breath shallowed until he scarcely took in air at all. It wasn't possible. It couldn't be. He'd watched her die without raising a hand to help.

Sobs wrenched him. *No, no, no.* Then he looked up, and she was there.

Burton stared at the space in front of Carl. Timbered wall, hung with every sort of tool, another lantern, and a first-aid kit. But Carl cried and talked and pleaded, then nodded, drinking in words only he could hear. "No, I won't forget. We'll do it just as you say."

His eyes had taken on a stare that didn't break when Burton shook him gently. "Carl. Carl, listen to me. You have to come with me now. Cooper's outside, and if you give yourself up . . ." He turned his son's jaw. "Carl, do you hear me?"

"I won't forget. Just as you say. Duke won't find us."

Burton swallowed hard. He'd seen broken souls, Carl's especially. But not a broken mind. Had the truth put him over the edge? He helped Carl to stand. "Come with me, son."

Carl walked, but what he saw and heard, only God knew.

———————

Steve woke with a raging crick in his neck. He rubbed it automatically. His lower back ached as well, and he leaned slowly into a stretch. Alessi hadn't gone in the night. Now they faced another day. He popped a square of gum into his mouth, then leaned over and kissed her.

He wished he'd been the one to give her breath instead of Ben. But what good had it done? They had only kept her from the peace that surely waited. Unless this time was for him. Maybe he was the one needing something. What was he supposed to learn? To love? Unguardedly? Everything he'd said to her was about what he wanted. But what would she want? The ache spread outward from his chest. Did he love her enough to let her go?

Lord. The pain was worse than he'd imagined. A little more than two weeks she'd been in his life and some of it unconscious. Would this morning be her last? Tears burned his eyes. *The greatest of these is love.* Could he love her into the Lord's presence?

A tear dropped from his chin. He looked into her face, studied each freckle she hadn't wanted photographed. He could not develop that roll. The pain of it would kill him. But this wasn't about him. *Faith, hope, and love.*

He had to love enough to give her what she needed. His voice didn't work the first try. Then he rasped, "If you have to go, Alessi, it's all right. I won't blame you." Heart laid open, he pressed her hand to his cheek, amazed to realize he meant it. He couldn't blame her for anything. Maybe he was through blaming. And he had given her the freedom she needed. Freedom to leave him, to be at peace. Tears streamed as he pressed her fingers to his mouth. He whispered, "I love you."

Alessi opened her eyes to a face haloed in light, but this light was wholly bearable. The fire had burned away, and she no longer saw the one with the stone. But someone was there, and slowly his features came clear. "Steve?" she whispered, though the effort was almost more than she could manage.

He held her hand so tightly it hurt. Pressing her knuckles to his mouth, he huffed out crazy breaths. His cheeks were wet. Why was he so worked up? He sucked breath through his nostrils and rasped, "Oh, God."

She searched his face. What on earth. . . ? She suddenly noticed the walls and ceiling, the metal rail he leaned on. "Where am I?"

He half laughed. "Chambers City Hospital."

Hospital. No, she couldn't remember a hospital.

"I see I'll have to repeat everything I said." His eyes teared up. "But that's okay." He leaned over and kissed her mouth.

An intense warmth not unlike the engulfing flames rushed through her. She couldn't think, couldn't . . . She closed her eyes and drifted until other voices broke out. Then she opened her eyes to unfamiliar faces. She felt as though she'd slept a hundred years in a glass coffin and was now the exhibit of the day. One woman stared at her as though she'd just walked through fire. But then, maybe she had. The flames were the clearest thing in her memory.

The woman came forward and said, "I'm Dr. Liz Deklin."

Alessi gathered her strength and said, "Hi."

Cheers broke out. Alessi startled.

"I told you she was speaking." Steve smiled as she'd never seen him smile. Maybe he'd had a hundred years' sleep as well. He wasn't growling.

The doctor pressed a button that raised the head of the bed. "I don't suppose you remember what's happened."

Alessi shook her head. She couldn't even figure out what was happening now. She met Steve's eyes and held them. He was happy; that much was sure.

The doctor said, "Do you know what day it is?"

Alessi shook her head.

"Who was the first president of the United States?"

She was joking, right? "George Washington."

"How old are you?"

"Twenty-one."

"Have you answered Steve's proposal?"

That stumped her. She glanced from the doctor to Steve, who looked as surprised as she.

He said, "You heard that?"

Dr. Deklin smiled. "I was at the nurses' station. We all heard it."

They all heard what? Alessi hadn't heard.

Steve scowled. "Well, she's confused enough. Leave it alone."

Alessi scanned the faces as a sigh circled the room.

"Is there a plan here?" Steve was growling again. That much was normal.

Dr. Deklin laughed softly. "I want to run some tests. But I guess what's happened here has more to do with you"—she pointed at Steve—"than me."

Alessi sank into the pillow. It would be nice to know what had happened, why she was there, and what Steve had to do with it.

"I'll want some time with her." Dr. Deklin nodded to one of the others who went out, then said to Steve, "Why don't you go home."

He opened his mouth, but the doctor laid a hand on his arm. "This is one for the record. I want to be thorough."

He nodded, met Alessi's eyes, sending that warmth rushing through her again. "I'll be back."

"Okay," she whispered. She actually felt it when he left the room, as though something vital had changed, some energy she had clung to evaporated. It was similar to the moment her mother's last breath seeped out.

She turned to the doctor. "Please tell me what's going on." She tried not to sound as lost as she felt.

Dr. Deklin shook her head. "I was hoping you'd tell me."

Great. Alessi struggled to think.

The doctor touched her hand. "No, I'm not serious. But Ms. Moore, I have to say, I may not have a medical answer for you."

Strange thing for a doctor to say. But answers wouldn't matter so much if she could only have a clue. "Could you just start with what happened?"

———————

Steve walked out to his truck. At least he thought he walked, though the ground was not too solid beneath his feet. He still could not grasp it. *I don't have to know, Lord. Not how or why. Just thank you. Thank you, Jesus.* He got into the truck and flew to the station.

"She's awake, Ben." He'd hardly burst through the door before the words were out.

"What?" The word slipped from Ben's mouth.

"Alessi's awake, talking, everything." Steve choked on the wonder.

Ben held himself up by the counter. "That's a miracle."

Steve pushed through the service door to find Dave and gave him the same message.

Dave hooted. "Praise God. I have to tell Diana."

Steve had others to tell, starting with Cooper.

The old man looked tired. "You mean she's recovered?"

"More than that. She's back from the dead."

Cooper's face eased. Maybe he'd cared more than he'd shown. "Well, that's good. It'll be good for Carl too."

Steve jolted. "Carl?"

"Brought him in last night."

Steve drew a slow breath. No, he couldn't hate the kid. Not now. Not with mercy flowing like a river. "He's in jail?"

Cooper nodded. "At least it won't be a murder charge." He tapped his head. "Cracked upstairs, though. Guess what happened to his mom was just too much."

There was some disconnect here. "His mom?"

"We found her body where Duke dumped it. Best guess is Carl saw her die. We're not getting anything too clear from him, though. Mostly keeps talking to the air."

Steve shook his head. He did not want to feel compassion for Carl. But . . . he'd seen Beth die? At Duke's hands? Probably forced to watch, probably helpless to stop it. Maybe felt guilty. When he saw Alessi . . . Had he simply cracked?

"What happens now?"

Cooper rubbed his face. "There'll be an inquiry. Who knows how that'll turn out, except I'll finally be done with this job." Both relief and regret in his voice.

Cooper deserved to retire, but it might not go well for him, failing to act on Duke's death. Things could be hard on Charity all around for a while. Steve leaned a hip to the desk. "Think it'll sort out?"

Cooper stretched out his legs. "After six years of carrying the blame together, who's even sure which ones dealt the blows?"

The ones who had certainly knew it. But it seemed Cooper was not planning to name names. Maybe it was right for everyone to accept the blame. Mob rage had contributed, fueled the fury. And the pastor had been right, that "Inasmuch as you think it in your heart, so you have done it."

Cooper rubbed his knee. "Beth's corpse is pretty clear evidence to the man's violence, and maybe self-defense isn't out of the question."

And not far from reality, Steve supposed, even if they had covered it up. He nodded. It would all come to light now, but it was in bigger hands than theirs.

Steve went to the Welshes' house, certain they'd be elsewhere, but Burton opened the door and braced himself for the expected news. No doubt he'd been pretty beat up lately. At least this wouldn't be a knock-out punch.

Steve said, "She's awake."

Burton stood speechless as the words penetrated, then rasped, "Recovered?"

Steve nodded. "It's a miracle."

"A miracle." The pastor sagged against the doorframe, eyes closed, and smiled. "And I had nothing at all to do with it."

Steve glimpsed the pressure that must have been on him these years, keeping the town together, keeping them believing, and trying so hard to bring good out of evil. He felt Burton's relief like a balm on torn and tired tissue.

"God is good," Burton said. "Too good."

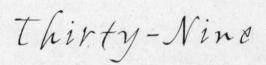

Thirty-Nine

THE EEG SHOWED NORMAL BRAIN FUNCTION. No residual damage except a lack of memory of the incident and the time that followed. Just hearing Dr. Deklin say it gave her chills. Alessi would just as soon not know how bad off she'd been, but the doctor hadn't held anything back.

Liz Deklin made no excuses either. Her original diagnosis was correct, and she had the first EEG to prove it. Nothing but minimal and failing brain activity. "There is no explanation for your recovery short of divine intervention." Liz Deklin rested her hands on her hips. "And I can't say I'd subscribed to that before."

Divine intervention. Alessi drank it in. God's miracle had finally come. Not in any way she could have imagined. But that was how it was. Miracles happened if you just had the eyes to see them.

She sat now in jeans and Amanda Bier's sweater as Dr. Deklin pulled the curtain of the cubicle to reveal the people waiting there. Steve and Ben and Dave. Karen and Diana, even Moll and Cooper Roehr. Ben could not stop smiling, and Mary beside him looked beatific. Alessi guessed the girls weren't allowed in.

Dr. Deklin said, "I don't believe I'm discharging this patient. But there's nothing more to do for her here." She shook her head and smiled. "Take her home."

Alessi liked the sound of that. Steve stood back, but everyone else closed in on her. There were too many congratulations to answer. She returned their hugs, amazed when Moll grabbed her up, saying, "Next chicken fried steak's on me."

"Sure sounds good." Alessi laughed. "I won't need a box."

Then Steve was beside her, one hand on her elbow. "Ready?" His voice sounded thick, his words charged with more than the surface meaning.

She nodded, her mind whirling as she was swept out with the crowd. They all seemed sincere as they packed the elevator down and dispersed into the lobby where the hugs and blessings repeated. She appreciated it all but was just as glad Steve suggested they give her some space.

Dr. Deklin had told her she might be overwhelmed for a while, and that was the truth. She blew out a soft breath as she got into the truck with Steve. He didn't talk as he drove, just sent occasional glances. He seemed to have recovered from his emotional state, yet there was plenty of energy between them.

He drove her to the house and let her in the door. "Are you hungry?"

"I don't think so." She looked around the small white-walled rooms as though she'd never seen them. It almost felt that way, though she knew she had.

Steve set his keys on the counter. "What's the last thing you remember?"

She crossed over to the Christmas tree and cradled a red-and-white bobber, smiling at the thoughts that rushed in. "I remember this."

Steve came up behind her. "Do you remember Christmas Eve?"

She tried to focus. "The power was out."

"We built a fire."

She narrowed her eyes at the fireplace. "I remember."

"Played chess."

She remembered that with a jolt. He circled her in his arms from behind. It both surprised and comforted her.

She sank against his chest. "I missed Christmas."

He rested his cheek on the side of her head. "I don't think so."

She glanced behind to look at him.

He turned her. "We have traditions and celebrations to remember Christ's coming. But I'd say He *came* to you."

Her heart surged. The bright Being with a coal setting her aflame. Not a babe in a manger, but power and glory.

"And just in case you're still feeling left out . . ."

Steve reached under the tree, handed her a tissue-wrapped bundle. He had a gift for her? She looked from it to his face and back. It wasn't a book by the weight of it. Not that she wouldn't like a book. . . .

"Open it."

She pulled the tape and opened the layers. A sweet face, white organdy and lace. Biting her lip, Alessi let the paper fall. He'd bought her an angel. *Guardian angels God will send thee, all through the night.* Stroking the gold wire halo, she fought her tears. "It's beautiful."

He took the angel and tucked her into the tree, where she smiled out between the bobbers and lures.

Alessi smiled. "She's supposed to be on top."

He didn't listen. His face had taken on that Heathcliff quality, and he pressed her to the wall, fervor back full force. "You walked out on me."

A memory flashed of her creeping out the door.

His silvery pine eyes smoldered. "I told you I would help."

He had. But her head had gone crazy with doubts. So many people had let her down. People she needed; people she loved. It had been easier to believe Steve the culprit than someone who might care. She looked into his face. "I'm sorry."

He caught her jaw between his hands. "I won the chess match."

She swallowed. "I know."

He brought his mouth to hers. Again flames engulfed her, but these were too potent to be healing. He drew back just enough. "Double or nothing." Then he took her mouth again.

Definite risk to her heart and, well, everything else.

His hands held her firmly. "I want to marry you."

Her breath staggered. "What?"

"You heard me this time. No coma excuse."

That was the proposal Dr. Deklin meant? She stared into his face, seeing bear, beast, and tragic hero. Not safe, not one bit safe. "I'm starting to think you're the one with the head injury."

"I know exactly what I'm saying." He stroked her with his eyes. "And I have an aversion to long engagements."

"Two weeks?" She half laughed.

"Pretend it's arranged." He kissed her temple.

"By whom?"

He caught two handfuls of hair and bunched them around her neck. "Who put the halo on the sun?"

"I guess God."

"That'll do." He smiled with purpose. "If God didn't ordain this, then explain the miracle."

How did you explain the magic? Heart throbbing, she tipped her head and narrowed her eyes. "Are you just trying to evade Amanda Bier and the schoolgirls?"

"You want me to take a knee?" He dropped down, caught her hand and kissed it. Then he looked up. "I love you."

Warmth as healing as the fire. She sank into it, knowing it couldn't last, but unable to resist.

"Come on, Alessi." Urgency and vulnerability—in Steve Bennet? But there it was, as easy to read as his wrong definitions.

She whispered, "You really mean it?"

"I'm not kneeling here for nothing."

She looked away, overwhelmed. He loved her. She tried to find the doubts, but they'd been swept away.

He stood up and stroked her cheek. "I'm thinking Alaska."

She bit her lip. "Alaska?"

"Honeymoon in the woods with elk and moose and grizzlies. Show you my waterfall."

HALOS

The picture formed in her mind. She could almost smell the woods.

He pressed in close. "I told you all this in the hospital, but you weren't listening."

She smiled. "If you say so." That had been a little beyond her control. But as she looked, it was there—with no light behind him at all.

319

More Highly Acclaimed Authors From Bethany House Publishers

A Wounded Heart...A Healing Grace...
Sophia Hess has never known genuine love. And she thinks she has arranged her life to get along just fine without it. But when she moves in with her nephew and his wife to finish out her days, their gifts of kindness reveal love's transforming power.

Winter Birds by Jamie Langston Turner

How Much Difference Can One Man Make?
In 1927, Pilotville, Louisiana, was an isolated outpost on the Mississippi River, an island of brotherly love in a sea of racism. But in the swamp beyond the cypress and the tupelo, veiled by Spanish moss, lies a lingering evil, and it will sleep no more. It will rain down on Pilotville, and nothing but a miracle can stop this awful flood.

River Rising by Athol Dickson

Mr. ...Mom?
When a bizarre accident leaves Mick Brannigan trading his hard hat and construction crew for laundry baskets and kids, he discovers that being "mom" isn't as easy as he thought. Struggling with the complete role reversal, he and his wife, Layne, finally learn what's truly important in life.

Summer of Light by W. Dale Cramer

What Price Would You Pay for The Cure?
Riley Keep, former man of God, now haunts the streets, a ghost of who he used to be. But in a last bid for survival, Riley sets out for a small town in Maine where miracles are happening...but sometimes the disease is not as dangerous as The Cure.

The Cure by Athol Dickson

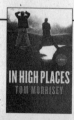

Sometimes There's No Place to Go But Up
As the loss of his wife drives Kevin Nolan to attempt increasingly dangerous and extreme rock climbs, his son, Patrick, is left to cope on his own. Can Kevin overcome his grief before he loses his son...and his life?

In High Places by Tom Morrisey